Brigid Delaney has worked as a lawyer and a journalist. Her writing has appeared in *The Age*, *Sydney Morning Herald*, *The Australian*, *The Guardian*, *The Spectator*, *Vogue* and *Griffith Review*.

She is also the author of the non-fiction book *This Restless Life* (MUP).

www.brigiddelaney.com.au
Twitter @BrigidWD

WILD THINGS

WILD THINGS

Brigid Delaney

FOURTH ESTATE

Fourth Estate
An imprint of HarperCollins*Publishers*

First published in Australia in 2014
by HarperCollins*Publishers* Australia Pty Limited
ABN 36 009 913 517
harpercollins.com.au

The lines quoted on page 336 are from 'Ode on a Grecian Urn' by John Keats.

HarperCollins*Publishers*
Level 13, 201 Elizabeth Street, Sydney NSW 2000, Australia
Unit D1, 63 Apollo Drive, Rosedale, Auckland 0632, New Zealand
A 53, Sector 57, Noida, UP, India
77–85 Fulham Palace Road, London W6 8JB, United Kingdom
2 Bloor Street East, 20th floor, Toronto, Ontario M4W 1A8, Canada
10 East 53rd Street, New York, NY 10022, USA

National Library of Australia Cataloguing-in-Publication data:

Delaney, Brigid.
 Wild things / Brigid Delaney.
 978 0 7322 9687 2 (paperback)
 978 1 7430 9919 3 (ebook)
 Bullying in schools – Fiction.
 College students – Fiction.
 Secrets – Fiction.
A823.4

Cover design by Darren Holt, HarperCollins Design Studio
Cover images by shutterstock.com
Author photo by James Brickwood
Typeset in 11/15 ITC New Baskerville by Kirby Jones

For my brothers:
Michael, Justin and Matthew Delaney

Fair youth, beneath the trees, thou canst not leave
Thy song, nor ever can those trees be bare
– John Keats, 'Ode on a Grecian Urn'

The man who has a conscience suffers whilst
acknowledging his sin. That is his punishment.
– Fyodor Dostoyevsky, *Crime and Punishment*

Alfred knew before he had been in the mountains three hours that they meant to harm him.

The game had gone on too long and when they went to tie him up he was too drunk to resist. Limp and passive, he felt pulled along in the direction this thing was going. It was as if it were a play and all the boys were characters who had performed this many times, who knew all the lines and where to stand, where to place the hood and when to light the fire.

A lot had happened – the blond boy called Hadrien had delivered a lengthy speech, some of which sounded not to be in English, a kangaroo had been dismembered, and a couple of the boys had been sick – by the time Alfred was freed from the restraints and ran out into the dark bush.

For one long, exhilarating moment it was as if he had woken up from a deep sleep. Strange and powerful chemicals surged through him, making him forget his cuts, welts and humiliations. He was Superman as he soared across the rocky paths, through the trees, over rocks, across a creek, and then down, down, down, down, down to a place where he merged with the night.

CHAPTER 1

Toby studied his teammates as they got out of the car and stretched their legs after the two-hour drive. They were all dressed in their college rugby jumpers and shorts, like it was a uniform. Their faces also seemed uniform – blank, world-weary. Nineteen, twenty years old and they had seen it all.

Not him, though. He was not like them. Even though he would turn twenty-one later this year, Toby was still experiencing sharp, pleasurable shocks of discovery.

From the day he had arrived at St Anton's it was like the world had remade itself. There was the college itself, a revelation after the portable classrooms of his country high school, with its library that was once the assembly hall, the scuffed grass on the oval. He had never realised before how makeshift his old school had been; it had none of the weight of history of St Anton's, where the chapel had always been the chapel and always would be, and where it was unthinkable that the gothic dining hall would ever be used for another purpose – an art studio, say, or a performance space.

From the outside, with its high stone walls, St Anton's resembled a fortress, but inside was a dazzling quadrangle as brilliantly green as ferns backlit in the tropics. Around it were arranged freshmen rooms, a chapel and an archway that led to another, smaller quadrangle, with rooms belonging to more senior students. The third quadrangle housed the tutors' quarters, the dining room and a second chapel. Behind the chapel were a velvety playing field, a pocket of farmland and a river. The St Anton's Master lived in a gabled cottage, set off to the side of the college beside a pond filled with gliding swans. The other colleges were also hemmed in by the river and by walls of stone, and they too had their own dining halls, chapels, computer rooms, tutors' lodges, playing fields, libraries, study rooms, billiard rooms, discussion rooms and smaller chapels for prayers and confession.

St Anton's was famous for the animals that grazed on its lawns – lambs, waterfowl, peacocks and pheasants. The job of feeding the animals went to members of the Senior Common Room. One might wake particularly early and see Dr Bath, the swollen-hipped modern history teacher, wandering among the peacocks and geese in his white nightgown and pale bare feet, his eyelids heavy, his lips mumbling either morning greetings to the birds, ancient battle speeches of Constantinople, or lines from a Gerard Manley Hopkins poem.

The college was home to two hundred students, both male and female, most of them aged between seventeen and twenty. There were a dozen tutors, a chaplain – old, feeble Dr Williams – and the head of the college, Locke Greenway, whom everyone just called the Master.

On his first day, more than two years ago now, Toby had stood in the first quadrangle gawping – at the buildings, at the animals, up at the spires, down at the lawn, at the other freshmen who moved around him with boxes and bags, in groups already, friends already. They didn't stare like hinge-jawed hicks at the llama being led by Dr Bath towards the river, nor were they conspicuously, almost violently alone, holding a much-loved cricket bat, a Gray-Nicolls Viper, the veteran of many games with his brothers. Yet still he gawped – in mad love with the place already but panicked that he did not belong here and would be found out at any moment.

'Do you play cricket?' A boy of about Toby's age had materialised by his side, wearing frayed khaki shorts, a navy-blue polo shirt, boat shoes and a cap bearing the legend *Wakelin Steel Guangdong Province.*

'Yes – do you?'

The boy nodded. 'Cricket tragic, actually. I spent the whole summer at the Test matches. I'm Ben.'

'Toby.'

'You should try out with me for the team,' said Ben. 'There's a bunch of us from my school going down to the oval this afternoon. I'll introduce you …' He was pointing to a group of boys gathered by the pond with cricket bats and pads. They were all dressed like Ben except for a small blond posh-looking boy who was, quite eccentrically, wearing a suit.

That first afternoon unfolded like a beautiful dream: a day of miraculous sixes and a stunning catch and the late afternoon sun toasty on his back, and later a strange dark English-style pub called the Red Lion, with a low ceiling and crossed rowing oars nailed above the bar, where he and Ben sat, drinking and talking easily. The feeling that he was an intruder, a lurker on the edges, slipped away so quickly that Toby felt strangely but happily unmoored from the past. His anchor was up. Nothing significant in his life had happened, or was fondly remembered before he got here.

As more time passed, he sometimes forgot that he wasn't from a rich family like Ben and the others. On his first visit back home at Easter break Toby's father warned him that it was more dangerous to hang around people with a lot of money than to have lots of money yourself, as it gave you an expectation of a certain lifestyle without the means of achieving it. It could lead to one of two things – perpetual frustration and bitterness at what you didn't have, or indentured servitude in a corporate law practice or merchant bank to feed your engorged sense of entitlement.

'Unhappiness and compromise are what come from that,' Toby's dad said. 'You are unhappy because you can't get what you think you deserve and so you compromise yourself in order to get it.'

'So I guess *you* can feel smug about being poor and having a boring life because you've never compromised,' Toby retorted.

He went home less frequently after that. Instead he visited the beach houses of his new friends Ben, Charlotte or Julian during the summer holidays. In winter he went on skiing trips with Julian, Roman, Charlotte and Ben.

Ben had become like another brother. By second year the new fresher girls had difficulty telling them apart. Toby had darker hair and was two inches taller, but through playing the same sports, studying for the same degree, having the same friends and sleeping with the same girls they became almost indistinguishable. Not that Toby minded: when there were two of them, it made him feel stronger.

Yet some transitions into this new world did not come easily. The boys from Ben's school – one of those famous and expensive schools where the boys all called each other by their surnames ('I was at school with Leeson for ten years, and I don't even know his first name!' said Ben) – were obsessed with some secret male-only club from the 1920s that their great-grandfathers had belonged to. Hadrien – the posh boy in the suit Toby had noticed on his first day – called it the Savage Society and would occasionally produce a red leather-bound book, in which complex initiation rituals were recorded in cursive script, and which they performed during the cricket away trips. In the past two years, Toby had been pressured to eat peyote (which made him throw up), have some hulking fourth-year threaten him with a dildo (waving it close to his face saying, 'You like cock? You like cock? You like cock, yeah!'), smoke opium from an eighteenth-century pipe Hadrien had found at some antique store in Shanghai and walk forty-six kilometres in the bush without his clothes.

Now, in late March, the cricket team was once more spending the night at Evelyn, the rundown college-owned camp in the mountains. As Toby had watched the cricketers ferrying slabs of beer and bottles of spirits from the car, he knew Hadrien would have organised some bizarre activity for the evening and he'd wondered if anyone would notice if he slipped out of the room and went to bed early. He didn't really do hazing rituals, just like he didn't speak Latin and had never owned a passport.

But the afternoon had been all right. They'd played cricket on the flat grassy area behind the house with their beer cans resting at their feet, the smokers sticking a smouldering cigarette behind their ear as they went for a lazy catch – and now this: the cocktails after the game.

Ben was opening the vodka and Ping, a cross-eyed, clumsy third-year, was trying to make dirty martinis. Ben shook his head and took over. Toby smiled – Ben had been the one to teach him how to make a martini, as well as how to read a stock report, how to pronounce French on a menu, when to clap at the Concert Hall, and how to ask a girl out confidently. Ben was often dismissed as a jock by those who didn't know him. He played cricket, football and tennis, and he rowed – you could set your watch by him as he crossed the quadrangle on his way to one training session or another. But Toby knew there was much more to Ben than his physical prowess; that beneath the surface he suffered from almost crippling bouts of unhappiness, dissatisfaction and shame, days – even a week here or there – of not leaving bed.

Toby guessed he would have to watch out for Ben tonight. When Ben drank too much he became a different person: mocking the accents of taxi drivers, being cruel to his friends and aggressive with girls, smoking too much, being kicked out of nightclubs, refused service for intoxication, getting into fights. The next day, unless he had forgotten his behaviour of the night before, he would be ill with remorse and shame. Then the depression would sink in, the self-loathing that it almost physically hurt Toby to witness. 'You're all right, mate, you're not a bad person – you just need to maybe get

some help, see a doctor or those people at Student Services,'
Toby would tell him. He had seen the signs around campus
asking 'R U OK?' But what did he know about depression?

Ben handed Toby a martini. Julian, his blond curls still
damp and cherubic face ruddy from the cricket game, took
photos on his phone. 'All you need is tuxedos and you'd both
pass for James Bond.'

They posed with their strong drinks and smiled.

Ben had been to Evelyn six times now but he still found it
creepy. It was isolated, set off the main road down a long dirt
track. The main block was a house made of stone. The ceilings
were high and the pink paint peeled off the walls like sunburnt
skin. A couple of small bedrooms, a long dorm-style bunkroom
and a games area had been tacked on later. The furniture was
sparse, old and springy with damp. Levi still spoke with horror
about the time he'd flopped on an easy chair only to hear a
squeak from under the cushion as a mouse uttered its last
following the impact of Levi's murderous backside.

But it could have been worse. An elderly caretaker visited
occasionally, killing the spiders and clearing cobwebs. The
linen was locked in an airtight cupboard to stop it from
getting damp and mouldy, and the showers were miraculous –
high pressure, with hot water that never ran out.

After a round of cocktails Leeson blew into the trumpet
that accompanied the team everywhere and the cricketers
gathered in the lounge room.

Hadrien walked in. 'Team, I bear a gift,' he announced.
'Prithee beat your drums, young fellows, for the time has

come to shake off the shackles of industry and propriety. Let us open the back of the van!'

They followed Hadrien outside. Ben watched as the other boys looked at each other and smirked. They guessed at what was coming. It was always the same. They would all be away – up in the mountains for the weekend, or at a five-star hotel, a casino or someone's parents' beach house – and as if by magic Hadrien would unveil something wonderful, subversive and strange. They'd be manic for a night, not themselves at all (for, as they would tell themselves beforehand, they had girlfriends, mothers and sisters; they *respected women*). Come Sunday night, a curious collective amnesia would descend, and after a long, silent drive back to college they would recall only a night of Scrabble, chess and boozy, boring conversations about sport.

Last year Hadrien had organised women. They were older than the cricketers and probably prostitutes. Ben hadn't seen them before or since. One night only. One night of dreamy fun.

Dr Bath had been there too, as a chaperone – blushing and stammering from the moment the women alighted from the jeep in their hotpants and the tight satin shirts that felt so delicious to touch. In the kitchen the next morning one of the women wore Ben's T-shirt and made toast. There were only three girls but that had been enough to go around – dirty chuckles and hands everywhere and things were slippery and someone was saying, 'Easy on the lube, dude' – and there was the rumble of someone's drunken snores from an old leather chair in the corner – Ping, probably, or Sam, one of the heavy guys, who were also heavy drinkers.

Ben still remembered the girls' strawberry lip gloss which tasted so sweet and their total lack of innocence and the drugs and lolling about on the rugs and the dawn broken by the *euww euewewe ewuewww* of birds and Dr Bath up early, blushing and not looking at them.

How could Hadrien top last year? Ben wondered, as they gathered outside under the sagging verandah.

Niall opened a bottle of tequila for shots and they stood around in shifty anticipation. Sam and Ping were whooping like sirens, others were silent but alert. Ben and Toby exchanged an apprehensive look. The motor stalled then switched off and Severin and Leeson got out of the car on either side of a thin, scared-looking Asian boy.

The whooping stopped.

The boy, whom Ben didn't recognise, wore his hair the way kids did in primary school – pushed forward and brushed to an almost reflective sheen. He had on brightly patterned shorts that seemed too big for his twiggy legs.

Someone growled, 'What the fuck?'

The boy looked back at them, also confused.

'It's okay. They're happy to have you here,' Hadrien said softly, placing an arm around the boy's thin shoulders.

The boy relaxed, smiled and nodded at each of them in turn. The cricketers nodded back, trying to be polite, but with furrowed brows.

Ben didn't want to look at Toby again. He felt his heart beat a bit faster.

Hadrien, who usually spoke so softly you had to lean in close to hear him, said loudly, 'Everyone, meet Alfred.

You may have seen him around college. He's a first-year Engineering student at St Anton's, and lives over in the Fraser Wing. Alfred's from Malaysia, but he speaks a bit of English. He's our special guest this weekend. Give Alfred a shot of tequila, Sam.'

'Where are the girls?' Ping demanded. 'I want something I can fuck.'

'Don't be so coarse, Ping. No girls this weekend. Sometimes it's good to have a boys' weekend – and in the interests of diversity, I thought I'd invite Alfred to join us.' Then Hadrien, still with his arm around the boy's shoulders, drew him in tight and said in that quiet way, 'As I told you in the van, this is how we mark the end of the cricket season. We won, by the way.'

A cheer went up.

Hadrien raised his voice again. 'So drink up, all of you, because tonight we're going to celebrate being WINNERS!'

It was 2 pm and unseasonably warm, so hot that the sun – blistering, powerful, full – seemed to cling to them, and yet up here in the mountains, away from everyone, it seemed to Ben that the night had already begun.

CHAPTER 2

It was Sunday night, and already Lucy was thinking about Monday. She looked forward to Monday night more than any other night of the week. It was *their* night. Their little group had fallen into a sweet rhythm that started in first year, chiefly to avoid the dreadful Monday night college dinners, which were assembled from the week's leftovers rather than cooked from scratch. Saturday's moussaka became Monday's shepherd's pie; a four-day-old lasagne was smothered with cheese and white sauce and passed off as macaroni cheese; elderly vegetables were bound together with eggs and became a vegetable bake.

So on Mondays Lucy and the others ate out, always at the same place, Angelica's, a quiet Italian bistro on Troutman Street that specialised in comfort food: pumpkin soup, risotto, lamb shanks with polenta, tiramisu. And it was always the same group that went: Toby, Ben, Julian, Levi, Lucy and Charlotte.

They had been close since first year. The casual couplings within the group could have made it awkward for them to socialise together, but instead they rationalised sex as a mere by-product of having had too much to drink, sort of like winding up at a bad nightclub or buying McDonald's at 3 am. Lucy liked to think that the looseness of the pairings and the lack of possessiveness gave their group an unusual degree of intimacy and sophistication. Like they were French or something.

Ben had known Charlotte since they were young, Toby had slept with her a few times in fresher year and Ben was with her now, in a tentative, anxious sort of way – more than fuck buddies but not a couple, each too courteous, or perhaps cautious, to talk about it deeply. Julian desired Charlotte but was unable to get past the 'just friends' stage. Levi and Lucy had had a drunken kiss that the next day had mortified them both and which they had never spoken of again. That Lucy loved Toby was apparent to everyone at college, but Toby had hooked up with someone over the summer break, an older woman named Lisa whom he had met in a laneway bar, though she had since been untagged from photos on his Facebook page and Lucy hoped it was over.

Lucy was in the college library when she heard the engines of the Land Rovers pulling into the car park. Her heart kicked against her chest. The boys were back!

She closed her books and moved to the window. Toby alighted from Niall's car, then the others followed, slamming the doors and grabbing their bags and cricket bats from the boot. But it was Toby she watched. She had watched him for so long, and so attentively, that she knew that he had not been kind to himself this weekend. He looked older – tired, sunburnt and hungover. Oh, Toby, when are you going to learn how to drink properly? she wondered, as he leant against the car and spat something gobby onto the ground. The others walked off quickly without looking over their shoulders. Lucy was tempted to call out to him but he had already pulled out his mobile.

Oh please, no, not Lisa, thought Lucy. Don't be calling her.

She knew these boys well, had studied them more closely than any textbook, and knew how these weekends away ended; it was the same every time. They returned to college looking sleazy and vulnerable, harbouring secrets and vague undercurrents of self-disgust. She knew that when they went back to their rooms and unpacked their things, and later when they were showering, their thoughts turned to women and comfort and a yearning for some sort of almost maternal softness.

Charlotte had told her of being summoned by a breathy phone call or plaintive text to hold boys on nights like these, heads on her chest, then they placed hands down there and fell into soft, whimpering sleep. And here was Toby on the phone at this vulnerable moment and there was Toby seconds later heading towards the Fraser Wing in the first quadrangle like he was flying. The Fraser Wing housed all the college's overseas students. Who did he know there? Lucy wondered. Was he with one of the Asian girls now? She had known him for over two years and she still didn't have a handle on his type. If he hadn't settled on a type she still had a chance, could still be the type he desired. There was time.

Lucy stayed by the window, holding her breath, and after a few minutes Toby emerged, pushing back the dark hair falling over one eye, taking the stairs down slowly now. She relaxed; whoever he had needed to see was not home.

After going to the Fraser Wing to see if Alfred was in his room (he was not), Toby, aching with fatigue, went back to his room and fell into a strange, deep sleep.

He woke disoriented and thirsty. What time was it? Had he missed his morning classes? Snatching up his phone to check the time, he was startled to see that it was Monday evening – he had slept for eighteen hours. On his phone were more than a dozen texts from Lucy, Ben, Julian and Levi. He rolled back to his sour-smelling pillow.

Ben's text was blunt. *Dinner tonight. Let's just keep to our usual routines.* Toby remembered Alfred and groaned. He deleted the text, trying to stop the rising feeling of dread. Maybe Alfred was back at college now. Or on his way back. He fired up his MacBook and checked some news websites but there was no mention of a boy missing in the Wycloffs.

A note had been slipped under his door while he was sleeping. *Remember the pact. Stick to it and we'll be fine. Break it and we're fucked.* No name. We're fucked anyway, thought Toby gloomily, as he tore up the note and put it in the bin.

After dinner at Angelica's he invited the others back to his room just like he always did. And as always, Levi brought the port, Charlotte coffee, Lucy chocolates and Ben cigarettes.

Toby dropped the needle on the old record player Ben had given him and the music of Mahler hushed the room. They adopted their usual positions: Ben sitting on the old leather swivel chair, Charlotte on the floor with her back resting against his legs, Julian in a beanbag covered in an academic gown, pillows between his back and the wall, Lucy lying on the floor on her stomach, chin in hands, and Toby wedged into a plastic chair stolen from a nearby pizzeria. The curtains were drawn but the orange sunset still seeped in, giving everything a mournful, end-of-days glow: the desk designed by Walter Burley Griffin, the books scattered everywhere, the scratched old wardrobe containing an academic gown, suits, a filthy tuxedo, and an evening dress whose wearer had slipped out wearing Toby's T-shirt and shorts one alcoholic sunrise, never to return.

Charlotte lit candles and then a joint, and dragged on it before passing it around. Ben opened the windows and a box of chocolates.

They were talking about nothing in particular and the joint had almost made its way around the circle when Lucy said: 'You're all very quiet tonight. What happened on the weekend? Did you do those horse tranquillisers again?'

The boys traded glances but stayed silent.

'What is it?' demanded Lucy. 'Did you fight?'

When no one responded Lucy sighed. 'I hate it when you go away on team trips without us. We could have gone down the coast instead – stayed at the beach house. It's hot enough.'

Toby tried to change the topic, to get them talking about the funny waiter at Angelica's who kept asking them if they wanted to taste the house wine, but Charlotte cut in, 'You all look wrecked – your eyes are really puffy.'

'I've just slept for eighteen hours,' said Toby.

'You must have had a lot to drink over the weekend. Ben, darling, you barely touched your wine tonight. God – what's wrong with your hands, Toby? They're all cut. What did you do out there?'

This time Toby didn't make eye contact with the other boys. 'We went for a long walk but we got lost. It was Ben's idea ...'

At that moment a sound like a fire alarm blared, making everyone jump.

'It's just my new ringtone,' Charlotte said, rummaging in her bag for her phone. 'It's Pharrell.' She held out her hand as she took the call to stop Toby from telling the story until she was finished.

Toby sighed. How could he tell a story he could barely even understand himself? Had it only been two nights ago? It felt like an age since Ben had loomed over his bed, saying in a panic-stricken voice, 'Alfred – Alfred's gone missing.'

At first Toby had thought it was Dr Bath in his room. Bath had been in a strange mood – would have talked all night about pre-war Germany if Toby hadn't invented a headache and gone to bed. Later, walking past Bath's room on the way to the toilets, he saw the portly tutor in his nightgown, swallowing some pills as Lance Vaine and the Musical Hellos sang *Midnight blue/And dreams of you/The stars at night/ Our candlelight,*' sounding tinny and awful on the portable radio. It was 1 am. Back in bed, he heard shouting from the other end of the house, then a door slam and a barking laugh that he recognised as Leeson's. He mumbled a protest at the noise, but he was sinking so fast into sleep it scarcely seemed worth the effort.

Then Ben's voice: 'Shit, Toby! Toby – wake up … oh God, oh God … We're fucked, fucked …'

Toby, groggy and still half asleep, registered how cold it was, how there weren't enough blankets on his bed, and that he probably should get up and get some more. Then he registered Ben's words. 'Huh? What are you talking about?' he asked Ben, rolling back to the wall and closing his eyes again.

'Oh fuck,' Ben was saying in a really strange voice. 'Fuck.' He sat on Toby's bed and tried to roll him over.

'Alfred – Alfred's gone missing,' Ben said. 'Out there.' He flung an arm towards the window before dropping it heavily onto Toby's head.

'Fuck off,' said Toby, hitting out in the dark with a punch that failed to connect, and landed softly somewhere near Ben's neck. 'Did you do something to Alfred?' he asked, waking up slowly.

There was silence.

'Ben, did you do something to Alfred?' Toby repeated. He nudged Ben, who fell to the ground.

'You're as pissed as a newt …'

At his door there was suddenly light and laughter. Julian and Levi were using a combination of the doorframe and each other to remain upright, but they were swaying as if trying to balance on a paddleboard in the ocean.

Julian started giggling and wheezing at the same time. 'Alfred's guilty,' he said, struggling to speak. 'That's the verdict … Alfred's guilty. But now the prisoner's absconded.'

'I checked out the back but I fell into the woodpile,' said Levi, who then lurched away abruptly. Toby heard the sound of noisy vomiting in the hall and the clatter of Levi's glasses as they fell from his nose onto the floor.

Julian turned to look at Levi and started laughing again. 'You missed the bin, retard! You dropped your glasses!'

'What happened to Alfred?' asked Toby sharply.

Ben spoke from somewhere on the floor. 'We were playing a game and then he ran off outside somewhere. He's probably hiding behind that thing – you know that thing?'

'Why don't you get the others to look for him? It's got nothing to do with me. I was busy being bored to death by Bath, then came up to bed.'

'The others don't care about Alfred,' said Ben. 'Please, Toby – you need to help us find him.'

'Alfred's guilty,' said Julian again, laughing.

Toby sighed, 'What does that even mean, Julian?' He stood up and found his clothes and shoes while Ben murmured, 'Thank you. Thank you, Toby. Your shirt is on backwards. I owe you, okay?'

Julian was in hysterics by the door, mimicking Ben. 'Love you, mate. Love you, mate.'

Even though Toby was still drunk, he knew several things: it was a bitterly cold night; it was dangerous outside, with all sorts of sudden drops and uneven paths; and Alfred, who had only been in the country for a month, must have been badly frightened to think of running off.

Toby poured a dram of port into his coffee mug, drank deeply and tried to avoid Lucy's intense gaze.

Charlotte finished her call and flung the phone back into her bag. 'Fuck – he's such a loser! Can't get the hint. What were you saying, Toby? You went for a walk and got lost?'

'Let someone else tell it,' Toby said.

'Let me!' said Julian, a gifted liar.

Levi, drowsy from the joint and the weekend's excesses, had fallen asleep, his arms thrown above his head in a way that suggested beachside abandon.

Julian made it sound like a lark, a first-day-of-spring sort of thing, a string of bucolic moments, a silly pastoral jaunt lit upon after a night of heavy drinking. No map or sunscreen, unprepared, ill thought out.

'Crazy. We were being crazy,' said Julian. 'Going for a bushwalk in the heat like that – not even wearing the right shoes. Ha! And Levi and Ben got so sunburnt that chunks of their faces fell off, and Toby cut his hands and Levi fell and twisted his knee. We ended up sleeping out there. Levi and I slept under a ledge and Toby and Ben roughed it on the rocks.'

Charlotte laughed at the picture Julian painted of them bumbling around in the bush, but Lucy stayed silent. Toby watched her watching him, and knew the deep study she made of things, her fledgling lawyer's mind already primed to find the holes in a story, to hear the verbal missteps. He knew she did not believe them.

CHAPTER 3

Halfway down the mountain stood a small red-brick building that could almost pass for a toilet block except for the sign that said SES, WYCLOFF REGION: SEARCH AND RESCUE. It had only been staffed intermittently since the government had centralised rescue services, and the answering machine directed callers to a call centre in the city before assuring them they could leave a message for local volunteers after the beep.

Gary opened the door then quickly unlatched the windows. The room smelt sour, closed and oppressive, like the summer had been. Someone had left milk out on the bench and the water in the kettle stood rank and sewerish. He refilled the kettle with fresh water then, as he waited for it to boil, flicked on the answering machine.

There was only one message.

The caller, young, male and seemingly drunk or distraught, rambled about someone called 'Alfred' who had gone missing from a house on the western side of the mountains.

Gary made some notes, but it was hard to follow – someone, 'Seven' or 'Sven', who had a pole, or was it 'Sven was a Pole'?

He could hear music and singing in the background. The caller was breathing heavily, like he had been running, then the phone cut out.

Gary checked the volunteer log book. In February Sue had been in. (So it was Sue who had left the milk out!) No one had been in since then.

'Hope the poor bastard's okay,' he said aloud. He rang the central office to see if they had received a call about an Alfred and if he had been found.

It was too early in the year to start going to the college library, yet Levi found Julian on Tuesday evening, squeezed in between the medical textbooks and the theology section, staring blankly at an open legal casebook.

'What are you doing here?' asked Levi. 'Is there an exam on that I don't know about?'

'No, I just thought I'd read about some cases,' said Julian.

'What cases?' asked Levi, surprised that his usually lazy friend, after more than two years of law school, was finally showing an interest in the course.

'Where people have been charged for being aware of a crime but not reporting it,' said Julian in a tight voice.

'Oh.' Levi was silent as he tried to read over Julian's shoulder. 'What happened to them?'

'They went to jail.'

'Oh.'

Levi flopped down awkwardly on a wooden chair. His knee was still throbbing from the fall in the mountains on the weekend.

'There was this one case,' Julian said, 'about this girl who worked at a chicken shop. They locked her in the cool room and left her there for a really long time – overnight, I think. She wasn't right in the head after that. It wasn't just the dudes that did it who were tried, but the other workers, the ones who just stood around and let it happen.'

Levi was quiet for a moment, contemplating what this meant for them. Even if they had not actually touched Alfred in the bunkroom they could still be found guilty of a crime.

In the library's hush, Levi could hear Julian's breathing, raspy and uneven. He looked at Julian with concern.

'Asthma,' explained Julian. 'It's come back. The other night I woke up and my chest was tight and I couldn't breathe … like a panic attack, almost.'

'It'll pass,' said Levi, trying to reassure himself as much as Julian. 'I'm sure Alfred's fine. He's probably back by now. Why don't we check his room?'

'Good idea.'

Levi tried to look nonchalant as they walked to the Fraser Wing, a place they had never had occasion to visit before.

'We don't even know what room he's in,' Julian noted.

'He's in 4A,' Levi said. 'I already checked the college directory. I was planning on going there anyway.'

Inside, the corridors were quiet. There was just the sound of computer games and the occasional disembodied voice seeping out with the light from under the doorways. But there was no light showing under Alfred's door.

'Knock, knock, knockin' on Alfred's door ...' sang Julian as he rapped on the door.

'Shut up,' hissed Levi.

'What does it matter? He's not here.'

'He might be asleep.'

Levi took a deep breath and knocked again, louder. 'I don't want anyone to see us.'

When Alfred didn't open the door they backed away, hoping he was inside in a deep sleep, not up there in the mountains still.

The next morning Toby, Ben, Julian and Levi sat down for breakfast at their usual table.

'I should have mentioned it at the pub last night, but before Julian and I left for the Lion we stopped by Alfred's room ... but he didn't answer the door,' said Levi, lowering his voice.

'Why did you do that?' asked Toby incredulously. 'Lurking around his room in the middle of the night is only going to attract attention. You don't even know anyone in Fraser. How are you going to explain what you were doing there?'

'I was there too,' said Ben. 'I dropped by around eleven, just to see if his light was on, but it wasn't.'

'Shit!' said Toby. Then, conscious of the echo of his voice in the dining hall, and keeping an eye out for Hadrien, he leant in and continued more quietly: 'I reckon we should forget the stupid pact we made and report this to the Master. It's what we should have done a couple of days ago. But we can still do it now – it's not too late.'

'I agree,' said Levi. 'I don't think I can live with myself knowing that we just left Alfred in the mountains and drove home without him. I mean, that's a really bad thing to do.'

'What about the … the game?' asked Ben faintly. 'All that will come out.'

Toby shrugged. 'I'm sorry, Ben, but that's not my problem. Let's skip the Master and go straight to the police. Maybe they can organise a search for Alfred.'

The others nodded, their toast stone-cold now, the tea tasting sour in their mouths, a visceral dread around them and the words drying up in their throats. But before they could decide anything more Octavia and Charlotte joined them, Octavia fretting about an overdue History essay, Charlotte a cracked iPhone screen. Ben listened to their distress, trying to suppress his own.

The chapel bells chimed nine times and the girls rushed out across the minty lawn to the university. Wordlessly the boys followed, only to veer off to Starr Street, which led to the police station. Ben felt a weird energy coursing between them, a sense of common purpose, like they were about to go skiing down a black run in the dark or drive a car the wrong way down a one-way street with the headlights off. Time seemed to stretch as they waited impatiently opposite the station for the lights to change. Julian told a joke, but it was feeble and no one could concentrate enough to absorb the punch line. Toby, trembling slightly, pressed the traffic-light button again and again with urgent jabs.

'Stop doing that,' muttered Ben tersely.

Just as the light turned green they saw Leeson. He was waving at them from further down Starr Street, shouting, 'They've found him! They've found Alfred!'

As Levi exhaled loudly, Ben's knees buckled under him. Toby was watching and grabbed him quickly by the elbow. Together, they walked towards Leeson.

CHAPTER 4

After a hiker spotted Alfred (his arm, gouged, blood-drenched, dangling from a ledge), rescuers came from as far as Fortune Hill in the west, Mount Difficult in the east and Yulapumda in the south. Men in yellow vests with ropey arms abseiled down the gorge. Later a helicopter winched them out along with a stretcher bearing the semi-conscious student. Alfred was airlifted to the city for emergency spinal and brain surgery and placed in an induced coma.

The hospital rang the Master on Sunday night – Alfred's student ID had been in his back pocket. The Master told them he would contact Alfred's parents.

From the window in his study, the Master had seen Severin and Leeson bundle Alfred into the van on Friday morning, had guessed Alfred was accompanying the cricketers to the mountains and knew it would probably end badly.

Initiations had moved underground since the 1980s, when one of the students in Minerva College had been killed during an O-Week stunt. Initiations were dark and edgy things, pseudo-sexual even – and more so now because of their illicitness.

The Master put thoughts of culpability or responsibility to one side; after all, the boys were adults and he could not stop their pranks. He rang the college's PR firm, Bassington Morley, and explained that one of his students had been in an accident – could they please help keep it out of the press?

Over port with Dr Bath in the Senior Common Room, the Master tried for a positive spin.

'It might frighten those revolting cricketers off ever performing stunts like this again,' said the Master. 'I could probably even get away with expelling some of the nastier elements. Get rid of Leeson, for example, and Severin. And of course that freak Hadrien. If only his family weren't such big donors.'

'Not Toby,' said Dr Bath. 'He wasn't involved.'

'No, not him,' said the Master. 'He's ... I don't know, moral or something ... that thing that country kids have. You know that thing?'

'I know that thing. Yes, he's very moral. Tell me, how is Alfred? I'm sorry I can't tell you more of what went on that night, except I stayed up with Toby by the fire. He was asking all sorts of questions about my PhD. I took really strong sleeping pills and slept soundly through the night.' Dr Bath sounded ashamed.

'It's okay, Bath,' the Master reassured him. 'The boys are adults, you can't keep a constant watch. But Alfred – yes, he's off the ventilator but his brain injuries are quite extensive. We have him on a list for a place in a nursing home nearby, then maybe later some sort of rehabilitation.'

'Oh, that *does* sound serious. Can I ask, Master, that you get someone else to chaperone the next trip? Maybe one of the younger members of the Senior Common Room?'

Gibbs, the porter, passed between them with a tray and the bottle of port. They fell silent until he moved away.

'Absolutely, Bath. I promise you'll never have to go on one of those wretched trips again, as long as you stick to what you just told me. You were out of it. You saw nothing.'

'Of course,' said Bath. 'Well – it is the truth.'

The Master nodded and tried not to appear irritated by the fact that in the short space of time they'd been together Dr Bath had already drunk four glasses of port.

Bassington Morley did an excellent job. Alfred's fall was reported on Sunday night as a small item on the local wire service. It was picked up by a national news website as a story off the homepage with a shelf life of an hour or two. The next day two newspapers ran it briefly:

> *A man in his late teens was rescued yesterday by emergency services at Plumley's Gap in the south-west Wycloffs. He had been camping alone when the accident happened. Emergency services, including the SavBank Chopper, assisted in winching the man to safety. He is in a serious but stable condition with suspected spinal and brain injuries at the Royal Prince Edward Hospital. His name has not yet been released.*

The college wasn't mentioned; keep the college out of it and no one would connect the incident to an initiation ritual gone wrong. Context was everything, a woman from Bassington Morley told the Master. 'If you give the media context they have a story. Provide only the bare facts – make it look routine or dull – and it gets overlooked. Which is what we want.'

The Master had viewed CCTV footage from the cameras set up in the Fraser Wing and had seen Alfred's last minutes at the college. (Leeson and Severin either side of him, twice his size! Alfred was wearing … what? His pyjamas?) He erased the tapes, trying not to think too much while he did it. It was an action that carried a curious echo of his childhood, when his mother would force him to eat the cold, rubbery vegetables left unwanted on his plate. He could do it, he could eat those terrible vegetables, he'd realised, if he deactivated the part of his brain that was aware of the act. In other words, he could do something unpleasant without experiencing the unpleasantness. What a discovery to make! It had proved a very useful skill to have.

Ben took the card from his wallet. It had been there since his first O-Week, two years ago. Funny that he had never thrown it away. He'd arrived at university as part of a pack – him, Leeson, Severin, Roman, Hadrien and a few others from his school. It was sunny, February – and they did a lap of the main quad, beers in hand, sneering at the stalls manned by the political activists, the university ski club, the Young Liberals, the horse-riding enthusiasts, the Friends of the Earth and the Womyn's Society.

''Tis sad,' said Hadrien, 'that these people need to sit here in their crummy little stalls advertising for friends. What is the Chocolate Appreciation Society other than a confectionary gulag for losers?'

They all laughed at that, although Julian did take free samples, and strode back to college for lunch. St Anton's had its own O-Week – steeped in ritual, drenched in booze, punctuated by hospital visits and 3 am arrests for the theft of road signs and, occasionally, assault. College O-Week was expensive, requiring the purchase of dinner suits, academic gowns, sporting kits and college and rugby tops. College O-Week required an empty brain, an uninquiring mind – these would be filled by the new language, hierarchy, songs, prayers, contempt, that would mark you as a member of St Anton's. So successful was the indoctrination that you pitied everyone else – all those *losers* at the university who had to live in other colleges or houses and missed out on such an incredible experience.

But before O-Week was over, Ben had gone back to the stalls on his own. He was drawn to the sincerity of those who waited at the card tables, keenly proffering brochures. At a barbecue in the Chemistry Courtyard for the Rock-Climbing Club, Ben enthusiastically pledged to spend every second weekend with this sinewy species – camping at the foot of Mount Stuyvesant, nights of warm beer and tinned meats at the base, and then at dawn, the climb. But he felt the same way meeting the young Amnesty International women: maybe the worst are full of passionate intensity, but they are also doe-eyed and lovely, with mouthfuls of marvellous intentions. Five minutes with them and he felt inspired to actually do something with his law degree – to visit prisoners, to fight oppressive regimes, to one day appear at the International Criminal Court in The Hague, verbally eviscerating some fat war criminal. He left their stall with a fistful of brochures, feeling purposeful: he could do something with his life!

The feeling stayed with him until he reached the college gates and saw Leeson retching into a bin, then passed an Amazonian third-year girl who had ordered him to undress in her room the previous night, then stared at his naked body with a dead look in her eyes before passing out like a poisoned queen. Ben walked back through those wrought-iron gates and instantly the special feeling of being able to save the world went away.

Yet back he went to university O-Week – each club's stall tickling some latent part of him, some hinterland heavy and potent with the promise of a new path. The Forest Alliance: direct action, habeas corpus between the tree and the bulldozer, a willingness to endure a criminal record for trespass. The Climate Sceptics: not afraid to be unpopular, but for God's sake, when will everyone see (as we do) that the emperor has no clothes? The Comedy Club: we will see live comedy – and one day, when we are ready, we will *do* live comedy.

But there was one stall to which Ben kept returning. Despite being in a prime position between the Socialist Alliance and Greenpeace, this stall was like the dead electrode in the quadrangle's circuitry hum. It was manned by a boy about Ben's age, always alone and kind of uncool – yet something unspoken passed between them, like it does sometimes between strangers: they were *interested* in each other. Sylvan's stall didn't promise weekends away at the university ski lodge, or midwinter black-tie balls, or exhilarating sex after a day of jumping from planes. Sylvan was trying to attract people to his church.

Sylvan was promising Jesus, but a certain sort of Jesus – a socialist Jesus. Unlike the Students for Christ and the University Christians, Sylvan's church didn't lure you in with basketball games, or group baptism followed by a gourmet sausage sizzle. It didn't have drug-free raves with Christian DJs; it didn't have a well-stocked bookshop, a radio station or an online Christian news portal.

The Jerusalems tried to live life as Jesus had lived it. One of their key tenets was living poorly – graciously and prayerfully, but poorly. The Jerusalems didn't have money; indeed, they went out of their way to reject money. They made their coin through enterprise – running cafes, selling woodwork and farming – and once they had food in their bellies, they gave away whatever was left.

'This frees you from so much,' Sylvan told Ben with real passion. 'If you reject money, you reject desire – and when you remove desire from your life, you remove so much pain, anger, disappointment. Those things that drag you down.'

Sylvan described Jesus in a kind of Religion 101 way, as if speaking to a simpleton. Sylvan's Jesus was constantly giving stuff away, was friends with all the people whom others shunned – people who worked for the Tax Office, hookers, security guards at detention centres. And he hated hypocrites, people who pretended to be pious but actually were pretty selfish and materialistic. Jesus was the guy who barracked for the team on the bottom of the ladder, who was mates with the guys who didn't always get the girls, who befriended the funny-looking kids at school, the ones who got stuffed in rubbish skips, locked in high-jump mat storage areas, heads held underwater too long at the school sports carnival.

The Jerusalems were all the things the other campus groups promised rolled into one: mountains and laughter, social justice and the environment, community and friendship. There was the sort of freedom and exhilaration you experienced when skydiving, but with the Jerusalems it was there all the time – the feeling was in you, you carried it.

Sylvan's group took their cues from Jesus' disciples and lived communally. Families who were part of the group all lived together ('Not polygamously!' he stressed) and pooled their resources: money, care of the animals, labour and childcare. They weren't much into preaching, Sylvan explained in his gentle way, but they did like to let people know that they existed. 'We don't want to shout it out – just, you know, "We're here, join us if you like."' Instead of a brochure he handed Ben a small card.

'It's got my number on the back. Call me anytime – I'll always remember who you are.'

And that was that, really. Over the next two years Ben saw Sylvan around, and an occasional acknowledgement would pass between them: a nod, a look, a half-wave. But college was its own cult, its own sect, and Ben fell into its slipstream, too passive to break away.

He thought of Sylvan from time to time, though – usually when he was with Hadrien, and active in or witness to some form of cruelty. But after a while Sylvan ceased to have a recognisable human form in his thoughts and instead came to resemble a concept – Sylvan was goodness.

Ben had thought of Sylvan when they were with Alfred in the bunkroom at Evelyn, though he had tried not to. And now that they were back from the mountains and Alfred was in hospital, he thought of Sylvan all the time.

Toby lay on his bed, checked his phone, then got up and sat at his desk, turned on his MacBook, checked his phone again, refreshed his Tumblr and his Instagram, checked Facebook, tried to think of a status update that didn't reveal his internal agitation, then went back to his bed, where he sat for a minute before standing up, more out of irritation than anything else. He just couldn't settle. Anything more than five minutes spent in front of his computer screen and he'd be pacing, putting on some music before tiring of the song, jiggling his leg, checking his phone, switching on the kettle, scratching his head, and opening and closing a textbook that had no hope of capturing his attention.

Alfred, Alfred, Alfred – that was all he could think about right now. Studying law was as much about disciplining your mind as learning the case law, training it to go down a certain path, follow certain logic, making the transition from unruliness to yielding to a hefty set of rules. Yet ever since the trip into the mountains his mind had been wandering, discursive as fuck.

Yesterday his family had driven to the city to attend some anti-war protest. He had drifted companionably with them through a throng down to the river. Occasionally they would shout out some slogan ('No Blood for Oil', 'Out of Gaza') or cheer at some speech, or kind of dance-walk behind a man playing a metal drum, but most of the time Toby spent with one arm linked through that of his mother and the other arm linked through his brother's, holding on more tightly than necessary as if their very matter would be strong and good enough to ameliorate the evil of last weekend.

He had been weak. Weak to help cover up what had happened to Alfred. Weak not to go to the police. But it wasn't too late, was it? He could still go and see them …

He tried to be shrewd – even cold – about it like the others seemed to be. He wondered if going to the police would get him into more trouble. He cursed himself for not having dialled triple zero when Ben first woke him. What valuable time they had lost! Even more, he hated how pathetic he had turned out to be. Instead of arranging Alfred's rescue, he had just delayed the whole process, no doubt making Alfred's injuries worse. They filled his mind when he closed his eyes: snapping of ribs, fluid bubbling from the mouth, the hiss of the collapsed lung like an air mattress deflating, the jumble of organs, muscles, bone, blood – under and breaking through the skin …

Toby thought back to the fruitless search, the night on the mountains, the return to Evelyn and the pact. After Ben, Julian and Levi had woken him in the pre-dawn, they had gathered in the kitchen.

'We need a bigger search party than this,' said Toby to his three friends. 'We need a *more sober* search party.'

Julian and Levi had showered while Toby made coffee, and when they returned the giggles and hilarity of the last hour had been replaced by a kind of woozy quietness.

'There's so much blood in the showers,' murmured Levi. 'I spewed again.'

'So did I,' said Julian. 'I didn't think it would be possible to spew again, but I did.'

'Whose blood?' Toby asked with alarm. 'Not Alfred's?'

'No, not Alfred's,' said Levi. 'I think there was an animal. Do you remember an animal, Ben?'

Ben said nothing.

'Wake the others,' Toby said. 'We'll eat now – you'll all feel better. I'll do a big fry-up and then we can get a search party together.'

'The others won't want to search,' said Ben, glowering. 'They won't want Alfred to be found. That's the worst thing that could happen as far as Hadrien is concerned.'

'What exactly did you do to Alfred?' asked Toby.

No one answered him.

He lifted a big steel frypan from the cupboard and inspected it for rust. 'Maybe we should just report Alfred missing – to the police, I mean, so they can call in Search and Rescue. Levi, where's your phone? Do you have credit left?'

'I think it's best if we find him ourselves,' mumbled Ben. He looked shifty.

'Christ – what on earth did you do to him?' Toby asked again.

'It doesn't matter at the moment, but trust me, it's better for everyone if we find him first,' said Ben emphatically, his voice still thick with alcohol. 'If we go to the police and they find him, we could get into a lot of trouble.'

'Did you hurt him?'

'He was hurt, yes.'

Pouring a leftover glass of wine down the sink – it was making him sick to look at it – Toby turned to Ben. 'I don't understand why the fuck you had to hurt him. The whole weekend's ruined now.'

'We didn't mean to.'

'Bullshit,' said Toby. 'Remember that girl who came up last year?'

'Oh, that … It's worse this time,' said Ben quietly. 'Hadrien and Severin insisted on it. We used to do a variation of it at boarding school. But you let them go in the end, they're not meant to run off into the night. God it's happened to me – it's happened to everyone.'

'It happened to me at my school,' admitted Julian. 'But I wouldn't do it anymore.'

'Why were you there, then? I saw you go off to the bunkroom with the others,' said Toby.

Julian blushed. 'I was in the room, but I was so drunk I passed out before anything happened.'

'What exactly went on?' asked Levi. 'I don't get this at all. Obviously I went to the wrong school,' he added sarcastically.

'Weren't you there?' asked Ben, confused. 'I thought I saw you there; you were wearing that Biggie Smalls mask.'

Levi was indignant. 'No way, I don't know exactly what went on, but I don't do shit like that. Never have. Never will. What did *you* do?'

'I watched mostly. I didn't do anything,' said Ben.

'Exactly,' said Toby. 'You did nothing.'

Ben shook his head. 'You don't understand.'

'So will this get on the internet? Did you film any of it?' asked Toby.

'No … I don't think so,' replied Ben, although he sounded uncertain. 'And even if it was filmed, we had hoods covering our faces.'

Toby sighed, feeling suddenly old and depressed. 'Maybe it's best not to talk about this now. Let's look for him, and we'll sort out the rest when we get back to college. Shall we wake everyone up and get a search party organised?'

'I can blow the horn,' said Julian, gesturing to the ancient brass instrument on the bench. 'We don't want to wake Bath, though.'

'I think he dropped some sedatives last night,' said Toby. 'I saw the packet in the bathroom. They're pretty strong. He'll sleep through anything, I reckon.'

Julian picked up the trumpet and walked down the hall, pausing before closed bedroom doors to blast out a wake-up call.

Toby, Ben and Levi followed him as if it were a funeral procession, their heads bowed, stepping over the broken glass, the smashed bottles, around the pools of … something … until they were all on the landing, the horn's echo still bouncing off the walls, until the others emerged from their rooms, eyes grotty with sleep.

'What do we have here? *Revenge of the Nerds*?' asked Hadrien, pulling the trumpet from Julian's lips. 'You fucking joker.' He pushed the trumpet deep into Julian's jellied abdomen, like he would a knife, before withdrawing it with a 'Hmph!' and turning to go back to bed.

Toby, quick and angry, blocked his way.

'What are you doing, you girl?' asked Hadrien. 'Fuck off.'

'What have you done to Alfred? Where is he?' asked Toby.

'What? Where's Alfred? Have you seen him, Severin?' asked Hadrien.

'Hell, no. Not for a good few hours now,' said Severin in his deep, gruff voice.

'What about you, Leeson? Seen Alfred?'

'No, I don't believe I have. In fact it is my belief that I have never seen Alfred. He hasn't been here, has he, Sam?'

'No, he hasn't been here ...' echoed Sam tiredly.

'Where's Alfred? Where's Alfred?' said Hadrien, doing a pretty good imitation of Toby's panic, albeit an octave higher. 'Ohhh – Alfred's gone! Ben, maybe you know where Alfred is. Actually, Ben, weren't you the last one to see Alfred?'

Hadrien was naked. He was smaller than the other boys, with none of the rippling muscle of Severin or Leeson, or the broad shoulders of Toby or Ben. He was an unusual-looking boy: he had white-blond hair and his skin had a metallic sheen like the moon – his mother rumoured to be an albino. Yet authority seemed to radiate from him in an almost palpable way. It was a murky authority, a quality that made Toby scared of him, yet ... yet ... here on the landing, in the half-dark, completely undressed and shining, he was spinning a new reality. Here in the cold dawn light he was making Alfred *disappear.*

'He was never here, was he, lads?' he said, turning back to address the rest of the cricket team.

There were a few 'yahs', enough support for him to suddenly spring on Toby, grabbing his wrist and twisting it in a fierce Chinese burn. 'You woke me up for this, you faggot?'

Severin and Leeson suddenly loomed over them. Toby drew back, only his shadow growing on the wall. Roman gave Levi a shove. In his sock-covered feet Levi slipped on the floor and fell backwards. A foot sprung out and struck him sharply under the chin.

'Oops – sorry, old chap,' said Hadrien, bending down to help Levi up. He turned and spoke to the cricketers behind him in the darkness. 'That was a low blow, whoever did that. We're a team.'

'Where is he?' asked Toby. 'Where's Alfred?'

'Cripes! Did you hear that?' Hadrien forced open a window and a blast of cold mountain air came in. The boys with bare chests shivered and hugged themselves.

'Alfred! Alfred!' Hadrien called out through the open window. The only answer was the sound of waking birds.

'Alfred! Alfred!' Hadrien's voice had an almost romantic, melancholy note now, making some of the boys snigger. 'Oh, Alfred! Don't hide from us!'

Silence.

'Mmmm, doesn't look like he's here, lads. Looks like he's gone, if he was ever here in the first place. But if he *is* gone – and let's pretend for a moment he was here – well, it's probably for the best. I think we'd all rather that he didn't talk to anyone about what happened when he was a guest of the cricket team.' Hadrien leant in close to Toby and said in his quiet, raspy voice: 'I don't know how much Benji told you about last night, but it wasn't pretty.'

The boys standing on the landing were becoming restless. Some looked defiantly at Toby, others were sheepish. They shuffled their feet around on the cold stone floor, hair wild, and looked longingly towards their bedroom doors, anxious to find the oblivion of sleep again.

Toby tried to read in their expressions which cricketers might feel guilty enough to join the search party. His eyes fell on Sam – a big, broad-shouldered, sandy-haired farm boy studying Ag Science; a powerful batsman, amicable, mostly good-natured, who followed the loudest voice, like a dumb work dog.

'C'mon, Sam – it's not like you to just let someone run off into the night. You know how rough it is out there. Come help us look for him. You too, Ping. Believe me, I don't care what happened in the bunkroom, but it'll only be worse if we don't find him. What if someone else finds him first? Or if he gets back to college without us and starts talking to the Master or goes to the police? That won't be good for any of you.'

No one moved.

Toby felt something hit him on the back. It wasn't hard. It felt like a rolled-up sock.

Surrounded by the team he had once captained, Toby felt a strange, new sort of menace in the air, an echo maybe of how Alfred had felt a few hours ago.

Then Hadrien's voice cut coolly through the silence. 'You won't find him. I know you won't. So many places to get lost. So many places to fall. You might fall yourself.'

He took the horn from Julian, drew it to his lips and blew it. 'Lads, to bed. Consider it not so deeply. Sleep off the night's mad adventures in your own little death and chaotic dreams. Know that what you did tonight is no different from what a soldier might do. They're our age too. We forget that. We are warriors, we are champions.'

A little cheer went up. Someone in underpants raised a cricket bat in the air. And then, with the milky daylight coming in through the open window, the boys dispersed – to sleep, not search.

Now, back at college, pacing in his room, everything dark except for the glow of the MacBook screen, it dawned on Toby that Ben and the others had got away with what they did to Alfred. No consequences! It didn't seem right; it upset his sense of how the universe should be ordered. But if he told the police, he would get his friends in terrible trouble. Maybe they would even go to jail.

'I mean, for Christ's sake,' said Toby aloud, trying to banish all thought of going to the police, 'I don't even know Alfred!'

But still it weighed on him, like a brick on his chest, when he went to bed that night.

CHAPTER 5

On the long, warm nights of that Indian summer, students took wine down to the marshy banks of the river and lit up the lawns with candles in the empty bottles. In each other's rooms, lying on the sun-brittle lawns, drinking by the night-time murmuring river, messaging each other on Facebook during a boring statistics seminar, Alfred was all anyone could talk about. Rumours spread: that Alfred was close to death, that the Master would have to make a decision about whether to take him off life support, that the last rites were being administered by one of the black-eyed Jesuits from St Sebastian's, that Alfred's parents were on a plane from Kuala Lumpur. Students started to crowd around the Master as he crossed the quadrangle, pressing presents and notes into his arms to pass on to Alfred, eyes wide and tearful, asking, 'Will he be all right, Master?' Even the latest hit by Lance Vaine and the Musical Hellos seemed to have an eerie resemblance to Alfred's fall: *'Brackish river, flowing fast/Holding a boy without a past/ Whispering darkly, "Nothing lasts."'*. Students sat in each other's rooms, listening to it on repeat.

At dinner on the Wednesday a week after Alfred was

found, the Master rang a bell and stood in his place at the High Table to address the students.

'Silence, please! I have an important announcement … about Alfred Khoo.'

The chatter abruptly died and became a silence that was palpable.

Toby felt flushed and sweaty in his heavy black gown, under which he wore a collar and tie – college rules for every evening meal, appropriated from England with no nod to the climate. He squirmed and loosened his tie and felt Julian press his leg under the table. He didn't make eye contact, concentrating instead on composing his face into a concerned, compassionate expression, partly for Lucy's benefit. She kept flicking him glances from across the table. He looked around anxiously for Ben. Where had he gone?

'I know you're all upset about Alfred's fall, but let me assure you he is receiving the very best medical care.' The Master's powerful voice easily reached all corners of the dining room without the benefit of a microphone. 'To all those students who have told me they are praying for Alfred – thank you. Prayers, although not proven in the field of medical science, are better than no prayers at all. If you don't believe in God then perhaps you can send your good vibes out to Alfred and I'm sure that will help him enormously.'

A student – one of the rowers – yelled out 'Amen' from the back of the dining hall. Toby couldn't tell if it was meant sarcastically.

'But we must remember that foolish behaviour has serious and real consequences. I know many of you here have left home or boarding school for the first time and are testing boundaries. That can be a lovely thing. It can also be very dangerous. Alfred left the college grounds and went on an unsupervised hike. Fair enough, he's not from here and so he doesn't know the topography, but I'm sure we would all agree that for such an intelligent, academically gifted young man, his behaviour was reckless. I should also note that he was found to have a rather high blood alcohol level. Let's all learn from Alfred's fall.'

Toby exhaled, returned Julian's nudge under the table and suddenly felt lighter. Alfred fell, that was all. It was unremarkable to have a hiking accident – boring even. When dinner was over Toby texted Ben saying, *I think it's going to be okay*, and then he, Julian, Lucy and Levi went back to Charlotte's room to drink wine and play each other funny clips on YouTube, not mentioning Alfred once.

But as the week went on Toby discovered that the Alfred situation wasn't boring, and that it hadn't been forgotten. The college, always susceptible to strange fads and strong emotions, relished the drama of Alfred's rescue, the cruelty of the bushland, the gravity of his injuries. The students of St Anton's loved him more in this broken state than when he was whole and new. He was the adopted Asian brother they never had, the Rotary Youth Exchange student who never came to stay, the whiz kid who could have explained the deep mysteries of engineering, mathematics and chemistry.

In half-death he was more alive than in life. Over the next few weeks in the overwrought hothouse atmosphere of the college, girls wept and wore black. Boys talked about their little buddy Alfred and his interest in football.

'He asked if the Magpies were a good team to barrack for and of course I said no,' declared Severin, swelling with sadness at his fraudulent recollection.

'Alfred was so cute,' said Charlotte, although once she had told Toby that most overseas students looked too similar to tell apart. 'Not only cute, but he had a real live-wire personality. Remember his crazy shorts?'

They weren't yet allowed to visit him in hospital but they prayed for him in the chapel and lit candles for him in the city cathedral. Some students started a Facebook page called HEAR FOR YOU (one of the rumoured side effects of his injuries was hearing loss). Many wrote old-fashioned letters to Alfred – some girls still using babyish handwriting, love hearts, stars and glitter in the margins – telling him he was in their hearts and prayers. The choir rehearsed a song for Alfred called 'Little Gentle Spirit' and Toby heard that even the Master was moved to tears when he heard snatches of it drifting down the cloister on balmy evenings.

In the beer garden of the Red Lion, amid a sea of rugby jumpers and stacked beer glasses, Octavia wept after too many drinks and said it was because of Alfred. Giles wondered about Alfred's parents: 'How can we show them our support? Are they on Facebook?' The students confessed they didn't know. How do you show someone you don't know the depths of your compassion? Alfred's fall had made them think about their own near misses – the hard fall onto asphalt from the monkey bars, the scraped knees while learning how to ride a bike, the drunken spills off scooters during holidays in Vietnam.

'Why was he the one to suffer while others stood up and brushed themselves off?' asked the college chaplain, Dr Williams, in one of his better attended sermons.

The students pondered the nature of God and the way He distributes his pain. The crying girls said it wasn't fair, and after comforting them at 3 am in a too-bright chip shop Toby wondered if it wasn't Alfred they were crying for, but themselves, and if at eighteen they had intuited, the way girls do, that adulthood was about pain and loss from which they could not escape.

And on it went – all that week.

Alfred Khoo – the slight memories of him, one month of him embellished until the memories became florid and too bright. Alfred holding forth on Malaysian politics in the dining room. Alfred dancing in his oversized Ken Done shorts. His arms flailing, his body too, spinning like a whirling dervish, into girls' soft bodies and away again. Alfred drinking punch in the cool dark on the parapet. Alfred hitting the vending machine to liberate a packet of chips. Alfred moving a motion in a Students' Club meeting that better quality coffee be provided in the Student Lounge and a greater choice of newspapers be available in the Reading Room. Alfred in the morning tearing across the quadrangle in flaming red pyjamas, trying not to miss breakfast. Alfred cheering the football team dressed in college colours. Alfred coxing at the rowing tryouts. 'He only weighs forty kilos,' jealous girls on the banks would whisper to one another. Alfred playing ping-pong. Alfred at the pub calling sculls. Alfred organising a Young Labor march on the city against increasing student fees, with a megaphone and dreamy left-wing women on his arm. Alfred joining the horse-riding club and cantering free and unbroken on the plains outside the city.

Although he felt guilty and complicit, Toby didn't want to break the mood, the intense, sweet, fragile melancholy that had swept through the college like summer flu. It was fragile because it rested on a lie: the Alfred of their collective imagination did not exist. In real life Alfred hadn't talked to anyone. Alfred was seventeen and didn't drink. Alfred stayed in his room and studied.

From what little Toby remembered of Alfred, usually from seeing him in the dining room, he smiled a lot, then looked away and frowned as he scraped the contents of his plate into the rubbish bins. He wrapped his dessert in a napkin and left the dining room. Alfred went to his classes, ate his meals, brushed his teeth, studied in the basement of the library, and had lunches alone at Kuao San Huou on campus, where the food stained your teeth yellow and there were rumours of MSG in the rice. Toby imagined Alfred tried not to see them – his fellow students – as animals, but it was difficult not to. Most of the kids at St Anton's revelled in their baseness, the elemental way in which they lived: drinking greedily then vomiting noisily, eating three serves of pasta for lunch. Cheering and talking too loudly when coming back from the pub or a football match – chanting as they passed the Fraser Wing, with its invisible foreign occupants. It was as if all their abundance could not be contained within them, so it spilt out around them, causing mess. The students were unable to contain things because they had too much of everything. The ritual of the place could have been humbling, but instead it seemed to draw out some monstrous pride. The singing in the dining room, the banging on tables covered in crystal and silverware, property casually destroyed, and the way some girls' noisy vomiting or tears drifted out of open windows at 4 am. The beer frothing and spilling out of sports trophies after the latest on-field victory, the students drinking deeply and passing them on. The way the boys would ignore the girls. The way some boys would ignore their deep attraction to each other. The way the lights would bounce off the stone walls and the lamps would be lit around the dining room and the huge boar would be carried aloft by footballers with backs like stone altars.

Alfred lived at St Anton's, but he wasn't of it. And if he hadn't been almost killed, no one would have noticed him at all.

CHAPTER 6

The rowers – Ben, Leeson, Severin and Roman – and their cox, Hadrien, had been training since January; or, as Ben thought of it, training to forget. All five of them had been in the bunkroom with Alfred.

Five o'clock starts on the river, another row in the afternoon and laps around the university oval in the evening ... The legacy was perfect bodies but dull looks in their eyes and this terrible secret between them. They said nothing to each other of Alfred during the drive in the dark through the city to the boatshed on the riverbank. They were drowsy and couldn't help but lean comfortably against one another in the overheated car, listening to the news on the radio and the *pip-pip*, *pop-pop*, *ratta-tat-tat* in the background as the foreign correspondents filed their reports from the Middle East.

Sometimes they passed small fires that had been lit around the wreckage of cars, the bodies removed but the twisted metal and shattered glass waiting until daybreak for the clean-up crews to arrive. Often they passed other bodies, seeming more dead than alive under a streetlight, not far from the Lazy Fox or the Grouse and Claret – pubs known for all-night lock-ins, refuges for the most dedicated drinkers. Driving past, Ben wondered about assaults and beatings, drunk tanks and domestic violence, wild sprees and blackouts, hungover mornings trying to both remember and forget the night before.

Padding into the boatshed in the still, balmy black, the rowers were so quiet it almost felt like a burglary; lifting the boat gently from its hooks and holds – all that heaving in the dark – Ben thought they might as well be wearing balaclavas and soft-soled shoes. The hush of it, the way no one spoke.

Then they were out on the water. There were false starts – an oar dragging and a great groan from the boy in front as he strained to play his part, his muscles still warming up and the water resistant at first. Then it happened. You found your rhythm and the water yielded to the boat. And although the boys were bent over, they remembered to look up and it was dark and still, but somewhere there was a little rip in the sky where the light got in and the birds knew this and they surged and sang as the sky ripped a little bit further open, until suddenly there were holes everywhere for the light to get in, until the night was torn to shreds and the sky was streaked with pink, blue and gold.

Already the crew were far, far away from that place where they first started, where they stole away in a boat in the night, and far, far away from St Anton's. Further down the river, as if by consent, the oars were dropped into the water and one by one the rowers fell onto their backs like dominoes, heads back and eyes to the sky, seeing dawn come in (hot, gusty, brilliant, promising you everything), their hands resting beneath the surface of the water as if to pet the fish. Another sunrise, this one upside-down, dripping fire. Oh God, the beauty of it all, thought Ben. Sometimes moans escaped from his throat that could have come from effort, but were actually a surrender to the waking life around them.

Yet in the boat and in the car, and later in the shower, and later still during breakfast, they didn't talk about the night on the mountains with Alfred. Twice a day they trained their bodies until they were each part of the same machine, but still they didn't mention Alfred. Jammed together in the car each morning, jammed together in the boat, this Alfred thing was like some lump they found on their bodies that they were too scared to acknowledge, too scared to diagnose, too scared to talk about.

There was so much none of them could talk about.

Dr Williams's wife led the St Anton's yoga classes, an initiative of the Master, who thought that 'The kids need some Eastern wisdom to mellow them out.' Mrs Williams, who'd visited an ashram in India in the 1960s and still practised at home each morning, taught every Tuesday night in a beautiful candlelit room under the dome of the college's roof.

She'd start the class by saying, 'I've seen the rains down in Indonesia and I've heard the Dalai Lama in India,' before leading them in a Sanskrit chant.

Sam liked it. Football season was about to start and he needed to limber up. It was hell on his back: guys piling on top of him, elbows and knees pressing rough and fast onto his spine; the joint-jarring early morning jogs in the cold around the athletics track; the way his muscles would lock up at night under the bright haloes of light on the oval, while they pushed through sit-ups and squats in the rain.

Lucy also did the yoga class. Sometimes they were the only two students who turned up. During the final meditation he watched her slightly out of the corner of his nearly closed eyes, her lips upturned in a small smile and he wondered what or who she was thinking about.

'That was good,' she said, looking sleepy and content one night after class. 'I feel like tea. Do you want some?'

Lucy's room was the opposite of his sparsely decorated quarters which he had no idea what to do with. Posters covered every square inch of her room and there was a massive bookshelf – 'Cheever, Fitzgerald, Hemingway, Austen, Sontag, Foucault, Arendt, Pynchon, Melville,' said Lucy running her fingers across their spines. 'Anytime you want to borrow anything, just ask ...'

Sam envied her. Her tastes seemed fully formed; he didn't know what to like.

There was an eerie Sufi chant playing from her computer, dark chilli chocolate broken into jagged pieces on her desk, a bag of black jelly-beans that spilt over photography books and magazines. There was a paperback copy of *Lolita* open on her pillow and a hardcover book that made him blush – *The Ballad of Sexual Dependency* – on her desk.

She saw him and said quickly, 'It's not a sex book – see?' She opened it to reveal pictures of punks and transvestites and shirtless guys splayed like snow angels across car bonnets. 'It's photography,' she said, flicking through the pages.

There was a vase of tulips on her desk, a marked-up copy of Zizek's *The Parallax View*, a tatty poster for last year's St Anton's Ball (theme: SCENE AND BE SEEN), a postcard tacked on her wall of Heath Ledger and Jake Gyllenhaal, their thumbs in the pockets of big trucker jackets.

'*Brokeback Mountain*,' said Lucy. 'You seen it?'

Sam shook his head.

'Farm boy like you? You may like it.'

'I've seen *The Dark Knight*. Heath Ledger was good as the Joker.'

She put a finger to her lips, then touched the postcard as reverently as you might a religious relic. 'Heath. I miss him.'

The only place for Sam to sit was on her bed. An old hard-drive took up all the room on her chair.

Slow, soft, sinking twilight, and she reached across the bed and undid the ribbons holding back the curtains. They fell across the windows like a girl's hair when you untied the clips.

'What music do you like?' she asked, sitting on the bed next to him.

Sam was quiet, thinking for a while before deciding to be honest. 'Whatever's on the radio. I'll hear a song and like it but won't necessarily remember it.'

'Commercial radio?'

'Yeah, sure, though I don't really like the ads.'

He felt intensely self-conscious, sitting so close to her on her bed. Every muscle was so tense that he had to keep making and unmaking a fist just to make sure the blood kept flowing.

'I don't mind U2 ...' She said nothing. 'Dad listens to Johnny Cash. He's good.'

'Yeah, he's cool,' she said encouragingly, maybe wanting him to say more. But he had nothing else to say.

She got up, killed the chanting on the laptop, put on a record and brewed some tea. Its odour was strong – almost chemical, like a cheap perfume yet unlike anything he'd smelt before.

'Lapsang Souchong,' she said, pouring it into small cups. 'So why do you do yoga? I wouldn't have picked it.'

'Football, my back … yoga loosens it. Don't tell Leeson or Hadrien or any of those guys – they'd probably have me killed or something for being a hippie. They hate hippies.'

'Yeah – I remember when Leeson had to be restrained from beating up that guy Lab Rat who used to play Hacky Sack in the quad …'

Sam nodded.

'I can massage a bit. Do you want me to massage your back? I mean, I'm probably not very good … but …' offered Lucy tentatively.

He couldn't talk. He just nodded.

She put the tea on the window sill and sat behind him – not quite with him between her legs, there was distance, but if she moved forward, and he moved back … The vapour rose from the teapot and the smoky smell was so novel, it was heady and he tried to sip his tea too soon and burnt his lip and she laughed. The vinyl record she had just put on felt scratchy and real; it had texture, like when it was cold and he put on his favourite jacket – he felt everything about it.

Fingers as stiff as pencils (and her asking tentatively, 'Is this all right?' and him lying and saying, 'Yes'), and his fear that the blood had stopped flowing through him, and the rich, bleak, flat vocals – 'Perfect Day' by Lou Reed, which was sad and beautiful. It had an undertone that made him shiver; Lucy told him it was about heroin. She was driving her pointy fingers into places on his back where there was a splay of bone, and it was uncomfortable and made him tense up more – and she pressed in harder and it was fairly awful. And the cascading minor chords of the song, and the candles she had lit in the room, placed in vermouth bottles from the wine bar on Marchmont Street, and the shadows they threw on the walls, and the thickness of the wax on the bottles made him think of tumours, and that guy was singing that he thought he was someone else, someone good – all suddenly made Sam want to get out of there. Lucy had the back of his neck in her hands and the guy on the record was singing with dark portent about reaping what you sow, and she was touching parts of him he was sure had never been touched before – a bone two inches into his hair, a nobbly bit of his head – and she wasn't meaning to hurt him but she was.

'You were on that cricket trip, weren't you?' she asked, her voice light and low.

'Which one?' he asked, now rigid.

'The most recent one, to Evelyn.'

'Yep, to celebrate winning the Cup.'

'No one will tell me, but you'd tell me wouldn't you? If something bad happened up there? Everything's changed, you see. Something's weird and no one's even talking about it,' said Lucy. 'I mean, Toby clams up whenever I try to raise it with him …'

She moved closer to Sam and slid her legs along the outside of his legs, her feet bare and she was so close he could smell the tea on her breath. 'I mean, what happened up there?'

'Nothing,' said Sam, inching slightly away from her.

Lucy was now kneading the flesh around his shoulders. 'God you're so tense,' she said.

It came out of Sam in a hurt, hot tumble, fast and ill-advised. 'I hate Hadrien, I really do. He hurts people, he *makes* people do things they don't want to do.'

'Who did he hurt?' asked Lucy. Her hands had moved down his arms.

He said, more cautiously, 'Someone.'

'Who? Ben?'

'No, not Ben – someone else.'

The song had finished. The needle was jumping; a pile of jewellery scattered in a ceramic bowl on the desk glinted in the lamplight.

Suddenly Sam sprang up from the bed and pulled his shirt down.

'Where are you going?'

'I just remembered I have to meet Roman – get some files off his ... zip drive.'

Lucy shrugged her hands back into the folds of her shirt. 'Oh, okay. Come back if you want to – I don't know – borrow a book or something.'

He pulled the door to her room shut behind him and outside in the cloister noticed he was breathing hard. He turned and went up the stairs and along the corridor to his bare room, glad for the moment of its blankness, and lay on his bed in the chill silence, trying not to think at all.

There was a knock on Toby's door just before the bell for dinner.

'Haven't seen you for days,' said Toby when he opened the door to Ben. It was two weeks since they had come back from the mountains but still everything seemed strange and unsettled. It was as if the cricket team had dissolved into twelve individuals – each separate, watchful and suspicious of the others.

'Rowing,' said Ben. 'They've added another training session just after lunch. I'm exhausted.'

They stood out on Toby's balcony and, fingers trembling a bit with the match, Ben lit a cigarette. His body was bulging almost grotesquely under a T-shirt, his eyes red and his hair tousled, and a faint sour tang – like he'd slept in his clothes – came off him.

'How's your essay on the Nigerian slave trade going?' asked Toby.

'Overdue.'

'Want a hand?'

'No, there's nothing you can do.'

The sun was setting behind the quadrangle; the clouds darkened and passed suddenly across the sky. Some freshers were helping Dr Bath bring the animals back to their pens for the night; one student caught Toby's eye and made a hopeful wave towards the balcony.

Toby felt strangely broody, moody, like he wanted to

separate himself from everyone and be alone. He turned and went inside without returning the wave.

Ben stubbed out his cigarette and followed.

'What's the latest on Alfred? I can't believe how worked up people are over him. Octavia – she didn't even know him ...' Ben sighed. 'Is he still in a coma?'

'Yep. Apparently they've operated on his back and neck.'

'The fall – or ...?'

'That must have been the fall.'

'So not us.'

'Not us. Well, definitely not me.'

They looked at each other.

Ben sighed. 'God, this is awful – we need to tell the Master. If only we had told the police.'

'I know, I know – awful. We should tell, definitely,' said Toby.

'I think about him all the time, especially when I'm rowing – too much time on the boat with those fuckwits.'

'If only we'd found him. That fucking search ...'

In the end, the search party had consisted of Toby, Ben, Levi and Julian. The sky grew milky and big around them as they entered the national park just after dawn on Saturday, and at first the gums were ragged, far apart and pathetic. The ground was hard and old. Gradually they moved into its density. The weather forecast was for 39 degrees.

They were silent as they crunched along the thin track, Julian peering intently into the passing scrub as if Alfred might suddenly spring out of the bushes and surprise them.

Toby tried to think of some jolly slogan that their cricket coach might use: 'You gotta be in it to win it' or 'The best part of the journey is the journey'. But nothing came to mind except for dark verses on death and forests.

The mountains loomed around them – vast and unknowable with sheer rock faces, labyrinths of caves and gullies, endless, endless green bush scarred by tracks and creek beds, and surveyed by the cockatoos, magpies and kookaburras that skirted its terrible heart: the gorge.

At first the boys stuck to the tracks and stayed close to each other. They carried compasses, maps and food. They walked single file up the mountain and later used sticks and their hands to climb the harder, higher parts – cleaving their bodies to the rocks, fixing their hot cheeks against the hot stone, their breathing becoming laboured.

Julian, the least fit among them, agreed to be the whip. Julian's only sport was cricket. He was happy fielding in a shady, forlorn spot, dreamy and vacant, slow to break into a run, taking ages to get to the boundary. And so it was here. They found a shady creek bed, and gathered to drink from it and wait for him, but he didn't arrive. They cried 'Cooee' in increasingly panicked voices; only the birds answered their calls. Toby doubled back down the mountain, its tracks so steep that he did not feel like he was walking so much as falling, until he found Julian perched on a tree stump, wide-eyed and staring at a wallaby.

'This is ridiculous,' said Toby when they were gathered again by the creek bed. 'We'll never find Alfred this way – we've got to split up so we can cover more ground.'

'Maybe Alfred will find his way back to the house this afternoon,' said Julian, ever the lazy optimist. Toby almost laughed at that. How could Alfred find his way back? They were in a place where bearings were the first thing you lost, where the trees and mountains seemed to stretch on forever, where you could wander hot and lost among them and not see another human being – just strange animals, straggly gums, bleached-out, bone-dry sticks.

So they split into pairs – Ben and Toby, Levi and Julian. They stuck red post-it notes to the trees. They called Alfred's name until they were hoarse, until the words became as dull as a mantra.

Deeper and deeper they went, until even things that were the background scenery of their lives – the roads and streetlights, the music and apps on their phones, the posters in their rooms – became distant memories, from another place, another time. Occasionally they'd hear a rushing sound that could have been water or a plane, but it was always nothing – an aural mirage. Other times they would be walking at a cracking pace when they were stopped short by a sudden drop as the land gave way. Death without sound or warning. Was Alfred down there? Had he plummeted like a stone?

Toby thought about Hadrien's words on the landing, how Alfred might fall. The thought made him feel vertiginous, yet he also had a perverse but strong impulse to throw himself off the ledge to see how it felt.

But the feeling passed and was replaced by boredom. What was there to do in the bush except walk and watch your step?

If Alfred were to die out here it would be the boredom that finished him off, not the animals or the sun or the starvation.

The heat beat on. Sunburn sang on their faces. Their shoes hurt. Toby wished he had brought some music – they had nothing to say to each other anymore that didn't involve some form of panic or blame. Then there was the monotony of the landscape, which dulled the senses: green on green, a sky that was a cloudless, piercing blue, the glitter and promise of a faraway creek, the brown dried-out leaves underfoot, and that was it, really. Even the magnificent views from the occasional lookouts depressed them. The mountains went on forever and they did not have forever to find Alfred.

Occasionally something exciting would happen and they would yelp for a bit before falling silent – the discovery of a pair of trousers and a hat (not Alfred's; he had not been wearing trousers or a hat), and moans that could have come from a boy with a crushed ankle but instead were from a kangaroo that had been attacked by … something. The contents of its stomach spilt out and the blood was setting like paint under the searing sun. Toby, desperate to put it out of its misery, tried to kill it by beating it around the head with a branch ripped from a half-dead tree. The sun beat on too, hitting them in waves. The surge of strength Toby had felt at first, inseparable from the surge of compassion for the dying animal, gradually deserted him, until he was not so much striking the kangaroo around the head and torso as sort of weakly chopping at it, all the while breathing uneasily and trying not to think of Alfred as the blood, fur and some kind of gelatinous stuff splattered his boots. In the sky an awful, large bird screamed then dropped too low for comfort. The animal's neck was only half broken and one eye had been dislodged, while the other one blinked at Toby until Levi was screaming, 'Stop it! Stop it! For God's sake, stop it, Toby! Please stop it!'

Ben, looking confused and slightly disgusted at Toby, grabbed the bloody stick from his hands, walked some distance away and hurled it off a lookout, where it made its noiseless descent far away from them all.

He returned, wiping some of the goo from his hands. 'Go ahead, I'll just catch my breath,' he told the others, as they headed along a neglected path towards the gorge, having decided to keep together from now on. Toby waited for him on a ledge, keeping a respectful distance, but he could still hear Ben cry for a bit and sing Alfred's name down the mountain, his voice following the stick down the drop.

Toby thought about the kangaroo for a long time afterwards, and was troubled by the horror of killing things and the horror of not killing things. It really was the worst day.

In Toby's room, as the chapel bells chimed around the college announcing dinner, Toby asked Ben the question that had been turning around in his head.

'What were you thinking that night? Why were you involved in that thing in the bunkroom?' He opened another beer.

'I don't know – it was a school thing,' said Ben, not looking at Toby. 'It got out of hand ... all those boys from boarding school. It was their idea.'

There was a silence, then, after a gulp of beer, Toby mentioned the kangaroo. 'Up there in the bush it had no natural predators – except for humans. So what happened?'

Ben was quiet for a bit, then murmured, 'Fuck.'

'It's sick,' said Toby. 'Sorry, mate – not having a go at you, but still … I just don't feel right about keeping quiet. I've protected you before – remember that guy in the nightclub last year? I didn't mind doing that – I thought he was going to glass you. But this is different. Alfred wasn't threatening you or anything. And there were, like, ten of you and only one of him. I mean, the size of Leeson and Severin … And you're not exactly small.'

'Stop it,' said Ben weakly. 'I know it was wrong – I know.'

'It's not too late – we can still speak up,' said Toby.

'I know, I know.'

'You'll get in trouble, though – not just with the Master but with the police …'

Ben nodded, and went to sip his drink, but it spilt instead over the sleeve of his academic gown.

'Maybe you'll just have to face the consequences. I mean, there's only so long any of us can get away with this shit. Out there in the real world it'll be different.'

'I know.'

'Let's be realistic. We're fucked. Julian and Levi are both complete messes since we got back. Julian can't sleep anymore and Levi's drinking a lot,' said Toby.

Ben shrugged. 'He always drinks a lot.'

'Well, now he's drinking more,' said Toby tartly. 'And you're smoking more.'

The sun dipped lower in its usual way and the animals bleated from their pens. Shaking, Ben lit another cigarette and stepped back out onto the balcony to smoke it in the cooling twilight. Giles and Jan lay entwined on the wet grass under the Faraway Tree, staving off dinner time in each other's arms.

The lamps were being lit all around the seniors' quadrangle and the chapel bells continued to chime. There was laughter from a distant room, then a harp, a cello, all their notes falling at once.

Like crows, students in black gowns descended on the quadrangle, where they lined up to file into the dining room.

'We should go to dinner,' said Toby.

'I'm not hungry.'

'We'll go to the Master after dinner. We have to.'

The two boys stared at each other in the almost-dark a powerful charge moving between them.

'Okay. I'm nervous, though. What if we get into trouble? My parents will kill me.'

'It's got to be better than feeling like this all the time,' replied Toby.

Ben sighed so heavily it came out like a moan. 'You're right. You're right.'

After dinner, when the students went off to the Junior Common Room for cups of tea and announcements ('The tryouts for women's netball are on Friday', 'Anyone interested in tutorials on the Great Depression and the Marshall Plan, give your name to Dr Bath', 'Donations to a floral tribute for Alfred can be given to Lucy'), the Master and his guests went through an oak-panelled door near the High Table to the Senior Common Room. Chesterfields were placed around the fire, there were tables covered in journals and week-old newspapers flown in from England, crystal on pewter trays, gin and vermouth on Art Deco drinks trolleys, and portraits of former Masters lined the walls.

The decor was strictly English gentlemen's club, St James or Piccadilly. But to the Master it sometimes felt shabby and provincial – like a decaying old presbytery in a once-prosperous country parish. And the other Masters, whose portraits were on the wall, well, they just looked dour. Not like him; he liked to think he gave the old bones of the building a splash of glamour. His wife was a magazine editor; his friends were in television, politics and the theatre. They wrote books, and they agonised over funding for their films. They knew about fashion and foreign cities and food. With his mane of silvery blond hair and expensive clothes, the Master was sophisticated, nonchalant, cool.

There were a couple of knocks on the old oak door, and Gibbs, morose as usual, opened it. 'Boys, you know you're not allowed in here.'

The Master, bored with his guests and actually fond of Toby and Ben, shooed Gibbs away. 'Let them in – give them a port. Where's the harm?'

But when Toby and Ben, clutching small port glasses in their large hands, asked to speak to the Master privately about a matter that concerned them greatly, the Master regretted his magnanimous gesture. When a student wants to speak to you alone, he thought, it's either something terribly boring, or terribly alarming.

He excused himself from his guests and led the boys off to the library.

The boys had barely sat down before they started talking about the weekend on the mountains. How awful it had been when Alfred disappeared. And even worse when they hadn't found him. And worse still when he had been found barely alive. How things had not been the same for them since.

'We think, sir,' said Toby, looking around uncertainly even though they were the only people there, 'that it is, um, advisable to talk, maybe, to the police.'

'The police? For heaven's sake, what could you possibly want to speak to the police about?' the Master asked.

'Alfred.'

'It's not a police matter,' said the Master firmly. 'It's now a medical matter, unfortunately. Doctors and the like.'

The Master went on in what he hoped was a mild, bland way about some medical procedure that Alfred had had the previous week that had involved punching a hole in his throat so they could insert a feeding tube.

'This whole thing with Alfred could even be good for the college,' he continued. 'Already the college staff are telling me how much nicer people are to each other since Alfred had his accident. It's like it's released some compassion, some tenderness, even among those kids who I've always thought of as being quite hard. Tran in the kitchen said students have even started saying hello to him, asking him about his family, asking him about Asia. That's a positive thing.'

Ben, who had been silent, gnawing at his knuckles as was his old, nervous habit, said in a rush, 'That's great about Tran, but Master, with respect, there were things that happened in the bunkroom before – before Alfred went missing … things that we – well, not Toby, but the rest of us – did to him. Illegal things. An initiation … of sorts.'

There was a silence, and for the Master, everything shifted in an instant.

What was solid liquefied. What he did know didn't amount to anything. What control he had was illusory. This was the library. This was *his* library This was his college. The students – each different, each a unique wonderful specimen, but in the end they were utterly predictable. And so young! Well, maybe that wasn't the case. He was hazy about what had gone on in the mountains and was desperate not to have clarity.

The boys standing before him suddenly seemed predatory and hostile. Somewhere he was flailing off the same cliff as Alfred; emitting the same astonished 'oh' when he realised he was no longer on firm ground. There was silence for a while as he fell. *Initiations.*

But Toby, as third-year law students were wont to do, spoilt the fragile balance, crashed through the poetry, didn't read the songlines in the silence. He stumbled in, wielding something blunt and heavy he had learnt only last week in Torts. He mispronounced Latin. He threw around phrases like 'vicarious liability', 'duty of care' and 'common law negligence' – the words still new and difficult on his tongue.

Suddenly the Master felt calm again. He knew now the boys were just showing off, testing out new knowledge on him, boasting. There was no deeper moral drive behind this meeting. He knew they didn't really care about Alfred – if they had, the incident wouldn't have happened in the first place! He stood to indicate the conversation was over.

'I'll take it on advice, boys. I'll take it on advice. So good of you to stop by and show your concern for Alfred. It shows we're a community. We care. We're only as strong as our weakest link, and our weakest link – poor old Alfred – is being well cared for.'

He guided the boys out while Toby was still gabbling about some dull case on his reading list, then closed the door and slumped against it. All around him legal casebooks stood behind glass – all of society's rules, all of the evolving precedents, all the ways people had tried to manage their interactions with one another. All that had come before, yet there it still was – the cruelty of boys to one another.

How he had come to resent saving the students from themselves! The boys with their odd rituals that sometimes resulted in violence and damage were a headache – and he couldn't control them all the time.

Eight o'clock and the sky was navy. The bells rang out across the quadrangles. The students were crows again, flapping back across the lawn in their black gowns after their feeding frenzy.

Ben and Toby stood near the fountain, separate from everyone.

'What do we do now?' asked Toby.

Ben shrugged, looking haunted again. 'Rowing training, essays … something, I guess.'

Toby said, 'The pub? Let's get Julian and Levi and go to the Red Lion.'

Ben shook his head. He didn't feel like it. He didn't feel like doing anything. These days he felt obscurely afraid whenever he left his room, but didn't want to tell Toby that. Toby had already seen too much – had probably heard him crying that morning in the mountains, had seen him shaking out on the balcony like an elderly person with Parkinson's.

He said goodbye and ducked into the cloister, head down, his gown slipping from his shoulders. He didn't want to see anyone, to have to stop and talk. He went back to his room and lit a candle and a cigarette. He had only smoked at parties before Evelyn, but now he wanted cigarettes all the time. They felt like a meditation – breathing in and breathing out, each inhalation slowing him down. How he needed comfort! But who would comfort him after what he'd done?

The shame of it felt so physical – like poison in him. Something vile travelling through his body. Except *he* was the something vile.

He tried to still his mind by scrolling across the apps on his iPad, but he couldn't stop thinking about the bunkroom and the search.

Up in the mountains, exhausted, Toby, Ben, Julian and Levi sat down on some rocks. The air was thick with heat and flies, which they tried to ignore as they ate their lunch of muesli bars and tins of cold spaghetti. Toby and Levi tentatively started to discuss the night before, talking around the issue, too scared to get near it, as if it were flames that might burn them. Each of them remembered something different about the night, and when they compared stories it was as if they were referring to many nights in many different places rather than just this one.

Levi adjusted his glasses and quietly recalled a sudden and violent storm that had rattled the windows and made him feel afraid.

'I wrapped myself up tighter in my blankets, but they smelt so bad I had to throw them off. I slept under my coat and a towel. I was awake for a long time.' Later in the night he got up to be sick. 'Cheap red wine and beer,' he remembered ruefully. 'Not pretty. I tried to clean it up but I was too drunk. It looked like someone had been disembowelled in the sink.'

Julian was also sick but couldn't remember the storm. 'I was coming back from the bathroom but got lost and couldn't find my way back to bed. It was horrible.'

'Remember you got up because you were frightened?' prompted Toby.

Julian winced. 'Was that after I saw the stick on fire? I guess that house gives me the creeps. I thought I heard the handle of my door turn, and it was either that spooky caretaker Frank Monk or Hadrien with his fucking mask on.'

Julian described walking along the corridor and how it had felt more like a dream or a hallucination than anything real. 'There was a boy running along the corridor ahead of me with a stick on fire.' From behind a closed door he heard grunts, moaning and a slapping sound. 'I also heard Hadrien talking about a ... a whip.'

He was silent for a moment, then said, 'I can barely remember getting to bed. How on earth did I get to bed?' He sounded mystified.

'I put you to bed, remember?' said Toby. 'You could hardly walk. I found you outside the bunkroom, slumped against the door. And it was me who put all those towels by your pillow in case you were sick in the night.'

'Which I was,' admitted Julian, belching then stretching out on the rocks. 'I woke up again later and went to get a glass of water, and there was a strange sound coming from the showers. I went and looked, and someone had turned them all on – all eight of them – and there was steam billowing up the top. It was like a sauna.'

'Strange time to shower,' mused Toby.

'It wasn't just that – the steam was pink. And there were red footprints on the floor.'

'Did you think it was blood?'

'I thought I was drunk and seeing things. Then I ran into Ben and Levi in the hall and that's when we came into your room to wake you.'

'Who was in the showers?' asked Toby. 'Who was covered in blood?'

'God, I don't know,' said Julian, slightly offended. 'I don't look that closely at men showering.'

'I was drunk – much drunker than I wanted to be,' said Toby. 'Got the head spins and everything. But I remember that at some point you all got up from your chairs and went with Alfred. Remember?' He was looking at Ben. 'He was so drunk you had to help him walk. And you all went into the bunkroom and closed the door.'

Ben knew the moment – there had been something orchestral about it, it had been so eerily synchronised. And helping Alfred up, his feet dragging along the floor.

'The next thing I remember, I was sinking into the bloody stinking old couch,' said Toby. 'I actually thought I might die of suffocation when suddenly Dr Bath was there.' He shook his head at the recollection: 'Maybe Bath saved my life by pulling me out of the couch. He made me a cup of tea and I guess I sort of sobered up. He talked a lot about the Second World War. I couldn't follow most of it, to be honest.'

'And then what happened?' asked Levi.

Toby shrugged. 'I fell asleep. Bath woke me up and I apologised then shuffled off to bed. Then the head spins ... When I got up to go to the toilet, I found you, Levi ...'

'And what about the moans and the slapping sound – did you hear them? Did you see someone with a torch?' asked Julian.

Toby shook his head. 'None of it. But maybe it happened after I'd gone to bed.'

Then the thing that had brought them all here. Sometime before dawn, Alfred had gone missing.

In his room, Ben turned off his iPad. It wasn't an oracle; it would provide no answers. He knew his friends would be discussing him at the Red Lion, talking about how evil he'd been in the bunkroom. He could feel the depression of last semester coming back again, stronger this time – yearnings, shame and loneliness that pulled him into himself like a tide.

He plugged his phone into his charger, switched on the kettle and thought of Sylvan again. More than two years had passed since he'd met Sylvan and still the card sat in his wallet, between those of recruiters who had visited campus last month scoping for graduates to work in their offices – management consulting firms, law firms, private equity firms, merchant banks. Sylvan's card felt flimsy among all those gold-embossed promises, but he couldn't quite bring himself to throw it out. It was because of the words on the card, strangely compelling. He pulled it out. *On sleeping soil, awaken to the call of your Lord. Enter Jerusalem today.*

He turned the card around in his hand, and asked himself the questions that he had been asking himself a lot lately. Were they going to get away with the terrible things they had done to Alfred? Did it not matter? Did Alfred not matter? Was Alfred really a person of no consequence? Was that what happened in life?

Ben had a horrible feeling that Alfred was in the process of being forgotten. The heat of the college's grief was cooling. It had been a month now since Alfred had been found.

'Awaken, awaken.' Ben wondered how long it was possible for him to live like this; to live with a self that was so at odds with what he thought he should be.

There was a knock on his door, sudden and urgent, and then his phone started to jump manically across the desk. It would be Charlotte, slumped outside his door, drunk-dialling him, he guessed. She'd been complaining that he never went drinking with her anymore.

'Rowing training,' he said, not wanting to say that actually, since that night in the mountains, since that stuff in the bunkroom, he'd mostly lost his taste for drinking. Sex had also become a problem. *Not while I'm training*, he'd written more than once in response to her frequent text messages. It was like all sexual desire had drained from his body after that night in the bunkroom with Alfred, and now the sight of Charlotte's revved-up eyes, those perfect tits, her expensive skin with its expensive sheen, made him feel a bit queasy.

'Benj, Benj, open the door, baby,' she said, almost purring. He opened the window instead and quietened her with a conciliatory but messy kiss on the mouth and a promise to seek her out once his Nigerian essay was done. He imagined that by then she'd be passed out on her bed, snoring, and they could avoid the inevitable confrontation.

'Don't you find me sexy anymore?' she would say, voice slurred, staring at her fingernails all pink and chipped. 'Don't you think I'm attractive? Or do you think I'm fat?'

'You are ... you are ... you are so beautiful.'

'Why won't you touch me, then?'

She left Ben at the window, placated by the thought of a 2 am tryst, her heels click-clacking along the cloister.

Ben stretched out on his bed, aware that after the rowing season he would no longer have the same battery of excuses. And there was this thought that he kept trying to suppress: that he no longer trusted his body after that night in the bunk room, a body so strong and capable of inflicting such violence.

It was quiet out on the quadrangle. From the nearby stables the goats bleated then sighed. A door slammed shut and a boy and girl laughed hysterically then suddenly stopped. The night was still, warm, close; even the air seemed muffled.

Ben looked at himself in the mirror; a blank boy with an unused face stared back.

There was still time. He no longer wanted to be asleep. He no longer wanted to hate himself. The card was in his hand, as it had been all this time, gathering moisture, curling at the edges.

Sylvan's number was on the back. *Awaken, awaken.* He dialled it, then held his breath until Sylvan came on the line.

All his life Toby had accepted that when he was tired he would fall straight to sleep, and sleep hard and fast, just as he accepted that when he was hungry he could swallow food.

But night-time had a new texture now: discomfort. His pillow was too hard, his mattress was too lumpy, his sheets were too scratchy.

And so he would give up just lying there (because after a while just lying there became the hardest thing in the world) and start to plug things in and turn things on. Suddenly there were lights and bleeps and bips and whirrs and things blinking and flashing in the dark – which was better than quiet and blackness.

While spinning around the internet, while mindlessly browsing status updates on Facebook, while cruising Twitter, part of his mind was tripping and sucking on the memories of how he used to sleep. Fast-falling, heavy, unbroken slumbers, a languorous weighty feeling in the limbs, that sense of being lost in a subterranean world of dreams, so that when it came time to waken he was still on the bottom of a deep ocean floor and he had to kick, kick, kick his way through the dense blue until there he was, in daylight, wrung out and refreshed all at once.

Some nights he had company. He knew his friends by their knocks – Ben's firm two-rap announcement (much less frequent since their return from the mountains); Julian, who did not bother to knock, would just shout out, 'Yo, Toby!' and tumble in; and Lucy's knock – hesitant and faint at first, as if she were standing nervously on some threshold, debating whether to announce herself, then louder as she gathered confidence. She would arrive at his door with a chessboard, a new playlist, a bottle of wine or a book and sit on his bed. They would drink from the bottle, passing it back and forth, docking her iPod to his speakers (Lance Vaine and the Musical Hellos crooning *'Silk stockings, crocodile skin, black leather/This is what it means darling to be together'*) and take it in turns to read aloud from her Introduction to Intermediate French course book.

'Je suis un architecte désireux d'élaborer mes plans pour un nouvel immeuble de bureaux,' he would say in an exaggerated, almost camp accent, while she would ask, *'Avez-vous chassé le jeu vous-même?'*

But then they would finish the wine, or they would tire of the French, or the music would stop, and Lucy would look at him – drunk, half expectant and half afraid – and maybe kick his foot accidentally–deliberately, and he would know she intended the night to have a Second Act.

That would be his cue to yawn or change the music to something jarring like Kanye or start texting one of the boys or some other girl – and she would waver, then slip out just as hesitantly and just as breathlessly as she had arrived. He would feel bad for a moment – but he would also feel relieved. He loved her as a friend, but as a girlfriend she just wasn't his type.

Last Tuesday night their usual rhythm had been broken. It had been late – maybe 2 am – and they'd been on his bed. They had been reading the lines of a play she was studying in her Jacobean Literature class. He had been reading the part of the Cardinal, she the Duchess. The curtain fell and everyone was dead. Then without warning she started asking about Alfred. Didn't the cricket team go away the weekend that Alfred went on his walk? Weren't they in the same mountain range? Did any of them see Alfred? And how come none of them had said anything about being there at the same time?

She didn't sound accusing, merely curious, like she was about everything Toby did.

But she was making links between the cricketers and Alfred, and Toby felt his heart lurch. He loathed himself for doing it, but he did it anyway: he grabbed her foot, and watched the blush spread up from her neck at the frank and unexpected contact.

'Before you go on,' he said, looking at her intensely, still holding her foot, 'I just remembered something I've been meaning to tell you all day. I had the most incredible dream about you last night ...'

His eyes were locked onto hers (her pupils suddenly dilated, like she'd been taking drugs), not letting her go, and it was as if Alfred had dropped down the gorge again. He was out of sight, and the round bone and soft skin of Lucy's ankle were in his hands, and her eyes were large and shining and still on his, and she was saying, 'What? What did you dream?'

He had stayed at the pub drinking until it closed, but now, back in his room, Levi couldn't settle. He was tempted just to move back home and put some distance between himself and the other cricketers. The revulsion he felt around them was overwhelming. And anyway, home wasn't too far away – just around the corner, in a terrace on one of the quiet streets that bordered the university. Others at college came from family homes surrounded by farmland the size of Belgium, with vast wheat plains, salt pans, ridges and ranges covering the distance between their narrow childhood bedrooms and the sandstone libraries and spires of the university. But Levi had grown up seeing the golden St Anton's lights from his attic room. On still, windless nights he could hear the braying of its famous animals as they were led to their pens at dusk. He had always dreamt of living there. It was like a fairy kingdom – beautiful, not quite real, a paradise at the end of the road.

Now he was at St Anton's he could do the reverse and look out from his balcony to his old room. His mother had turned it into a study. She kept strange hours. Sometimes in the early morning when he was coming home from the pub he would see the attic light burning and would wonder idly what she was working on. Another book? She published one every few years – the latest about the rise of patriotism among young people. She had written her first book when she was a young woman. It had been described by critics as 'momentous' and full of passion and rage, lighting up her generation like a flare. But Levi had never bothered to read it; it was not about his time. Someone else would write that book and when they did he would read it.

His parents didn't understand his decision to move to St Anton's. After all, they lived just across from the university. He could go home for lunch, he could study late at night in the law library and not have to suffer a long ride home in a half-empty train carriage with ugly 'tagging' and energy drink cans dribbling and rolling along the aisles. The library would shut and ten minutes later he would be sipping green tea with his parents, watching *Lateline*, all three of them screaming insults at the conservative politicians.

But it wasn't just an issue of proximity. His bearded, balding academic father would say with some distaste, 'College people aren't really our sort.' How was the professor to know that the slight curl of his lips, his thin tone of contempt, had been enough to drive his son out the door and over to the lawns, the playing fields and the strange ways of St Anton's? How was he to know that this decision would lead eventually to Hadrien, to that dark, awful night in the bunkroom?

Levi's parents had often been described on radio and in newspapers as 'public intellectuals' – but what did they know? thought Levi with contempt. They hadn't been travelling at great speed down a river to some gaping, dark, rotting-toothed mouth. That concept for them existed only in novels. But he had seen it, he had been there!

He wondered what he would do now. Could he just move back home? Then it would be like the bunkroom had never happened and he'd never have to see the cricketers ever again. He could take all his classes online, and just stay at home with his parents … if they'd have him.

Levi winced as he remembered what had happened yesterday. He'd been having a late afternoon beer with Toby in one of the Italian bars near the university, where the old Europeans and gangsters idled and plotted into the twilight. He and Toby were deep in another of their infernal, circular conversations about Alfred, when Levi's mother walked past with one of her friends. They were all cropped silver feminist hair, purple lipstick and bright scarves, with their bulky bags – carrying notes for their lectures, students' essays to mark and hardback art history books – banging hard against their thighs. They were talking and laughing so loudly that the old men playing cards at the next table paused to frown and look up.

She was his embarrassment. She was his mum. Why couldn't she be more poised and elegant, like Ben's mother?

As she paused in front of him, her mouth opening to utter a greeting, he cut his eyes away from her and continued talking to Toby. He hadn't really meant to, but he had done it: he had just disowned his own mother. It was as if some new citizenship had been conferred in the bunkroom, some exam had been passed, some initiation were over.

He didn't look at her, but he could sense her looking at him, sensed that she had understood the shift within him, and he had felt such sadness that he thought he might cry then and there but didn't, because Toby was talking about 'fucking Hadrien and that fucking initiation' with a kind of compelling panic.

When Levi looked up again his mum was gone. College was his mother and his father, his bad parents. He realised he could not go back home – at least, not yet. He would have to lie low, study, drink port, play sport, look after his friends, wait for it all to blow over.

He leant over from his desk to the bin, stuck his fingers as far down his throat as he could manage, and prodded a couple of times until he started vomiting – just like a bulimic ex of his had shown him.

He would feel better tomorrow. Ugly now. Better tomorrow.

CHAPTER 7

Toby wondered if anyone would miss him if he didn't go to the Scholars' Dinner. When he'd received an invitation on thick pearl-coloured paper at the start of term he'd been thrilled. Not everyone was invited to the annual dinner, just the cream, the Master had said almost lasciviously. Toby had been so proud to be invited he'd even texted his parents with the news. But now the thought of it made him anxious.

The bells chimed six and Toby wasn't even in his dinner suit when Levi turned up at his door.

'You *have* to come,' Levi implored. 'Otherwise it'll just be me and Ben.'

'What's wrong with that?' Toby asked.

Levi shrugged. 'I feel a bit weird around him now. You know, because of the Alfred stuff. I think it's kind of creepy what he did.'

'What do you mean "what he did"? How do you know what he did? I thought you weren't there.'

'I ... I wasn't. I'm just going on what Roman and Severin told me.'

'Don't listen to them! Ben's better than ten of those guys.'

Toby sighed, feeling even more reluctant now. 'Let's just go to this bloody dinner and get it over with, all right?'

In the cool, dark hall, forefathers stared out from the walls as the Master looked at each student in turn to check that every gown was in place, the dinner shirt underneath wasn't too tatty and the student had sufficient background on the academic they were to be paired with.

'Levi, Professor Connelly will try to talk to you about some geopolitical situation – which one I do not know. Please pretend to be interested. Ben, you can mention your father. No harm in that. Toby, Professor Figgis's husband has just left her. Be sympathetic but don't cross the line. Lucy, I'm afraid Dr Childs is a bit dull – just left a seminary, you see. Keep talking at him and you'll be fine. Dr Bath will be circulating in the Senior Common Room later to rescue anyone in conversational difficulty, and of course I'll be omnipresent – which means, children, I'll be everywhere. Don't talk about Alfred.'

Toby watched, feeling quite detached as he and the other students shook hands with the academics lined up in the wings to take their allocated seats at the High Table. They started the night deferential and meek, but at dinner, nervy and depressed, they all drank too much. They forgot the Master's advice and it wasn't long before they became careless with their hands and their claims. They defied their academics on the canon and canonical law. They dismissed *Ulysses* and the poetry of Adrienne Rich. The Master tried to smooth things over with university gossip, and by offering more wine to his guests while withholding it from the students. During dessert, Toby whispered into the crook of Professor Figgis's neck and touched her hand with a tenderness that seemed to unnerve her. He supposed he was flirting with her, but he wanted her to think about him for a long time afterwards with bittersweet sighs, with desire that had teeth.

Dinner ended with a prayer, followed by that dreadful sound of two hundred chairs being scraped back on the floorboards. The select students were condemned to more small talk in the Senior Common Room, where Gibbs moved glumly about with a tray of thimble-sized port glasses and a decanter.

Toby felt that on nights like this something legendary should happen – some crackling energy between the students and academics should be coursing through the air and the talk should start reverently and end in the orchestra pit, with some bearded sage conducting things with a fury as other voices and views chimed in from all over the room, and revelations were drawn out of the din.

He felt the talk should go on late into the night, that they should be blinded by terrible insights into the way the world really operates in all its majesty, magic and misery. The academics should almost feel not human, but like lightning rods – pure instruments from which knowledge flows. At night's end the academics would ride home a bit drunk and exhilarated on wobbly bicycles and the students would lie awake in their beds, the energy of the evening coursing through them. They had been woken after sleepwalking all this time. And from open windows they would hear sirens and then the morning's first birdsong, but how could they sleep when they had discovered so much, when they felt cut open in the best possible way?

Instead, they went back to the Senior Common Room for port and stilted conversation about the marks needed to get an internship at a global management consultancy or one of the good law firms. Professor Figgis was not meeting his eye.

Toby sensed Alfred close to him, closer than he'd been since his first and last bright smile on the mountains. It may have been the weeks without sleep, but Toby had a feeling that Alfred was there, standing ghostly and frail near the sideboard eating cheese and studying the portrait of the founding Master.

Leeson, hulking and black-haired, entered the room without knocking, also more like a dream than a real boy. He had a long scar on his temple that Levi once cruelly described as a coathanger mark from an abortion gone wrong. Toby shuddered involuntarily when he saw him. Bearing a gas lamp and looking jaundiced in the half-light, he seemed somehow more vulnerable without Severin, Roman and Niall flanking him, and now that he was not drawing energy from the dark source of Hadrien.

He approached Toby, not caring that the academics hovered close, hoovering up their port and clutching grapes, and said without preamble, 'We had a meeting with the Master about Alfred. He said there was no point going to the police but that we could be sent down – because of what happened in the mountains, in the bunkroom. Sent down – even though we're going to win the rowing for this fucking college!'

And on he went – how could they be sent down? Back home to distant and reproachful parents, into share houses (God forbid, Saturday mornings outside the letting agent armed to the teeth with false credentials and fifty-dollar notes), or to the beds of older, more sophisticated girlfriends who would love them for two weeks then tire of their drinking and their friends.

Then there were all his previous years of hard work, of the ground being prepared: playing slave to the older boys, first at boarding school and then St Anton's; the time he was almost electrocuted in the bath because the older boys made him strip and lie in the cold water, and shaved off his eyebrows with an electric razor while they cheered and took photos on their phones and uploaded them to Facebook and Instagram. He'd passed that test and it was his turn now to be on top of the pile, with access to the hottest girls, the best rooms and other boys on whom to vent his inadequacy, longing and cruelty. Okay, he hadn't taken the temperature recently and obviously things had changed; there were things it was unacceptable to do. 'We know that now,' he said a little hysterically.

'Stop talking! Stop talking to me about this!' hissed Toby, moving Leeson away from Lucy and her academic who were talking to the law tutor, Dr Heath. 'No wonder you're all so screwed up.'

But Leeson didn't seem to hear him, was ploughing on, saying that yes, things had gone too far in the mountains, they hadn't meant to let them go so far. Toby thought with alarm that Leeson might cry.

Suddenly the room was hot and oppressive. Every encounter seemed loaded with jeopardy. Ben looked sick, but he always looked sick now – sick and quiet. Levi was drinking too much and seemed to be talking to himself.

Like a ghost, Severin materialised beside Toby – like Leeson, carrying a lamp that let off a sulphurous smell and was almost burnt down to the wick. He whispered, 'Did you hear?' then lurched in a heavy and dangerous way towards Dr Bath, his breath beery and his eyes bloodshot. The Master, trying to extract himself from a circular and pointless conversation on global warming, moved towards Severin, saying, 'We'll talk about this business tomorrow in my office. But not now. Not now.'

As Toby watched the Master was cornered by Dr Heath, who had heard a disturbing rumour of a student being tortured by one of the sporting teams.

'Surely initiations don't go on anymore?' Dr Heath asked, and Toby couldn't tell if he was hoping for reassurance or a ghoulish anecdote.

The Master laughed and placed a hand on Dr Heath's back. 'Now then, Heath, you know initiations were outlawed years ago. The student in question had a hiking accident, that's all. He's in hospital now. An overseas student, you know. We try to integrate them, teach them our ways, but if they go off on their own into unfamiliar territory it can lead to unfortunate incidents.'

Toby found Ben by the drinks trolley. 'You look sad,' he told him. 'Is everything all all right?'

Ben said nothing, just shrugged a little wistfully, before his academic strolled over, wanting a top-up.

Suddenly the Senior Common Room seemed like the most

perilous place in the world to be. If there was a frontline in the room, it was not fixed. Troops and alliances shifted. Toby could not recognise the enemy anymore. He had drunk too much and not slept enough and was giddy with a sort of remorse and lack of a compass. What Leeson had said frightened him. He scanned the room for Professor Figgis but she had gone. He sensed Lucy staring at him from across the room and tried not to feel irritated. With a jolt of recklessness, he suddenly felt he could say anything, could even talk about Alfred. There was only the Master, watchful and poised, to stop him.

Lucy watched and listened and knew something awful was unfolding. But what?

She glanced over at Toby, trying to catch his eye. She was feeling upset and hurt by his behaviour at dinner. He had sleazed all over his professor right through the meal, *everyone* was talking about it. Lucy knew the signs well enough: first he would have been talking in a low, quiet voice and the professor would have had to lean in; he'd maintain eye contact for one beat too long; he'd lay a hand on her arm when he was making a point.

He'd done it to Lucy herself early on, in their fresher O-Week: all smouldering stares and pet names, tugging her ponytail in the line at breakfast, lingering hugs, kisses on the cheek that went too close to her mouth. The way he'd nuzzle her when he'd had too much to drink. Professor Figgis mustn't have been keen, though: she'd left after only one port.

Lucy wondered if Toby had been trying to make her jealous. She'd read on some online forum that some men would flirt with one woman to arouse another. Well, it had worked. Everything was sexual with him. It disgusted her! (But also, confusingly, enthralled her.) Over dinner she had felt her desire sharpening to a point as fine as a needle. Meanwhile, she was stuck with Dr Childs, a youngish but already balding academic recently returned from a Jesuit training college in Cambridge, where he'd studied sixteenth-century manuscripts and lived with forty other men. Lucy pondered whether he was like her, lying in bed at night in his narrow bed, his body starved, the feeling of loneliness penetrating to the marrow. Each night she lay in bed in Gregor House, her blood pumping with desire that had only one object. It affected her terribly. Some nights when she thought of him, she couldn't sleep, she was just so turned on (skin dry and burning hot, masturbating but not coming, grinding unhappily against her pillow).

When she stepped out into the world tired the following day, she was filled with a vast and uncontrollable tenderness. Her eyes welled with tears at the sight of a *Big Issue* vendor with one leg and an awful, loving dog. How she longed to reach out to the nervy woman who fumbled for change at the supermarket till. How she longed to touch everyone, even that dumb footballer Sam, rubbing his back that night. How she longed to subsume the thing that contaminated everything – this unrequited love.

Lucy wondered if she and Dr Childs had this loneliness in common. He looked like he might know what it was like, could perhaps teach her how to survive it. But how to make that leap? How to talk about it? When he asked her about herself things came pouring out in a disconnected jumble: a

hockey final, a masked ball, a friend with an eating disorder –
then she was talking about the war, a market town hit in
friendly fire, and then her gluten intolerance. The academic
looked confused and she knew that she was gabbling, her eyes
constantly darting to Toby, but she was helpless to stop it.

Dr Bath stood off to the side of the room. The sleeves of his
jacket were too short, the port too sweet, the night full of non
sequiturs and a strange discordant feeling. The Master kept
saying to him in an urgent whisper, 'We must not talk about
Alfred.' And then the strange selection of students. Mostly
the athletic and moneyed set. The old set. Not really the sort
you'd want to represent the face of the college in these times.
Not entirely appropriate for a Scholars' Dinner. They all
seemed drunk or on drugs. They could not meet his eye.

He stood on the outside of a small circle of academics, while
the Master got caught in some intractable and increasingly
heated conversation about global warming. 'Don't listen to
him,' Dr Bath wanted to say to the others in the group, but
didn't. 'The Master knows nothing about science and even
less about climate change.'

Ben, once his favourite, seemed even more introspective
than what was now usual. Last semester he'd had to take
some time off for treatment of depression. Maybe the disease
had come back. Standing by a portrait of an old Master
(*Professor Comma, 1964–1972*), he looked like he might slit
his wrists any moment.

Dr Bath wondered if family issues were contributing to the
boy's problems. He had met Ben's father, had been the victim

of the man's aggressive handshake and the withering glance at the length and fabric of Bath's jacket sleeves, at his paunchy, undisciplined body. They were holders of high standards, Ben's parents – too high, really, for this flawed world. But Ben was a good kid. Fabulous manners, a quiet intelligence, handsome and good at games – yet all of it encased in this melancholy skin.

Dr Bath ambled over to him. 'You all right, Ben? You had a good night?'

'Hello, Dr Bath. Yes, it's been most stimulating. My academic was an immunologist, so we had a fascinating conversation about disease.'

'Oh, that's good.'

They stood there for a bit, not talking, until Ben, not looking at Dr Bath, broke the silence.

'That night up there in the mountains, that Friday night ... what do you remember?'

Dr Bath hesitated, then said quietly, 'Nothing. I don't remember a thing. I take these strong pills to sleep, you see, and they really wipe me out.'

Ben nodded, but didn't speak, and that night hung there between them like a contaminated mist until, unsettled by the silence and the depression and tremors radiating off Ben, Bath took an inferior bottle of wine, put it under his gown, and went back up to his room.

These horrible occasions with students and academics. What a desperate mix. Only Toby seemed to be swimming above it all. Student prince; how could someone so beautiful move so casually among them?

CHAPTER 8

Gary put in another call from his home to the central office of Search and Rescue.

'I'm a volunteer from the Wycloff regional branch,' he said. 'We received a message on the answering machine about a man who went missing in our area on 25 March, and I just want to know what happened to him … First name Alfred, no last name given.'

Gary was put on hold. He held the phone away from his head to avoid the awful music, a Hammond organ version of 'Greensleeves'.

The young woman at the central office came back on the line and said, 'My supervisor says we cannot give out that sort of information over the phone. You'll need to put your request in writing.' Then she lowered her voice. 'But I have the information right here in front of me.'

Gary, speaking softly too now (although he wasn't sure why), assured her that he would be discreet.

'Let's see … It says here Alfred Khoo was rescued from Plumley's Gap on the afternoon of 27 March, and is now in a serious but stable condition at Royal Prince Edward Hospital. A hiking accident, according to the notes. He's a student, from Malaysia. He went out there alone, didn't tell anyone where he was going. His injuries are awful. Another few hours down there and he probably would have died. He's young, too – only seventeen.'

They were both silent for a moment, then Gary murmured, 'Gee, that really is awful.' The girl agreed and hung up.

If Alfred had been alone in the mountains, who had rung the regional centre to say he'd gone missing from a house up there? Gary wondered. Was there some way of tracing the call?

He walked into the kitchen, where his wife was bathing their twelve-week-old baby in a tub over the sink. The sight of his daughter made him feel his heart might explode; he ran his hand over her small soapy head and thought of the boy in hospital, only seventeen and so far from home.

'Do you and the little one fancy a trip to the city tomorrow?' he asked his wife. 'If we left early we could make a day of it, visit the shops and your mum.'

'What's on in the city?' his wife asked, puzzled.

'There's someone I want to see in hospital.'

Alfred lay on his back in the ward, his eyes covered with surgical tape, plaster casts right up to the thighs of both legs, fluids being drained from some internal cavity to an external plastic bag that sat at the head of his bed. According to the clipboard that hung on the side of his bed, his condition was stable. Gary was his only visitor.

'Can I touch him?' Gary asked the nurse. It felt important to him that Alfred be touched, gently, carefully.

'Just be careful of the tubes,' said the nurse.

Gary put a hand on Alfred's clammy forehead and his wife took Alfred's hand. They sat like that with the baby sleeping in a basket at their feet for almost an hour, until Gary registered someone at the door – a boy, perhaps Alfred's age, tall, in a rugby jumper.

'Hey – hey, mate,' said Gary, getting up and moving towards him.

The boy, looking startled, moved quickly away from the door and bolted down the corridor, around a corner.

'Hey – wait! Are you a friend of Alfred's? Do you know what happened to him?'

Was he the one? Gary wondered. Was that the boy who had rung Search and Rescue?

Sylvan had the kind of haircut that no one Ben knew had ever worn after grade three. Ben was quietly proud of his own hair – dark blond and plentiful, cut for $70 by a lisping Spanish brunette who was thirty-eight and had tattoos older than him up her arms. She also had the unnerving ability to give him an erection with her borderline-erotic head massages.

Sylvan's hair looked like it had never been acquainted with product in its life, while Sylvan himself seemed unacquainted with erotic head massages. But it wasn't just Sylvan's hair; there was also the beard. Ben didn't know anyone who had a full beard. Toby appeared most days at twilight with a five o'clock shadow, but the next day it would always be gone. Some of the cricket team – like Severin, Roman or even Levi – could get a bit bristly over swot vac or on away trips, but with

Sylvan, it was if he were trying to will the hair to grow out of his face but his face was only half complying. There were little bits of beard here and there, an encouraging few hairs that sprouted from the left side of his jaw and some more down his chin, but there were also vast areas of pink, hairless skin. It was embarrassing, that beard.

The other Jerusalem men were also bearded. Ben was introduced to them (shaking their hands solemnly, sure that he'd never be able to tell one from the other) one unseasonably cold day at their small cafe next to Jacaranda Station, the Pleasing Sands.

Pleasing Sands, Pleasing Sands ... When Sylvan had told him about it, Ben had said, 'I don't think I've been there. Is it in the *Good Cafe Guide*?'

It wasn't. The Pleasing Sands did not make good coffee and the interior, designed by Sylvan's uncle, made customers feel as if they had entered a tree house. There were tree trunks in the middle of the floor, baskets of sugar sachets hung from branches, the seats were wooden stumps and you couldn't turn around without hitting a tree branch glued to some surface. The Pleasing Sands was a world dreamt up by Sylvan's family – every chair hand-carved, each wooden placemat lovingly sanded down – a place not only created by them but also a kind of sanctuary for them. It had been running for three years now, and all the proceeds went back into the work of the Jerusalems.

Ben had never met a family like Sylvan's. He was not even sure they were an actual family. They might have been just a collection of individuals who dressed in a similar way, all worked in the cafe and had identical beliefs. Even though

Sylvan referred to them as his auntie, cousin or brother, it wasn't clear whether they were bound by blood or religion.

In the cafe the female 'relatives' stood behind the counter and cooked. None of them wore makeup or jewellery, and they all wore floral headscarves and had long hair worn in a plait down their back. The dresses were long and shapeless, the colour of oatmeal, and they had white aprons tied loosely over the top and sandals on their feet. The toenails of the older women, Ben couldn't help but notice, looked thick, yellow and tough.

These women glanced at Ben with clear, pale eyes then looked quickly away. Just as they were all shapeless here, they were also ageless: the difference between mother and daughter was defined only by a certain heaviness in the jaw, greying hair – and their feet. These women were so different from his own mother, Anne, forever blonde with a painted smile and weekly pedicure.

In appearance the men were all older versions of Sylvan – beards and work shirts, loose pants, basic work boots. There was a plainness about their manner, too – something about them that said, 'We've got no tricks, we're as plain as our clothes.'

The Pleasing Sands was crowded with Jerusalems – everyone busy, the place humming, the women in the kitchen, the men taking orders from customers, many of whom giggled and took photos with their phones of the strange, religious waiters moving among the foliage.

Were the customers here to have a coffee or to see the freak show? More to the point, what was *he* doing here?

All Ben knew was that when he was at the Pleasing Sands he started to relax. Something in him loosened, just a little bit. It was only on the train on the way back to college that he felt his chest tighten again, a burble of acid in his gut, butterflies released and swarming.

Although Sam had hoped desperately for a miracle, the search party had never really stood a chance. After returning from a day and night spent in the upper reaches of the mountains, Julian gave him the rundown: the food had run out, there had been bickering about who did what to whom in the bunkroom, they had suffered from sunstroke and dehydration, and Levi had slipped and twisted his knee, and almost broken his glasses.

When the search party showed up the rest of the cricket team were just emerging from their beds after another night of heavy drinking.

'I guess you didn't find him, huh?' said Leeson with a shrug. 'Let's lock up and get out of here. I have an Economics test tomorrow. I can't believe it. Haven't cracked a book all year. Oh, by the way, Hadrien's gone back to college with Dr Bath. He's going to find out how much Bath knows about Friday night.'

Leeson sounded unconcerned, but Sam could tell that some of the other boys were not so relaxed about Alfred's disappearance. They had assumed Alfred would come back after an hour or two of sulking in the bush, or that the searchers would have found him.

Toby tried to persuade them to stay and keep searching. 'We owe it to Alfred,' he pleaded. 'Plus we can't leave the house in this kind of mess. We need to get the spew off the walls.'

But the others – tired, jittery, hungover, coming down – just wanted to leave as quickly as possible: withdraw, retreat, pretend they were never there in the first place.

'We should never have brought him up here at all,' said Sam nervously.

Leeson gave him a murderous look. 'We can't undo what happened, but we can shut the fuck up about it from now on,' he said.

The team gathered outside under a desolate stringybark to put it to the vote. Toby argued convincingly that they should stay to look for Alfred, and was backed up by Ben, Julian and Levi.

Leeson was just as persuasive when he argued in favour of leaving. Self-preservation, reputation, their golden futures … The brutal hand gestures and the cold, compelling logic of his barrister father had been handed down to the son.

'We cannot move forward if we stay back here,' he said, gesturing to the sagging camp.

'Let's just leave now,' Sam said, suddenly and inexplicably afraid. 'I don't like it here anymore.'

Roman, who despite his tremendous tanned bulk had always seemed unformed, like gelatine still shivering and wet in its mould, looked from Toby to Leeson, confused. 'Yo, what's the least likely to get us into shit? That's all *I* care about. I don't want to get into any trouble over that Korean dude.'

Four hands went up for staying and six for leaving and then very quickly, as if their decision might result in their being hunted or pursued, the boys packed up the cars, left the vomit on the walls, threw the key back near the woodpile and sped off, looking for all the world like a normal group of friends, like a young hunting party returning to the city empty-handed, having killed nothing.

Now that the cricket season had ended, Sam saw the rest of them infrequently. They were a bit more intellectual than he was, spent more time in the library. He had a voice built to carry across fields and crowded pubs, and when all this college stuff was over he'd go back to the farm. Julian, Levi, Toby and Ben, with their expensive clothes and the pretty girls they hung out with, the games of chess in their rooms late at night, the restaurants they ate at and the difficult novels they discussed in the dining hall, left Sam feeling a bit uncomfortable, like he didn't quite measure up.

'One of life's natural-born followers,' said Toby once as Sam, on a dare, stood on a table at the pub and drank beer poured from a funnel straight down his gullet. Sam flinched when he overheard Toby's words but kept drinking anyway.

'You right, Sammy?' Toby asked when he passed him later in a laneway behind the Red Lion being sick – foamy, thin liquid pouring from his chapped farmer's lips.

Sam nodded, his eyes watering. 'I'm okay, sort of ...' Then he plunged in. 'Do you ever think about ... what happened?'

'What?'

'You know – Alfred.' It had been more than a month since the mountains, and Sam still thought of little else.

'Yes, of course. But let's not talk about it here,' said Toby, looking around furtively.

Once or twice since then Sam had made other approaches – to Toby, mainly, and once to Julian. He would be drunk, or it would be early in the morning before everyone was up, and he'd seek out Toby on the running track or in his room.

Late one evening he found Toby in the all-night library and said urgently, 'Hey, I want to talk to you about that night. The night with Alfred. I can't get it out of my head. I think we did something bad. I don't want to be caught, I mean we'd have to go to jail – even you, mate, you'd go to jail as well for keeping quiet – but what the fuck? What the actual fuck? I still can't believe the things we did.'

Yet Toby seemed strangely unmoved by Sam's panic. He just reminded him of the pact they'd made. 'It's too bloody late now, all right? We had our chance back there at the house, and now it's too late.'

'It's not too late! Why are you saying it's too late?'

'Because it won't change the fact that Alfred is badly injured. We can't undo it. You do understand that, don't you? Christ! Just go and do some good deeds – even the ledger that way.'

Later that week in one of his Politics classes Sam came across a term he hadn't heard before: whistleblower. Good God, those people were brave – Bradley Manning, Daniel Ellsberg, Edward Snowden. They weren't just taking on some old traditions and an individual like Hadrien – they were up against whole governments!

Meanwhile the year rolled on, just like the previous two years at St Anton's had. He was back in footy training again, his essays were returned with credits and passes, he broke a record standing from the 1990s for drinking the greatest volume of beer straight from a keg through a hose, and then there was that surreal night with Lucy. Her questions about the cricket trip didn't mean anything, he told himself. What was important was the massage, the tea and the brief hour feeling cloistered in her room – a time that was private and dense, like he was a plant receiving some rare, intense nutrients. All this happened – life moved on around him, and he moved with it – yet he couldn't help thinking of those people, the whistleblowers. Late at night, alone in his room, he'd Google them and read their stories – and when he did, something in him became less afraid.

CHAPTER 9

Week ten of the academic year and the seasons were changing. In blew the first of many late autumn storms. Leaves from Viola Street flew into the quadrangles and the animals were spooked and had to be coaxed out of their pens. Some students lay down with them in the dark by the river and scratched their bellies with bark, and for a while the animals were not so scared and the students did not feel so temporal. On other days the scent of pine needles blew in from the forests in the east, and at night the sky was not black but grey and full of clouds. The air pressure dropped, Levi's grandmother started knitting him a jumper and Julian's older brothers – one in a law firm, the other at a merchant bank – took Toby, Julian, Levi, Charlotte and Lucy out to good restaurants and bought them red wine, steaks and puddings. They settled the bills and talked of global warming, scrambled weather patterns and how the students should make sure they enjoyed these, the best days of their lives.

Toby watched the other members of the cricket team as they trudged in a group across the quadrangles to their classes, but couldn't help noticing that they were falling behind, that the Alfred incident was affecting everyone, though in different ways.

Ben was becoming remote, spacy and disengaged. Toby presumed he was busy tackling his long overdue essay on the Nigerian slave trade, or was steeling himself for another bout of depression. But gossip around the college said otherwise: Ben had turned political, had dumped Charlotte and was hanging out with some university people in the Bio-med cafe. Julian, a little hysterically, passed on the rumour that after the rowing finals Ben was going to give up sport. Lucy said she heard from Octavia that Ben had joined some weird religious group on campus – which was strange, she said, because he'd always been an atheist. But it wasn't strange, Toby thought to himself. Religion gave people meaning, solace ... But why hadn't Ben come to him to talk about it all? They talked about everything.

One Tuesday morning Toby got up early and waited outside the dining hall for the rowers to come in after training.

'Hey,' he said, grabbing Ben's arm. 'You're a hard one to catch.'

'Well, here I am,' said Ben. 'You had breakfast?'

'I thought I'd wait for you.'

They lined up by the industrial-sized toasters, an uneasy silence between them as they waited for their bread to brown. Words echoed around the dining hall at that hour – there were only a few Science students with early pracs, a couple of the part-time tutors with city jobs, and the rowers.

Toby led Ben to a small table away from the rowers.

'You haven't responded to my texts. Or my calls.'

'Sorry, I've had my phone switched off.'

'Why?'

'It's a challenge I've set for myself. I don't want to be reliant on technology anymore, I want to see what happens when I go without it for a while.'

'Like a digital detox?'

'Sort of.'

'When will you be back on the grid?'

'I don't know. Maybe if it works okay I'll stay off – just jump on when I need to submit assignments or listen to a lecture or something.'

'Ben, that's crazy. No one can live without the internet. Has this got anything to do with those people – the religious group Octavia saw you with?'

'You say "those people" like there's something wrong with them,' said Ben, his jaw tensing up.

'They're Christians.'

'And that's a bad thing?'

'Well, some Christians can be pretty weird; it's like they're not right in the head.'

Ben looked over at the rowers. 'You think those guys are right in the head? You think Hadrien is right in the head?'

'Shush, Ben – keep your voice down.'

'Why are you so afraid of them? Has Hadrien threatened you?'

'Threatened me? Why would he threaten me?' asked Toby, still whispering.

'I don't know. But you're not being very cool with me at the moment. I just have this … this stuff that I need to work out, okay?'

Ben's voice had grown so loud that even the cooks had stopped chatting and were staring at him. From the rowers' table, Hadrien was looking at him with an inscrutable face, eyebrows slightly raised.

Levi was worried about Julian. Initially, Julian's anxiety over Alfred had manifested itself in an almost pathological need to speak to his parents at least twice a day – before they went to work and then a longer conversation with them in the evening, about nothing, really – his day, their day, the dog. Julian told Levi that hearing his father describe a particularly tetchy business meeting, or the precise shade of blue ('power blue, not powder blue') of the new car he was going to buy, or the quality of the food on a short-haul flight, was soothing somehow. The banality of their conversations, even the words themselves ('beige settee', 'tangy mushroom sauce', 'new set of golf clubs'), had the almost magical effect of keeping thoughts of Alfred at bay.

'I think I'm freaking them out,' Julian confided. 'At first Dad was suspicious, thinking I was after money or had got into trouble, but now they think, I dunno, that I'm suddenly interested in them or something.'

'That's the opposite of my parents,' said Levi. 'I went home to get some books the other day and had a big fight with Dad. He said I was becoming an arsehole.'

'That's not true, you're not an arsehole,' said Julian.

'Thanks, dude. And you know what? Maybe this Alfred thing and all the bad shit that's happened this semester, maybe it's made you feel closer to your parents. That's not so bad, you know.'

But after a week or two this new closeness passed and Julian returned to what seemed like his old self – a sort of happy laziness that was his default setting. He barely bothered to contact his parents unless he wanted money, and even then he preferred to text in the request rather than actually have to talk to them. He slept through breakfast (Toby left dry toast and a pat of butter on a plate by his door), he slept through classes (Levi gave him his notes), and during a play or an evening lecture he'd doze like a brandy-soaked old uncle on Christmas Day, nodding off in his chair. Yet despite his return to his natural nonchalant state, despite the frequent appearance of his lopsided smile and the dimples in his apple cheeks, something was happening to him. His asthma flared up more often, and once or twice a week Octavia, who had the room to his left, and Charlotte to his right would be woken in the middle of the night by his screams.

'It was so sweet,' Octavia told Levi after one of these nights. 'He was calling out for Alfred, like he was looking for him or something. But then he started screaming like someone had come into his room.'

Levi knew Julian was not dreaming that someone was in his room – instead, just like him, Julian had never left the bunkroom. He was still standing near Alfred, still chanting in a voice he didn't recognise, still strong and angry, still sweating, slightly delirious and most definitely drunk, still staring at the blood splattered on his trainers. He was still *there*.

As well as being unable to escape the night in the bunkroom, Levi often – daily, nightly – thought of the night after: the night he, Toby, Ben and Julian had spent in the bush.

After their lunch of muesli bars, and a pointless argument between Toby and Julian about who had taken the last one, they had continued searching in a higher part of the mountains, where it was colder and there were fewer trees, and strange animal noises. They searched for hours, crying 'Cooooeeee!' until they were hoarse. When darkness fell and the stars sharpened, they came together – for safety, to formulate a new plan, their torches pulsing out SOS, their toes getting cold. They decided to stay on the mountain overnight, signalling with a torch and calling out Alfred's name.

They passed that night on a perilous ledge, hoping that the advantage of height and the air's stillness would carry their voices to Alfred. And they wanted to share some of his pain. He was alone out there. They had failed him back at the house but they would not fail him now.

The bush changed at night. Black against black, the sky and the trees moved as one. The chatter between animals and insects did not seem so different from one of their parents' dinner parties: the light, low voices of women; the booming laugh of a man who'd had too much to drink coming in over the top; a short, tight argument at the end of the table between a man and a woman who knew they'd been married too long; then the explosion of all the sounds at once, a *Haw haw haw, rah tarah, rah tarah, rah tarah, crah, crah, arghha ha ha ha!* screaming across the sky.

At the navy-blue time of night, Julian and Levi found a rock that hung over the ledge, creating a small protected cavity. They nestled inside like a pair of lungs.

'Did you see much in the bunkroom?' whispered Levi. 'Did you see what they did to him?'

'No, I was too drunk. I can barely remember a thing. What about you?' asked Julian.

Levi faltered. 'I wasn't there. At least, I'm pretty sure I wasn't there. I can't remember anything except for hearing someone being beaten.' He sighed. 'I feel bad.' Levi could feel the heat of Julian's breath on his back and wished he could withdraw from the stench of the previous night's alcohol, still oozing from both their skins. 'We really lived up to our name last night – we were savages, all right.'

'I feel bad too,' said Julian. 'I'd like to resign from that stupid society. It's not nearly as much fun with Hadrien running the show – it was better when Edward was in charge. What happened to him?'

'In America doing something at the Kennedy School,' said Levi.

'Oh, that's right. Well, he wouldn't have stood for that trial bullshit last night,' said Julian.

'You're right, it was stupid,' said Levi. 'I've been thinking about it all day – whether if I hadn't been so drunk I could have stopped them. But you know what it's like going up against Hadrien. Impossible ...'

'Do you really believe Alfred's a terrorist?' asked Julian.

'Nah – that was just Hadrien's excuse. Anyway, he's too young; terrorists are usually in their twenties,' said Levi.

Julian shivered and could feel his bones contract; even under the ledge it was bitterly cold. 'What kind of animals do you think are out here? Do you think they'd attack us?'

Levi said without humour, 'I guess if we're eaten by wild dingoes we sort of deserve it.'

At 4 am Levi thought he heard Alfred, but it was only Ben standing on the ledge, looking towards the outer darkness, muttering something nonsensical to himself. Levi jumped up, restraining Ben from going alone back into the miserable tangle of the bush.

'But what happened to Alfred was my fault,' he said hoarsely. And Levi said it wasn't, even though he did not know why he was comforting Ben, because right now he really hated him – for playing a part in such a terrible game, for knowing such a terrible game.

'We should have been happy tonight, drunk back at the house, playing cards,' said Levi wistfully as he moved a stone from under his head and stretched out under the hard, glistening stars.

Later, towards dawn – a full twenty-four hours since they had left the house – they all had their turn at hating and fretting. They feared they would be up on the mountain forever, and that Alfred was nearby, his bones and back broken, the few words of English he knew stuck like cotton in his throat. He would smell of beer and the rain and not hear their cries. He would be fearful of the strange animals that ran across him and he would be fearful of his rescuers. Had a person ever been so far from home?

Levi wondered if his father was right, if he had become an arsehole. It had felt weird to hear his dad, who chose all his words so carefully, call him that. Normally Levi would have turned on him, started a blue, but lately everything was disordered, like he'd gone through Alice's looking glass. He had begun to feel odd, manic almost.

Last week he'd used up the once-yearly privilege of increasing the limit on his Visa card. Up he'd gone. He was now at $15,000, which made him feel sick but also giddy with possibility. He'd bought a ticket to New York for a big end-of-the-year trip, and one day he'd taken Charlotte into the city and they'd drunk champagne at one of the grand Victorian-era hotels, and then he'd gone and put all these expensive clothes on his card. The clothes were still in their bags, tags attached – ridiculous things that he didn't need, like neckties in fourteen colours, a velvet blazer from Jack English that fitted tightly across his chest and a pair of green crocodile-skin loafers.

He and Charlotte had been tipsy when he'd gone on his spree. He'd bought her some bright pink knickers and a bra that she'd allowed him to inspect on her in the fitting room. They were both so drunk, but that kind of giggly, bright-yellow drunk that belongs to afternoons and expensive hotels and champagne. He'd flicked the knickers' elastic at Charlotte's hip then fallen backwards through the fitting-room door. The washed-out-looking sales assistant – a girl about their age, lips pursed to disappearance, who probably thought they'd been fucking in the change room and didn't look at either of them except to throw Charlotte a hateful glance – wrapped the package tightly and took Levi's credit card. He held his breath – had the increase been approved yet? And when the card was accepted and she slid over the slip and said 'Sign here' with a toneless sort of hate, he and Charlotte had whooped and hugged, like the approval of the increase in credit was a prize they had won, and he would never have to pay the money back.

Now, in his room, on his bed, Levi took a navy tie out of its tissue paper and tied it in a slipknot around his neck, following instructions he'd found on the internet. He tightened it a little, just to see how it would feel – silk cutting into skin, restriction of breath, a cellular sort of panic – before he relaxed the knot again.

He couldn't admit it to anyone, but since they had been up on the mountains, since the thing with Alfred, he felt different. Life around him vibrated with a different frequency. Or maybe it was him vibrating with a different frequency. He wondered – and also tried not to wonder – if the violence and chaos of that night had turned him on, making everything seem more vivid, intense and close to the surface.

Maybe that was what had been missing from his life so far – from his family's terrace house, filled with books and arguments and people dropping in from the university to spill their opinions all over the place. 'Opinions, not blood – that's what you all spill,' he imagined saying to his appalled parents ('*Watch it, you're becoming an arsehole, Levi*'). The thought gave him a thrill. He'd had some experience of violence now;

he'd had a different experience of life from them and now he felt he was a different person from them.

Like his parents, he had always lived mostly in his head – and now, after this thing with Alfred, he could feel his body awakening. It was the strangest feeling – and not all bad, just ... different. He rubbed the silk of the tie across his chest, feeling the blood rush up to meet the touch.

After this he started skipping some classes – just a few here and there – and while it was still warm enough he took a blanket down to the quadrangle closest to the river, drinking wine from an old thermos so as not to get in trouble with the chaplain. When the weather got cooler he drank in his room, sometimes alone, sometimes with girls from the university – girls who, like him, wore heavy-framed glasses, girls who were different from the ones he knew at college. These girls wore lots of makeup and black clothes, had tattoos and were political or bisexual or often both. They were happy to drink his awful white wine while lying in his bed in the middle of the day, painting their fingernails black and listening to the *Goldberg Variations*.

Julian barely noticed the change in Levi, but Toby did. He kept asking him if something was wrong, if he needed to talk. It was, quite frankly, very irritating, Levi thought.

'Come on, Levi,' said Toby. 'You can't sit in your room and drink all day, it's unhealthy. Let's go watch the lacrosse final.'

'I don't watch lacrosse with cunts,' Levi replied.

'What?'

'You know what I mean. You and Ben are both cunts.'

'Why are you saying that?' asked Toby, visibly stung.

Levi just shrugged and walked away, not really knowing why he'd said it. He was frequently assailed by a reckless impulse to set fire to his life and everyone in it. Stand back, watch it burn.

But still Toby persisted, calling by Levi's room, waiting for him at the door of the dining hall, dropping into the seat next to him in a lecture.

Levi could tell when Toby was at the door. He had a certain knock, his footsteps had a particular cadence as he walked up the cloister. 'Shhhh,' he would tell the girl beside him, holding a hand over her bright-red mouth. 'It's Toby … and we're not home, okay?'

And they would hold their breath until his footsteps died away.

It was on one of these white-wine afternoons that he got himself in a bit of trouble. He was with two girls from his ICEPIC class – Introduction to Contemporary European Politics, Ideology and Culture, probably his favourite subject. In ICEPIC he often sat with Georgie and Jen, who he had at first thought were girlfriends, but he later discovered they were a little more ambiguous than that. One morning, when the class was watching *Betty Blue*, he felt Jen's hand on his leg. Both girls accepted his invitation to come back to his room after class for a glass of wine. He drew the curtains, blocking out the sun that had been warming his bed.

They were sweet girls – soft and dreamy, planting kisses on his neck and ears, their half-empty mugs of wine on the nightstand, the Smiths playing from his phone. He was grateful for the third-year privilege of a double bed and manoeuvred himself so he was between the girls. Jen passed a joint to him, and after he'd inhaled he blew the smoke into Georgie's mouth and rubbed his hand along her side tentatively, up near her breasts. When she didn't object he stroked then cupped them, before leaning over and kissing Jen, who had the joint. Soon he was all sensation, just a mouth and hands and a dick, blood and skin, cells that were firing off dopamine so fast that Levi found himself moaning with pleasure and—

'What the fuck? What the fuck?' Georgie propelled herself out of bed towards the door in a couple of deft, energetic moves. Her pants were down and her shirt was open.

'What?' asked Levi, puzzled. 'What?'

'Did you just finger me?' she asked with disgust.

Levi, confused – the dopamine chemicals now in flight, his skin clammy and cooling – said, 'Yes, I fingered you – what's your problem with that?'

A pillar of ash from the joint that Jen was holding fell onto the sheets. At that moment it looked to Levi like the collapse of the World Trade Center done in miniature.

'You're meant to *ask*!' said Georgie, shaking with anger as she buttoned up her shirt. 'You can't just *go in there*!'

She grabbed Jen, who looked very stoned, and pulled her from the bed, and Jen kept saying, 'Where did I put my shoes?' and the Smiths were playing 'Reel Around the Fountain', and then the girls were gone and Levi didn't even get to say, 'Hey, Georgie, your buttons are done up all wrong.'

After that the frequency changed again. Instead of the intense colour and drenched meaning he felt in everything around him, life drained of meaning. Everything became flat and pointless, lost its tone and texture, and Levi found himself longing for the tumult and terror of that night in March.

Ben discovered it was not always easy to be Sylvan's friend in the supposedly tolerant and 'anything goes' atmosphere of the university. Sylvan was known around campus as a Jesus freak and his classmates gave him a wide berth, avoiding his grey eyes if he sat next to them in a lecture or tutorial. But sometimes Sylvan created the distance himself. In the cafeteria, he would pull a tambourine from his hemp rucksack. Ben always thought – but never said – 'Oh no, don't! Put it away!'

But when Sylvan played the tambourine his eyes looked unfocused and far away, like he was meditating or something, and before too long he was lost in a jangling song. Ben didn't have the heart to rouse him out of it for appearance's sake. Not that Sylvan cared about appearances – he didn't notice the students sniggering and laughing. Soon Ben stopped being embarrassed for Sylvan and became angry and protective.

'Fuck off,' he told some nasty, drunken Engineering students. 'It's a free country – he can sing if he wants.'

'Homos,' they replied.

Sylvan shrugged softly and kept shaking his tambourine. 'Don't get angry,' he said to Ben.

Actually, what Sylvan really said was: 'Don't get angry, brother.'

Since Ben had started going to the cafe and staying back to talk and sing (but not to pray, not yet), Sylvan had called him 'brother'. It jolted Ben to be called that, but in a good way. An only child, until now he had been no one's brother. Toby was the closest he had to one. Ben winced, as he often did when he thought about Toby. Toby had seen Ben at his worst, and Ben's instinct was to avoid him right now.

Sometimes Ben and Sylvan were joined by a younger girl, Katie, who dressed like all the Jerusalem women, tripping over her long skirt while finding a seat in the lecture hall, adjusting her slipping headscarf. She obviously loved Sylvan so dearly that Ben sometimes felt awkward about hanging out with them – like he was the third wheel in a love affair (or, his unchaste mind sometimes suggested, like it was a spiritual ménage à trois with Sylvan as its hot, loving centre).

'If you and Katie want to be alone that's okay, I can go back to college for lunch,' said Ben on one occasion, although he actually wanted to be right there, with them, and nowhere else.

But Sylvan shook his head (and his tambourine). 'Please stay – Katie and I don't need to be alone; she is my sister.'

'What, literally or figuratively?'

Sylvan shrugged as if to say, 'What does it matter?' Aloud he said, 'All men are my brothers. All women are my sisters.'

When they were alone Sylvan would talk to Ben about which bits of the Bible meant the most to him. It was the message of poverty that appealed to Sylvan. He quoted the Gospels, where Jesus had said to the poor, *'Blessed are you who are poor, for yours is the kingdom of God.'* To the rich he said, *'Do not store up for yourselves treasures on earth'* and *'Go, sell your possessions, and give the money to the poor and you will have treasure in heaven.'*

Sylvan recited some lines from memory: *"'I was hungry and you gave me food, I was thirsty and you gave me something to drink, I was a stranger and you welcomed me, I was naked and you gave me clothing, I was sick and you took care of me, I was in prison and you visited me.'"*

Ben tried hard to be nonchalant, but how could he be cool when presented with the awesome power of 'as you did to one of the least of these my brethren, you did to me'?

'What was that again?' asked Ben, all his senses (everything, really) bristling.

Sylvan paraphrased it: 'Whatever you do to the least of my brothers you do to me … It's great, isn't it? It's a whole way of being in that one sentence. How you treat the humblest person, the lowest man on the pole, the least important – that is how you are treating God. It informs everything we do. You give your money to the poor, you work to improve the conditions of the least well-off in the world, and you are working for God. Turn your back on the suffering and you turn your back on God.'

They talked of other things, not just Sylvan's God but all gods: 'You've gotta worship *something* – you choose,' said Sylvan passionately. 'But make a choice, make a conscious decision. Don't just drift. There's no real consciousness to be found there. Whether it's via me or something else, it doesn't matter, but I want you to be awake in your life!'

This kind of talk was new and radical for Ben. St Antonians frowned on involvement in student politics or religion, regarding it as suspect or uncool. To fight for social justice was also seen as weird. It wasn't like all the students at St Anton's were cynics, but they prided themselves on their pragmatism – looking life in the eye and seeing it for what it really was: an unfair game where often the people who held all the cards were the least deserving. Power, they felt, did not contain a moral aspect. Their parents had schooled them in this. Follow power, they exhorted, rather than trying to change the power structures. Be wary of those who don't have power but claim self-righteously that it should be shared. That is all they have: self-righteousness – not the skills needed to wield power, to grip it when it's hot and dangerous.

Anyway, what were college and that terrible, cruel school Ben went to other than an extended lesson in working with power? 'Go to the source of power,' Ben's father had said, 'and work with it.' But here was his spiritual brother, Sylvan, telling him that it did not have to be this way – that the world had gone wrong somewhere along the line, and for him it was not too early, it was not too late: the time for change was now.

CHAPTER 10

'We're here, join us if you like.' The great thing about the Pleasing Sands cafe, thought Ben, was that he could drop in anytime and just hang out. Alighting at Jacaranda Station, he would take his laptop and his reading list and sit at a far table surrounded by bonsai plants and work on an essay or read case law. When it got busy he threw on an apron and helped out. If only his mum could see him now! She had tried (half-heartedly, it was true, since they had a dishwasher and a cleaner) to get him to help around the house many times, but had eventually given up. But now here he was, bicep-deep in water, wearing some hard-core rubber gloves, suds floating like dandelions through the air, scrubbing an enormous, crusty lasagne tray. And singing. With his eyes closed.

The Jerusalems were great singers. Often they would close up the cafe before opening up their lungs, but, said Sylvan, 'If the spirit moves you, sing it.' Customers would look up from their coffee and cake with embarrassment at first, but as more voices were heard from the kitchen and the floor swelled with song those looks changed to wonder. Sometimes the customers even joined in, their phones forgotten on their tables – their selves forgotten, too. It was special when that happened. Poetry in motion.

Sylvan also said that song and prayer were ways of releasing joy and hope. That combination of words (song, prayer, joy, hope) would have been enough to elicit spirit-deflating sniggers and soul-smashing rolling of eyes from the cricket team, but they hadn't been here, they hadn't heard the music – they didn't understand.

On the train on the way back to college one day, still buzzing, Ben tried to work out why the cleaning and the singing made him so happy. He didn't think he was finding God – after all, he didn't believe in God. But if he wasn't finding God, what *was* he finding? Whatever it was, something about the Jerusalems lit a fire in him. Filled with this warmth, he no longer felt so anxious. When he sang and he cleaned, he too was forgetting himself, the words almost rinsing him clean of memories of the bunkroom, almost wiping out allegiance to that dangerous pact.

The pact ... He turned it over and over in his mind until it was like a playing card worn at the edges. Could he undo it? Was it a binding contract, like the ones he'd been taught about in the first week of Contracts Law? During the vote at the stringybark, he had been on autopilot, numb and silent.

He had been central to the voting, yet something in him was detached. He hadn't slept in a couple of nights, and was close to hallucinating. The light was soft, the trees were dark, sounds merged. As usual he let Toby do the talking for him, but Toby hadn't been able to get them over the line. The vote seemed rushed. They packed up the cars quickly, almost in a panic. Boys were stuffing bottles of gin and muddy walking books into duffle bags along with squashed paperbacks tangled in iPhone chargers.

On the drive home Ben stared ahead like a zombie. The white lines steadied him and kept him from waking up, from jumping out of the car and running back up to the mountains to look for Alfred.

When they stopped to get petrol at some forlorn station, Leeson was waiting for them.

'Let's get a drink,' he said.

'No, I'm tired, I think we should just go straight back,' said Toby.

'I want a fucking drink,' said Leeson, almost emotionally.

'So do I,' said Julian. 'Badly.'

They swung off the main road to a rundown little pub called the Sea Sisters, near the foot of the mountains. It was a dark, low-roofed place, decorated with portraits of a younger Queen wearing a golden sash, the heads of things that had been caught in a hunt and spoons from all over the world – Zurich, Potsdam, Leeds, Basel, Mumbai, Mount Gambier – arranged in a wooden rack.

When the cricket team walked in, dragging the cool mountain air behind them, they felt the mood in the tavern shift, as the five or six locals bolted to the bar stools somehow simultaneously ignored them and stared.

The publican ('You boys not from round here, are ya?') led them to a quiet table near a fire and Toby, always comfortable talking with barmen, cooks, waitresses and cleaners, ordered for the table.

'We're hungry, so we'll have whatever's easiest for the cook, whatever's handy in the kitchen.'

'Well, I'm the cook,' she said shyly. '*And* the waitress, and the cleaner, and the barmaid ...' Then she looked like she regretted telling them that she was so downtrodden – as if they would understand.

'I'm sure whatever you cook will be lovely,' said Toby.

She returned with plates of bread and butter. She seemed caught in Toby's gaze, and for a long moment, her hand almost outstretched, it seemed she was about to run her hand through his tangled brown hair to shake out the sticks and leaves lodged there.

As she walked away Leeson muttered, 'What are you trying to do, Toby – pick her up? She's old enough to be your grandmother – and ugly enough.'

'She's rough,' agreed Roman.

'Why are we even talking about this?' asked Ben, the feeling of detachment starting to wear off. 'We need to talk about Alfred. What are we going to say to the Master when we get back? And what will we say to the police?'

Leeson, gouging holes in the soft white bread with chunks of hard butter, said, 'Leave all that to Hadrien, old boy. Don't worry about the Master or the cops. All we have to do is shut up.' His mouth full of bread, he swung the butter knife close to Ben's face. 'Don't take it outside the college gates, okay? Just don't. And don't tell Charlotte or Lucy or whichever fur you happen to be screwing.'

He swallowed and leant towards Toby, almost leering. 'Especially you. Don't squeal.'

'But look at you all!' said Toby. Leeson, Severin, Sam and Roman were covered in cuts and bruises, dried blood in their hair and behind their ears from where they had hit each other in the strange games of Friday night.

The publican approached carrying a tray laden with heavy, mismatched crockery, deep soup spoons and a bottle of merlot. The boys fell silent. Leeson's words hung in the air. Julian let out an involuntary groan of pain as his sunburn settled in for the night. Ben's foot was bleeding under the table. Levi's knee was swelling and turning black. Sam had gone to the bathroom to be sick. The smell of alcohol and sweat hung around them, and the deeper, richer scent of a fire.

'Now listen up, team – it's time to talk plans,' said Leeson. He had won the vote under the stringybark. He had the authority. 'We have to stick together in this. If one of us breaks ranks then that's it for all of us – we're finished.'

'Hang on,' said Levi. 'I was asleep, and so were Julian and Toby. Why should *we* get in trouble? Why should we be part of this to protect you?'

Leeson looked at Levi slyly. 'Are you sure you were asleep? You don't just kick footballs well, Leev.'

Levi blushed and looked away.

'And you, Toby – you don't want to say anything that might get Bath in trouble, do you?' asked Severin. 'Because he really didn't supervise us properly, the old poof. I can't believe he missed the whole thing. Wouldn't it be weird if *he* went down.'

'No one going down, all right? We keep our mouths shut and they can't get us because there's no evidence.'

'There's Alfred, for God's sake!' said Toby. 'Alfred is the evidence. Gross, Severin – you're bleeding for fucksakes.'

'Not necessarily,' said Severin, running a napkin over his face and dabbing at a bloody spot under his eye. 'Even if he is found and does remember, he'll be too scared to say anything.'

'Why? Why would he be scared?' asked Toby.

No one answered him.

'How do we explain that we've come back without Alfred?' asked Levi.

'We don't,' said Leeson. 'No one knows he came here with us.'

Toby shook his head. 'Not possible. He could have told any number of people where he was going.'

Leeson smirked. 'He can't have told anyone because he didn't have time. We took him by surprise. Hadrien, Severin and I knocked on his door. He was alone, wearing some sort of tai chi clothes – or maybe they were his pyjamas or shorts … whatever. We introduced ourselves, said we were from the cricket team and were going away to celebrate the end of the season, told him we had a spare seat in the car and asked if he'd like to come with us. He said yes, packed a little bag, put on some shoes and came down to the car park with us.'

'He was delighted, wasn't he?' said Severin to Leeson.

'Yes, delighted to be invited,' replied Leeson. He shrugged. 'And that's it. We stopped to get booze and a pie each. Alfred had a chicken one. We tried to warn him against it.'

'They're never nice,' Severin chimed in.

'But no one saw Alfred,' Leeson concluded.

'No,' Severin confirmed. 'No one saw Alfred.'

'I mean, it wasn't like we threw a pillowslip over his head and made him lie under the seat – but no one saw him.'

'Because there was no one around to see him.'

'And if no one saw him, then he wasn't there, was he?'

'I can't believe this,' muttered Toby in disbelief. 'How do you think you can get away with it? Are you totally nuts?'

Leeson motioned for another bottle of wine to be brought to the table. Everyone was silent until he said quietly, 'I thought we had just explained that to you. God, sometimes you really are so thick I can't believe you got into university.'

Roman started singing softly, 'He's just a poor boy from a poor family ...'

'Don't you feel bad?' asked Toby, his voice cracking. Ben worried his friend would start to cry.

'Don't ask that question,' said Leeson tightly. 'We all *feel bad* at some level. Of course we do. But we'd feel worse in prison. Unless maybe you're longing to get raped by some bikie?'

'*I* feel bad,' said Ben emphatically.

No one said anything at that, but Severin and Roman rolled their eyes.

'Oh, for fuck's sake – we stick together on this or we go down, okay?' Leeson said. 'That's what it comes down to. United we stand, divided we fall. I'm just being practical.'

'If Alfred has made it back before us he's probably gone to the police,' said Levi.

'No,' said Leeson confidently. 'He's an overseas student – they don't think to do things like that. He'll just think what happened to him in the bunkroom is part of our way of life. What would he know? He's only been here a month. Trust me, we have nothing to worry about. We can get away with this ... Don't you see that?'

Ben waited for Toby to stand up and denounce the cricket team, its so-called mateship. He waited and waited for Toby to put forward some inspiring argument about how individuals are responsible for their own actions, good and bad. Of course, this would be disastrous for everyone, except for Toby himself, the only truly innocent member of the team. Toby could walk away that night and be okay.

But Toby just sat there, mute, listening to Leeson and becoming more complicit by the minute.

'Don't bind yourself to us!' Ben wanted to urge him. 'You're too good for us!' But instead he looked at Toby from across the table and mouthed the words, 'Be careful.'

Leeson held his glass up in the air. 'Let's drink a toast – to sticking together.'

The other boys – arms weak from punches thrown or from climbing rocks in the hunt for Alfred – managed to raise their glasses and say the words out loud: 'To sticking together.'

Outside twilight sank down into the mountains and the cockatoos suddenly started up a riotous noise. The birds, even the birds, were trying to send a warning: 'Don't promise anything!'

❋

Ben's train pulled into the station, and he got on a tram that took him back up to college. Toby shouldn't have got involved, he thought, as he took out his phone – the one that he'd promised himself he'd stop using. Maybe he could just ring Toby and talk properly – or at least text. But something stopped him, something instinctual. Instead he went on to Toby's Facebook page and his Instagram account, smiling as he scrolled through the status updates, the photos and the links.

Oh, he missed him! But this was nice, keeping close at this distance, checking on him, making sure he was safe and okay, until this thing brewing inside him blew over.

Toby was surprised how quickly Alfred's absence was forgotten after the initial hysteria. Even Vincent, Ricky, Chi and others who lived with Alfred in the 'Ching Wing' seemed to move on quite quickly and too easily. They became absorbed in their lectures, their self-directed study groups, their games of chess in the quadrangle, sitting cross-legged in patches of sunlit grass. Footballs bounced too close to the board and sometimes hit them on the back but they did not look up. 'Norwegian Wood' leaked from their earphones and sometimes they smiled. In the dining room Toby noticed that their appetites returned. He again heard the pop-pop sound of ping-pong balls coming from the Games Room. Play had resumed, and after the first weeks of hysteria it was as if nothing had ever happened. Just before Easter, Gong moved into Alfred's room and the erasure was complete.

Gong was from Vietnam, a rumoured maths genius, and unlike Alfred he was a careful dresser. He wore expensive trainers, cargo pants and bright red and yellow T-shirts bearing incongruous slogans: *My dog lies down now* and *Wasabi ahhh wassabi!*

For Toby, though, everything hung in a state of suspension. Alfred was either getting better or getting worse. Who knew? Alfred could either identify or not identify his attackers. Who knew? Toby was either culpable for shielding the cricket team or not. Well – this one he knew the answer to.

How long could he stand at this crossroads, hedging his bets, hoping for the best? The coward in him believed that the best outcome would be if Alfred made a full recovery except for the part of his brain able to recall the events in the bunkroom.

Toby was aware (how could he not be?) of the case of the cruise-ship woman. Sex, a drug overdose on a ship, a group of men ... Sometime in the night she died and they did nothing – they closed ranks, they vowed not to talk, despite immense moral and legal pressure. Did he want to be like those men?

And all those rugby league teams, with their bunning and roasting and all that suspect group sex. They never broke ranks, did they? They never talked, never dobbed. They were watertight – no weak links, and no criminal convictions. But did the cricket team of St Anton's really want to be like them? Of course not! They were university men, well bred and well read. Men of calibre. They were meant to be better than that. He thought of that line from *Crime and Punishment*. It had a fresh, awful resonance. *'You're a gentleman ... You shouldn't have gone murdering people with a hatchet; that's no occupation for a gentleman.'*

The more he considered it, the more he was convinced that he should go to the police, no matter what the Master said. He could talk Ben, Julian and Levi around, couldn't he? Appeal to their better selves? Right this ship.

But when he mentioned the plan to Julian – just sounding him out – Julian became quite hysterical. Flinging himself across Toby's bed, he pleaded with him tearfully to give it just a little more time. A week, a month … 'Let's just wait and see. We're not in any danger. We're not going to get caught. Now is not the time to panic and go to the cops. Please. Wait until after semester break. I have this Psychology test coming up; it's worth thirty-five percent of my mark for this semester … Oh God, Toby, I'm not a terrible person – you know that. I don't know what came over me that night. Really. But please, *please*, don't go to the police just now, okay? Think about it some more. Sleep on it.'

Toby sighed. How could he turn Julian in? Julian was like an overgrown boy; he was somehow still developing. But how could Toby 'sleep on it' when he was finding it impossible to sleep? He was sure his inability to decide about Alfred had a lot to do with the fact that since they had come down from the mountain, after that first mammoth eighteen-hour coma, he hadn't slept for more than four hours at a stretch.

He decided to take a tram through the city and across the river to see his older ex-girlfriend Lisa, whose own experiences of sleep deprivation were quite legendary; she claimed to have not slept properly in sixteen years. She had dumped Toby at the end of summer, citing the age gap as the reason – they had 'no future' – though Toby wondered whether, after sixteen years of poor sleep, she was not thinking straight.

Before Lisa, anyone over twenty-five had seemed impossibly old to Toby. He had a brother who was twenty-five, almost twenty-six. Matt was a farmer and seemed fully formed, whereas Toby, particularly now he saw less of Ben, felt like a hologram. Matt had opinions on the government, tax subsidies, international trade and produce prices, climate change and organic pesticides. He knew about the cosmos, and the seasons and science and the whole cycle of life and death of the farm animals he kept. He had delivered calves into the silent 4 am frost and murdered others that slid onto the yielding hay with extra limbs and filmy eyes. Meanwhile, Toby was still living in his college bubble and had delivered nothing except for double-spaced essays and wordy toasts at the annual Debaters' Dinner.

His first glimpse into the world of adults (as opposed to the world of parents, which was an entirely different world altogether) occurred that summer when he started dating Lisa. She was thirty years old. He had a thirty-year-old lover. He used to whisper the fact of her to himself – thrilled and not a little frightened. Lisa was his window on the world; through her he could astral-travel down the years to see the world that was waiting for him in a decade or so.

It wasn't just that she looked different from the girls he had been with – the glamorous ingénue Charlotte; the childlike urchin Octavia, with her pinafore and pixie cut; Suzanne, who despite being twenty-one was always asked for ID. Lisa had a different energy. She pushed herself in a way that the girls at college didn't. She worked (at an investment bank) to the point of exhaustion, and when she wasn't at work she seemed preoccupied by it – by her fraught and difficult projects and her fraught and difficult colleagues. When Lisa wasn't at work, worrying about work, or analysing her colleagues, she was exercising – either jogging around the city in the dark or meeting her personal trainer in the morning almost-dark for a series of chilling, ritualistic 'drills' that left her exhausted but happy. She was his lean, weary, gorgeous secret.

When Julian, Ben and Levi found out about Lisa they teased him about his cougar, but they didn't understand that it wasn't like that. She was preoccupied and busy; work was her primary motivator in life, not notches on her bedpost. She had hardly any room left, and that was why, on an unseasonably cold November night in the Still/Life bar near Parliament House, she had lit upon him and his unlined features. Ten years her junior – or was it eleven? Picked because he would take up the least amount of space, was someone she could easily climb over on her way to her morning run.

Though she ran and worked like an engine, she couldn't manage the sleep thing very well. 'Too wound up,' she would say. On particularly bad nights she would take a pill and then drop like a rock into unconsciousness.

Now it had been months since he had seen her. He was as nervous as he had been on their first night together. She opened the door a crack, greeted him and said, 'I'd invite you in but I'm busy.'

Toby was fearful for a moment, expecting there to be another lover in her apartment, but he peeked around the door and saw that it wasn't a different boy but two laptops and an enormous screen, side by side, the figures on the screen churning so fast they were the digital approximation of falling snow.

When he stammered about his problem with sleeplessness she pressed a packet of Xarbol into his hand and said almost tenderly, 'I know how much it can suck.'

Back at college, Toby started taking the pills straight away. They put him into a dreamless sleep, but they also impaired things when he was awake. He felt blurry and far away all the time, as if he were lying under ten blankets. In this state he became strangely slow and vulnerable. At a Criminal Law lecture he was a beat and a half behind the class. He tried to keep up with what the lecturer was saying, but his mind was still chewing over the majority judgements while the rest of the class were debating the dissent. He thought he saw Ben after class, waiting for him in the usual place by the water fountain. But when he got there – waving, too excited – he realised he had been waving at a boy in some massive poster about domestic violence, and it wasn't Ben at all. It didn't even look like him.

A week later and the effect of the pills was even more pronounced. After a few beers at the Red Lion with Levi and Julian, Toby felt anxious and paranoid, certain that the prescription drugs and alcohol in his system would conspire to shut him down and switch him off, the way they had done to so many young Hollywood stars. He must not fall asleep, he announced to his startled friends after a drab few hands of UNO. He poked and pulled at his skin, he pinched his arms to stay awake. Back in his room he made foul brews from instant coffee and Red Bull.

And so, in what he figured was pretty neat irony, he was striving to avoid what he had so strenuously tried to get: sleep. Wakefulness now became the desired state lest he wanted to die in an embarrassing and, to his parents, puzzling way – the fit young man, the cricketer whose pill-addled body rattled like maracas, with such a confusion of chemistry that it had simply thrown its hands up and stopped.

Finally he sought the assistance of Niall, whose partially completed medical degree conferred on him an almost shaman-like status among the college's sick and anxious. Niall knew when a cold would become flu, the difference between a break and a sprain, when a lump on the body was a bomb or just a bump. Niall was cool and detached, a stark contrast to the overly familiar camaraderie that was a feature of college life, particularly among the sporting cliques with their crow-like calls of 'Maaaayte' across the quadrangle, their backslaps and manly embraces. Niall stood apart from all of this, watching with heavy-lidded eyes. (What had he been like in the bunkroom? Toby wondered. Still detached? Still cool?)

When Levi and Julian had left Toby's room after yet another evening of furtive talk about Alfred, and now about Ben too, Toby pulled on some shoes and a hoodie and headed out towards the candles that flickered and burnt on Niall's balcony like the remnants of a Roman Mass.

At his desk, Niall bent over Lisa's Xarbol tablets like an old apothecary and dismissed them quickly. 'Those won't do shit,' he said. 'You need to take these.' He produced a film canister from his bar fridge containing blue pills. 'These are for night and these –' he shook a handful of shiny red capsules into Toby's hands '– are for the day. Preferably when you first wake up, or you'll be foggy. Don't smoke weed, and lay off the booze, okay?'

In this disorder of colour (greens and purples would later be added to blues and reds), Toby felt his life was like one massive CGI special effect. The impact of the pills was dazzling: the sharp shard of light that danced through Charlotte's hair, the clouds that rushed to meet him in a hilarious marshmallow embrace, and the fluffy fat kookaburra perched on a low branch near the Master's office that opened its gullet and sang melodies in rhymes and riddles as nonsensical as K-pop. It was easy in this dazzling dreamscape just to lie in the quadrangle all day in the weak sunlight and get lecture notes from Julian and Levi – because who could be bothered going to class when all this beauty spun around you like a top?

Sylvan and the other Jerusalems lived in a big disused school on the edge of the city, shut down in the 1990s because of asbestos fears. The old schoolhouse was stone, with a high ceiling and dark wooden beams overhead. Bunting hung from the beams in faded colours, like the flags of countries that no longer existed. There was a fireplace and cushions and even a blackboard, though the chalk and the dusters were long gone.

In the clearing around the schoolhouse was a confusion of portable classrooms, a toilet block with low, shrunken seats – suitable for schoolchildren – as well as shower facilities and a long, crudely rigged up kitchen. Tin pots hung from nails banged into poles, gas burners stood in rows, their workings exposed and brutal-looking, but despite its makeshift appearance, the benches were steel and spotless – a non-distorting mirror, should you wish to gaze down and tidy your hair.

The families slept in the portable classrooms, the women cooked in the jerry-rigged kitchen, and they all gathered in the old schoolhouse for meals, for non-worship meetings, and for the occasional late-night guitar session or game of Scrabble.

Great care had been taken in the building of a chapel, which sat away from the portable classrooms in another, smaller clearing. It was mud brick and finished with wattle and daub. The altar was like a clay wave that had set before breaking on some distant shore, with fresh wildflowers picked by the children each day and placed in clay bowls or little vases. 'It's our Shangri-La,' said Sylvan as he showed Ben around. 'That's what we call it.'

Beyond the clearing was a lake ringed by high fir trees, giving it an exotic look, like the whole scene had been transported there from another world, or at least from northern Europe.

Ben loved it there: so close to nature, so close to grace. He sometimes stayed over, sleeping in a swag in the schoolhouse, the dying fire and the dogs warming him, a child creeping in now and then in the middle of the night to gaze at him like he was Gulliver. He would wake to see the child curled round a dog, and the dawn coming in through the classroom windows like the sun was being wrung out all over them.

'*Grrhhmmm*,' a dog would murmur in its half-sleep.

'*Hurrrumph*,' Ben would reply, climbing out of his sack to bathe in the lake, then head to the little chapel for the morning service.

He would see them all there in their pews – Katie and Sylvan and Sylvan's uncles sitting together. He knew that fresh tea would be brewing back in the kitchen, and that there would be damper and fruit and porridge for breakfast.

Then it would be off to work for most of them – in the cafe, or the workshop, or with the children under the shade-cloth that was a classroom.

All this was sweet – so sweet yet so temporary.

Soon enough the camp would be packed up and the kitchen dismantled. The wagons would be hitched and then – like the great traveller, St Paul – they would move on to the next place.

The Jerusalems had worked with, and had great respect for, the traditions of the Romany Gypsies – stateless, long persecuted, mocked by adults and children alike, effigies of them burnt on bonfire nights. The Jerusalems took some cues from them: the storytelling and the folk-singing, the lack of allegiance to a flag, intermarrying and travelling.

'It gets tiring,' Sylvan admitted to him once. 'Never staying in one place.'

'Then stay here,' said Ben, trying not to sound pleading, trying to buy something from the Jerusalems despite their non-materialist code – time, just a little more time.

Unless you had been in the bunkroom with Alfred, unless you had tried to sleep overnight on a spooky crag while searching for him, unless he had visited you each night in a kind of hot vision or nightmare, the memory of him would probably fade fast.

But for Levi, Alfred loomed larger than ever. Lately, Levi had become convinced that some retributory force was at work, that punishment was being meted out not by the Master or the police but by some malevolent metaphysical instrument. He paid close attention to Severin, who wasn't his friend, but who took some of the same classes and was in the football team with him.

Severin had been the most violent in the bunkroom. Levi shivered when he thought about his pale, dead eyes that night and remembered the splatters of blood on his face. Since the Scholars' Dinner, Severin had looked markedly unwell, zombified almost – he had already been a man of limited facial expressions, but now his face looked blanker than ever. Abruptly he took time off and had to take incompletes on three or four subjects. Rumours of illness went around the college: chronic fatigue, tuberculosis, hep C. Whatever it was, it worked on Severin quickly – his muscles seemed to be wasting away at such a rate it was as if they were deflating under his skin like shrunken balloons. He played with his food in the dining hall, his eyes refused to fix on yours, and then one day he even resigned from the football team.

During his last match he sat on the sidelines fumbling with his boots, frustrated tears not quite making the necessary journey down his granite face. The next Monday he had left college in a taxi, only to return a month later – colour back, the yellow gone from his eyes but a fresh, deeper nastiness there, as if he had tasted what it was like to be weak, not to be part of a winning team.

How could Levi help but suspect that this, his mysterious rapid illness, was connected to Alfred? That the rot of the skin was a manifestation of the rot of the soul? What were the rapid jaundicing of Severin's skin and eyes, the wasting of his muscles and talent on the football team, but signs that no bad deed went unpunished? The Alfred secret was acting like a tumour. Levi became suspicious and paranoid – reading his (and Toby's, Ben's and Julian's) horoscopes in the women's magazines left behind by the college maids, searching for answers in cold tea leaves, timidly knocking on the door of an elderly clairvoyant who lived by the beach in a shack that shook in the wind.

'Where do you see us all in a year?' he asked the clairvoyant nervously. 'In a happy place? Settled? Maybe in healthy relationships? Or on student exchange to … the Netherlands?'

Salt over the shoulder, ladders avoided, a shiver when he saw a black cat.

When he wasn't drunk and angry, or scared and confused, when he wasn't removing his glasses and applying mascara to his lashes with the door locked (and then staring for a while in the mirror before furiously washing it off), when he wasn't flicking through the *Crimes Act*, he felt sick with dread. He couldn't continue like this, but neither could he forget what he had seen in the bunkhouse. Had he kicked Alfred? Well, maybe there had been a kick here or there.

Levi wished he could eradicate certain charnel-house scenes from his memory – certain smells and cries, certain boys' excited responses.

'How are we going to be punished?' he whispered to Toby one night, when they were at an off-campus party, lying on a bed together with five others after having taken ecstasy. He was high and wanted to be reassured like a child. Bon Iver was playing from the iPod dock and the music moved through him like a religious visitation. Curled on his side, his lips pressed against Toby's ear, he asked: 'Will it all be okay? It'll be all right, won't it?'

Toby, eyes fixed on the ceiling and his hand stroking some girl's hair, murmured, almost too quietly for Levi to hear, 'Nothing will happen to us. Stick together, remember? As long as we all keep the pact we can protect each other.'

They were quiet for a while, the music changed to Massive Attack, and Toby murmured something that surprised him, but in a good way: 'You know I love you, man.'

Levi replied, 'Yeah, I know, dude. I love you too.' And at that moment he really did.

CHAPTER 11

'I didn't know you were in the choir,' said Levi to Charlotte, sounding pleasantly surprised. The tryouts had been on before dinner and they were walking back down the cloister, their academic gowns slung unevenly across their shoulders. The setting sun shining through the gothic tracery made diamond patterns on the tiled ground.

'And I didn't know you wanted to be in the choir,' Charlotte batted back.

It annoyed her that people assumed all choristers were nerds. She loved singing the hymns but they didn't mean anything to her – they were only words that, when sung with others, created a gorgeous billowing curtain of sound.

'I had a vaguely hostile conversation with my parents the other day,' said Levi. 'They want me to do something other than play sport. I thought the choir would make them happy.'

'I take it they don't really approve of your life at St Anton's,' said Charlotte archly.

'How do you know?'

'Your mum taught me Gender and Society in first year. I liked her, but, I don't know – I can't really see her coming along to Parents' Day and fawning over the Master. She's ... not like the other mothers.'

'Did she assign you her own books in class?'

'Yes,' said Charlotte, laughing. 'But I didn't mind. That one on collectivism is quite good. It was lovely of her to dedicate it to you. Did you adore it?'

'I haven't read it.'

They reached the dining room, and Charlotte looked around for Lucy, Julian, Toby or Ben.

'What's happened to our little group, do you think? We're all dispersing. I can never seem to find anyone in the same place.'

'I saw Ben out on Troutman Street waiting for a tram. He's going to his parents' for dinner tonight. But I haven't hung out with him for a while ... I think he's been sick,' said Levi carefully. 'Toby's got a late lecture; I'm not sure about the others. But at least you have me. I'm not as weird as Ben.'

'It's okay, I understand Ben. He goes away and he comes back. He's always been like that.' She leant into Levi and said huskily, 'I just miss his cock, that's all.'

'I don't even want to know. Don't tell me this stuff,' said Levi as he pulled out a chair for her next to Sam.

Ben had no longer been able to ignore his mother's phone calls asking him to come home for dinner and to stay the night.

'You don't have to get me a present for my birthday this year – this could be it, you home for dinner.'

She knew how to stick the knife in, to make him react, to bring him back. So there he was, standing on the platform waiting for the train, and the air smelt of jasmine and gasoline. Then in a crowded carriage smelling of fast food and the inside of office buildings – coffee breath, a papery smell, sweat trapped between skin and polyester shirts, loneliness channelled into Sudoku. Then home.

There were too many pots and bouquets of flowers in the long, dark hall, and for a moment Ben thought someone had died and he had not been told or, worse, he had been told and then forgotten about it, but once he was in the kitchen, with the light pouring in from the patio and his dog Sandy – now blind in one eye and drooling – nestled with love and habit against his leg, his mother appeared and reminded him of his father's OAM. She recited the names of the flowers and the giver: hydrangeas and the Mayberrys, roses and the Galbraiths, lilies and the Bassingtons.

He stood nodding but feeling drowsy already from the fragrances and the late afternoon light that soared and tumbled in through the windows.

His mother was talking about other things now – a neighbour diagnosed with bone cancer, a woman she knew from Ben's old school who'd collapsed on the tennis court with a heart attack and then the people she had met at a colonic place in Indonesia and how there had been a terrorist attack not on their island but on the next one. 'But thanks for asking and showing your concern,' she said, even though he hadn't. He hadn't even thought about her when he heard about the bombs.

Dinner was soup, lamb chops and mashed potatoes with roasted vegetables. 'Honest food,' said his father heartily, opening a bottle of wine and pouring himself and Ben a big, messy glass of red each. His mother, looking pinched and too thin, was still sipping her pre-dinner gin and tonic.

Dinner started neutrally enough with polite inquiries about the Master, who Ben's dad, Gerald, thought was a dandy and a dilettante, not to be taken at all seriously. 'The Showbiz Master', members of the College Council called him behind his back.

'Champagne Charlie. Vain academics – they're the worst,' said Gerald. 'The tweedy, shabby academics bore you at dinner parties, but at least they don't bore you with their narcissism – not like this one with his ridiculous hair and that bloody wife who works in the media.' He went on about trendy degrees (in Cultural Studies) and television appearances. 'His style is more American than English and that just doesn't work at St Anton's.'

The College Council were all old boys of St Anton's, like Gerald, and their decisions about the college were the decisions of men who were frozen in time, back in the fifties or the sixties or seventies, when they were eighteen. When they talked of their college days, it was like they were there again: wearing shorts, lying on some patch of lawn – elbows propped up on ... what? A tennis racquet, a hula hoop, a croquet mallet? Some object that belonged to that time and place – not part of their world now. And that was why they paid all that money: for their children to lie on that same lawn, decades later. So they too could enjoy the prison of nothingness – being trapped in a quadrangle with music and animals and books and each other.

'Is he still considering leasing the grounds for filming in December?' Gerald asked Ben. An American film production company had expressed interest in filming a literary adaptation starring Cate Blanchett and George Clooney. Set in the nineties, it would be based on the real-life story of a sexual harassment scandal at a university college. Blanchett would play a feisty journalist determined to get to the truth of the matter. Clooney was cast as the beleaguered Master fighting for his reputation. The two would fall in love.

There was a buzz around the filming – not only at the college but also across the whole campus. Guests from the media, academia and politics had started replying to the Master's invitations for dinner or volunteering as after-dinner speakers. In recent weeks there had been an embarrassment of riches: two High Court judges, an award-winning documentary maker, an architect from a TV reality show and two important scientists had all filed through the Junior Common Room, addressing the students from an armchair by the fire then taking port in the Senior Common Room. Some even went to the pub with the students when the port bottles had been emptied. It was only around 11 pm, when they started to sway and feel like they might either vomit or kiss someone on the mouth, that they remembered they weren't eighteen. It was a sweaty moment of realisation pierced with a tinge of sadness. But they rallied at the thought that they might be invited back during filming, and actually meet one of the stars.

Ben had heard the Master talk as if he and Cate Blanchett were already confidants, already close enough to spark rumours around campus that maybe there was something – you know – *going on*. The Master had confided to Ben at the Scholars' Dinner that during gaps in filming he planned to discuss his specialty with her: the Belgian Post-Structuralists. 'And when the conversation gets too heavy for her she can play with the cat' (Marmaduke, rheumy-eyed, a hisser) 'and I'll help her learn her lines.'

But there was one impediment to the movie being made on the college grounds: the College Council. Stodgy old boys, old Antonians, who didn't seemed swayed at all by celebrity – in fact, quite the opposite. The idea caused them to wrinkle their already wrinkly old brows in distaste. They had weird hang-ups about privacy that would have been quaint if only they hadn't had the power to veto filming.

Gerald, a fourth-generation Antonian, had considerable influence on the council, and right now he was attacking his chops with aggression at the thought of even having to consider the request that a movie be made.

'Silly thing, this movie stuff. St Anton's is a place for serious learning. It's not a glorified movie set – although those dreadful film people seem to think, bizarrely, that we'd somehow be flattered by their offer.' He gave a dry chuckle.

'But the staircase is pretty unique,' said Ben.

'Granted – but it would be demeaning to have all those actors traipsing all over the place. Outsiders.'

And with that Ben saw his chance of being chosen as an extra in a Hollywood movie vanish, and with this also vanished the possibility of a producer seeing him and saying, 'That's our kid.' Now he would never be plucked from obscurity and university (same thing, really) and rescued from a lifetime in the law, to become an actor and live in LA! Ah, impossible dream. So silly he dared not even dream it when alone.

Although Sylvan didn't hate anyone, he didn't have a lot of patience when talk turned to actors or TV shows. Fame was an empty pursuit, Sylvan said. When you chased God, chasing anything else suddenly seemed worthless. Celebrity culture was the embodiment of everything that was wrong with the world. Seen in that light, Sylvan and Ben's father – otherwise polar opposites – were actually kindred spirits: two grumps railing against the state of the modern world.

Ben wondered if he was subconsciously seeking to destroy his relationship with his father only to align himself with a younger, Christian, more socialist version of the same man? He shivered at the vaguely Freudian thought and suddenly didn't feel hungry anymore.

'I presume they'd want to film the animals roaming around the quadrangle,' his father was saying, 'and they'd want some of you boys – maybe Toby and Julian – to walk around in academic gowns and mortar boards, arm in arm, like something from *Brideshead Revisited*. Ridiculous. Hammy.'

Brideshead's gone bad, Ben wanted to say, but didn't.

Pudding was a chocolate soufflé that Ben's father insisted be accompanied by Cole Porter singing 'I've Got You Under My Skin'. His mother seemed to have lockjaw she was so tense, and Sandy chewed on the discarded cutlet bones until she started to choke and her one good eye bulged horrifically. Ben had to stick his fingers deep into her mouth (past her tiny, crumbling teeth) to clear her airway. His mother looked stricken at this and another bottle of wine (a second? a third?) was opened, and a look passed between Ben's mother and father that was historic, complicated and heavy. A look that only develops in old marriages. Ben realised his mother had not spoken all night – not spoken since she said, '*Bon appetit*!' Suddenly he felt like an arsehole for some reason. But his father was talking about other things now. His firm's plans to move their customer service operations to India and the huge cost saving this represented, and his recent trip to Germany that was part pleasure (the wine, the Rhine) and part business (property speculation in the former East Germany). And Cole Porter was singing 'Night and Day' and Gerald was talking in almost mellow tones about the apartments he saw: derelict but with soaring ceilings and marble staircases, veined and pale like palliative patients, and communist carpet and red velvet moth-eaten brocade draped on couches sunk under the weight of their own mildew, dusty chandeliers that swayed in a dangerous way, the weak northern hemisphere light and the cracked claw-foot baths. Out on the streets things were not so well preserved. Borders were open and a tsunami of people was moving in and through: endless, uneasy migration.

'Berlin …' said his father with the certainty of someone who had spent a week there on business, 'high unemployment, refugees everywhere, Africans selling bootleg CDs and DVDs spread out on blankets in the streets, and a huge Muslim population, so many women in headscarves, some fully veiled with hardly even their eyes showing.' And the airport security. The tedium of flying. The way the man ran his hand up your inner thigh in the airport queue and you had to pretend that you felt okay about it all. No liquids, no sharp objects, no nail clippers – the sheer boredom of terrorism. 'Should call it boreism.' And in Berlin they were building this thing, right near the Reichstag – a mega-mosque. Ha! The communist fathers not even cold in their graves, and look how much their world had changed.

Ben saw his chance. 'I've sort of become interested in ...'

'What?' asked his father almost impatiently, almost stamping his foot, excited that Ben was at last interested in something. 'Learning German? Property speculation? You're not too young at your age to be thinking about investment properties. We could help you out, of course. Get you started.'

Ben, too excited to hesitate, said no, no, he hadn't been thinking about that. He'd been thinking about religion ... how it had some things to recommend it. In fact, he'd been to a Christian community not far from here and he'd found the whole thing really, really valuable and was likely to go again. Ben described how the Jerusalems lived communally, how they didn't believe in private ownership, how they gave everything they had away, how they travelled and preached, how radical their humanism felt to him, how 'I don't know ... exciting' he found their austerity.

But his father started to smirk, then chuckle. 'Religion ... Really? I'm embarrassed for you. Why can't you be normal and have a drug problem or something, like everyone else?'

Ben suddenly felt furious. He wanted to reach over and throttle him.

His mother leapt in, eager to change the subject. 'Did your father tell you we got an email from your cousin Gilbert? He's having a good time in France. He's staying at the house. Did you know that? He's staying at the house.'

Gerald had stopped smirking and now looked almost angry. He exchanged another heavy, historically charged look with his wife and cleared his throat. 'Yes. Maybe you should arrange to meet him over there at term break – have a holiday. Get away from … things.'

'Yes,' said his mother. 'By the way, how's Charlotte? You haven't mentioned her at all tonight.'

Anne never asked about Charlotte. It was Toby whom she usually mentioned, whom she invited to family occasions, holidays, even Christmas.

'Charlotte? She's lovely. She's … I don't know … in the choir. And we play tennis together. She'll be twenty next week. I got her some perfume … Chanel. But let me tell you about Sylvan, the guy I met from this Christian group …'

Suddenly, without warning, his parents both excused themselves and Ben was left alone at the table with only the grateful dog for company. Where had they gone? He poured himself another glass of wine and sat there for a while, with so much to tell them about Sylvan. His parents didn't always understand him (in fact, he felt they had never understood him – the tides and eddies, the secret yearnings, the too-numerous fears, the flashes of happiness that were so sweet he almost felt like weeping at their arrival), but they were his parents nonetheless. So he sat there for a very long time, draining his glass and filling it up again amid the half-eaten soufflés, a half-remembered Cole Porter tune, and his half-prepared speech.

'Mum, Dad, I've got these new friends and they don't make me feel so dead inside.'

He wanted to tell them how these new friends had shown him what faith meant; it should have been his birthright but instead he'd inherited the cold, sad certainties of atheism. Hardly jolly, was it? To be brought up to believe in nothing?

And these new friends, they made this horrible world make sense as well. The horrible shit on the news. They had it all figured out – this geopolitical situation, they called it. It was all connected – the global financial crisis, Third World debt, anxiety and depression in the First World, governments spying on citizens, the terror training camps in the Middle East, hotel bombings, all that Syria shit – why hadn't he known before that it was all connected? And so *we* are all connected, he wanted to say. All of us. And *this* is all part of something too – the uneaten soufflés, the lights blazing in every room, the East Berlin property grab, moving the factory to India, Mum's unhappiness, the talk of movie stars and mega-mosques, Sylvan and Alfred, especially Alfred – everything is connected.

'Don't you understand?' he implored the dog. 'Why doesn't anyone in this house understand?'

It was only an hour or so later that his slight mother had to put her weight under his six-foot rower's frame and help him to bed. It was all foggy for Ben. Had he really drunk that much? He leant heavily against his mother. How embarrassing that she had to help him up and how sad the intimations he felt – he was the cross, she Christ and this was the stooped walk and stumble towards Calvary.

'Goodnight, dog. Goodnight, Mum,' he said, falling on the bed, the lights and his shoes still on.

'What are you trying to do to us?' he heard his mother say before he drifted off, and he felt that special mother knife twist in his heart again. But 'Hmphff' was all he could manage in response.

CHAPTER 12

Toby was confused and angered by Ben's snubs – he'd put himself on the line for Ben, and all he got in return was radio-silence. There was that old Evelyn Waugh truism: you spend your first term at university trying to make friends and the rest of your degree trying to shed them. Now it was almost halfway through third year and it seemed Ben was doing his best to shed Toby – shed everyone, really. It was quite an ambitious project, thought Toby as he set out across the quadrangle to see if Ben was in the library. Trying to ditch friends at college was almost a physical impossibility, considering that most classes were taken together, all meals were eaten together, and at night all two hundred students were locked in together, like prisoners in a particularly beautiful, hedonistic jail.

Each night was a riot but there was no escape from each other. A lit lamp in your room was an invitation for tea and sympathy with the college's lonely drunks and insomniacs. A spare seat at your table was a licence to dine together. Walk through the gates to get a coffee down Burton Street and suddenly you'd have an entourage. Going to the library? Let's study together.

'You never need be alone,' one of the older students said to Toby in first year. 'Even if you *want* to be alone – it's impossible.'

Not impossible if you were Ben, though.

He wasn't in the library. And he hadn't been in the Reading Room or student bar or on the lawn or with Charlotte either. Each night Toby would knock on his door before dinner and there would be no answer. Toby would save him a seat at dinner and Ben would not be there, or if he was he would not take it. Instead, in a bizarre kind of 'fuck you' gesture, he would sit in Siberia with the overseas students who barely spoke English. It seemed like a joke at first – as if Ben were doing it for a dare or a laugh, or the rowers had put him up to it. But meal after meal he sat next to Vincent or Chi or Ricky or half a dozen others whose names Toby didn't know. The sniggers that came from the rowers' table grew less mocking and more uneasy. What was Ben doing sitting with Alfred's friends?

'I'm not trying to stalk you,' said Toby in yet another voicemail message. 'Is your digital detox still on? Look, I'm worried about you – we're all worried about you. You don't seem to want to hang out anymore. Did I do something wrong? Is this about Alfred? Because if it's about Alfred I should be mad at you, not the other way round. You were the one who got me involved in the first place – so how come you're the one making me feel like a dick here?'

And on it went – messages, texts and emails, veering all over the place from concerned to angry to confused to petulant, seeking explanations, positing theories, pushing for an answer. Toby wished he didn't sound so much like a jilted lover; he wished he could keep the whine out of his voice when he left yet another rambling message. But really he just wanted to talk to Ben, clear this whole thing up, return to the way things had been last summer.

It had been a good summer. Ben's parents' beach house: bright cool mornings on his own surfing, bringing Ben back takeaway coffee and returning to bed; Ben bidding for Cartier watches online and reading Graham Greene; afternoons of exhausting mid-distance ocean swims; staying out until closing time at the surf-club bar, moonlight and walks back home along the beach, drunk on cheap beer; or stoned in Ben's room playing computer games and laughing at … nothing, really … Hazy, almost featureless days, hilarious but indistinct nights, where the only signs of time passing were their tans deepening and hair lightening in the sun. One hot day, borrowing Ben's mum's BMW and taking Lucy and Charlotte for lunch at a winery, and the small shiver of apprehension they all felt watching a wedding party among the vines – people not much older than themselves making vows – and Lucy driving them back to the beach house, and cicadas and the white wine in ice buckets; sweating in the dark garden, asking each other, 'What's the worst thing you've ever done? Promise not to tell anyone'. Back in the city, long, athletic fucks with Lisa in her air-conditioned apartment on the fourteenth floor, meeting Ben for lunch at his father's club, the ceiling fans hypnotic overhead and Ben saying, 'I think we drink too much', then not looking at Toby as he ordered another drink. Days at the Test cricket with Ben, Julian and Levi; sunburn and music festivals in laneways, heavy metal bands and girls with too many tattoos and too few clothes slipping garlands over their necks; cold beers in rooftop bars where the sun looked like a lozenge dropping down the sky; getting in fights with drunk suburban guys at taxi ranks. Sitting through a really boring play that Levi was in; going to Julian's house to swim, where Charlotte raised her eyebrows at the pool furniture and said, 'Very bourgeois', and at another rooftop bar, high on ecstasy, where Ben suddenly gripped his shoulders and said intensely, 'Look, Toby, I'm being serious – you're my palace, you're my palace,' and Toby laughed not knowing what he meant, but thinking it had something to do with Ben's depression of last semester, and the shelter you could find in each other.

He and Ben had once known everything about one another. Nothing had seemed real or permanent in his life until he told Ben about it. And now Toby missed him – really missed him. He was still there – still at college, still in the much-coveted room that looked over the stables –yet at the same time he wasn't there at all.

And it wasn't just Ben whom Toby missed; it was himself. That was the great gift of friendship: your friends gave you *you* – the idea of yourself that is your best self.

So long as Ben was like this, nothing was real for Toby. How could you tell your friend that the girl in your class, the one you've been watching for a while, has started watching you back? Or that your mother's friends, women you have known and loved all your life, have started coming down with cancer like it's the flu? And of course you're worried that your mum will get sick too. And how could you communicate to your friend the nameless dread you sometimes feel at a party, or going for a run, or when your head is resting on some girl's chest?

How could you make it real when your friend turns into something else entirely – slippery and suspicious, strange and unknowable, receding gradually at first, then suddenly distant and unreachable?

Toby thought of his father, a soft, gentle man, overly fond of poly-fleeces, saying to him almost casually that adulthood was a process of loss. Each year you lost a little bit more until you were down to your bones. It was a lot easier if you loosened your grip. If things weren't so precious to you. 'Don't value things so much,' he'd urge. Did he mean friendship? By covering things up for Ben he'd sacrificed some sort of moral code, and now he was in deep – here in this place where he did not want to be, where nothing made sense.

Was that what his father meant by loss: that it was actually possible to lose yourself? To get too close to your own bones and then beyond, to … nothingness?

He wondered if he should take another pill, or maybe ease off. He was losing track of what he was taking and it was playing havoc with his appetite. He would stop eating for days, then wake one morning with a raging hunger.

He went outside, where the quadrangle glistened like it had been freshly washed. A Sufi chant was drifting out of Lucy's room ('La Ilaha Illallah Allah Hu Akbar'), and languorous, almost ethereal students were leaning out of windows, Charlotte the most gorgeous among them. She was dressed in chiffon that was suffused with light and whispered lemony promises; she seemed more like an angel than a real girl. Ben should be up there holding her hand, not with those odd Christians, like the wan girl Toby sometimes saw him with who dressed in long Victorian-era nightgowns.

Toby checked his phone. Nothing. The light was falling quickly. It was getting towards June, and the shortest day of the year. He checked his phone again. Nothing. Ben, where are you?

He thought of one bad afternoon at the beach. Watching the ocean under a dramatic and heavy sky, a swimmer dragged out by a rip and struggling against it, trying to move across it to the other side. It was the intuitive thing – fight when in danger – but the rip would not be beaten and the man was being taken further and further away. 'Don't fight it – swim with it!' he yelled from the foamy shore before plunging in to bring the man back from death's grip.

'Go with it' was what his father always said. Go with it in the ocean and go with it on the land. But Toby was in the same sort of panic as the drowning man; he didn't want to just go with it. It was the same with what happened to Alfred. He didn't want to just go with the cricketers, go with the pact. His instinct was to swim against it.

Toby went back inside to his room and lay on his bed, the dying sun spilling from the window across his body, warming him, making him drowsy. He looked out the window to the quadrangle. It felt like a lifetime of bland, sunny days had passed since that one hot weekend on the mountain. But outside nothing had changed. There were still girls sitting in a circle drinking wine from a thermos, haloed in wintry sunlight, dandelion pollen suspended in mid-air, the peacock strutting on the lawn, suddenly interested in the plants. The gardener was laughing and petting the peacock and the girls were laughing too and the pollen was falling. The peacock fanned his feathers in a way that made Toby smile, as if he were really seeing the feathers for the first time.

But the feeling of normality stopped when he saw Ben walk across the grass, looking so cross again, not even stopping to look up at Charlotte, and Toby remembered that a lot had changed and not for the best.

He stopped himself from calling out and waving but could not stop himself from whispering, 'Ben, I have so much to tell you.'

Gary bought a VB and sat among a group of about six other local men at one of the two outdoor tables at the Sea Sisters. They sat facing the empty road and smoked and drank in silence. He'd just driven back from the hospital, where he'd seen Alfred and had a distressing conversation with the young man's treating physician. So now he was putting the cans away more quickly than usual.

Yes, admitted the surgeon who had treated Alfred, his injuries were puzzling. 'But the main concern when he arrived was to stabilise him,' he said somewhat defensively as he stood, arms folded, by the door. 'Brain injuries, spinal injuries, hypothermia, early stages of pneumonia, frostbite, sunburn, two broken legs. He was in a bad way. I really can't say much more on privacy grounds.'

One of the nurses – older, an Islander woman – was more forthcoming.

'I shouldn't be doing this, but … well, I think we should be going to the police on this one.'

'Really? Why?' asked Gary.

'Take a look.' She slid Alfred's file in his direction.

Photos of Alfred's torso taken during his admission showed some evil-looking burns, bruising, cracked ribs and pronounced swelling along his abdomen. In another photo his buttocks were crisscrossed with cuts, and the doctor on duty had recorded in his notes that there was light bleeding from his anus.

'Oh my God,' said Gary, horrified. 'Is this consistent with some sort of sexual assault?'

The nurse grimaced. 'It looks that way but we can't prove it.' The registrar who had admitted Alfred noted internal injuries, bleeding and bruising, she explained, 'but he said it was consistent with a fall or several falls in that type of environment. The cuts and bruises could have been from trying to haul himself up one of those rock faces; the anal tearing from a fall.'

As to whether Alfred had been assaulted the night he went missing, it was possible, probable even, said the nurse, 'but impossible to prove unless Alfred regains consciousness and gives some kind of account. But maybe you have some other kind of proof?' she said hopefully.

Sitting outside the Sea Sisters, the images Gary had seen in the file went around and around in his head, almost making him sick. Proof, proof – that was what he needed. All he had now were suspicions, and no-one to pin them on. But Alfred hadn't been alone on the mountains, he knew it. He could feel it in his bones. And then there was the phone call. Someone had been worried about him, or someone had hurt him. *Something* had happened.

He went into the bar and bought another round, then rejoined the men out at the decaying picnic table. 'Remember those young guys that came here in March?'

'Jesus, Gary – narrow it down a bit, it was a long bloody time ago.'

'We were talking about Colin's combine harvester – you know, the one that blew up – and all those young blokes came in looking like they'd been in a fight. Remember? They dressed weird and spoke weird. Jan, do you remember the ones I'm talking about?'

The publican was picking up glasses at the next table. 'Those boys who came here back in March? Yeah, I remember them. They sounded posh, like they had English accents or something.'

'Yeah, now I've got you,' one of the men said. 'One of them said they were in the same cricket team, I think. What about them?'

'A cricket team ... Can you remember when they were here? Was there a match on?'

'Well, it was after the fire at the bluff but before Noorcat Show. I remember it was a Sunday because it was the last day before I went north.'

'Maybe the twenty-seventh of March?'

'Maybe.'

The air cooled, the sun dropped below the mountains and the night sky was a sudden, beautiful purple that surged with birdsong. Alfred had been found on 28 March.

Ben came across two Jerusalem girls at uni in the Bio-med cafe – Sasha and Celeste. They were peeling oranges and drinking tea, pale-haired and quiet, wearing headscarves and those long shapeless dresses that looked like nightgowns.

'Nice to put names to faces,' said Ben warmly. 'I've seen you in the Pleasing Sands, and wanted to say hello.' They smiled back, but then looked down and returned to peeling their oranges, which they did with overly intense concentration.

The Jerusalems, Ben was beginning to realise, didn't really do flirting. He was pretty sure that Sylvan was a virgin. As for the girls, they looked like Sylvan's blood relations – in fact, they could have been his sisters. There was a familial atmosphere at the cafe and at Shangri-La that was a stark contrast to the hypersexuality of St Anton's, where everybody was up for grabs, and up for it, all the time.

Ben thought about all the girls he had been with through the prism of sex and seasons. The girls of summer. Looming above him, and a languid pull of their bikini strings … how the fabric would come off into his hands and feel lighter than air. Wet, humid nights and wet, humid mouths on his chest, roaming down to his groin. And then the hot surging sweetness, skies covered by a thousand expanding stars. Sylvan had probably never known such nights. Such sweet, sweet delights.

Then the girls of winter. How cold and dry their hands felt at first contact. The heating on high or a fire lit in the front room and the layers they wore, the deepening puddle of scarves and coats on the floor, the chill of their skin, the warmth of their kisses.

But as Ben found out, after time, after great warmth, a hollow feeling comes.

Ben considered his cousin Gilbert. Ben's father, at times of great disappointment in his own son, would say, 'Look at Gilbert, for God's sake. There are worse people whose book you could take a leaf from.' Gilbert, his role model: that said it all, really. Gilbert had gone to St Anton's then done a business degree at Cornell. He was now working as a venture capitalist … where? London? Buenos Aires? Hong Kong? Sydney? All of the above, probably. He went around the world 'doing deals' but was unable to explain exactly what it was that he did. When asked directly, a confused, panicked look would flash across his face until he recovered and let out a stream of words that almost sounded like obscenities. Modelling. Derivatives. Risk analysis. Data. Hedging.

Last September, when Gilbert was in town, he had taken Ben and some banking colleagues out to a bar owned by a young millionaire always pictured in Sunday gossip columns wearing too much hair product. Gilbert ordered vintage champagne and chocolate pudding. He was bloated and losing his hair and looked kind of ill, but had a marvellous confidence, particularly when talking about women.

'Let me tell you about women, Ben,' he said. 'That "I'm a feminist" stuff? Run a mile.'

Ben nodded, feeling sad.

The friends, the other bankers, chimed in, talking about their girlfriends in various parts of the world.

'Asian women are the best,' said Peter. The others murmured their agreement.

'Some Latina women still have respect, know how to be proper women.'

'Thai girls, they know how to be a woman,' said Mike. 'They'll take your money and shop all day, but they don't complain about giving head.' He launched into a bitter tirade against Amanda, his Caucasian former fiancée, who would passively–aggressively withhold pleasure.

Cousin Gilbert, magnanimous, expansive, feeling so much like the Master of the Universe that he knew himself to be, turned to Ben and said, 'The girls at St Anton's will talk about feminism – even if they don't use the word, that's what's behind it. If they do, just tune straight out. They're not the ones for you. They'll compete with you, they're all ego. You want a real woman – not someone who's half-man.'

The others nodded, looking slightly haunted, and Ben wondered how this had happened to them. Had they each woken up one dark morning, looked at the slight, breathing figure beside them and recoiled with a new awareness? That it was no longer about meeting a woman and finding out what she was like, but about making judgements at some broader level, a decoding of DNA, a reading of ancestors' songlines, hints revealed in how she wore a dress, how she moved, the motions of her eyes. Their relief at the way she never complained or talked back, and how her personality was a kind of mist: ungraspable, shape shifting, elusive.

Ben couldn't help it – sometimes hated himself for it! – but he was now seeing Charlotte through new eyes: Christian eyes. Acres of skin exposed, a practised pout, the tough talk of empowerment that seemed to hit false notes and the self-conscious use of the word 'cunt' when describing their particularly tough Semiotics lecturer. Through his newly opened eyes he saw a mechanical and derivative sexuality; an inauthentic, piecemeal personality. He shouldn't have given her the Chanel No 5 for her birthday. She had sent him a Snapchat naked selfie, lying on a rabbit-fur coat spread out on the floor. *I'm wearing your present. Cum&smell-me.*

He didn't reply, feeling he'd rather be alone. Alone, alone. But wasn't that the opposite of what Sylvan promised? What he'd told Ben he'd never be?

Alone, even though college life hummed around him – his friends and their world of balls, parties, sport, the pub. Even though he was there standing in the second quadrangle, staring at a passing waterfowl, it all seemed to be a distant shore and he was drifting, drifting to a place of greater certainty, where the men were committed, austere, serious somehow. All the things he hadn't been. Where the women were modest, self-possessed and unknown. All the things the girls in his life hadn't been. He wondered if he should share these new insights with Toby, if Toby would understand. But as he watched him, in a dinner suit, helping Lucy, in very high heels, get into a taxi, he saw a sort of rupture between them – Toby so fully part of a material world, Gilbert's world, and Ben breaking away, moving towards Sylvan and the promise of Shangri-La.

CHAPTER 13

Toby had not had a lengthy conversation with Hadrien in all those months since they came down from the mountain, but each day, passing each other in the dining room, crossing the quads, in the Reading Room, they made eye contact and unspoken things flowed between them.

By the time they did finally speak, leaves were dying all around them and the mornings had a sharp chill, fog rolling in across the quadrangle, shrouding the animals. In the dining room girls wore their pyjama bottoms under their skirts and sheepskin slippers.

At night, Toby unpacked his bar heater from the linen press in his room and fired it up; it glowed like a demon's eye. At around 11 pm he mixed some Lemsip, feeling the beginnings of a cold in his throat that was sure to move into his bones. He took a red pill and settled back to make the transition from wakefulness to sleep. It was a fast transition: as the pill took effect the Lemsip was only partially drunk. Slowly he began to sink into the bed, drifting downwards – until the handle of his door shook, the door opened, and in the dark there materialised someone who came to sit close to him on the bed.

'Sorry to disturb, old chap.' It was Hadrien. 'No need to

get dressed – just thought I'd drop by. You should really lock your door, by the way. Anyone can just walk in.'

Hadrien was wearing a green-flecked suit of Irish tweed and a yellow tie and, even though it was late, he was carrying a pair of sunglasses. His almost-silver hair was slicked back off his face, his eyes as cold and pale as the moon.

Toby's voice was thick and slow. 'Ya sh'da rung first.'

Hadrien sniffed at the steaming Lemsip on the bedside table and tipped it down the sink, pursing his rosebud lips. 'You shouldn't mix Lemsip with those pills, you old soak. Lemsip contains paracetamol.'

'Oh no – really?' said Toby, trying to sit up. 'What does that mean?'

Hadrien sighed. 'Don't you know anything? Niall tells me you're becoming something of a pill head. Always popping around for a pick-me-up or –' he examined the pack of pills Toby had left by the sink '– a pull-me-down.' He regarded Toby with curiosity. 'Look at your eyes. Wouldn't have expected it from you. You used to be such a brick. And so pure! Well, you used to be, anyway.'

'I'm having difficulty sleeping,' replied Toby. 'It's driving me mad … Why have you got sunglasses? Is it bright outside?'

'My future's so bright I have to wear shades. So you can't sleep? Insomnia is a curse,' said Hadrien with sudden apparent empathy.

'Yeah,' said Toby, his head lolling back on his pillow.

Hadrien prodded Toby with the arm of his sunglasses, then cradled the back of Toby's skull quite tenderly and arranged his head higher on the pillow.

'Stop it, stop it,' said Toby in a slow voice that barely seemed to have the energy to travel out of him (and also made him sound like his deaf cousin, whose speech patterns he had mocked as a child).

But Hadrien kept on touching him, leaning too close, his pale skin glowing red by the light of the two-bar heater, saying almost soothingly, 'I can help you, Toby. I know why you're falling apart. Things will improve. I can promise you that.'

Toby could feel his eyes rolling back in his head. The medicines were working quickly.

Hadrien vaporised along with his promise, the yellow of his tie being the last thing to fade, the door quietly shutting the last sound Toby heard.

After trying to avoid Hadrien all the rest of that week, Toby, stupefied by the pills (he was forgetting which ones were to pull him up and which were to bring him down), was too addled to refuse Hadrien and Leeson's late-night invitation to the bar in the Junior Common Room. The bar was raffish, like a gentlemen's club gone to the dogs. The carpet was worn and discoloured, faintly seedy-looking foam was spilling from the chairs, and then there were the pictures on the walls: boys rowing, boys playing cricket, boys holding tennis racquets – dusty and strange among posters of Bob Marley (looking chilled, man), Kurt Cobain (looking tortured, in a cardigan, circa 1990) and Jimi Hendrix (looking stoned, holding a guitar).

Possums got stuck in the chimney and fell dead into the fireplace. Take down a set of Scrabble from the shelf and you'd find all the vowels missing and the board stuck together with bits of tape. The bar's library hadn't been updated since the 1950s; it featured Biggles, *Tom Brown's School Days* and some falling-apart book on Australian explorers (Douglas Mawson, Blaxland, Burke and Wills).

'Oh, you've got the fire working,' said Toby as he walked in and saw Hadrien poking a small flame with a stick.

'Fire is my specialty,' said Hadrien, without turning around.

Leeson poured some red wine from a bottle usually kept locked in the drinks cabinet.

Hadrien flopped on the couch almost dramatically and raised his glass. 'It's been a while, Toby. Cheers.'

Toby took his glass, but didn't clink Hadrien's.

Hadrien dropped his arm and smirked. 'Still pissed off, are we? I would never have guessed. Tell me – what's your fur situation these days? Are you still nailing Lisa? She's practically menopausal, isn't she? Elderly, right? Tell me – are her tits real?'

'You wouldn't know a tit if it hit you in the face.'

'Fair enough, you don't want to talk about Lisa. So do you mind telling us what's going on with Ben?'

'I was going to ask you the same question.'

'Ben doesn't speak to us anymore, except when we're rowing.'

'Not that he talks much then,' said Leeson yawning. 'He's not talking to Charlotte either. Rejecting her advances is what I'm hearing around the cloisters.'

'Charlotte is upset, isn't she? She tries to make herself feel better by getting absolutely wasted. Can't walk properly most nights. Needs assistance,' said Hadrien.

Hadrien and Leeson laughed and Leeson said, 'Yeah, assistance being fucked.'

Toby, tired and bored by them, asked, 'What do you guys want? Seriously, what do you want? If you want to know about Ben, since that thing in the mountains he's been really distant. He barely talks to me anymore, sits with those weird Asian students.'

'Do you know about Sylvan?' asked Leeson.

Hadrien looked at Toby with dead eyes. 'He's been going to Christian meetings. He's been attending – I don't know – fucking séances in that weird cafe at Jacaranda Station. Obviously we don't care about what he does, but we *are* worried that this thing with Alfred has given him a guilty conscience.'

Toby laughed, incredulous that they would feel threatened by someone's guilty conscience. 'Trying to purge it through religion sounds like a great idea – better that than getting sick like Severin or what Levi and Sam are doing: trying to drink their way through it.'

'Maybe, maybe,' said Hadrien, his sharp features relaxing into an almost compassionate expression. 'But something about it seems dangerous or defiant. Ben's a potential threat to us. What if he tells these new friends of his about Alfred?'

'For fuck's sake – I'm leaving,' said Toby, standing up. 'I am not involved. I wasn't in the bunkroom. Just leave me out of it.'

'I know you weren't there, but you're involved now,' said Hadrien, smirking. 'You know that too. Also, as much as Levi and Julian like to pretend they weren't there, they were – at least at the start. So let's be honest for once, shall we? Come on, sit back down.'

Toby remained standing. Leeson heaved another massive log onto the fire, which gave off an arc of sparks.

'If any of you really cared,' Hadrien continued, 'you would have protected Alfred. Stopped what happened, or maybe rung the cops. *First they came for the Jews and because I was not a Jew I did not protest, then they came for the—*

'Shut up,' said Toby.

'I would have respected you more if you had actually done something,' said Hadrien. 'It's all retrospective angst with you, isn't it? Someone's been visiting Alfred in hospital – is it you? I'm sure he won't thank you when he comes out of a coma and sees your face. As far as he knew you were in the bunkroom with us. We were all wearing masks, you see. What would stop him from thinking it was you who threw the petrol on him? Or Levi? Or Julian? After all, he was drinking with you all afternoon. You're part of the cricket team – what's to say you weren't part of everything else that happened that night?'

'I'm sure Toby was there in the bunkroom,' Leeson said almost mildly in his lazy, posh drawl. 'He was wearing a woman's stocking over his head.' He was standing behind Toby, flicking through an old almanac, as if the conversation were of no consequence at all.

'That's right, he was, too,' said Hadrien, laughing. 'He was so drunk he's probably forgotten that it was his very distinctive Celtics scarf that was used to tie Alfred up.'

'Oh, the scarf in the photos?' asked Leeson casually, leaning over to show Toby a photo on his iPhone of someone masked and draped across the bleeding, bare back of another boy. The person in the mask was wearing Toby's scarf, knotted in an almost jaunty way around his neck.

'Whoa!' said Toby. 'What the fuck is going on in that picture?'

'That's Toby's scarf,' replied Hadrien, who was squinting at the phone.

'You guys are sick,' said Toby.

'You were very drunk, Toby old chap, but you were there. Remember?'

All the air went out of Toby suddenly and he thought he might throw up.

'Bath can vouch for me; I was with Bath,' said Toby.

'Bath can't vouch for *himself*. He can't remember anything past seven o'clock,' said Hadrien breezily.

'Bath can't remember what year it is!' said Leeson, laughing.

'What do you want from me?' Toby asked.

'I'm controlling *my* boys. I have them on a tight leash. Niall, Roman, Ping, Severin. Sam, too. And Bath was sedated. I know there are no squeaky wheels in that bunch,' said Hadrien.

Leeson grunted in assent.

'I give them pep talks about the need to stick together, about the need to keep quiet. I remind them about supermax and anal rape and jail-cell weddings. Valid practising certificates for our legal careers, an unblemished record for the Rhodes or Fulbright applications, just *fucking graduating* ... There's a lot at stake. But what about *your* boys, Toby? What about Ben, Julian and Levi? Especially Ben. You see, I'm worried about Ben – and I reckon you must be worried too. We're only as strong as our weakest link and right now we are not in a strong position. You don't have control of your side of the team.'

'My side of the team? I didn't think a team had sides,' said Toby.

'Of course it has sides – you, Ben, Julian and Levi, men of certain sensibilities, have always formed a little cabal. I see you together drinking cappuccinos down Marchmont Street like a bunch of middle-aged women. What do you talk about? Your children?' sneered Hadrien. 'The fucking selective school you want to get them into?' He sighed. 'I just want to ensure that you don't feel so separate from us, so removed from what happened in the bunkroom, that you feel you can just blab about it to anyone. As if you had no responsibility or stake in the matter. Because we feel you do have a stake in the matter, don't we, Leeson?'

Leeson, his beady eyes boring into Toby's, nodded. 'Yes, and your stake is quite high. As high as ours, in fact. We have a common purpose.'

Toby could suddenly see Leeson a few years from now: his scar shining and silver, completely bald, his big hulking head fully exposed, his dark eyes glinting, almost reclining on a couch, as he was now, in front of a nasty CEO in a large office, helping to plan a merger that would swallow up a smaller, more vulnerable company, or sending swarms of hooded scab labour into a union-only site, or closing down textile mills, independent bookstores, buying up farmland for 'light-industrial commercial-redevelopment purposes'.

Hadrien was talking about other things now: 'Hence the insomnia. Hence the pills. I bet you feel burdened.' His voice had softened slightly. 'I bet you feel afraid. Well, you're right to feel both. I mean, look at you. You're falling apart. I was watching you in Torts the other day – you looked wired. Pull yourself together! I'm telling Niall not to give you any more of those pills. You know they're diet pills, right? Pharma-grade speed. You look like you have AIDS. You need to be clear-headed for this, for what comes next. Because there is a next. You need to keep a closer eye on Ben; he's drifting. Keep Levi and Julian on the path. No weak links, okay? We need to talk more often, you and I – make sure the cricket team is united.'

Toby was still trembling when he went down the stairs. He felt incredibly weak and hoped that he might meet someone pulling an all-nighter whose conversations about exams, holidays, parties and sport would help erase the conversation he had just had in the Junior Common Room bar. Distraction, he needed distraction!

Suddenly his legs gave way on the stairwell and he banged his knee on the banister. He howled sharply and sort of slid the rest of the way back to his room, where he hoisted himself up onto his bed.

All of the pills that Niall had given him were still on the nightstand. Lance Vaine and the Musical Hellos were playing in his head ('*The birds cry out in pain and sorrow/This can't be fixed/ Vale, vale, tomorrow*'). He twisted until he was eye to eye with his medicines. Diet pills? Really? Then, without even a prelude of sadness, he started to cry – strong emotion breaking through the delightful spell of the pills. It all rushed up through his body, expressing itself violently. He stuck his head into the pillow and howled. Everything within his rib cage hurt.

Ben, Ben, Ben. What have you done?

They had studied *Crime and Punishment* last year. '*Do you understand, sir, do you understand what it means when you have absolutely nowhere to turn?*' Marmeladov's question came suddenly into his mind '*for every man must have somewhere to turn …*'

He understood now. And he had never felt so desolate.

He imagined taking enough of the nightstand pills to sleep some eternal sleep; then he would no longer have to deal with Hadrien, he would no longer have to fret about Ben, he wouldn't have to speculate about Levi and Julian, he wouldn't have the guilt about Alfred. I'll just slip away, and I'll be gone …

He cupped his hand and poured some pills out. Would these be enough to do the trick? Other images flooded in: his parents, of course, and his brothers, and Eunice, the Jamaican maid who would find him in the morning.

Still crying, his T-shirt pulled up to his face and wet with tears, nothing profound hitting him except his own loneliness, Toby slowly placed the pills back on the nightstand. They were greasy and slick now with the sweat of his hands. This is all Ben's fault, he thought.

But perhaps Hadrien had been right: they were all in this together. And that was why, very soon after the conversation in the Junior Common Room, Toby began to take fewer pills and started monitoring his friends for any sign that they might weaken or dob or talk about what happened in the bunkroom with someone who hadn't been there. It was why every Sunday at 1 am he went to Hadrien's tower to assure him that everyone was keeping quiet, performing their part; that they were keeping it together, still playing as a team, even though the nights were lengthening, the chill in the air had sharpened, and the cricket season was well and truly over.

'So how is Alfred?' the Master's wife asked her husband as she poured a drink from the chilled bottle of riesling on the bench.

'They say he's going to live to fight another day, but it's too risky to move him back to Malaysia,' said the Master. 'His poor parents – I don't think they speak any English. I'm not sure they really know what's going on.'

At first – until Alfred's parents had arrived from Malaysia a week after the accident – he had visited the boy fairly regularly, but he didn't really have the time, and anyway it was boring visiting someone in a coma. They didn't contribute to the conversation. They did not banter. They were not witty. But then, he told himself ruefully, Alfred had probably not been a great wit before he had his accident.

'What's he like?' asked his wife.

'Who, Alfred? I don't remember interviewing him,' said the Master. 'Maybe old Williams did that one.'

'Or maybe all overseas students seem the same to you,' said his wife archly.

'Oh, that's not true, my cynical, cynical love,' said the Master. 'Each student, no matter where they are from, is a human being. They each have potential and personality. Or a potential personality. Ha! And they have needs,' he said, warming up. 'Each set of needs is different. Each specific and paramount to the owner of that need. Some students are vegan – though thankfully not many. Others are lactose-intolerant or syphilitic or coeliac or sibilant. Others require vast amounts of medication to control their various mood disorders. Some must be offered obscure sports like fencing, others will only pass if you threaten to send them down or banish them to the overseas students' wing, others require special tutoring and coaxing and praise and stroking. And some like it if you ignore them, because in a strange way you might remind them of their much-hated over-attentive parents. Some are, in turn, hated by their parents. Some are loved. Many are ignored. I do not think of them as one homogenous lump. You know that. Remember dear little Barney?'

He took his wine to the couch, and muted the sound of the 7 pm news.

The Master's wife said she did remember Barney, but not fondly. Since Barney had come into their lives, she'd insisted on a ban on students just dropping into their cottage.

'It's like Barney's moved in!' she would say when she came home from a long, hard day in what she termed 'the real world', and there would be this boy with his feet up watching television with the Master, or mixing a sharp, complicated cocktail that shrivelled her lips on the first sip, or saying with disdain, boredom even, 'Salinger is so overrated.'

Barney's ubiquitous presence had been the result of the Master's decision to turn the entire college into a wi-fi hotspot, starting with their cottage. But for some reason, the Master – so used to just making things happen (dinner parties for twelve, guest speakers gifted in cell biology, intercollegiate hockey tournaments, seminars on the post-colonial novel) – had wrestled with the technology. He had been forever on hold talking to Telstra, beet-red and screaming at the automated-response system: 'I said no! No!' He had been forever loitering about somewhere near the college gates, hoping to meet a phantom technician who never came, forever standing somewhere with a confused, cross look on his face holding cables in his outstretched hand, staring at them like they were stigmata.

It was at some painful moment when the Master had literally become tangled in the cables that Barney, passing by on his way to the dining hall, had offered first to unravel him, then to connect wi-fi in his cottage. Then Barney had started coming over for dinner and staying long after he'd downloaded iTunes or installed Skype or activated the modem. After a month of having him underfoot – to the Master's wife's horror, he had become the spectre of the child they'd never had – she laid down some ground rules.

The Master had acceded to his wife's demand for 'some space, please, from these goddamn strange teenagers!' and become a bit more remote from the students, a bit hazy on their personal details and sometimes even their names, and had eventually realised that the college worked quite tolerably if he just let the students flow around him, as if he were a rock in a stream. And so they flowed on, each new year bringing with it a new stream.

And so to Alfred, whom – the Master had had to admit to his brilliant, brittle wife – he really didn't know at all.

CHAPTER 14

First term is usually the quickest and the sweetest: all care, no responsibility. It's not too late! The die has not been cast; scramble, scramble and it's still possible to withdraw from some poorly chosen and infrequently attended subjects. The grunt work of the end of the year is still a long way off, the paint in the rooms still new smelling, flowers still smiling in the garden bed, sports still being played on some distant oval, the animals still roaming in the quad, sniffing the evening air.

But then comes second term: essays due, football season, jackets, scarves and gloves, hot buttered toast and tea for breakfast, lights burning later in the library. It's always been this cold and you've always been feeling this tired, and night seems to arrive abruptly in the afternoons.

Toby made the semester-break journey home on a crowded coast-bound train. The luggage hold was filled with rucksacks, tartan canvas bags and laptop cases. Bags for dirty laundry and books were thrown on the overhead racks and rowdy greetings travelled down the carriages.

There were backs being slapped and laughter from in-jokes and private nicknames, and anyone not travelling with this coalition of young hearties felt immediately outside something splendid, vigorous and alive.

Fizzy drinks, chips and microwaved pies were ferried from the snack bar, and the hellos turned to goodbyes as the train pulled into dusty little coastal stations. As it chugged further from the city, deeper along the coast, the air became thick with salt and the scent of brine, and in the glittering dark children from these small hamlets gathered along back fences to wave at the train, before being led back into their fragile little houses. The light from the train windows would illuminate the dark gullies, where it could have been a fox running alongside the train, but might have been a small child.

When the lights of the train threw shadows across the familiar shapes of familiar buildings, Toby pulled his bags from the rack and stepped onto the platform. Home: the remote magic kingdom, the snow dome that contained his childhood. Here were ships in bottles, surfboards drying on the lawn, soup simmering on the stove top, a tinkling of ragtime on the piano from the next room. Here the air was so heavy with salt that it settled like dew on his clothes. He could hear and smell the Southern Ocean.

His brother Matt met him at the station, helped him with his heavy bags and embraced him, before looking at him a little more closely in the car with the light on and saying, 'Jeez, you look like shit.'

'I haven't been sleeping,' mumbled Toby, not mentioning that he was also withdrawing from several strong medications.

While Toby's younger twin brothers were away touring with their band, their mother kept the curtains in their bedroom drawn and used it as a 'meditation cave'. That was where he found her – amid the amps and cords, the abandoned laptops, the skateboards and the retro posters of the Dead Kennedys and Frank Black. She was sitting very erect on a pancake-flat cushion with her eyes closed.

She barely flickered at his presence. In the hush he could hear her murmuring Sanskrit under her breath. She had just arrived back from India, where she had found another guru. Some horrible new incense was burning.

Toby felt like he watched her a very long time. The dark, the quiet stress she put on certain words and the almost violent sucking in and spitting out of the waves outside gave the 'cave' a womb-like texture. He felt a sudden raging desire to be close to his mother, close like he was in the olden days of packed lunches, balled school socks, all those evenings where the headlights were shining in the rain, as she waited for him to finish football practice. She must have felt it too, because she raised her arms slightly from their prayerful pose so there was enough room for him to slide his head across her lap and feel her creased maternal fingers moving through his hair and across his brow. Yet she did not miss a beat in her chanting.

Later in the break, Toby and his dad walked on the beach behind the house, the Southern Ocean roaring towards them, grey and white, holding its memories of Antarctic ice floes and polar caps and silence. Toby longed to unburden himself, tell his dad about what had happened on the cricket trip, how they now had this secret, how badly injured Alfred was in his fathomless coma, about the pills that he had been taking, the way he had fallen behind in class, and about Ben. If only his dad would ask! But his father was preoccupied and didn't sense his son's anxiety. Instead, he talked to Toby about his wife's dying friends and other things Toby didn't want to hear. How people become ghosts – people you've known and touched.

'People die young,' his father said. 'When you least expect it. Or they drop out of your life and you can't get them back again.'

Toby wondered why they were talking about this on the darkening beach, and wished his father did not seem so vulnerable right now, so introspective.

'But they walk among us, Tobes, sometimes closer than they did in life. You dream about them and you see them everywhere. The living and the dead walk so close together that they bump into each other.'

Toby was silent, but his father continued quietly, in his usual mystical way, almost as if he were talking to himself. 'I feel like I need to prepare for loss. How do I do it? Perhaps if you aren't willing to lose someone they won't go away. They'll turn into dreams or they'll walk beside you down the street or along the beach. Perhaps those whom you love will always be around you.'

That night, as the ocean pulled back and forth under his window, Toby dreamt of Ben ... the process of loss, the process of not letting go. The great tug-of-war of life.

The week continued without incident. He slept a lot, ate what was put in front of him, watched a stack of movies on his computer, and switched his phone off to avoid his school friends and his older brother, only switching it back on from time to time to see if Ben had called. He missed his friend so much that late at night he looked back over old Gmail chats they'd had with each other – in part to reassure himself that he hadn't just made the whole friendship up, that he wasn't deluded or exaggerating their closeness. But there was the evidence: thousands of words a day flying between each other on Instant Messenger, even as they were sitting alongside each other in class –observations, jokes, links, quotes, stuff about feelings, stuff about what to get for lunch. Fuck, he hated missing him – how could they have travelled from there to here so quickly?

Ben obviously didn't miss *him* at all. He'd found some new friends. What were they doing now? Were they at that horrid cafe singing 'Kumbaya' and making bad coffee? He started a text for the twentieth time – '*Hey – we need to talk*' – but saved it to Drafts. Why was he the one doing the chasing? Meanwhile he was getting texts from Hadrien that he deleted as soon as he'd read them – weird, threatening messages about spying on Ben, or checking up on Levi and Julian. They always ended with a string of emojis, which somehow made the words seem even more sinister, as if a cactus, banana, broken heart and panda were codes to carry out something too awful to be named.

During the break Toby tried to read the William Faulkner book he'd been assigned in Deep South American Lit, but couldn't concentrate long enough to make sense of it. Instead he went online to see what other people thought of it, then drifted off through links to other articles, clicking and clicking until he got further and further away from what he was meant to be doing and five or six hours had passed and he still didn't know anything new about *The Sound and the Fury*. He heard his mother's voice in the kitchen one night asking his preoccupied father, 'Is Toby depressed? Do you think he's depressed? He's not acting like himself.'

He braced himself for an intervention, but it never happened. His parents had a New Age style of parenting. They took courses – including an odious American import called Positive Parenting, which saw them meeting with other parents for discussions and role-playing games. There'd been parents of some of Toby's school friends there, and parents who had kids in their forties and were still having difficulties, parents who had given up pretending to have all the answers, who complained over tea and sweet biscuits, 'Gee, this parenting thing is tough.'

Toby's parents' new mantra after graduating from Positive Parenting could have been 'Openness at all costs'. They hid nothing from their children – not financial worries or work concerns or, most embarrassingly, their psychosexual problems of two years ago, during which Toby's dad slept in the shed and Toby's mum stopped wearing makeup and impractical shoes, stopped bothering with certain things ('It's a revelation,' she told her sons, 'when you just let go') and instead started to meditate.

Openness, openness, openness.

'You can tell us anything – anything, mate,' said Toby's dad through tears after the police brought Toby home when he'd been caught driving his mate's dad's ute while drunk and unlicensed. Steaming pots of tea at 2 am, rain severe against the window, and his dad's tears.

'If you want to get drunk, you can get drunk here with me.'

'If you want to drive a car, we can go out to the paddock in my car and you can have the run of it.'

'If you ever need to talk, you can talk to me.'

Openness, openness, openness.

As open as his mum's blank Buddha face and feet in sandals; as open as his dad's tears and, later, his arms; as open as those small, sad groups of parents gathered around the plate of lemon slice after the lounge-room Positive Parenting meetings.

Could this be the rebellion that had long been anticipated by his parents, but had never quite arrived? That he was going to *reject* openness? That he was now someone with a secret?

Levi usually looked forward to semester break. His parents went away each year to some little village on the south-west coast, and he had the run of the house. He used to invite friends over for blurry days and nights playing Xbox, smoking dope, ordering pizzas, generally making a mess. So it was a bit of a nuisance when his aunt texted saying she was coming around with dinner, as the two of them were overdue for a conversation.

His Aunt Primrose wasn't really his aunt, she was a family friend, someone who'd been at university with his parents and was still there, quite high up in the Languages Faculty now. She was like his second mother, and there was an earthy robustness to their discussions. She was blunt but never unkind.

Primrose had barely finished ladling out some delicious-smelling Balinese curry when she drew first blood. 'Your mum's seen some graffiti about you – and so have I.'

'Is it in the Botany toilets?'

'Yes.'

Levi groaned, embarrassed. 'Don't believe everything you read, Primrose. There were these girls from my ICEPIC class and, I don't know, things got weird one day, that's all. Seriously, don't believe some random toilet graffiti.'

She looked at him with shrewd blue eyes. 'Of course I don't believe everything I read, but I believe some things. And sometimes I notice grains of truth in the lies.'

Levi blushed.

'I hear things, too, about those girls – among other things. And I see things. Those boys I've seen you round campus with. Those – what are they, football players?'

'Cricketers.'

'Well, whoever they are, I don't have a good feeling about them. Your mum says she saw you in the street with one of them and you pretended not to know her.'

Levi said nothing, but shame flushed right through his body in a way that was almost chemical.

'No one's saying you have to be a feminist, but you have to do better than this.'

'Is Mum upset?'

'Yes, and your father too. They're very worried about these boys you're hanging out with – about how you've been acting.' Primrose topped up their wine glasses.

'Dad called me an arsehole,' said Levi, still aggrieved.

'I know things are tense,' said Primrose. 'I've discussed this with your parents, and if you don't want to live at home with them, if you want some independence, you don't have to live at college – you can come and live with me. I'll give you a key, leave you pretty much alone, just drag you along as my plus-one to the occasional book party. You have options, okay? It's no big deal if you want to leave St Anton's.'

Levi nodded, and felt as if he might cry, though he couldn't locate the precise source of this emotion – shame maybe, or relief. He had options, he could leave, he didn't have to go back.

One rainy day, towards the end of the break, Toby was in the kitchen with his mother, who was baking a batch of muesli bars. She stirred the mixture with one hand, and with the other reached over to ruffle Toby's hair.

'What is it, Tobes? You seem so unhappy at the moment. Is it a girl? That Lisa girl? Or one of your friends? You've barely mentioned Ben – have you had a fight?'

Toby's face crumpled and the hair-ruffle turned into a hug. Toby held his mother tight, near tears, the sticky spatula suspended behind his back, his face in her long, greying hair. He felt she was almost there, she had almost broken the hex that had been woven around the Alfred thing, she had almost got through to the part of him that was timid and frightened and undecided and needed to be led out by the hand.

He sighed into her neck. I am part of an injustice, he wanted to say. I am aiding an injustice. And I miss my friend. And I don't know who I am anymore.

Some batter fell onto his sleeve. The phone rang. Toby's mother broke the embrace and turned away to answer it. It was one of Toby's younger brothers, overseas with their band, calling from Austin, Texas. The phone call wouldn't be quick.

Toby exhaled – disappointed, yet also relieved, marvelling at how close he had been to telling his mum everything. I am part of an injustice was all he would have had to say, and that would have been it. The whole woozy charade, the secrecy, the energy that went into maintaining that secrecy would have collapsed with that one sentence. She would take him to the cops for sure. She would dob in the whole lot of them.

Yet the tension that lay within him had not eased. He felt he should be happy that they were getting away with it. But the fact he had not been brought to account provided him with no happiness at all.

He remembered what Hadrien said in the Common Room: 'For fuck's sake, pull yourself together, man … You need to be clear-headed for this, for what comes next.' On the train back to college he felt a new hardness and resolve settling upon him. He had kept his mouth closed and in doing so felt his heart closing too, and this made him feel glad and defiant all at once.

CHAPTER 15

Toby sat with Julian, Charlotte and Lucy on the banks of the river. They drank wine and watched the St Anton's crew win the intercollegiate rowing, the final race coming at the end of a long day. It lasted twenty-six minutes and finished around the bend, where the boys lay back, their oars heavy against their chests, all of them sobbing with fatigue in the hull of the briny boat.

The student spectators could never appreciate all the sunrises the rowers had witnessed during countless dawn training sessions – and while the girls admired their bodies and the boys their strength, after the crowd had been drinking all day, anything more than the win itself went unremarked. Students from the other eight colleges sat in their college jerseys in demarcated sections along the riverbank, waving their flags and their colours, singing their awful songs and drinking their cases of beer. The students of St Martine's had brought watermelons to throw at the students of St Anton's and a fight broke out between the students of King's and St Sebastian's. Ping knocked out the front teeth of a boy in a kilt who called *him* a faggot.

Some girls from Minerva who really needed to go to the bathroom but could not be bothered queuing went to the area belonging to the girls from Persephone, pulled down their pants and urinated on their picnic blankets, and some boys cheered and took photos on their phones. Students were sick and a boy called George had to be taken to hospital after being concussed by a flying watermelon that split the softest part of his skull.

The rowers, with all their precision and grace, glided past and the crowd missed it. They missed it all.

Toby went to find Ben after the race to congratulate him. He was a college legend now. He wouldn't have to do another thing; his status for the rest of the year was secured. There would be queues in the pub tonight to stand him and the other rowers a round.

But Ben had left, without even having one drink – without even a shower or hugs from the girls who lined the banks just for him. 'Just chucked on a hoodie,' Roman complained, 'and got the fuck out of here.' He missed the celebrations that continued all night back at the college.

The Master approved an impromptu black-tie dinner and the rowers were carried in by the footballers. Their grotesque trophy was also carried aloft. They all sat at the High Table, bare-chested under their gowns and so drunk they were falling – almost comically, in the manner of a Laurel and Hardy skit – into their food. The dining-hall roof shook with all the singing and the violent banging of cutlery, which cut grooves into the tables, and the awful trophy was passed around like a body crowd-surfing at a concert. It was touched, sometimes on its most intimate parts, before being passed to the next pair of hands, and all those who touched it felt at once that they were somehow part of this great victory. And standing above it all was the Master. In his black gown, smiling and silent with the candles flaring behind him, he appeared not like a human but like a golden, glowing god.

All night Julian, Toby and Levi sat together, refusing to sing or touch the trophy, texting Ben instead.

'He's probably been kidnapped by that cult,' muttered Levi angrily.

But, thought Toby, maybe Ben had disappeared because he wanted to – gliding along the river at speed, past the knocked-out teeth, the girls with their pants down displaying their waxed vaginas, past the postgraduate students with their bongo drums and beer guts, past the two students from St Sebastian's attacking each other with up-ended broken champagne bottles.

What beauty was there on the riverbank, or here in the dining hall?

Later that night there was a smoko. People and things were set on fire. A girl broke her leg, she said from 'dancing too much'. The Master was drunk, and in the Junior Common Room, hair wild and eyes wild too, he was swaying in time not to the music but to a beat that only he could hear, dancing in a way that seemed to suggest control had been lost a long time ago.

Toby watched, feeling separate from all the others, as Dr Bath held back the hair of a lonesome girl being sick over the parapet walls. He saw another girl under the Faraway Tree attempting to perform fellatio on a rower so drunk that only the tree's enormous and ancient trunk was holding him up.

When he let go of her hair, she collapsed at his feet and he listed and gripped the trunk.

Past the Faraway Tree, a lamb that should have been locked up for the night peered up at Toby, looking amused, not at all disgusted by the scene. Toby and the lamb looked at each other for a while, before the lamb got bored and roamed away towards the library.

'Innocence,' said Toby – suddenly remembering it was the lamb's name, not a reference to anything else around him.

He wandered over to help Dr Bath carry the sick girl to her room.

Ben checked into an expensive hotel as a celebrity exhausted from touring might check into rehab. It was a desperate, spontaneous decision, only half thought through but born of an instinct deep in his gut that all was not right and there was no one around to fix it. Not even Sylvan, who seemed to have so many of life's answers. Retreat. Retreat. It was the same instinct that drove his mother to check into the luxury spas of South-East Asia and his father to disappear into the belly of a European vineyard. Maybe he was genetically programmed to hide away somewhere expensive.

In the boat that day, and in the boat all the other days, and in the mountains he had been haunted by the word *excavation*. Up in the mountains on the second day, teamed with the useless Julian who talked of a recent trip to Spain and his favourite actresses, he sang the word to himself: *Excavation, excavation, tra-la-la, la, la la la la la*. In the boat, with each stroke and pull of the oars, the hateful back of Leeson (and those nasty, powerful muscles that had so thoroughly worked on Alfred's body) pulling and sliding in front of him, ripe for a knife, he whispered it to himself: *Excavation, excavation, excavation.*

Sometimes even with Sylvan and the others, when they were talking about things that scared him – the gorgeousness of sacrifice, the nobility of poverty, the Garden of Gethsemane, a suffering Christ, the nails and the thorns, the tomb and the shroud – he saw the word *excavation* flashing before his eyes, anchoring him in a safe place, way underground. He said it and sang it and thought it until its meaning became so large and bright he could scarcely contain it; or until its meaning deflated into nothingness.

So, saying it again to himself, trying not to think of anything, he went and checked into a top hotel – credit card in hand, no luggage, still dripping with sweat, river water and the champagne they had sprayed over him when he returned to the bank a victor.

That was his part of the college deal done. Now that the early-morning starts were over he could attend Jerusalem meetings without falling asleep and feeling guilty. He would make a pledge, commit to something good, then the business of change could begin. There would be the grave and serious act of submission of his individuality into a larger, badly dressed 'group'. Already he had begun the financial process – transferring money and stocks that had been in his name over to the Jerusalems, stripping his bedroom of things that could be sold or given away. Soon he would have nothing. His affluence was a bland, featureless and arid pile that had failed to enrich him. Anyway, it was just 'stuff' that he was giving away – his watch collection, his Mac products, his clothes.

The process both scared and excited him. But it had been a long time since he had felt so alive.

The aftermath of the thing with Alfred had revealed what had already been there: a loneliness that didn't just follow him around but was in him all the time. He could no longer ignore it or try to block it out with drinking.

'Shit, Toby! Toby – wake up … oh God, oh God … I'm fucked, fucked …'

'Huh? What are you talking about?'

'Oh fuck. Fuck.'

Ben sat on Toby's bed and tried to roll him over.

'Alfred – Alfred's gone missing. Out there.'

That fucking haunted, heavy feeling was there when he was awake, was there when he was asleep. It seemed unalienable. He wished he could confess to someone what he had done to Alfred in the bunkroom, relieve the terrible burden of self-disgust. He knew Toby didn't understand, but to be around anyone from that night, anyone from the cricket team – even Toby, who was essentially blameless – felt like a continuation of the initial act of violence. Only being with Sylvan helped him to feel better, calmed him somehow. It was the goodness he exuded; it was the fact that he had some kind of moral code, in contrast to the hedonism and decadence of St Anton's.

Ben opened the curtains with the remote control and the city spread out below him in a way that suggested limitless temptation. But he had everything he needed right here.

A hot bath, television, wi-fi, a comfortable bed, solitude. *Excavation, excavation, excavation.*

He drew a bath, putting in some girly Jo Malone bath products that created great peaks and crests of froth. While the bath was filling, he stepped into the shower and turned on all three shower heads. He supposed this was what couples did when they rented rooms like this for dirty weekends. Water poured onto him and down him, stinging his eyes, boring through his head, coursing down the back of his neck, across his body, already sore and stiffening from the effort in the boat. He was a rock pounded by surf – and below him, through the floor-to-ceiling windows, he saw the lights of the city's bridges turn on, like jewels being draped across a lovely neck. He stepped from the shower into the bath and lowered himself down. *Excavation, excavation, excavation.*

CHAPTER 16

Everything continued. The year would turn out all right after all, thought the Master with relief. His osteopath had expressed shock at the amount of tension the Master was carrying between his shoulders, and until recently he'd been forced to use one of those wheat bag things regularly to loosen it up.

But things were slowly getting better. The debating team won their heat with the argument that threats to national security should override human rights. 'But we were prepared to argue the other side,' the third speaker for the affirmative, Octavia, reassured him. The three members of the team walked around for a week like mini Aristotles – speaking with gravitas and using dramatic gestures when discussing the weather; reciting the recipe for their mother's shepherd's pie as if to a panel of adjudicators.

The women's hockey team, too, won their heat, and they stood a bit taller and spoke a bit louder in the dining room, wielding their cutlery like sticks, bludgeoning their veal, splicing their vegetables as if going for a goal.

The Dramatic Society re-formed for another year. Boys with Byronic hair and girls who wore too many scarves collided happily in the quadrangles or on their way to Philosophy tutorials. They discussed with a theatrical world-weariness the relative merits of staging Sondheim versus Ionesco or Stoppard versus Pinter. Soon their time would come (when the curtain was raised and there they stood, poised and ready) to be admired by their peers.

After such a wonky start, self-esteem was back in surfeit! You could feel its levels rising with each minor trophy won, with each prize awarded, with each article published in each little journal (Sarah Hardy: 'Student Debt: Fuck off, Treasury!' *Et Diias* Vol. 5; 'Meat is Still Murder!' *Green Left Weekly*) until the Master himself could feel it, walking through the cloisters and out onto the lawns. The sheer love these kids felt for themselves was a gift, he told his doubtful wife. She shook her head and tried to explain that you could be arrogant and egotistical and have dreadfully low self-esteem at the same time.

'The way they are told all the time how privileged they are, and how all the prime ministers and poets came here – it makes them feel that if they're not somebody, they're nobody,' she said.

'Nonsense,' said the Master. 'They know they can fail here. Put on a bad play or form a choir that can't sing or lose the ping-pong final – I'm not going to judge them. We give them the self-esteem to fail gloriously. So do their families. These kids were raised on self-esteem – it's practically a food group for them.'

'If that were the case, then you'd be obese,' said his wife, poking his belly, and they laughed at that and the Master felt happy – happy because his wife was laughing, and happy because 'the Alfred situation' seemed to have passed without any fuss.

Gary accompanied Alfred and his parents as he was transferred to a rehabilitation facility one Sunday. An ambulance without a siren sat in traffic, pulled up to get petrol, stood with its motor idling while the drivers changed over, and glided down a long, long highway to a low-rise modern building. The child of one of his nurses had made Alfred a bracelet from things she had found at the seaside – small shells, a green stone, an old button, a chipped piece of clay. The bracelet hung off Alfred's wrist and caught on the ambulance officer's watch as the stretcher was lifted from the car. The officer swore as the bracelet broke, its elements cascading to the ground in a pip-pip pop-pop rattle. Alfred shifted slightly on the stretcher. A dog barked in a distant yard, a door slammed shut somewhere, the Top 40 countdown sounded tinny and almost inaudible on the ambulance radio. The sounds of Sunday, Alfred deaf to them all.

CHAPTER 17

Late afternoon and the sun was still high in the sky, and a light breeze sailed through the cloisters and ruffled sheet music and hair. Everything was heightened; even the college's stone walls and cobbled grounds seemed alive, coursing with anticipation.

No one went to classes on the afternoon of the St Anton's Ball. Charlotte always promised herself she would listen to the lectures later online, but never did. Instead, the boys played touch football in the quadrangle and the girls went in and out of city day spas with foils in their hair and the skin below their eyebrows red from waxing and tweezing. They took Nurofen while getting a Brazilian wax – chewing on the chalky tablets and on the insides of their cheeks. And once everything was waxed, their skin spray-tanned and dewy, they leavened their eyelids with charcoal and ran a clear slick of gloss over their lips.

Charlotte knew tonight was important. More important than the looming exams, more important than her overdue essay on Robespierre. There was a list on her phone of things she had to do. Highlights in her hair, a blow-dry, spray tan, leg wax, bikini wax, eyebrow wax, manicure and pedicure.

In the mirror her nose, too Roman, was a sort of reproach. She was almost old enough to change it. Pictures of noses ripped from magazines were stuffed in her diary, lined the mirror and were trampled underfoot like autumn leaves as they came unstuck from the walls. Miley Cyrus – she had the best nose. And so it was the Cyrus schnoz that blew around the room when the windows were open, that stuck to the bottoms of her shoes like stubborn loo paper.

Her parents hadn't let her have the nose operation when she was at school, but they had said, 'When you're older you can do what you like with your own body.' It was worth thinking about. Ah, the great project of self. What to conceal (her stomach – too much beer over the summer), what to reveal (long, tanned legs; really great hair). The deepest part of her realised this knowledge was worth more than a bunch of facts about some long-dead dude called Robespierre.

This knowledge of herself was the map to guide her through life. She was the path and the destination. Her cousin Sophia, a few years ahead of her at university, had applied herself to her studies but had let her body go – put on the fresher stone, plus a couple more. What use were all the As in the world if you weren't looked at? If you had just started on a course of anti-depressants because the world did not accept you as you really were? She scrolled back down her to-do list. She should have had her waxing yesterday – it was crazy scheduling it so close to the spray tan. Her legs would be all gross and rashy.

Balls were the exam, the test you took to prove that you knew the subject matter – the subject matter of self. Around

10 pm – that was when you knew if you were flying or if some dreadful error had been made early in the night and you were stuck on a bad track. Angry or crying with your friends in the toilets, taking too many drugs or drinking too much and being sick on yourself and others, spending too much time with the wrong boy.

Ben, Toby, Hadrien, Leeson, Roman – even Levi and Julian: she followed their eyes at the start of the night and clues were divined. Where did their attention rest? On her or her or her? She watched them watching others and was only happy when she felt them watching her. Anything physical that flowed from that was nice, but nothing compared with the feeling she got when she knew she was being watched and desired. It was power – or it was how power should feel. There was a sense of all the boys' energy flowing to her, surging like a star towards dark matter.

Her mother, unsmiling now because of all the Botox, had told her that the pursuit of beauty was harsh but was its own reward.

Charlotte stepped over the mountain of clothes on the floor and peered under her bed looking for a missing blue stiletto. It was seriously gross under there. Sometimes she fell asleep while reading or eating pot noodles or trying to knit a scarf, and so everything tipped onto the floor and was pushed under the bed.

A song floated past her window: the strange band that had been everywhere last summer, Lance Vaine and the Musical Hellos, singing *'Princess lies alone in her tower/The rope's been snapped/Ash and tears and a summer shower'*. She thought their music was sad, particularly after Levi told her all their songs were actually about the war.

Charlotte took a yellow silk Prada dress out of its dry-cleaning plastic. She eased it over her head and it slipped on like a sheath. She felt some internal part of herself swell with pride. Hot, hot, hot. Well, almost hot. Except for the nose and a few other bits. She put Beyoncé on and danced around the room but lingered longest before the mirror to see herself as others would see her tonight at the ball: free, young, beautiful and dancing.

Levi spent the day in his room feeling out of sorts. He took off his glasses and lay on his bed in his underwear staring at the walls, unable to focus on the history textbook he was meant to be reading. He experimented again with the little sticks of makeup that girls had left behind in his room. A bit of this under his eyes, some white powder across his cheeks and, most daringly, red lipstick. With the curtains drawn and door locked he stared at himself in the mirror for a long time – an hour or more – pouting and tilting his head to different angles, mouthing the words, 'Hey, honey baby.' He knew he was not pretty enough to pass as a girl – he had a sort of bulgy face, googly eyes, glasses, lips that were as thin as an afterthought. He would forever look like a geeky teenage boy, probably even when he was forty.

He imagined what it would be like to go to the ball tonight wearing makeup; 'Hey, honey baby.' He could probably get away with it – tell people it was ironic or something. They might forgive it, thinking it one of his hipster quirks. He could say he was dressed as a young Lou Reed – except Lou looked so much tougher with lipstick on.

Maybe he wouldn't go at all. He wasn't really in the mood. He had been to dozens of balls in the past two and a half years – the Commerce Balls, the Law Balls, the Architecture and Medicine and Engineering Balls. They were all the same. But not only that: they all made him *feel* the same, sad and anxious, as if they were a promise so great that they couldn't help but not be fulfilled. The excitement was too high to be realised and he knew this time tomorrow there would be dreadful hangovers and regrets.

People would be left alone on the dance floor, their lips unkissed; girls unused to drink would slip from their heels into the arms of footballers too cavalier to hold on too long after they'd been caught.

Flirtations that might have been brewing all semester long fell over under the weight of anticipation. Nothing could fulfil such great expectations. Why hadn't someone explained to him when he was in first year how it felt to walk home by himself at 2 am, the headlights of every passing car rendering him more visible? He could have read the minds of the drivers: a young man in a tuxedo, walking along Marchmont Street, head down, smoking, alone. The cars would flash by, their tail-lights bright then fading, and he would long to hide. The other boys thought he was such a stud – slept with a different girl each week, was some sort of campus Lothario. Hey, he'd even had a threesome! What a disaster. He had stopped going to ICEPIC lectures and he'd had to send Charlotte into the Botany loos to white-out the graffiti calling him a rapist.

There was all that. There was all that, plus his sexual response to the Alfred thing, which had really freaked him out, plus the fact that his second most sensible friend had joined a cult, and his parents hated him. What a shitty year.

Maybe it would be better simply not to go tonight. Take a sleeping pill or watch some porn. He knew that everyone would be too drunk and signals would be confused or not picked up. The girls would morph into their infernal dancing circles around handbags, smiling sadly to themselves at their failure to connect. Or they'd wait until later to make their move, but sometimes later was too late. The boy would be drunk and they would be too, so they'd say things that they really meant but didn't mean to say and hope that the next morning all would be forgotten. (There was always a particular shame about revealing yourself too early, letting them in on your secret fears and hang-ups – more personal than fucking and harder to recover from.) Or they'd fall down drunk or vomit on themselves or spend the night in the bathroom crying about some childhood upset – their parents' divorce, a cruel older sibling, the boy from school who took their virginity and failed to text them the next day.

The boys would sit at the tables in their teams and packs and talk about girls and football and their older brothers. They'd get drunk and get pulled onto the dance floor before they remembered they didn't know how to dance. So a girl with too-tanned skin dressed like a butterfly would dance around them while they stood swaying and shuffling, unsure where to place their hands.

The cricketers would end up in Leeson's room or in the tower with Hadrien, dressing in women's clothes and calling each other a faggot. And the legend of the Savage Society would grow. All of them would be wearing makeup (so perhaps his own unfurling interest in cosmetics wasn't so weird after all). They would run like warmongers through the college corridors and smash in doors and windows with some girl's discarded high-heeled shoes. They would threaten to torture the animals that were locked up for the night, sleepless in their pens. They would have to be held back from hurting vulnerable old Dr Bath. They would wander across busy streets, forcing the traffic to stop for them, feeling all-powerful, singing some boarding-school shanty, and try to break into other colleges with their road signs and cans of paint and only the haziest of intentions.

Sometimes they would return to their rooms and find the girl they'd tried to dance with lying there, really like a butterfly now, her clothes spread out beneath her, her eyelids fluttering in a Morse code of inebriation, and in an abstract state of need they'd unpeel their fishnets and wipe off their makeup before flipping her over.

Since the Alfred thing Levi had a desperate longing to be somewhere, anywhere else. He wished he was in Brooklyn writing a novel rather than in this decadent little hell-hole. Little girls trying to be their mothers, trying to court men who could have been their brothers. Then after college there would be travel, then jobs, then marriage and babies. Why didn't they just get it over and done with now and then die!

Worked up into a furious state, he reached over and fastened his curtains together with a clothes peg so he could lie on the bed pants down and masturbate. He wrung himself out, then scrubbed the makeup from his face with some exfoliant he had stolen from Lucy, and didn't wish everyone dead or feel so much like crying anymore.

Lucy sat in her room and cursed all the drinking she had done at the start of the year. Her dress clung too tightly around her hips and stomach – the fabric creased, rippled and stretched. She threw a cashmere wrap across her shoulders and drew a belt around her waist (as her mother often did, beautiful still, though thickening now), but she realised these accessories only drew attention to her bulges so she flung them back on her bed. She was so angry these days – angry, angry, angry! Where had they come from, these feelings of rage?

Maybe because of her own body ... If she were to look in the mirror she would see her skin was too pale and her legs lumpy with cellulite. She had been invited to a tanning salon party that morning, but wasn't in the mood; she would remain pale and her legs would stay unwaxed. Her best features – her eyes – were useless on ball night. The light was too dim and always it was about the dresses and the bodies under them. That was what the boys would see when they did an inventory of the girls at 8 pm. Not that she cared about them. She dressed for Toby, she read for Toby, she listened to certain bands for Toby; she stood back from herself, always, to see herself as he would see her.

Someone down the corridor was playing Lance Vaine and the Musical Hellos and she knew she should be getting excited about tonight. Looking out her window she saw Toby and Julian walking across the quadrangle. If she didn't eat lunch, would her dress fit tonight? If the dress did fit, would she be brave enough to kiss him at the ball? Actually, why should *she* be kissing *him*? He should make the first move; he should find her irresistible! How she wished to get away from this looping, interminable dialogue – the way her mind strategised and bargained with itself. If she tried a little bit harder, would he love her a bit more?

If she changed her timetable to match his, would they become closer?

If she dyed her hair brown, like Lisa's, would he suddenly see a different person – one he wanted to sleep with?

It wasn't madness, then, it was *strategy* when she left her room (can't find keys, door unlocked, never mind) and walked in sort of a daze out across the car park and playing fields, through the university's Humanities Building and along tree-lined Marchmont Street, past the cafes where the King's and Minerva students sucked on Marlboro Lights and discussed their own balls, which were also happening that night, and talked and texted and smoked and surreptitiously looked her up and down for evidence of a spray-on tan or $200 haircut.

In the supermarket she looked at all the boxes of dye – all featuring the same even-featured, forgettable women on the front, with hair that looked like a wig. The colours they promoted sounded like lines from a poem ... Ash Blonde, Golden Dusk Yellow, Deep Chestnut Brown, Honeyed Brown, Whispering Silver. She chose Ravishing Raven, but felt a weird mixture of excitement and shame about her selection, as if some essential part of her character were being revealed through this purchase. They didn't cost too much, these little boxes, but they promised a lot. Tonight, nothing short of transformation would do.

Back in her room she filled the sink and opened the box. Its elements spilt out: a plastic cap; a container of whitish cream and a sachet filled with brown goo that she was meant to mix and spread on her dark blonde hair for how long? No more than thirty minutes and she would be raven; she would be utterly different.

The goo was a cold, tingling shock on her scalp. She put the stereo on – Fiona Apple singing about wanting to feel everything – and sat at her desk to wait. From the postcard on her wall Heath Ledger looked back at her with a steady gaze. The thirty-minute wait felt not dissimilar to the last hours before the ball – cells alert with anticipation; alive to all things, particularly potential. For a minute or two she felt aware of everything – a certain speed in the breeze; a certain heat in the air; a soprano practising in the Music Room, her voice carrying across the quadrangle, even her notes bearing the promise of transcendence.

Toby looked up and saw Lucy staring at him through her curtains. Why was she always watching him when she thought he couldn't see? He could feel it when she did. She had a strange plastic cap on her head. He hoped she wouldn't wear it tonight as some absurd fashion statement. Sometimes he really didn't understand girls.

Three o'clock. The drinking would start soon. Cocktail parties in people's rooms or parents' houses, dinner at some restaurant and then the ball. A deep yearning to be very far away struck him as he crossed the quadrangle. Niall kicked a football to him and he smoothly handballed it back, careful not to hit the Asian chess players on the back or Jan and Giles lying together, wrapped up in each other, studying the patterns the clouds made as they moved across the sky. The chaplain, Dr Williams, walked past and inquired as to Toby's spiritual wellbeing.

'It's in rude health sir,' said Toby.

Dr Williams nodded and said, 'Good, good,' and limped off towards the library.

Suzanne was sitting in a transparent white dress on the landing outside Hadrien's tower, blowing bubbles into the air through a wand. She tossed Toby a kiss and shouted something to him in French that he couldn't understand.

Ben, acting strangely as usual, had his curtains drawn and a reading light on. No doubt he was sitting up there in the semi-dark with a sulky face and a highlighter, going through the New Testament.

After a great deal of pleading, Toby had managed to convince Ben to come with them to Octavia's pre-ball turn at her parents' apartment in the city. Toby wondered if something was up ... if Ben was planning something. Perhaps Ben, under the chandeliers, amid the champagne and the canapes and the silk gowns and bare, perfumed skin, would start shouting about how very WRONG! it all was – how they should all stop caring so much about their appearance, how they should, you know, make a live organ donation – say, a kidney – to a stranger, because that was the pure meaning of altruism and you only need one kidney anyway.

And where was Levi? Still reading Camus and drinking wine in the middle of the day? Sometimes he was manic and talked a mile a minute about some new band, or anti-globalisation or the Paleo Diet. And sometimes his face looked too pale, like he was wearing powder. Was he turning from a hipster into an emo? Toby hoped not. He was beginning to suspect that he didn't like it when people turned into different things – that he didn't like change particularly much.

Weary, weary now, even though it was only mid-afternoon. And more girls walked by and waved and he felt them looking at him after he had passed, and more footballs were kicked to him and the strange Dr Bath opened his window and sang out to him, waving ... He had an armful of flowers and was saying, 'Beautiful day, beautiful day' in that high-pitched sing-song voice of his. Why did this strange, lonely feeling of homesickness always visit Toby on the brightest days, when there were blossoms and melodies carried on the air (*'Listless bruises and cut lips/Gin and swollen knuckles/Lost at sea with capsized ships'*)?

Home. Home. Far from this artificial world and the evening's ball, where everyone was young and fit. Where no one ever had to clean their rooms or make a meal because someone did it for them and, if you wanted to, you could kick a football back and forth all day or lie on your back watching passing clouds and losing yourself in the tangle of a girl's hair. Or you read Tolstoy or the Bible or the Koran by the half-light in your room and then looked in the mirror and saw that the book had shifted the planes of your face and the knowledge had made you different somehow. Such an artificial world. Toby was sure it would cost him something sooner or later.

That lonely feeling was still there. He thought of Alfred, and of a man he had seen in the city last year, an image seared on his brain because it symbolised something of his future, all of their futures. The man had been a businessman, maybe in his fifties; he still had some of his white hair left. The man was drunk. He was wearing a pinstripe suit and his eyes would not focus. He looked lost in every sense of the word. He was about to cross the road but hesitated at the lights, as if the decision to cross was a grave one.

Toby watched him, recognising a fellow traveller, something in this man that he knew, and saw him fall halfway across the crossing. The man let out a small 'Oh', a wounded, boyish sound. His suit was ripped and there was blood coming from somewhere – maybe his head.

The women came first – all eye contact and action. Gripping the man by the elbow, a young mother with her other hand on a pram tried to help him up, while a strident young woman with a high ponytail was punching numbers into her phone. But the man had begun to soil himself, a stain and a smell spreading across his suit pants. 'Ohhh.' That sound again, but this time coming from deep in his gut.

Now it was the men, including Toby, who moved to the man, taking his arm from the young woman, saying to all the young women around, 'It's okay, we've got him.' The man was whimpering now and ashamed. The men moved inwards, towards him – protecting him somehow. You get old. You piss yourself. You lose dignity. You are King Lear at the pedestrian crossing. It's only those who recognise themselves in you who will save and protect you. Cover you and cover for you. Pretend that you have lost nothing and that life goes on as usual. Toby thought of Alfred, how he – and everyone – had failed to protect him. Was it because they didn't recognise themselves in him – Asian, Islamic, small, a strange species of man–boy? Had they even tried? On the mountains that cold night, and in the blooming heat of the day that followed, there had been some terrible kind of failure. It probably started there – as a failure of recognition.

Toby passed the Master, coming in through the gate as he was going out.

The Master said, 'Toby – deep in thought?'

Toby wanted to say, 'Yes, I am; I'm thinking about Alfred.'

But the Master was already walking away, still talking. 'I bet you're thinking about the ball and what young women you're going to bestow your magnificence on tonight, you jammy bastard.'

Ben was in the library. He should have been studying for his Property exam but instead he'd logged into an online chat room for young people new to Christianity. He had found a group, based in America, of young people who had been raised by atheist parents but wanted to be Christian.

The chat room was interesting; it discussed how to tell your parents and friends, and how to be religiously observant in a sneering and secular world. But he was yet to tell those closest to him who he was becoming, as he unsheathed his true self. He was wondering in particular how to tell Toby. Maybe he could introduce Toby to Sylvan somewhere neutral, like the vegan caf in Patton Place ...

Someone slid into the seat next to Ben and he quickly minimised the window. It was Grace, Alfred's friend. He had never spoken to her properly before. She smiled shyly.

'Hi.'

'Hi.'

'You off to the ball tonight?' asked Ben.

'No, no, I have some work to do – an assignment due Monday,' she said.

Ben nodded. 'I don't think I'll go either.' The theme this year was Elysian Fields, but to Ben it sounded more like his idea of hell. Toby had been pressuring him to go, and was expecting him at Octavia's pre-ball turn. Julian had sent him a text: *It'll be like old times*. Ah, the good old days ... Well, there *were* no good old days. Still, he felt a bit guilty at the thought of letting Toby down.

Maybe he and Grace should have dinner together sometime. When he wasn't doing a shift at the Pleasing Sands, they definitely should have dinner.

'You're really close friends with Alfred, aren't you? How's he doing?' asked Ben.

The question startled her and she took a moment to recover. Her eyes filled with tears and, looking back at him, she said, 'Alfred – he's not so good.'

'Oh no – really? I thought I heard from someone that he was on the mend.'

With that, Ben wanted to talk to this slight girl in the library all night with his churning heart and his muddled head and the painful parts of him just waking up. He wanted to tell her all about that night in the mountains, and how he had been with Alfred in the bunkroom alone after the other boys had run out into the bush.

But what would he say? How bad stuff had just happened in the bunkroom, and how outside the creatures of the bush had rioted?

Hadrien, Leeson, Niall, Roman and Ping had lit a bonfire, drunk more, been sick, covered their faces with mud and covered the night with their screaming – their screaming for no good reason at all. Someone half-killed a kangaroo and they all came back to the house, their arms wet from having been plunged deep into the kangaroo's stomach, discarding a joey from her pouch. Innards dripped from their hands, entrails still steaming in their arms. Hadrien was covered in blood. It ran through his silvery-blond hair and down his face. His shirt was off. All their shirts were off. The blood and some mucousy, muscly stuff was smeared along their chests. Everyone was so drunk – except Hadrien, who was sober. They approached Alfred, holding something that seemed still to be beating. Maybe it was the mutilated, undead joey. Later Alfred ran, not even screaming, into the night, deep into the unquiet bush.

He wanted to tell Grace all this and more, but couldn't. He opened and shut his mouth like a fairground clown, no sound coming out. Yet his face was slick with snot and tears. Grace sat almost impassive, watching him.

'It's okay, it's okay, Alfred's okay,' she said softly.

'No, he's not okay,' said Ben. 'I am so ashamed. He's not okay and no one cares.'

CHAPTER 18

Toby looked in the mirror and straightened his bowtie. It was an unseasonable night. Humid almost, with a charge in the air – electrical currents and the currents between each other. The weatherman had forecast storms.

The Master was away for the evening. The tutors took Serepax with their port and retired for an early night and a chemical sleep. The animals were locked up. An old Lance Vaine and the Musical Hellos song was playing from the Games Room. *'I try but I can't escape the ghost of you'* travelled along the breeze.

Private security guards roamed the perimeters of the playing fields and along the corridors and parapets. They unlocked and locked the library and chapel, ran their torches along the altar and down the book stacks, across the old copies of *The Spectator* read by tutors still dreaming of England, and swept past the glass cabinet, where old biology textbooks sat opened at yellowed pictures of engorged hearts captioned in Latin.

Toby – who was usually pretty lax about security – locked his door and shoved the key down his sock. Students from other colleges broke in on nights like this. In the past they'd stolen laptops, iPads and BlackBerries. They'd smashed the statues around the grounds and thrown food dye in the pond. They'd sprayed pesticide on the lawns and poisoned trees. They'd stamped on rosebushes and left lurid graffiti on the walls (*Severin sucks Hadrien's cock and has AIDS*) and wrenched doors off their hinges. They'd sung the college song but substituted lines about St Antonians being homosexuals, fond of bestiality and hopeless at sport.

So the security men roamed the perimeter fences with their guard dogs and their torches, while across town the cricketers drank until they fell over – until they forgot themselves and what they did to Alfred but still remembered the words to the college song.

Too drunk already, and having misplaced his dinner jacket, Sam was sick of the prancing and the dancing and the drinking and his fellow St Antonians and how feral they were on ball nights.

It was after 11 pm when the major sponsor of the ball started handing out chocolate-coated vanilla ice creams on sticks. Called Indulge, they had been the big luxury food craze last summer. Each ice cream boasted a calorie count in the thousands. Ads urged consumers to ignore the politically correct anti-obesity message and gorge themselves sick: *Go On – Indulge!*

There were ice-cream fights and chocolatey white blobs on sticks sailing across the hall and landing in the elaborate beehive hairdo of a laughing girl, or splattering across the back of a broad-shouldered footballer, who then leant against a girl and smeared Indulge along her bare arm.

Sam pitched an Indulge at the back of a particularly annoying girl, and even though it smeared almost pornographically down her back he still didn't feel satisfied. He looked around, hoping no one had seen him do it, but Hadrien was watching him from the bar. Hadrien was watching him a lot these days – but not in the way you look out for your mates; in a way that suggested Sam was being monitored. And he *was* being monitored.

'Stop going to the hospital, Sammy – no need to visit him,' said Hadrien when he had dropped into Sam's room late one night the previous week.

'But the kid's got no friends,' said Sam, thinking, How the fuck do you know about those visits?

'And neither will you if we get caught,' returned Hadrien lightly.

Was that a threat? Sam now wondered dumbly as he watched yet another girl slip over in a puddle of Indulge. He was too paranoid now to enjoy himself at college. The first two years had been fun, like paradise. Could this be real, he used to think, this life? It was too good to be true. But this year had taken a nightmarish turn.

Hadrien was standing alone, a bottle of mineral water in his hand, wearing a tuxedo with his pale hair slicked back. If you didn't know him you might almost think he was a puritan – the way he didn't drink and always looked so prim and clean. He was still looking at Sam. Their eyes met and Hadrien raised a finger to his lips. 'Shhh,' he seemed to be saying. 'Be silent.'

❀

On that awful night in the mountains, even though he had been really pissed and had already spewed twice, Sam had known that what they did to Alfred was not right. He's not a terrorist, he'd thought quite early on in the piece, even before they staged their mock trial. (Hadrien had even produced wigs and gowns! You could tell which boys were taking Trial Practice and Advocacy that semester; they were really good.) Alfred was found guilty and sentenced to a variety of physical punishments.

Sam had shoved a sock in Alfred's mouth to muffle his screams and had stood and watched as the other boys did things to him – things he had never seen done before, things he hadn't even thought you could possibly do to someone else, things that disgusted him. It was like they were all fucking homos. It wasn't right. Then they killed an animal, or tried to kill an animal, but they did it badly; they didn't finish the job properly, not like he'd been taught on the farm.

Later, after Alfred had run off somewhere and the other boys were in the shower and the bunkroom itself looked spent, exhausted and defiled, Sam found his sock. It was soaked in blood and saliva, and some other vomity stuff; it was dripping wet. Horrified and suddenly sober, Sam pitched it out into the bush. Was Alfred out there walking in the dark, or had he hidden in one of the sheds? He hoped Alfred was hiding, not walking.

Sam's phone had felt chunky in his pocket, nestled against his thigh with a pressure that seemed to be telling him something. The number for the local branch of Search and Rescue was stored in his SIM card from the last time they had been up there and had gone for a long walk.

He was not a dobber – never had been, but … but … this was different. He took a deep breath and dialled the number. He got an answering machine but left a message anyway – he just needed to tell someone. It was a bit garbled, he probably went on too long, but he said what he needed to say – about how Alfred had gone missing and he wasn't a terrorist.

Charlotte spun into Julian's arms, and could feel him burying his face in her hair. Men were so unsubtle sometimes!

'Stop sniffing my head – I can feel it when you do that!' she complained, but yielded her crown to his snout anyway.

A slow Frank Ocean song was playing and all around her were girls falling into ice-cream puddles and chocolatey kisses were exchanged, white evening shirts were suddenly transformed from starched nothingness to a delectable treat. More things were getting thrown and people kept slipping over, and that idiot Ping fell heavily and started laughing hysterically, even though he was bleeding from the head. The blood mixed in with the chocolate and he put a towel up to the wound and went right on dancing, saying he didn't feel a thing.

There were no fights yet – just love, love, love. At this point of the night everyone still believed in love and knew it could be theirs for the taking. Even those who just minutes to midnight hadn't yet found love, hadn't yet had their desires requited, still believed that the night had some magic left, that there was the possibility of romance. They all heard the promise of it in the last song of the night, by Lance Vaine and the Musical Hellos (*'Hot lips on your bare skin/Too aware of your traitorous heart/Slow waltzing to Vera Lynn'*). They just had to wander into the right pair of arms.

Last drinks were called and everyone walked up Monte Street to Isolodes Towers. Charlotte linked arms with Julian, wishing it were Ben. But Ben's phone was switched off and no one had seen him all night.

Maybe he's jumped off a bridge, she thought harshly. Finally done what he's always said he would do.

Julian paid her admission to Isolodes. It was a notorious dark den where gangsters snorted cocaine openly at the gaming tables, blondes in lamé twisted and arched on their laps, young royals on gap-year jaunts danced badly and visiting film stars took refuge in the dark, telling themselves that this feeling of loneliness would pass.

To the St Antonians, Isolodes Towers seemed like some sort of descent into Hades from the floral innocence of the Elysian Fields, and they knew that, once there, they would explore darker forms of love. Impulse was made physical. Girls danced with each other and slipped their tongues into one another's mouths. They felt around for the soft underpart of each other's breasts, sharply drew in their breath and rocked to the beat. The boys sat around not even pretending to be nonchalant. They rubbed the sweat from their palms onto their pants and let the music – Daft Punk or Chemical Brothers or Vampire Weekend – course through their bodies like a virus.

❊

Back at college Dr Bath awoke with a start. What was it that woke him? He thought it sounded like a gun or a scream or a flock of geese shrieking across the moonless sky.

There was still heat in the air. It was a close night. He thought about opening his window then decided against it. What if the skies were to break open in a thunderstorm and the rain were to sweep in and soak his bookshelves and all the papers he had prepared for Monday's seminar? What would he do then?

He had fallen asleep at an odd angle and the latest tome by Sir Charles Motion was digging into his left shoulder blade like a dull knife. He had nodded off at page 117 of a particularly tedious account of the fall of Stalingrad. The wireless was on BBC World Service. London was waking up to the news that there had been another attempted bombing, this time at a busy nightclub in Piccadilly Circus. Had that happened while he slept and dreamt, or did it happen when he was awake and racing through the more exciting earlier chapters – in particular Chapter Five? News of a thwarted terror attack on the wireless, sharp corners of the book sticking into his back, faint feelings of lust and disgust and a sharper one of excitement when he remembered he'd had that dream again – the one about Toby and the rowing boat, the sun low and hot in the sky, his hand trailing in the water (cool, silky), the sweat drifting down Toby's neck and arms and the oars beating on. The flock of birds, a gunshot, the scream of a woman. Toby shirtless, looming above, then smiling at him. In that smile a whole lost world was found.

The security guards passed under his window, then torchlight swung across the quadrangle and continued its sweeping path across his bed and the floor of his room. Dr Bath froze as the light swept past, like he was about to be caught doing something he shouldn't. But of course he was doing nothing. He was just a middle-aged man in a nightshirt sitting up alone in his bed. It was only his thoughts that were crowded with bodies and sin and moans of pleasure – by him and for him.

From a distant place, maybe the Games Room, some swoony song from Lance Vaine and the Musical Hellos floated past before fading away (*'I'll pick you up some gin, darling/The cruelty of your painted mouth/The gravity of our sin'*). The sirens rising and falling in the background, he finally realised, weren't from out on the street but were sounding from the wireless with reports from London.

Dr Bath wondered briefly about the animals – if they would be okay in their pens tonight, if the students could be trusted to stay away, not to harm them. (He couldn't forget the blood of the last time, sprayed around the walls of the pen, the bits of matted fur, the smears of something on his car, and the smell.)

The clock said 2 am. He did what he sometimes did when he felt alone and afraid (and had done since he was a child): he prayed.

Even though he thought prayers were for hopeful fools and religion for the ignorant, he uttered the half-remembered words of the Lord's Prayer and then, trailing off, added his own coda: 'And please, Lord, look after the animals and myself and anyone hurt, and the souls of the terrorists who planned the attack in London. And look after Toby, and the Master, and all the students, protect all the students – particularly on a night like this.'

He spoke the words out loud, but as he did his eyes darted around his empty room and he felt a bit self-conscious, worried that someone might hear. He was also aware of the contradiction in this: he didn't want anyone to hear, but that was why he prayed, because he wanted to be heard.

The Master had booked a suite at the Park Hyatt, as he did every year on the night of the St Anton's Ball. He liked to get off campus when there was a big student function such as a ball or a football grand final. He would return when the cleaning crews had come and gone and the place was wiped clear of the vomit and excrement, tidied of the spent shells of fireworks, the shrunken balloons and the clumps of melted candles and crayfish tails.

He knew the students could be animals but he liked the term 'wilful blindness'. He could turn away when they went feral. He chose not to know and thus remained unaccountable. What he wanted to see were his scholar princes and trust-fund princesses. Privileged, good-looking, intelligent, articulate, athletic and well-mannered.

His wife snorted when he told her this. From her reclining position on the biggest bed in the hotel (not just king-sized; it was called 'the Royal Family') she told him again that most of the students were animals. 'It's just like *Lord of the Flies*. Look at Alfred,' she reminded him. 'C'mon, Locke, what about what they did to Alfred?'

'Let's not talk about Alfred,' said the Master firmly.

His wife was a beautiful redhead. She was also not infatuated with young people the way he was. She did not regard youth as anything more than another time of life that one usually lived in a certain squalor and ignorance.

On the giant bed, flicking the remote at the big TV, she was like a fairy queen with a wand. The Master opened the champagne while she went on about some horrible boy: 'Ping is his name, I think … He looked at me once like he wanted to rape me.'

'Like this?' asked the Master, and fixed her with a terrifying impersonation of Ping, whose eyes were buried in an overly fleshy forehead like raisins in dough.

'It's no way to look at a woman,' she said. 'What about when he goes out into the real world and has a female boss or clients? He's going to get Pinged for sexual harassment.' And she laughed a little at her own joke.

The Master agreed with her but without much concern for Ping's future. 'He's a bit of a lame duck. His whole life is spent trying to get the other boys from the cricket team to throw him a crumb of recognition – it's a terrible way to live.'

The champagne cork popped. The Master slid onto the bed and waved across the vast distance of the mattress to his wife, who was still laughing about Ping and was now laughing at her husband.

They too loved the night of St Anton's Ball, but for their own, historic reasons.

CHAPTER 19

Lucy had lost track of Toby between the Town Hall and Isolodes Towers. He had danced with her (well, with her and Octavia and Charlotte – there was a group of them) and she had yelled in his ear, 'Nightclub?'

He had yelled back, 'Yeah, come and find me,' and danced away from them.

It wasn't long after that the lights came on, too abruptly, and when they did everyone seemed startled, as if they had been caught wearing a complicated expression that they usually only wore alone in their rooms.

By the side door, under the full bloom of the lights, Suzanne was weeping with unusual violence. There was a rash across her chest and her face was slick with snot and tears. Empathetic girls and sympathetic boys gathered around her, absorbing her gusty sobs into their shoulders.

The girls of St Anton's, the ones with eating disorders and alcohol problems, had relinquished their much-cherished self-control many hours previously. They had crossed some threshold of excess from which they could not return and so they walked through the dark warren of the nightclub to find a bathroom that promised a refuge of cool tiles, running water and silence. Their mouths and the backs of their throats tasted of the not-unpleasant cocaine burn, and it was then, at 2 am, that they felt such a deep dread, the dread that they worked so hard to keep at bay, that they thought it would be okay if they died now, on the floor of this nightclub, because at least there would be release and relief. So close to the bathroom now, so close to disappearing, and they wondered why their mothers had never explained how this would feel. All that money on school fees, all the French learnt and still – still – they were unable to negotiate the darkness of their own matter. Why could they learn about poetry and physics but not themselves?

Lucy had done a lap of the Town Hall looking for Toby but all she could see were kids walking round looking lost, kids crying, kids slipping on the floor, kids trying to remember where they'd left their dinner jacket or wondering where they could buy cigarettes. Bewildered kids. Sad kids. Kids being carried out by ambulance officers. Kids so drunk that they could no longer remember their own names. It was the most jarring, unlovely part of the evening.

Lucy had walked to the nightclub with Nicky, a boy in second year who lived in the room below the parapet in Gregor House. She hadn't seen him all night but he materialised on the Town Hall steps just after she had been on another fruitless search for Toby, or even Charlotte, Julian or Levi. She felt drunk and bereft, as if she had lost everybody important to her and they would never be recovered.

'Your hair looks good that colour,' Nicky said, and she touched it lightly; she had forgotten that she had dyed it that afternoon.

'It was sort of an impulse thing; I got it at the supermarket.' She sighed. Toby must have gone on. 'Shall we walk to Isolodes Towers?'

Raindrops was coming down as hard as gunfire now; there had been foul weather brewing all that humid night and now the almost spicy smell of fresh rain filled the air. They walked slowly under shop awnings, avoiding cracks in the footpath while Nicky (tall, black-haired, a rumour – what had it been? Last year – drugs, a nervous breakdown ... Was that him?) talked of the internship he did in the summer at a legal centre in some desert township. Red river gums, fine orange dirt, huge black skies that billowed like a sheet, ripped away by the light each morning. The way people talked through their teeth or didn't talk at all, their slow blinking eyes. They were like lizards, scaly, coarsened, muted and made strange by the heat. Wary of outsiders, taciturn, grave.

'I felt like I was in another country, but of course I wasn't,' said Nicky.

But of course you were, thought Lucy, but didn't say anything.

He talked and talked, fixated on Ben and how he'd seen him last week. 'He was working – can you believe it? – at that religious cafe by Jacaranda Station. I mean, we were just there for a laugh, we didn't think we'd run into Ben Winchester, of all people.'

Lucy nodded and said, 'Yeah, yeah, I hear he's there a lot,' but was thinking about Toby. When he'd said she was 'really interesting' did he mean it? And did that mean sexy, or was 'interesting' a polite way of saying 'not sexy'. And what about the other week in his room when he told her she'd been in his dream? What did that mean? She was on his mind, that was what it meant. On his mind, in his subconscious – and now was the time for her to swim to the surface.

Nicky was talking about other things now – a bus trip across the Nullarbor, Valiums at sundown, feeling groggy at an outback service station, the monotony of the trip broken up by sunsets and road kill.

She would find Toby and dance with him. Be near him and walk home with him, along Marchmont Street with its sheltering elms. She would go with him back to his room, put the kettle on – not very sexy, she thought ruefully, but she couldn't think of what else to do once she was in his room. (She could say, 'I will never let go of your heart.') She would make him tea. Then dawn. In the light he would notice the new colour of her hair. And it would all be new, new, new.

Now Nicky was talking about how he'd been beaten up after the rowing regatta by a boy from another college who he'd always thought had Down's syndrome ('But once the first punch was thrown I knew he didn't') and how anyone studying journalism was deluding themselves about job prospects.

Isolodes Towers, and they lined up at the door, holding their wrists out to be scanned. Dawn would come and she'd be lying on Toby's bed saying, 'Come here.' And he, tired and not really drinking his milky sweet tea – only sipping it out of habit – would lie down beside her, his arm over her shoulder and she could ... well, she'd be close enough to stroke his thick brown hair and she would whisper hoarsely how long and dearly she had loved him. On the radio Lance Vaine and the Musical Hellos would be singing ('*When I told you I loved you, my dear/You whistled through your crooked teeth/And you sighed in my ear*'). He would only have to move his face a fraction of an inch and they would be kissing and he would be murmuring into her mouth, 'Oh, me too, me too.'

She was following Nicky down some stairs that led to the centre of the club, to a place called 'the Pit', packed with a hot, writhing mass of bodies. Some retro pop was blasting – an old Blur song about boys who like girls who like boys who like girls – and there were professional dancers in cages. (Why, oh why, thought Lucy, do they always put the dancers in cages?) The St Anton's girls danced with glitter on their shoulders, cocaine up their noses, the curls of their hair loosening. Their limbs made little shapes like starfish under the light and Nicky, who had been talking all this time, who had not shut up, suddenly stopped and looked down into the Pit and said: 'My God, it looks very hot down there.'

Toby, Toby – why didn't you wait for me?

Nicky went to the bar to get drinks (wrist out, barman scans your skin, some debit is arranged) and Lucy wandered off to find Toby. Peering into the Tambourine Room, with its mass of cushions and some Jay-Z song being piped through that merged into Rihanna, she saw a gaunt man in an armchair in the corner pressing two small dice into the palm of his hand, and a dramatic-looking woman with cropped blue hair sitting very still, as if hoping the man who had gone to buy her drinks would not come back. On one of the couches, Hadrien sat next to Suzanne. When Lucy passed him and saw a flash of teeth she shivered and was reminded of a blue-eyed, white-haired vampire. Toby had told her when he was very drunk last week that Hadrien was a murderer, that he had killed Alfred. 'But Alfred's still alive,' she had replied, confused. Toby had been sick on himself that night, and had wanted to sleep in a flowerbed despite the forecast of 5 degrees. She had rapped on Julian's window and they had both taken Toby under his arms and put him in bed.

She'd heard rumours of the all-male secret society from the 1920s that Hadrien was obsessed with – the Savage Society – and the late-night games and Russian roulette in someone's country house, and how he carried syringes to parties and drew blood from the arms of stupefied girls and made ridiculous art works on the walls. Maybe the strangest thing about him was that in a place marked by such alcoholic excess, she had never seen Hadrien drinking. He always looked in control and immaculate in his perfectly cut lounge suits. Did he have a tailor? She'd heard he saw someone in London. She had also heard of a massive fortune he was to inherit when he turned twenty-one and how he was distantly related to the British royal family, and alternatively that he was entirely self-made, a creation of his own imagining, who had walked chimera-like into the college grounds with a neat but vague history, when really he'd been raised as a cub by lions in the Western Plains Zoo in Dubbo or hatched this new version of himself in the council houses of Sunshine. That his father had disappeared, that his father was a disgraced policeman, that his father was a recluse who owned department stores, that his father provided funding to the violent militias in West Papua. That his mother was a prostitute, that his mother was a movie star, that his mother was a senator. Who were they really, these parents of a boy possessed of such creepy charisma? A boy who made people feel afraid and unsure when they were near him. And how was it that the air around him always seemed chilled? She supposed he amassed these followers because he was fabulously wealthy, a real one-percenter. Otherwise she didn't really get it.

In the pool room the football team and their girlfriends lounged together in careworn tuxedos and tired lamé. They prodded each other playfully on the rump with the pool cues before becoming suddenly overcome with fatigue, and so the cues were up-ended and used as props for their heavy heads. Lucy moved quickly through the room, not wanting to catch Sam's eye, not wanting to … what? Not wanting to start something with him. But of course that would be the easiest thing in the world – to start something with him.

The next room was roped off. Nestled in its red-velvet lushness, like a flower waiting to bud, was the small, tired figure of Sam Tooth, a soap star with a well-documented morphine addiction. At another booth was a Labor Party politician with a woman who was not his wife. They sat in silence and – it was apparent even to the casual observer – turmoil.

Lucy brushed past a rapper she recognised from Saturday morning music video clips, swinging gold chains and blinding her with his white trainers, and all around her were St Anton's students, walking past or sliding down the walls or emerging hologram-like from other rooms or heard as distant voices – chemically affected, unseeing, drunk, disappointed, undone. She passed some poor boy on his knees whispering, 'My lost Albion, off course now, of course …' A very beautiful girl walked past wearing sunglasses and a boy who had cut his hand on broken glass was slumped and bloody in an otherwise empty room.

In another room a masked jazz trio played some wild, discordant bop, the music and the masks making everything seem so, so sinister. Lucy worried that if she sat beneath the mellow pool of lamplight and fixed her face to the stage she would be hypnotised, transported and stranded in a place from which she could not return.

But luckily all corridors led her back to the Pit, where Nicky stood with her sweating glass of vodka tonic, still mouthing the words to the Blur song.

She touched her hair again and, passing a mirror, got a shock when she saw herself. The dye had not made her a Ravishing Raven any more than being blonde had made her sexy. But it didn't matter. If she looked different it followed that things would be different.

Sam didn't like to admit it, but he was bored and he'd had too much to drink and they were at this terrible nightclub playing pool and someone was handing out cigars. He took one but when he drew back on it he almost choked, and after that he began to feel incredibly unwell. But at least the pre-ball parties had been good. There'd been cocaine passed around at Suzanne's but he'd been unsure if it was meant for him, so he'd just stood near the sushi and kept shovelling nori rolls into his mouth. He'd met Suzanne's cousin, who was sixteen but looked younger, and she had glanced at him off and on in a way that he could only describe as dirty. He felt confused about how he should respond, so he'd stayed there, by the food, glancing at her probably too often and then turning away from her as if to get something back for himself. As he was leaving, she stood too close and he could feel her breasts on his chest, and she said, 'I love your tiny eyes.' Little minx. But then at the ball, the night had got boring, particularly after some dickhead had brought boxes of those disgusting Indulge ice creams and they'd melted all over the floor and got on his tux and somehow in his hair. Lucy kept dancing away from him, or not looking at him, and he was surprised at how hurt he felt, and just stood there dumbly by the bar for most of the night, and drank steadily.

Niall made a wild, aggressive shot and the white ball bounced off the pool table. On the way to the bathrooms Sam saw Severin on his knees in the corridor and he seemed to be crying, and the room was getting dense with smoke. All around him were girls with their dresses slipping off their shoulders and their breasts exposed (in a way that seemed tired and matter-of-fact, not sexy). They tugged at his sleeve, screaming, 'Get us while we're hot. Get us while we're hot,' which confused him but also turned him on, until Roman explained (as if talking to a moron) that they were just singing along to a Lana Del Rey song.

In the next room he found Hadrien, who looked at him with those dead eyes. Suzanne's hand lay on his crotch casually and almost without intimacy, as if it were an armrest or a shoulder, and her eyes were all bloodshot and unable to focus. It was like she'd been crying or perhaps hit.

'Are you bored as well?' Hadrien asked him. Sam nodded. 'We should go back to college then, get started,' said Hadrien.

He heard Leeson exhale sharply behind him as a new kind of energy flew between them. The boys around the pool table looked for their jackets, smoothed down their hair, and got ready to leave.

CHAPTER 20

After the evening meal the Jerusalems gathered together by a fire under blankets in the cool night air. They were just up the hill from the commune. The little boys were helping the men split the wood, other children were carrying canoes and singing as they came back from the lake. The women had picked leaves for tea which they were brewing overnight for breakfast in the morning – mint, lemongrass and honeysuckle. In a circle by the fire, their fingers worked over the leaves, shearing them off into a bowl.

One of them offered Ben mint tea and he went over to sit with a man called Ted who was alone and staring into the fire. Ted was not that much older than Ben but looked different – rougher. His was a face that had been used, over which so much had passed, but some sort of pain had stopped there and decided to hang out for a while.

On the other side of Ted was an almost gothic-looking little group Ben had seen around the cafe, first as customers then as tentative, strange waiters. They were dressed in black – young, but with wily faces, nicotine-yellow fingers, and sharp little teeth like fangs.

Where do I fit in here? Ben wondered, but then thought, It doesn't matter – I just do.

Sylvan had told Ben that Ted had a drinking problem and had joined the Jerusalems when he was unable to pay his bill at a rehab facility. The group of young smokers were also recovering addicts who couldn't afford detox treatment. They had all met five years ago in the far west, on farmland leased to the Jerusalems.

The Jerusalems' creed was work and hospitality, explained Ted. 'They worked that land like they work the cafe – toil, toil, toil. It was fucking back-breaking. As for hospitality, you turn up in the middle of the night fucked up, half-crazed from driving all night, knuckles throbbing from belting your missus or the wall or some poor bloke – your brother, just as sad and lonesome as you at the bar. No questions asked. A bed. Food. Rest, routine, prayer. When they moved on, I moved with them.'

The shadows of the fire moved around his face as he went into a reverie about those days on the farm – the prayers before dawn, throughout the day and into the night, the Vespers and the Complines, the chanting and the bells, the massive skies, the huge flat soft land, the way you couldn't hide from God there, the way you couldn't hide from yourself. A million stars and you underneath them, having terrible dreams. You cried in the furthest fields, away from the others. You wept in your comfortless single bed. Suddenly you had so much feeling in you, so much flowing out, you thought you might break open. You were as soft as a newspaper that'd been left on the porch in the rain. One touch and you'd fall apart. Except that you were too tender for touches. So tender you couldn't even bear to be looked at. Way out in the back fields you raged and you whimpered; you yearned for an anaesthetic.

'Those things that hid it, the booze and drugs, the sport and the hours of TV you would watch all night, are gone. Remember, you're at the end of the line, unable to run anymore,' Ted said, not even really talking to Ben any longer, just talking to the fire. 'You're raw and fragile and you can't stop weeping. You don't feel like a man anymore.

'That's where God takes you, right there under the all-seeing sky, when you're at your lowest. He takes you and settles you. You etherise yourself on prayer and work and silence. In this there is finally peace. I guess that's what they talk about when they talk about healing. I guess it's also what they mean when they talk about religion. You can't do all of this on your own. You need something bigger than yourself.'

Ted poked the fire with a stick. 'But you can't stay there forever. The Jerusalems are like the gypsies; they move on, and on, and on. I followed some of them down here.'

'Are they going to move again soon?' asked Ben, suddenly afraid he would be abandoned just when he had found something.

'It's likely. I've heard whispers. Three years here. I reckon this is the longest they've stayed anywhere for a while. And with Sylvan set to graduate soon ...'

Ben nodded, and they settled into a companionable silence, but his mind was whirring and restless. He wanted to experience what Ted had experienced, that thing that was bigger than himself.

When Charlotte came to, getting up was a gradual and painful process. Her eyes were clagged shut with … stuff, and her mouth was also claggy with other … stuff. Gross. But before she could get up off the floor, there were a number of body parts competing for her immediate attention. First there was her head, pain bright and dull all at once behind her claggy eyes. Then a non-specific ache that ran down her legs like she had gone for a long run without warming down. But the worst was her stomach, an organ whose various pains were right now competing in some sort of hangover arms race: hunger was fighting nausea; anxiety was, of course, ever present. She hadn't eaten for – how long? – days now, after she'd taken one of Suzanne's Duromine pills, and she was starving. She could have chewed her arm off had her jaw not felt so exhausted and incapable, utterly incapable of movement. But while her stomach was begging for food, the nausea she felt made her certain her stomach would reject it. It would be a battle to the death, with the nausea winning as usual. It was her old friend. She knew it well, and she knew she would be sick. Yellow bile from a part of her body that she didn't really understand and those great gasps for air in between retching that gave her the hiccups and then the stuff that came out of her nose – yellow and toxic – and suddenly she would be sweating like she did in Bikram Yoga. Gross. Sweating and spewing and heaving and hiccupping – and sometimes this would all be going on not even in private, but in some boy's room with him on the bed, looking at her with disgust, looking sick himself while she said between dry heaves, 'So sorry, darling.'

She scraped the gunk from her eyelids with one long, bright fingernail so she could better see exactly where she was. A bedroom. But whose? It was still dark outside. Out the window she could see the glint of the spire of St Anton's Chapel, St Martine's tower, the college quadrangles, and in the distance the skyscrapers of the city shrouded in a soft violet-coloured pollution. She was in the tower – Hadrien's bedroom. Of course: last night with the Savages; it was coming back to her. She was naked under a scratchy Union Jack flag, and cold, and there was some blood and other mucousy stuff between her legs and, fucking Jesus, it hurt to stand up, and when she did she fell over again, sliding on a shiny textbook, then tripping on – what? A perspex dagger … that she had mounted …? Gross. She didn't like to think about it (the fragments she could remember). But she had some dim recollection of one of the boys saying to someone, 'Let's fuck her with the perspex dagger.' Weird. Or had it been a football trophy? They had wanted to fuck her with a football trophy but it had been too big and she had been worried the cheap gold finish would give her a rash.

Where was her dress? Where were the other women? She hadn't known them but they had appeared in the tower like creatures from a grotesque dream, with their hard faces and fingers, their cold, purple skin and their hollowness, their absence of either joy or desire – and their wrinkles! She remembered Leeson kicking the oldest one and saying, 'You're diseased. You're fucking diseased. Don't touch me.'

Where was everyone? Why was she here alone?

Could she wear the Union Jack back to her room? Cover up her bloody legs and the cuts on her belly (had she done that to herself earlier in the day? She couldn't remember) and those strange puncture marks on her arm? Gross. They looked like a bite. One of those monstrous boys had taken a bite out of her arm, or maybe it had been one of the women, unused to these boys; they had been like wild animals, panicked and afraid, trying to escape. All around the room was expensive film equipment and on the wall hung an enormous flat-screen TV – huge, perversely so; pornographic in its dimensions. So the women had fled without committing the theft that Hadrien had foreshadowed. 'I will kill you if you take anything. I will actually kill you,' he had told them calmly, while she had sat there rolling her eyes, saying, 'Don't be so bloody melodramatic, Hadrien.'

The room stunk of stale cigar smoke and spilt Dewar's. Under the mess Charlotte found a cat food bowl filled with champagne and flicked some onto her face. It woke her up a bit, and that was when she decided that once she walked out of Hadrien's room she would never think of this night again. She had been deviant before, really deviant, but never like this. She knew if she thought about it she would get depressed again and have those panic attacks and would not be able to go out (well, not much) and the worst possible thing would happen: she would become frigid and fat and no man would want her.

Hadrien's cat, a peevish and sleek Burmese called Janet, sprung out from behind a pot plant, opened her mouth and said, '*Hsssssssssssssssss.*'

Charlotte tried to swat then kick her but slipped again on the textbook (Luntz and Hambly, *Equity and Trusts*, the latest edition). The pain in all her body parts was singing too loudly to ignore now, and she was sick in exactly the way she'd imagined she would be, yellow crinkly stuff coming out of her nose and mouth, the struggle for breath and the way her stomach contracted and inflated as if to a beat. Then the sweat came pouring out and she was hot, cold, hot, cold to another, different beat. She was sick into the Union Jack. Oh God, Hadrien would kill her. Janet looked disgusted and disappeared behind the curtains. The flag now smelt of the chemicals her body had made – a sour, hot concentrate. Double gross. Where *was* everyone? More blood was coming out of her nose now and more blood was running down her legs. Maybe they *had* put the perspex dagger up her arse ...

She finally found her dress and struggled back into it. It was torn at the shoulder. She took Hadrien's academic gown from the wardrobe and slipped it over her ruined Prada (which she did not dare look down at, now that she had made the vow to herself – the vow of forgetting). It was still dark and rain was falling in a way that could only be described as biblical. She crossed the quadrangle, the gown saturated and her hair frizzing in the rain. Some lights were still blazing from bedroom windows, the study room and the Reading Room, but it was so quiet. She thought she saw Dr Bath walking back from the animals' pens but it could have just been a shadow lengthening then shrinking under the moon. It was only her and the rain and the end of this night. There was not even morning birdsong to tell her that this was a new day and the previous one didn't matter, it really didn't matter at all.

On the way back to her room she passed the cricket oval. There she saw four figures standing far away in the pre-dawn gloom. They appeared to be – what was it? – playing croquet? The scene looked almost otherworldly, composed like a painting – a tableau from a hundred years ago, in another country, not here. Young men with straight backs and excellent eyesight hitting a croquet ball carefully in the mist. The mallets made a satisfying *clonk* sound every time they hit the ball.

She walked towards these ghostly figures; it was as if she too were in a dream-like painting. They knew her, or seemed to know her. They were calling her name, waving her over.

A light drizzle. The warm sensation of blood running down her inner thigh. Its iron scent. Birdsong.

She got closer, but there was something not quite right. There was another figure with the men. It was motionless and lying on the grass. It was one of the older women from the tower, a prostitute, the one Leeson had kicked and called diseased. She appeared to be sleeping, the game going on around her. But the croquet hoops were set around her wrists like bracelets.

The ghostly men with the mallets were calling Charlotte's name louder now, telling her to come on, come join them for a game. *Clonk* went the ball. The woman did not move. *Clonk, clonk, clonk.*

CHAPTER 21

Students staggered out to the oval and ringed it like druids. A woman was spreadeagled on the wet grass. Her dark hair was spread out under her like a stain. Her wrists and ankles were fastened to the earth by croquet hoops. She was naked except for a torn dress, which was draped around her in folds. Through the mist it looked like she was carved from marble. A toppled garden statue of Venus de Milo, thought Dr Bath, his mind free associating before panic set in.

One of the overseas students – Grace, it looked like to Dr Bath – was standing over the woman, wearing pyjama bottoms, a sopping T-shirt bearing the legend *Too Cute* and hot-pink trainers. She made a sight almost as arresting as the woman pinned to the oval by croquet hoops. Grace's wet hair was plastered to the sides of her face. Her mouth was hanging open, with a tremendous sound coming out of it. Her screams, sounding at dawn like an oddly inverted call to prayer, had brought the St Antonians from their beds, out of the daisy-chains and tangles of each other's arms, up from the floors of bathrooms where they'd lain retching, shaking and spent.

Many students were still in tuxedos or evening dresses. Some of the girls were wearing men's shirts, their coltish bare legs poking out beneath the tails. Others had hastily dressed, freshly arrived from sleep, shivering in T-shirts on back to front, sarongs covering legs, a few in ratty dressing gowns and shameful nightwear: stained T-shirts, girls in their father's old business shirts or a beloved older brother's pyjama bottoms – nothing on top – or a former lover's boxer shorts that still smelt of his skin.

Grace's screaming did not stir the woman on the oval. Her head lay cocked to the side, her open mouth kissing the wet grass. A mallet and ball stood between Grace and the body, like an invitation to play. The woman was, said a panting medical student leaning over the body, still breathing but concussed.

Dr Bath had been the first member of staff to attend the scene. He had emerged from behind the football stand in bare feet and his nightshirt, white like a large baby's christening dress, billowing behind him. Yet although he was the first staff member there, he felt like someone always destined to hear news too late, to be too slow to react, to always be the last to know, to miss the crucial things like when the heart beats and when it stops. He was in charge for the night while the Master rolled with his beautiful wife in the Royal Family bed and laughed and muted the sound on the wall-mounted TV and drank champagne from the hollow of her neck. And forgot. Forgot all about the students.

As Dr Bath ran out to the oval his gown became soaked and clung to his body like a negligee, and his naked feet sank into the mud. Could the students read the fear on his face? What he had seen from his window in the weak dawn light had been his own distortion: the animals had come to harm! He had thought the students ringing the oval had torches and knives. Their ball gowns were the robes of some strange priestly cult. These unknowable creatures, the students with their strange habits, their blood lust, their pack mentality, had finally found themselves on the dark side of the moon. The girl standing in the middle of the oval with her arms above her head, her slight build, her electric-pink shoes, had been transformed into a voodoo princess, elected to perform sacrificial rites. The body on the ground, pale and wounded, ready to be set on and torn apart by the robed mob, had looked to Dr Bath like a peacock, skinned and plucked, or a lamb, shorn and battered, or a shaved and humiliated dog.

And so he had torn out onto the oval, right into its centre, and bent to free the animal from its restraints, and when he saw it was not an animal but a woman ('Oh please, don't let it be one of our students!' he begged shamefully, silently), he shrank back, and that was when Grace started screaming again and some flag was planted, some spell was broken and people dug into their suit pockets for their mobile phones and the police were called. And later there were sirens and police tape and five milligrams of Valium for Grace, and one of the students – was it Julian? – led Dr Bath gently by the arm away from the oval, and he sat in a room – was it Giles's? – with some crouching students as they gave him whisky and tried to warm him up. One of the boys gave him a jacket that was exquisitely soft, and the student murmured, 'Calvin Klein', and Dr Bath looked at him and said, 'Thank you, Calvin', and he felt like he was in another land – he was Gulliver and they were Lilliputians and he knew nothing of what was going on around him. He was in a foreign land, you see. He was very, very far from home.

Maybe it was being so close to the Jerusalems, or the wine going to his head, or Ted's story, or the singing or the moonlight, but for once Ben didn't want to be outside some experience observing. He wanted to be in it and made of it.

He found Sylvan and grabbed his arm. 'Baptise me,' he whispered.

'What?'

'I want to be baptised – tonight. I want to join.'

'It doesn't work like that. You have to – I don't know – study, meet with a priest. There are certificates you have to get. You need to be sponsored. Paperwork. You actually need to know the Bible, and it's early days for you in that respect,' said Sylvan, sounding almost irritated. 'In any case, I have no power to make you a Jerusalem.'

Ben shrank back in the dark, crestfallen at this sudden turn from the divine to the mundane. *Paperwork? Sponsorship?*

'What about going where the Spirit moves you – that sort of thing?' he muttered angrily. Maybe his parents were right: perhaps religion *was* ridiculous, a crutch for those too weak to stand on their own. Why did he want to drag behind him all that history and hate, that elaborately crafted jewellery box (but open it and it's empty). The little gaggles of Jerusalems – Ted and the smokers, the mothers, the workshop men – suddenly seemed to recede from him. The trees moved as one in the darkening forest, and all matter in the universe seemed connected. The moon was yellow. The camp dogs groaned and rolled like cogs in their sleep.

Despite what his parents had told him, Ben had a longing for the sacred. He wanted to feel full up with something, heavier somehow, and people could only give you so much.

To have been baptised when he felt such a yearning for a sacrament, to receive God when he felt so broken open and porous – well, it would have felt right. He would have been – in the proper sense of the word – revived.

More of the children were coming in from the lake, hair wet and flat like caps on their heads, stirring the supine dogs with sticks. The sweet smell of treacly tea drifted over from the fire.

'There's still another boat out there,' one child said, nestled against Sylvan's leg. 'They say they are going to stay out there all night. They say they are looking for treasure.'

The thin, long tail of the Jerusalem's song could be heard travelling over tree tops. The women by the fire picked it up casually as they might their sewing needles and began singing in rounds.

Mother, I adore you,
I lay my life before you,
How I love you.
Spirit, I adore you,
I lay my life before you,
How I love you.

Suddenly Sylvan seized his hand.

'What are you doing?' asked Ben, pissed off, but not pulling away.

'Come with me,' said Sylvan, his eyes bright, his cheeks daubed with colour.

This is very odd, thought Ben, as he and Sylvan walked hand in hand into the forest. Sylvan's grip was light but deliberate. This was no accidental brushing of his hand, this was proper hand-holding. Ben had never held hands with another man before, and although Sylvan's were very soft, they were also large and it felt weird.

But still Ben didn't pull away.

Katie was trailing behind them, singing a little – fading in and out like a badly tuned radio.

They reached the lake, and at the water's edge Sylvan gripped Katie's hand with his spare hand as the three of them stood staring out into the teeming dark. It felt as if they were teetering on the edge of a precipice, as if they were opening themselves up to something big and powerful that lay just beyond their sight line, something that would bring them to their knees. But what?

The children floated on their craft, far away across the water. Some of them lay dozing on the pontoon, the moonlight catching their silver bodies, making them appear like freshly caught fish.

'I will baptise you now,' said Sylvan.

'But you're not qualified,' said Ben.

'Forget that. Forget what I said – this feels as it should be. The moment feels ... I don't know ... holy.'

The three of them left their shoes on the bank but kept their clothes on. They walked into the water up to their waists. Katie and Sylvan were either side of Ben, tipping him over gently and supporting his torso. *Whoosh, whoosh*, down he went into the cool, still water, submerged then brought up again.

He lay on the surface of the lake, their hands under him. Clouds blew across the moon.

'I baptise you in the name of the Father, the Son and the Holy Spirit.'

Down Ben went again into the mysterious deep. He felt the tickle of a fish against his trouser cuffs, currents moved across him like cold shocks and he gasped; his clothes filled with water and pulled him down.

They were holding him. They would always be holding him. He would always feel held.

Sylvan's hand was cupped and pouring water over Ben's head. He was smoothing Ben's brow, he was saying, 'Whatever you do to the least of my brothers ...'

Ah – that was the great, grounding line he needed to hear. He loved Sylvan, the way he and the other Jerusalems walked the line between the worldly and the divine, between the mud and the clouds and the stars.

He went down again into the water, for longer this time. He came up gasping with deep, sweet hurt in the night air.

Had he really been crying all this time? He must have been. How else could his body process the sacred? How else could it cope with such a release of tenderness?

On the bank the three of them stood together, cold but not uncomfortable in their wet clothes. The children across the water kept singing, another old song in rounds.

Scotland's burning! Scotland's burning!
Look out! Look out!
Fire! Fire!
Fire! Fire!
Pour on water! Pour on water!

Would the children ever get sick of it? Would they ever come in? Ben imagined them out here forever, the Jerusalem children – never getting older, never sad, always singing or resting on the pontoon or floating around the lake like elderly, cranky fishermen, drifting, drifting, not needing their parents, not needing anyone, their hair grown long and tangled, wild like the river reeds.

Katie walked on ahead, and Ben slowed and asked Sylvan if he could make a confession.

Once again, Sylvan said it wasn't official, then laughed and said, 'Well, darn that! Once you've broken one rule I guess you can break them all. Go ahead – speak if you want to speak from your heart.'

'It may take a while,' said Ben, suddenly joyful that there was this mechanism of confession, that atonement could be formalised and spiritualised and recognised all at once.

'Well let's lie down together while you make it. You can direct it up to the sky and the stars and the moon.'

They walked for a bit and lay down in a place near the commune where the owls looked on and the bats talked behind their wings.

It was time, yes. But where to start?

'It was a hot day up in the mountains and we had won the cricket season. There's this one guy, Hadrien, who's … I don't know – strange, deviant. He organised a surprise for us. He always organised a surprise, but instead of a girl or girls, it was a boy this time. His name was Alfred …'

CHAPTER 22

Lucy went back to her room, in shock after what she had seen on the oval. She sat before the mirror, winter sun coming in, warm and full even though the curtains were shut. Mottled patterns of light, refracted through the curtains, skipped along the floor. Someone was playing Arcade Fire in the Billiards Room. She picked up some scissors and started chopping off large chunks of hair, and these too went skipping along the floor, tumbling away, liberated from her awful head.

She would never forget what she had seen: Toby on the oval – mouth hanging open, looking like he was about to be sick, but still, somehow, looking cool. Clinging to him was Octavia, and Lucy took her eyes off the injured woman on the ground every second heartbeat to stare at them. Suddenly her whole body became nothing but a vessel for hot, fierce rage. 'See you at Isolodes Towers.' Yeah, right.

Octavia had buried her face in his chest and he had kissed the top of her head and held the back of her neck in a way that was more tender and intimate than any kiss. He had not looked at Lucy even once! Not even to see if she was all right. Who was comforting *her*? It was meant to be him!

She kept cutting away at her hair until she realised with horror what she was doing and how horribly different she looked. Yet there was some small consolation in this. If she looked different it followed that things would be different.

It was just after breakfast when Levi got home (*home* home, not college home), right after he had seen the woman trapped by croquet hoops on the cricket oval, not quite dead. Hadrien, Leeson and Severin. The Savages, it had to be them.

He had sprinted from the oval with all the gaping, brainless debutantes and their gormless dates and gone back to his room. He'd moved around quickly, packing without folding his clothes, throwing his books into garbage bags. He'd ripped the silly posters from the walls and put them in the bin. He'd thrown out the makeup and the ugly clothes he sometimes wore – the Blundstone and R.M. Williams boots, the chambray shirts, the rugby jumpers, the tracksuit pants, the football socks and the cricket stuff – *especially* the cricket stuff. *Brideshead* fucking *Revisited*. With self-disgust that suddenly flooded every cell, he couldn't believe what he had become. Was it only last week he wore his *cream cricket jumper* out in public? His stuff was his identity and he'd adapted to this middle-aged grazier look without a second thought.

But it wasn't just that. He had been so quiet and complicit in the bunkroom; not hitting Alfred, but holding him down while Ping tied him up. *He had held someone down.* He had never held anyone down in his life. Yet there he'd been, leaping to his feet – they didn't even have to ask him! – using strange muscles he'd never even flexed before to overpower this young Asian guy.

Before leaving college he'd hesitated but then, deciding it was the right thing to do, he'd written notes to Julian and Toby and slipped them under their doors – saying sorry, and don't take it personally, but perhaps it would be better if they weren't in contact for a while. He'd gone to the Facebook app on his phone, unfriended them and everyone else from St Anton's, then decided to deactivate his account entirely. He'd also, with a pang, deactivated his Instagram account, *memento mori*, filled with hundreds of pictures of them all together.

Looking around his room, Levi had seen there was very little he needed to take with him – just a framed poem he had written in first year that had won him the Walter Hawke Memorial Prize ('*Grandfather wore numbers on his hand/ Inscriptions from an evil land*'). He had walked off down Troutman Street, turned a corner, turned another corner and turned a key and there he was, in that familiar terrace, which had seen a dinner party the previous night. There were still-wet wine bottles, Rizla papers and an open tobacco pouch, bits of risotto stuck to the bottom of a pan, dishes in the sink.

His lovely bohemian parents were no doubt still in bed staving off mild hangovers, and would stay in bed until he knocked on their door with conciliatory coffees and said, 'I'm sorry. Promise I'll change. Can I please come home?'

CHAPTER 23

Two days after the ball, the police moved in. Unlike the Alfred incident, the Master found it impossible to conceal the sexual assault of a woman on the cricket oval.

'I wash my hands of you,' he told Hadrien through gritted teeth as he passed him on the way to an evening lecture on the future of the monarchy, to be given by a visiting professor.

Hadrien, dressed in what looked like a new charcoal suit with a natty red tie and poppy in the buttonhole, looked back at him blankly. 'I don't know what you're talking about.'

'Yes you do, you little freak,' the Master muttered. 'No protection, not from me, not anymore.'

'Just out of interest, are you for or against the monarchy?' Hadrien asked. But the Master had already strode away, his black gown flying behind him like a cape.

The university colleges thrived on gossip at the best of times, but now the rumour mill went into overdrive. Around College Crescent Chinese whispers travelled swiftly from the dining rooms to the libraries, from the dance floors to the lecture halls. Hadrien had brought prostitutes into the college; Hadrien had organised a sort of *Eyes Wide Shut* S&M orgy on the oval the night of the ball; Hadrien had watched while

Leeson and Severin had sex with Charlotte, who had passed out; some of the animals had been involved; there had been no doubt to anyone who was there that night that Hadrien was *bisexual*.

All this gossip was vulgar, thought the Master. The children should be allowed to develop their sexuality in private, he argued to his wife.

Furious, but also frightened, she was having none of it: 'While you moon around the place talking about movies and models and Cate Blanchett, the students are tearing the college down! That thing with Alfred, that woman found injured on the oval are not problems because they might hold up filming or be leaked to the media – *they are problems in and of themselves*!'

She was pushing for them both to move to a hotel, she was checking deals on Wotif.com, she was angry. 'The whole goddamn circus tent is going to collapse on us, Locke.'

He was safe inside the stone walls of the college, yet the Master felt besieged. He worried about how he could leave the college grounds without being pelted with eggs. Ratty feminists and hysterical student politicians were threatening him. On his phone were messages left by at least a dozen reporters. And now the police! How had he lost control so quickly? he wondered. He got his assistant to schedule another meeting with the PR people, this being the only way he could think of to get it back.

Initially the police cast their net wide and visited every college to question the students about the night of the balls. Did they know the woman? Did they have any idea how she had happened to get there? Had they heard any rumours about who might have placed the croquet hoops around her wrists and ankles? No, no, no.

The investigation was led by Detective Diane Tarrant. She and her colleagues, Detectives Tony Lowell and Paul Sanderson, found it deeply unpleasant. The colleges all had a smell about them: subterranean, cold. The buildings were grand, designed to intimidate; so were those in charge. Sitting with all these men in their dark studies (what strange titles they gave themselves, like 'Master'), the officers were unsettled by the lack of concern displayed for the woman who had been found on the oval. ('She's not one of ours,' said a dark-eyed Jesuit, the Master of St Sebastian's, speaking from the gloom like an El Greco half come to life.) They chafed at the defensive way these masters spoke of their students – as if they needed to be protected from themselves.

The students too had a disturbing air about them. They were confident, haughty even. The girls had long shiny hair and private-school accents. They were very attractive and this was accentuated by the fact that they were only half aware of it. By the time they really knew, their beauty would be gone.

The boys were also at some sort of peak – lustrous hair, hulking shoulders, thigh muscles that bulged beneath football shorts, their French accents probably well lubricated from summers spent in Aix-en-Provence, holding forth on why *Ulysses* is culturally important. They looked the police straight in the eye and kept their curtains and windows open. They acted as if they had nothing to hide.

Yet there was something deeply wrong with the picture, Tarrant told her colleagues, puzzled. There was an *absence* of something. Maybe it was tenderness. St Anton's oval was surely a beacon for the curious and distressed – a place for students to stand huddled, exclaiming or even crying over the crime, perhaps even launching a Facebook page for the victim. Instead they withdrew into their hangovers and their rooms.

The police overheard conversations, on the oval and in the dining rooms, about the injured woman.

'What a skank! A total pro.'

'Yeah – gross, she looked totally gross. I was so totally grossed out. I'm going to apply to get Special Consid.'

'Yeah, me too. Good idea!'

Did they not care?

Whatever it was, it was collective. When Detective Lowell later requested a transfer (declined) to Operation Saurus, surveying terror cells, he observed to Sanderson and Tarrant that the terrorists and jihadists seemed like a less Machiavellian and disturbed group than the students.

'These places give me the creeps,' said Sanderson. But the investigating team moved in to St Anton's anyway, placing a sign on the side of the cricket oval appealing for witnesses and setting up an office in the Reading Room after the Master, on the advice of his PR team, reluctantly agreed to allow them to use the space.

Toby ran into Levi as he was leaving his Criminal Law and Procedure lecture.

'Hey!' he said, grabbing Levi roughly by the arm. 'What's going on? Why have you left college? And you've changed your phone number!'

Levi, wearing all black and a complicated scarf that looked like a hospital bandage, tried to wrench his arm away.

Toby tried the handle of a nearby empty seminar room, and pushed Levi in there.

'Don't look so frightened, for fuck's sake – I'm not going to hurt you,' said Toby. 'I just want to know why you've gone. I mean, first Ben, and now you ...'

'I don't feel safe at St Anton's,' said Levi. 'I haven't for a while.'

'What are you talking about? It's great there. College is great.'

'No, it's not great. It's awful – and getting worse. I don't know – I just had a feeling, building up since that Alfred thing, that something bad, something really bad was going to happen to us. And you know what? It's happening now. Mum says there's a police investigation going on – top cops on it and all that stuff. They're going to find out.'

'Find out what?'

'Find out everything. You should go too – now, before it's too late ...'

'But I have nowhere to go,' said Toby.

Levi hesitated, looked like he was about to say something, then changed his mind, reached for the door handle and quickly walked away.

That night, unable to sleep, Toby rang Julian, waking him to recycle and recirculate rumours he'd heard about the police:

that they were part of a bigger conspiracy to shut down the colleges; that there would be a massive drug raid ('Octavia is sure she overheard them say "Dog Squad" when she passed them in the cloister on the way to the ATM the other day'); that the Master was being investigated for fraud.

'They couldn't know about Alfred, surely,' said Toby. Yet for him, the fact that the police were on campus was a constant reminder of the crime that had so far gone unpunished. 'We need to find out if they know. Maybe I could seduce her, find out? She'd take me, I reckon.'

'Who? Who are you talking about now?' asked Julian, annoyed.

'The female cop. Tarrant.'

'Stop it, Toby, you're delusional. She's, like, forty.'

'She's a hot forty.'

'No.'

'No – you don't think she's hot?'

'No – I don't think you should go anywhere near her. She's all right, but I think we should keep away from the police,' said Julian. He stifled a yawn. 'It's four in the morning and you've woken me for *this*?'

'I'll go now. You should – I don't know – get some sleep or something. What are you still doing up?'

'You woke me up.'

A few hours later Toby was at Julian's door, his hair sticking out at wild angles.

'C'mon, dude, we gotta talk to them, see what they know.'

Julian, too tired to argue, shrugged and followed Toby down the cloister.

There were no doughnuts in the Reading Room, but there was a freshly brewed pot of tea and an open window so the air did not become too close with three officers working in such a confined space. The officers greeted Toby and Julian crisply. They all seemed to be around the same age and to be sharing authority over the investigation. Toby guessed this was modern policing, and reflected that it didn't conform to the usual stereotypes (binary oppositions, really) played out in all the movies and TV shows – junior cop/senior cop, good cop/bad cop, black cop/white cop, man cop/woman cop.

The police had a map of the university grounds on the wall and manila files were spread before them. The radio, on low, was tuned to intelligent talkback.

Suddenly Toby didn't feel so confident anymore. It wasn't just that these people were the police, but they were also, in every sense of the word, grown-ups. The very fact of it threw him off balance from the get-go. They seemed shrewd and observant, mature in a way that all the other adults in his life weren't – the academics with their funny old clothes and alcoholic fumblings, his distracted parents, even the Master himself, with the games he played, the way he bent the rules for the students and did it with a knowing wink.

The police were a different type of adult and suddenly he didn't feel so sure around them. What games would *they* play?

'How's it all going? I mean, with the investigation?' asked Toby politely, suddenly self-conscious and patting down his hair. 'We – my friend Julian and I – are law students, so we thought we'd drop in and see if we could help. Maybe sort through documents or transcribe witness statements.'

The three officers laughed, although not unkindly.

'That won't be necessary, thanks,' said Sanderson.

'What we want from you guys is information,' said Tarrant. 'That's why we're here. This space is cramped but it's important to be on site. People with information find it less intimidating to drop in here than go to a police station.'

'I'd agree with that,' said Julian.

As the small talk was unspooling Toby became aware that the other two police officers were watching him and Julian closely. They probably saw two casually dressed young men with a look on their faces that said: We're here for a reason and we're scared. We are not as casual as our clothes.

'Well, why don't you both sit down, have some tea?' said Tarrant. 'It would be great to have a chat about your experience of college.'

'Yes,' said Lowell. 'We're quite curious about the parties you guys have here. I mean, I've had a lot of nights out in my time,' he went on, chuckling, 'but you guys really seem to know how to party ...'

'Love to – really would – we'll get back to you with a time,' said Julian, who had grabbed Toby by the sleeve and was edging out of the room. 'We're going to be late for class.'

CHAPTER 24

The Master tried to look grave and concerned as the police outlined their suspicions about some of his students. He wasn't sure if he had his features arranged impassively enough, or if they instead reflected his interior state – a grimace or, even worse, panic.

'As well as the students at the party in the tower room there may have been several sex workers present. We need to establish which students were in the tower and who the sex workers were, which agency they came from, and whether they've all been accounted for following the party,' said Detective Lowell, his shadow angling across the Master's desk. The police had been offered neither coffee nor chairs when they arrived at the Master's office to talk about the investigation.

'We also need to establish whether the sex that occurred at the party was consensual,' said Detective Tarrant.

'Do you know of a group called the Firestarters?' Detective Lowell asked the Master.

'Not personally,' replied the Master, now trying to sound jovial. 'Is that a lesbian group? You'd be better off speaking to St Jerome's, in that case. We don't really go in for that sort of thing here.' And the Master laughed, but the police didn't seem to get the joke.

'Actually, it does have its genesis in the university's women's groups,' said Lowell. 'But they've become a bit more radical than the usual campus group. They're publishing all sorts of allegations about sexual harassment and rape at the colleges. A student of yours is involved – Lucy Mason.'

Sanderson leafed through a folder and pulled out a photo of Lucy. She was a Vermeer maiden in a cocktail dress, with calm, pretty features and long, straight, blonde hair. It looked like a party picture they had lifted from Facebook, thought the Master. He would have to tell the students to adjust the privacy settings on their accounts.

'I don't believe it,' he told Sanderson. 'Lucy's from a good family – an old family.'

Sanderson sighed and muttered that every family was old. 'We're keeping an eye on the group; they have the potential to become quite inflammatory. But we need to make a thorough investigation of their claims, which I'm sure you are aware extend beyond the sexual assault case and cover other matters – including some animal-cruelty allegations. It's early days.'

The Master gave a sharp intake of breath but tried to look calm. He would have to ring his lawyers and the PR firm (again! The college was becoming their best client) after the police had gone.

There was silence and some long, long minutes during which the dust falling through the air in the study was lit by the heavy afternoon sunlight, and looked so much like phosphorescence that the Master began to feel as if they were all underwater and the oxygen was running out and they were moving slowly through the water and then not moving at all.

Phosphorescence glittered and fell.

Finally he replied, 'Yes, of course. Well, the students are over eighteen, and if they choose to engage the services of prostitutes, that's their business. It wasn't illegal the last time I checked. I mean, we are talking about boys who are at their sexual peak. Has anyone even made an allegation of rape?'

'The woman found on the oval is still not talking.'

'Well, until she does, why worry about it? She's made a full recovery, hasn't she? She'd just had too much to drink or too many drugs, hadn't she? There's this new thing on the market – what's it called? Got a funny name. All the kids are talking about it …' He trailed off, before murmuring, 'It's a shame that it was Grace who had to find her. She's still very upset.'

'So what the Firestarters have said—' Tarrant began.

'It's common after incidents like this for these ragtag feminist groups to spring up and act all outraged,' the Master interrupted. 'I don't know if you're on Twitter, but some of the worst abuse is there. I'm being cyber-bullied myself! Usually their allegations are baseless. You need to solve the crime at hand, not some other crime that you imagine might have occurred – a crime that hasn't even been reported. The Firestarters are clearly troublemakers. I may ask the college lawyers to consider making a complaint of defamation.'

'Something else, Master,' said Sanderson, the word 'Master' sounding heavy on his tongue. 'When we've talked to your students about the woman on the oval, many have said, "Just like Alfred" but have then refused to elaborate or even to tell us who this Alfred person is.'

'No – no students here called Alfred.'

The police looked at each other in a way that made the Master nervous (so many unanswered questions!) before pulling out search warrants for the college's CCTV footage and its computer files on each of the students. The air was thick, then there was no air at all.

'This is ridiculous!' the Master said peevishly. 'Why don't you just go back on Facebook to get what you need? Check their status updates. They're all on it. You're not going through my computer files – not that I have anything to hide. But there's sensitive stuff in there about a movie that's going to be made here – with Cate Blanchett. And it's really none of your business, and – and we have lawyers, and my wife works in the media – wait until she hears about this!'

But the oxygen in the room had run out and it seemed the police didn't care. Soon enough they would begin to seize things from the students – laptops, modems, cameras, SIM cards, memory sticks and mobile phones. They obviously knew what they were looking for … things from the night of the ball. And these students – with their expensive technology and their narcissism and their intense desire to communicate all the time and to tag and be tagged and to 'like' and be 'liked' and to be filmed and to record *everything* – would load the police up with all the information they would need.

After going through the CCTV footage, the police had over a hundred stills of the human traffic down the college's main cloister – all taken between 2 and 6 am on the night of the St Anton's Ball. The police turned on a dictaphone and asked the Master to read out the number of each photograph, and identify the people in it.

Even though the quality of the stills was bad, the Master recognised most of the people captured in them and was able to enunciate their names clearly onto the tape.

First up was Dr Bath, wearing a bathrobe and standing outside Toby's room. He was just standing there doing nothing – for almost twenty minutes, according to the footage.

'He's a bit odd,' explained the Master clearly into the microphone. 'Dr Bath, one of the tutors. Lives at college. Obsessed with World War II and the animals – and Toby, by the looks of it.'

Then there was Julian. What a tosser! He was ridiculously posh, quite stupid – and would no doubt end up in some banking job earning obscene amounts of money, just like his father. At 4 am, still dressed in his tuxedo, he was knocking on Charlotte's door. Then he slumped against it before banging his head repeatedly against the wood. 'Looks like he thought he might get lucky with her,' the Master said by way of commentary, 'but failed. It happens to the best of us.'

The next set of prints featured Charlotte with Leeson on one side of her and Severin on the other. Their arms were linked and they appeared to be skipping down the cloister – heads thrown back, knees up high, locked into one another. They seemed to be very drunk and were heading in the direction of the tower. Hadrien followed at a distance. Behind him were three women the Master didn't recognise. They were wearing heavy fur coats.

'Charlotte, Severin, Leeson, Hadrien … and I don't know the others,' he said. 'But you can't get through the gates unless you come in with someone from the college, so I'd say those women would have been with Hadrien.'

Roman and Ping then followed them down the cloister. 'They're wearing women's clothing,' Tarrant observed. There was a blur of feather boa and a flash of stockinged legs, strangely muscular, under a stretched silk slip.

'That's what can happen after a ball,' explained the Master. 'They're all charged up – they've had their party fuel. They get changed when they come home and go up to Hadrien's tower for another turn. I've never had any problems with the parties before. I stay out of it. As you know, I wasn't even at the college on the evening of the ball. I – well, my wife and I – always spend the evening of the ball at the Park Hyatt. Do you need proof? Do you want to see my credit card statements?'

An odd assortment of photos followed. Ben, whom the Master hadn't seen around the college for quite some time, walked along with a young man wearing … were they robes? 'Ben is a very well-respected student around the college. Plays all the sports, studies Law – look how handsome he is! The girls adore him. Family's very wealthy. Although I'm not sure who that is he's with. Maybe they've been to a costume party.'

Then there was a range of stills showing packs of students coming back from the ball – paired up or unpaired, depending on how the night had served them. Some were filmed vomiting violently into the rosebushes that lined the seniors' quadrangle, others drifted over to the animals asleep in their pens.

There were girls in evening gowns with bodices torn, straps ripped, hems muddied; their beehive hairdos had collapsed, and makeup drizzled down their faces like the ink on a letter left out in the rain. They were mostly barefoot, their painful shoes long since discarded or lost. The boys lurched around the cloisters drunk, their clothes also ripped but their shoes still on. It was their bowties that were missing – probably left in suit jacket pockets, draped over the backs of chairs at the Town Hall, or trampled on the dance floor at Isolodes Towers. Back they all came, looking like creatures who had survived some terrible natural disaster with their clothes barely intact.

Then there were pictures of Lucy in the cloister. 'Lucy Mason. The one who's creating all this trouble with the feminist group. She has an agenda. A gender ... get it?'

In the CCTV footage Lucy sat at Toby's door for an hour, her face in her hands, arriving just after Dr Bath left.

'Toby gets a lot of traffic,' murmured the Master. 'He's quite popular, and his twin brothers are in that band – they're touring in America right now. They have that song – you know the one: N*ah, nah, nah-nah* ...'

Then, around 5 am, the three women in fur coats walked back down the cloister from Hadrien's room. Leeson and Severin followed.

'Are you sure you don't know who those women are?' asked Lowell.

'No, they're not familiar. They don't look like college girls. They look older.'

'Could they be sex workers?'

'That's possible. Look, I really don't know – I've never actually met a prostitute, would you believe it?'

The last shot, with a time of 6 am, the Master could have framed. Even though it was grainy, it was stunning: Charlotte, like Aphrodite, drifting along the cloister, her hair in waves down her bare back, her body wrapped in what looked like an academic gown, her eyes enormous and expressive.

When Charlotte failed to meet the police for the confidential chat they'd organised in the Reading Room, they knocked on her door.

Lowell was aggrieved, saying they shouldn't be making house calls, especially to princesses, but Tarrant told him to hold back, to go gently. And so gently they went, starting with a gentle knock on the door and a gentle look on their faces – until they registered the mess. The girl didn't seem to have bathed or dressed for days. And the room ... it was spacious, one of the largest they'd seen at the colleges – yet it was packed with rubbish and clutter.

In the bin were bloody tampons, and across the floor were puddles of used underwear, rogue bobby pins stuck into the carpet, and wax strips, having performed their duty, were tossed on the ground and stuck to all the other discarded bits of her – bangles, scarves, exaggerated rings in garish colours, silk ribbons, empty bottles of spray tan, stockings that still smelt of Chanel No 5, lip gloss and nail vanish missing their lids and ground into the carpet.

Tarrant had never seen so many clothes. Great colourful swathes of them covered every surface and were piled up on each other so that the stacks resembled tottering, soft pyramids. Under the bed were bits of uneaten food: noodles congealing in a pot, chip packets, and bags of childish sweets pressed between her bed and the wall – jelly babies, Snakes Alive, chocolate bullets, Redskins. Some brightly coloured sticks of candy, indented with the marks her molars had made, lay on the carpet. The police shuffled uncomfortably – there was nowhere for them to stand, let alone sit in this room – and Tarrant had to fight the urge to open some windows.

The girl herself was at first nothing more than a shape among all this stuff – a blonde under blankets. She turned to them with a face that was probably pretty under normal circumstances but now was creased from the bed and looked like a poached egg – pale and runny, her features seeming as if they were about to slide down her head. Tarrant was alarmed at the black marks round her eyes until she realised the girl had not been hit, it was just makeup – kohl that she hadn't bothered to wipe off.

'It's an easy mistake to make,' Charlotte said when Tarrant remarked on it, 'but that's the look these days anyway – the bashed look.' She laughed and turned her enormous eyes on Lowell and Sanderson. 'I'd call the cops, except you're already here.'

Tarrant was thrown not only by the smells and the mess, but by the fact that even in this state the girl was so confident – was flirting with the men like it was her default setting.

But they said nothing and did not flirt back.

'Maybe, Miss Barnsley, we could chat in the Reading Room; it might be more comfortable,' said Lowell.

'I have nothing to say,' said Charlotte defiantly, sitting up in bed. 'I saw that girl on the oval, just like a hundred other kids that turned up, but I didn't know her. God, I was blasted – like, totally blotto. Anyway, now's not a good time, if you know what I mean.'

Tarrant did know what she meant. But that didn't matter – Charlotte rolled over to face the wall and all the lolly packets squished there.

Lowell said, 'Well it's not really the oval that we've come to talk to you about. It's the party you went to before, in the room in the tower, with the boys who call themselves the Savages.'

Charlotte shrugged.

'We know you were at that party and we think the injured woman might have been there too,' said Lowell.

'What did she tell you?'

'She's not saying much. As you probably know, someone was filming what happened that night in the tower. We have a lot of footage of you.'

'Did you see it on YouTube or download it from the internet?' Charlotte asked.

Tarrant cleared her throat, feeling the claustrophobia of the room keenly. She was sick of the flirting and the weird silences, the mess, the way the girl wouldn't face them, after they had seen so much more than her face. She spoke sharply. 'We'll be in the Reading Room. Get up and shower and we'll see you there in fifteen minutes.'

'Evidence is an interesting concept,' Dr Heath said to Toby as they walked out of a lecture theatre into the Law School quadrangle, lined with the skeletons of leafless winter trees. 'Is it truth? You see, we have a legal system that says if you provide evidence of a crime being committed and the evidence is tested under cross-examination in the witness box with skilled barristers – duelling, if you like, with the evidence – and then someone decides after the duel, after the evidence has been supported or discounted, or a witness cracks or doesn't crack, that the evidence wins, does that make it the truth? Or is it the best spinner of certain facts who wins? If it's the latter, it's really not about evidence at all, it's about presentation. It's about story. It's about narrative – getting bits and pieces and constructing a story out of them. Whoever tells the best story wins.'

Toby nodded and re-knotted his scarf, trying not to look anxious.

'Have you done discovery?' Dr Heath asked. 'Don't worry – you will should you decide to embark on a career in the law. You sit in a horrible little room with other clerks and lists and lists and lists of things, and you catalogue them. Documents, files, tapes, images, reports: evidence. But what is it really? Bits of things, fragments of the past, snatches of conversation, unhinged from context, free of fixed meaning, which in skilful hands and twisted the right way could be affixed to anything – could mean anything. Evidence can hang you or help you, depending on your skill in delivering it.'

Toby wondered what evidence the police had of what happened that night to Alfred. Had the cricketers filmed it? Yes, they had – and they had disguised their faces with hoods, and someone was wearing Toby's scarf, and his alibi, Dr Bath, was often so vague that if you asked him his own name he'd stammer the wrong words and look away.

Toby said goodbye to Dr Heath and started jogging across the car park towards Levi's room to talk about his alibi, until he remembered Levi had gone. Prick. Coward. He and Ben both. Hadrien was right: they were both weak and worthless.

He couldn't help being struck by the dreadful irony. He was the one who hadn't been involved, who had tried to rescue Alfred, yet here he was: the one who stuck around and took the punishment for everyone else.

Dr Bath walked across the darkened quadrangle. He felt almost pulled to the pens, to check that the animals were okay. He wanted comfort, that was it most of all. The objects in his room – his electric kettle, his hot-water bottle, all his books, his wireless, his notes – they were comforters in their way, but they weren't enough. Only hours earlier he had locked the animals away but he wanted to be near them again.

Why was he being so stealthy? Why did he feel so guilty? There was something in him that felt furtive. As if he should be self-contained, as if a hot-water bottle and a volume of Auden's poetry should be enough. They weren't. So to the pens he went, and they smelt dense, alive and seething.

He carried a torch, which he flashed around in a random way. How they slept! So different from us. The peacock, his feathers away for the night, standing up, but looking so reduced, so not himself. Then the sheep, really no different from when they were awake – so hard to tell if their eyes were even closed. And the dogs, lying on their sides and snorting occasionally, something in the way they shook suggesting that they too had vivid dreams. He crept past all the animals in various attitudes of repose, until he came to Innocence, the lamb.

Gently he woke her, throwing a rope around her neck and leading her out of the pen. Let no one know! he told the sleeping animals. He led Innocence by the rope, drowsy and slow, across the quadrangle. The lights were on in the Reading Room and the library and Octavia's room, of course – her all-night parlour of wailing, wine and chess. He and Innocence padded across the cool grass, in the cool night, back to his quarters. Once inside she seemed to fully wake up and become frightened, kicking a little, before she settled down. He heated some milk for a bottle for her and poured himself a sherry. His little bolthole. She would like it in here. He turned the wireless on low: the BBC World Service, broadcasting tonight from Nairobi. He and Innocence had their little drinkies and regarded each other companionably. This was all he wanted, really.

He climbed into bed, but not before helping Innocence up. She was confused and tired but she did not question his intent. She lay at the end of his bed, heavy, her hoofs marking the blankets. The bed whispered then groaned. It felt good, the weight of something other than him on the bed, thought Dr Bath. He adjusted his legs so Innocence had more room.

He hoped there would be no emergency with the students tonight. Sometimes at odd hours, when one of them had

had too much to drink or fallen off the music-room roof or been hit by a car, they charged into his room without even knocking.

He tried not to think about how it had come to this. He was forty-nine now and so lost he looked to the animals for comfort. Had he forsaken other people or had they forsaken him? Forty-nine – but really no different from when he was fourteen. He was back in adolescence, in a place where he felt utterly alone, like he did now. Had he taken a lot of wrong turns between fourteen and forty-nine, or was this what the poets called 'the full circle'?

Innocence snored but slept on. Dr Bath ran an uncertain hand through her oily wool, then settled back on his pillows, drank a second sherry in a gulp. Best not to think too much about what gave him solace now. Best not to think about the only places where solace was available.

It was raining. Long, loose slaps of water fell against the Reading Room windows. The door was locked and Tarrant, Lowell and Sanderson were sitting together under the mellow lamplight.

In this setting, thought Tarrant, they could have been mistaken for tutors, with their looks of concentration, the scratching of their pens and the *tap-tap-tap Enter* on the keyboard. But instead of books they had spread before them a more forensic collection: things in plastic bags, mobile phones, USB sticks and memory cards, mobile SIMs and computer hard drives, lists of names and room numbers and folders containing student records. After cataloguing them at the college it was back to police headquarters to sift through the data to see whom they could build a case against.

Even with Tarrant's subtle probing, their interview with Charlotte had gone badly awry. She had given a no-comment interview, bringing with her a golden-haired law student called Roman who looked like a young Jude Law and stood behind her, staring down at the police with a contemptuous gaze. 'You don't have to answer that,' he would tell Charlotte with monotonous regularity.

'We're trying to help her – we're not looking to charge her with anything,' said Tarrant, exasperated.

As the police pored over the evidence, they tried to think their way around the impasse. How could you mount a case if neither of the victims would talk to you?

Towards the end of the day, in the hush of the Reading Room, the three officers could hear protesters gathering outside, even though it was wet – young women mostly, but some men – calling for an end to violence against women.

The chanting of the crowds and the words of some strident socialist on a megaphone were muffled within the stone fortress, but the hum of youth and anger heightened something for the police in the Reading Room: a sense of drama but also of futility. How could they investigate these athletes when no one close to them was prepared to speak out?

'I feel like we'll be torn apart if we go out through the front,' said Sanderson. 'They see every man who walks out the gates as a rapist.'

Lowell chuckled and said, 'You're a bit outside the demographic, mate.'

Tarrant's laptop glowed like a lamp in the darkening room. She looked again at the photos of Charlotte. She was beautiful, like an old-fashioned movie star with that cascading blonde hair, the huge, slanted blue eyes ringed in kohl and the sensual lips. She noticed that Sanderson avoided looking too closely at the picture – as if even to glance at it were to become enchanted.

'It could be a one-night stand that got a little bit out of hand, or she could be into rough sex, but since she's not telling us all we can do is guess,' said Tarrant, who had spent a frustrating hour trying to establish whether a crime had been committed, even playing back to Charlotte the clip that had been uploaded onto YouTube. Charlotte had looked a bit uncomfortable, and embarrassed by the filming style, which was so obviously trying to imitate a porno in the emphasis on all things anal. But she had also been defiant.

'That's just the way things are here,' she had said more than once, over Roman's insistence that she make no comment. 'Did you hear me saying no? Well that's because I didn't say no. I wanted it. I wanted all of it.'

And she was right: the word 'no' had never been uttered; she'd just made indistinct and inauthentic noises that were meant to signify pleasure but instead sounded like an actress pretending to be in a pornographic film, pretending to be turned on.

As for the sex worker found on the oval, could they mount a charge that she was kidnapped, falsely imprisoned and raped? Maybe – but she'd thrown up a wall of extreme indifference. She wasn't talking and hadn't turned up for her interview with the police. When Lowell rang her, the mobile was switched off, and a few days later it had been disconnected.

Yet other things were emerging – the fragments of other stories, other occasions, other students, other cricket seasons that seemed to suggest that this type of violence, consensual or not, was not a one-off but something woven so deeply into the fabric of the college that those wrapped up in it were so close they couldn't see the violence anymore.

'We may not get the athletes for this particular thing,' said Tarrant. 'I think we all know that. But we'll find other things in here.' She gestured to the gathered evidence. 'We will find something, somewhere.'

'Good,' said Sanderson. 'I fucking hate these kids. I really do.'

Tarrant murmured in agreement. Then suddenly she remembered something the Master had said. 'Lucy Mason!'

'The Firestarter activist? What about her?' asked Sanderson.

'She might be worth talking to if some particular thing has upset her, turned her political. She's in a lot of Facebook photos with Charlotte; maybe they're close friends. Maybe Charlotte's confided in Lucy.'

'Great,' said Lowell. 'Let's get her in.'

CHAPTER 25

Ben sat desolate – not helping, not even singing – as Ted and the Jerusalem men removed all the foliage, all the sugar shakers, all the helpful religious literature from the Pleasing Sands.

'Why?' Ben asked Sylvan again. 'Why are you leaving?'

Sylvan sat down next to him in the denuded cafe.

'Because sometimes you have to go to the people rather than wait for them to come to you. Because if we didn't move around I would never have met you.'

'I don't even know how to say goodbye to you.'

'Then come with us,' Sylvan suggested.

'I can't. I've still got two years of uni left. You always said if I was a lawyer I could do something, something to do with social justice.'

'Of course,' said Sylvan. 'Just don't forget to become what you've promised yourself to be.'

Ben nodded. Things were going to change, he vowed to himself and to Sylvan and to the whispering woods down at Shangri-La. College was over for him. So was home. He wanted to live in a big messy terrace with other students on Viola Street – students who studied chemistry and theology and modern history … anything really. As long as they didn't play sport obsessively, as long as they weren't old boys from his school or college kids. Just normal students.

Before the Jerusalems left, Sylvan extracted a promise from Ben: that he would tell the police about Alfred. Confessing to Sylvan had made Ben feel light, like some internal clamp had been released. But Sylvan said it wasn't enough that he felt good. He had to *do* good. The timing was right. Ever since he'd got back from the Jerusalems' compound he'd seen an unusual number of police on campus, including an ad near the cricket pitch for Crime Stoppers. He'd taken a closer look and realised they wanted information about a woman sexually assaulted on the St Anton's oval and his heart sank. He knew immediately it would be Hadrien. His attempt to resurrect the Savage Society had gone too far.

In the queue at the university bookshop Ben heard two hipster girls gossiping bitchily about the ball, and how Charlotte Barnsley had been gangbanged by some of the cricketers in Hadrien's tower and how it had got 'a bit out of control'.

'She's always been an incredible slut,' said one girl with enormous glasses and a purple trilby. 'Even at school. She lost her virginity when she was, like, thirteen.'

'Yeah, to me,' he wanted to say. 'So what? We were young, and now we're fine.' But he kept quiet and put his headphones on to block them out.

Charlotte was the most sexually uninhibited girl he knew, and proud of it, but still … still, it was a fine line she walked. She got completely drunk and sometimes became quite passive and let things happen to her that were borderline illegal.

One day he used the men's urinals in the Law quadrangle and someone had written the URL of a Vimeo clip filmed on the night of the ball, and underneath it the words: CHARLOTTE SUCKS AND FUCKS AGAIN. AND AGAIN. AND AGAIN.

Ben had flicked a stream of piss up at it – thinking not about Charlotte but about the boy who had written the words. 'I piss on you, I piss on you, I piss on you,' he said to the wall.

On Roman's and Severin's phones Tarrant found some strange photos, and Roman's also contained a bizarre seven-second video.

Tarrant, Lowell and Sanderson gathered around the screen.

'Holy hell,' said Lowell.

The photos were immediately shocking in their similarity to the infamous pictures of Iraqi torture victims taken at Abu Ghraib by American soldiers. They had the same haunting, unusual composition. But these featured a hooded figure in robes with arms and legs fastened to some wooden structure in the manner of Jesus on the Cross. The head was bowed.

'It looks like a crucifixion,' said Sanderson. 'Can you enlarge it at all?'

'This is as big as we can make it without it getting too pixelated,' said Tarrant. 'But the quality's not too bad.'

There were no other figures in the pictures and behind the figure were white walls. The photo appeared to have been taken with a flash – maybe at night. Had it been taken at the university, or at the college, or was it a picture taken of a picture in a magazine? Was the person on the cross a consenting participant, or were they there under duress? Was it a man or a woman? It was impossible to tell due to the hood and the robes. There was something quietly evil about the picture, but also something compelling. Who was under the hood? Where was he or she now? Was this a criminal act or was it some sort of third-year art project (*Abu Ghraib: The New Aesthetics of War*)?

The video, which they played on Roman's iPhone, started with a flash of the figure on the cross, and then swung behind a door where someone big, wearing small shorts and a mask, seemed to be wrestling with … what was it? A flash of fur – a tail. Could it be … surely it wasn't … a kangaroo? The camera had moved again and there were several excruciating, precious seconds wasted on a shot of the floorboards, before it swung up and a giant night-time skeleton of gum loomed into the shot.

The animal, the tree … The footage wasn't filmed in the city – it was shot in the bush.

The police debated among themselves the merit of investigating something that looked like it could be a crime, but was really nothing more than a series of blurry pictures and seven shaky seconds of camera-phone footage. But Tarrant's gut feeling was that the pictures meant something, that they led somewhere.

'I think these guys – Roman and Severin – are trying to hide something. We might not get them on the prostitute assault, but we might get them on something else.'

'But what?' asked Lowell. 'I mean, who is that in the hood? Is it even a crime to put a hood on someone and tie them up?

We already know these guys are pretty sick – it could just be one of them having a laugh.'

Tarrant shook her head. 'No – I think something is happening in these pictures. Cruelty to an animal or human. We can get them on something, I'm sure of it – we just need to dig a bit deeper.'

She opened a folder and showed her colleagues a title search she had done on properties owned by the college. 'I found this: a place called Evelyn up on the western side of the Wycloff Mountains. It's used for retreats, sporting camps and weekends away. The students have to be chaperoned by an academic. It doesn't seem to be used much anymore, but the records show that the cricket team went up there in March for a weekend under the supervision of Dr Bath, the History tutor – he's your classic absent-minded professor.' She swiped to his picture on her iPad. It was blurry, and Bath, balding and plump, was looking at something out of the frame. 'We could follow it up with him.'

'And how about the interview with Lucy Mason?' asked Sanderson. 'Any luck there?'

'I was in contact yesterday,' said Lowell. 'She's scared, but also angry. She'll speak to us, but not here. We're booked in tomorrow to interview her at headquarters in the city.'

Lucy was nervous, but she knew she had nothing to hide, so she went to the police station alone, without a lawyer. The interview room was like the seminar rooms at university, with cheap furniture and bad carpets. An officer called Diane Tarrant asked her questions in a clipped but not unfriendly manner. Her colleague Tony Lowell, whom Lucy had seen around college, sat behind Tarrant, maintaining intense eye contact with Lucy. In the corners of the ceiling were CCTV cameras, moving like eyes.

'What do you know about Evelyn? Have you ever been there?'

'Yes. Charlotte and I went up there once. We'd been at a day spa on the other side of the mountains for her nineteenth, and even though it wasn't on the way home, we were curious about it and stopped by.'

'What did you think?'

'It was pretty awful – very basic. We didn't stay long; there were mice droppings on the ground, and it smelt damp … it was pretty gross.'

'So you've never been invited to Evelyn by any of the boys?'

'No, never. It's been a bit of a sore point, actually. We didn't want to go there, but we did want to go away with Toby, Ben, Julian and Levi, and couldn't understand why they'd go off on these end-of-season trips with the other boys when they could have gone somewhere nicer with us. Since first year they've been going up to the mountains once or twice a year, usually with the cricket or football team. I suppose they binge-drink or take drugs; they come back in really bad shape. Ben is always depressed afterwards. Just ask Charlotte. It's like he becomes infected with something up there. But it passes, and things return to normal. Then they go back there and the cycle starts again.'

'When was the last time they went?'

'March – just after the cricket season. They went up there to celebrate winning the intercollegiate comp.'

'Can you tell us who went?'

'Leeson, Hadrien, Severin, Ping, Sam, Roman, Niall, Levi, Julian, Toby, Ben – and Dr Bath, I think.'

'That was it?'

'I'm pretty sure that was all. I saw them come back.'

'And what were they like when they returned?'

'Terrible. I went by Toby's room. His door was unlocked and he was sleeping, it was like 5 pm. He was totally out of it. He told me later he slept for eighteen hours. We went for dinner on Monday night – which is what we usually did back then – at a place called Angelica's on Troutman Street. But the boys were acting really weird. They were quite sunburnt and were covered in cuts and bruises. Levi could hardly walk. He'd twisted his knee. Julian told some bizarre story about getting lost in the bush and how they had to sleep outside.'

'Did you believe him?'

'Yes, I did. They looked like they'd slept rough for the night and they seemed kind of traumatised by it. But I felt like they weren't telling the whole story.'

'And what do you think that story is?'

'I don't know. But something else happened that weekend that – well, even if you do believe in coincidences, which I don't, is too weird to be a coincidence.'

'What was that?'

'The same weekend, another St Anton's student got lost in the bush in the same part of the mountains – Plumley's Gap. His name is Alfred Khoo; it was on the news at the time and was a big deal at college for a while. He's a fresher – you know, a first year. An overseas student from Malaysia. But there was really nothing to connect the cricket team with Alfred. He didn't play cricket, he'd probably never even spoken to them – and anyway, he'd only been at college a few weeks.'

'So where's the coincidence?'

'Well, I guess the fact that Alfred was there in the first place was weird. I've spoken to some of his friends – there's a girl called Grace who you've probably met, and a guy called Ricky. They said he'd never shown any interest in bushwalking, had never talked about going into the bush – I mean, he didn't even have transport. No Australian driver's licence or car. None of his friends could believe he had gone off alone, and they had no idea how he could have got there.'

'So what happened to him?'

'He's still in hospital. He had a terrible fall that caused a brain injury. Apparently he can't remember anything about his accident, including how he ended up in the bush in the first place.'

'Okay – and how is this connected with the cricket team?'

'Well, at first I wasn't sure. It was just a feeling – but a strong one. It was a big deal when Alfred was found and we were told by the Master how bad his injuries were. People at college are really close – we're a community – and when something happens to someone in that community, even someone new, we all feel it really keenly. I mean, when we weren't sure if he was going to pull through, I just remember people in the dining hall crying about it, people weeping in the cloisters. The choir wrote him a song. It was a real shock.

But whenever we tried to talk about Alfred to any of the cricketers they shut the conversation down. Especially Toby. He'd change the subject or he'd start tickling me or something stupid, like he wanted to distract me.'

'That's Tobias Murphy?' Tarrant asked, and opened a file on her computer containing pictures of all the students of St Anton's taken from their student IDs. 'This one here?' She pointed to a picture of Toby taken when he was a fresher – brown hair, green eyes, strong jaw.

'Looks like Zac Efron,' said Sanderson. 'My daughter has a screensaver of him ...'

'That's him,' said Lucy ruefully. 'Toby wasn't being straight with me. There was this one night when I started talking to someone else who was on the trip to Evelyn, a guy called Sam – one of the cricketers. He's all right. Came over to my room once after yoga. We made tea, talked, whatever. He said a bit about that weekend, seemed really bothered by it – said that Hadrien had hurt someone. That's what he said: "He hurts people". But who did he hurt? I thought it might have been Ben – Ben Winchester, Toby's best mate. Ben completely shut down when he got back from the mountains. It was bizarre. He stopped seeing so much of us and started spending time with these Christians – bells and smells, giving stuff away, forsaking the internet, that sort of thing. It was totally weird. Ben was like something from *GQ* magazine – then suddenly he completely changed his image, tried to grow a beard and stuff.'

The police were nodding, Lowell was listening intently as Lucy talked.

'But none of the cricketing guys were talking about it. I mean, Ben was going off the rails and no one was even *mentioning* it. So that set off alarm bells ... and I thought maybe something had happened to Ben up there – and something so bad that the others couldn't talk about it. But Ben is strong, he can take care of himself. And Toby would protect him, of course – so it didn't seem right.

'Then something interesting happened. One day I was at the Royal Prince Edward Hospital seeing my cousin, who was having a baby, and I ran into Sam. He looked really surprised to see me and was sort of caught off guard. He got really red in the face and blurted out that he'd been visiting Alfred. Alfred, the overseas student ... I mean, why? And that's when I started thinking: maybe *Alfred* was the person that he'd been talking about, the person that had been hurt! After all, the dates matched up.'

The police nodded, their faces remaining expressionless.

'That's an interesting theory,' said Sanderson.

'If we show you some footage from one of the cricketers' phones that we suspect was taken at Evelyn, would you be able to help us identity who is in it and if it is in fact Evelyn?' asked Tarrant.

'Yes.'

'We must warn you: the footage we have is graphic and distressing.'

'That's okay. I'd like to see it.'

Toby stayed in his room, scared. Rumours were flying around college that were wild, yet plausible: Levi had been arrested at a nightclub in the city; Julian had become a police informant; the boys who had been at Hadrien's party might be prevented by some sort of ethics committee from practising law when they graduated; Niall was leaking information about the Savage Society to newspaper reporters; Lucy was booked to do a television interview to talk about university colleges and misogyny; the university Vice-Chancellor had requested an urgent meeting with the Master; prominent old boys were circling, offering to make statements to the media, to arbitrate with the university, to *handle* the police.

The cricketers kept to themselves. 'Lie low,' Hadrien kept saying. But they did meet and did talk, through texts or voice calls on mobile phones using a variety of disposable SIM cards purchased by a paranoid Toby. They gathered in each other's rooms, or in Levi's old room, which by now had been converted into a bar by Leeson.

'What did the police seize from you? Who have they been talking to?' they'd ask each other.

At night they would slip in and out of different rooms and beds at a pace that might have alarmed them at a more sober time. In dark rooms and narrow beds they were sexually promiscuous but emotionally closed, nestled in some girl's collarbone, clutching fistfuls of her hair almost with violence and digging deeply between her legs. They tried to fuck away their fears, and for ten or fifteen minutes after coming they felt at ease. Then, like possums, they would slip out before dawn's tepid light and scarper across the damp quadrangle to their own beds, feet and pyjama bottoms wet, their own beds cold.

In the morning and at night Hadrien's words were never far from their thoughts: 'The police are moving in on us.'

Toby noticed how each of them was seized by his own singular panic, how stress drew out the truths of character. Sam desperately wanted to go back to the farm, and had packed his bags a dozen times. Toby heard from Julian that Sam had actually been intercepted by Hadrien at the station one evening, on one of the country platforms, and Hadrien had said something that frightened Sam so much he had come back to college like a dog brought to heel, meek and silent. He cowered whenever Hadrien addressed him.

Julian confided to Toby that he was also feeling frightened – that the urge to go home, back to Mum and Dad, was strong. His parents came and took him out for dinner one night with his godparents to La Sabrine, the most expensive restaurant in town. In the car on the way back to college his mother had rebuked him. Why did they have such a dull boy for a son? It was embarrassing how he'd just sat there and played with his food, with nothing sensible to say, even though he was halfway through two degrees. Back at college Julian had felt the first melancholy stirrings of loneliness; he must have texted Levi a hundred times. *Where are you? Come back, I need you.* And then anger: *I cannot believe you have abandoned me here with these freaks.*

Severin, Leeson, Roman and Hadrien looked less worried than the others – impassive almost, as if they had located a quiet, impenetrable part of themselves and decided to reside there until this thing blew over. Toby, on the other hand, was a wreck. He was only twenty but he felt much older. He was finding sleep more elusive than ever, and begged Niall to give him something to help him relax. The new pills gave everything he touched a thick, viscous texture but he was grateful for it. He had never felt so distant from the realm of logic and emotion. He was just a mass of physical sensation, all tingles and burning eyes, warm blood and weightlessness, dreams where he moved like a ghost through lost cities – Atlantis, Petra, Machu Picchu, Herculaneum, Troy. Hadrien started calling him The Oxymoron – and when he accidently glanced at himself in the mirror what looked back were sad, glassy eyes.

Lucy knocked on Charlotte's door, holding a salmon bagel. When she pushed the door open she saw Charlotte sitting up in bed, watching something on her MacBook.

'I haven't seen you in the dining hall all week. I brought you a bagel.'

Charlotte slid across the bed and Lucy climbed in. 'What are you watching?'

'*Game of Thrones.*'

'I've heard that's good.'

Charlotte took a bite of the bagel. 'Yum. It's addictive. That's why I haven't been over to the dining room or uni. This show – it just sucks time.'

'Do you want to talk about what happened the night of the ball?' asked Lucy quietly.

Charlotte shook her head. 'Not really.'

They watched the MacBook for a while, not talking.

'Did *you* have a good time, the night of the ball?' Charlotte said after about an hour.

'Not really. I suppose you heard about Toby?' asked Lucy.

'And Octavia? Yes. You should have hooked up with Sam – your yoga buddy. He's all right. And he actually likes you.'

'You know I'm not in love with him,' said Lucy, feeling almost in pain to be talking like this.

'You're such a romantic, Lucy – a hopeless romantic,' said Charlotte. She picked up the half-eaten bagel from the bed and pitched it high in the air towards the bin. Lucy heard a soft thud as it landed on the floor.

'Did you just put emphasis on the word *hopeless*?' she asked.

'Don't be so sensitive,' said Charlotte, snuggling deeper under the quilt and nestling against Lucy.

Lucy bristled. 'Do you think I'm hopeless?'

'I don't think you're hopeless. But I think things with Toby are hopeless,' said Charlotte.

'You've been encouraging me to chase him for the last two years! So what's with him and Octavia? Are they together? It's just a hook-up, isn't it?'

'I don't know,' said Charlotte. 'She's liked him for a while. They make sense. Why can't you just enjoy his friendship?'

'Because I've invested two years in him. Because I don't like anybody else.'

'Does that mean you're still a virgin?' asked Charlotte, sitting up.

'Why are you saying it like that?'

'Like what?' Charlotte shut down her MacBook.

'Like it's a bad thing.'

'You're being too sensitive.'

'Stop saying that. I'm not like you. I don't think it's a virtue to spend my time at college trying to hook up with as many guys as possible,' said Lucy.

'Well then, you're missing out,' said Charlotte.

'Missing out? *Missing out?* People are watching you on the internet! It looks like you're being raped,' said Lucy, grabbing the MacBook. 'Do you want me to show you?'

'You're loving rubbing my face in it,' said Charlotte, seizing the computer from Lucy.

'No – I brought it up because everyone is talking about it. Not just here at college, but all over uni. You've gone viral.' Lucy climbed out of the bed and went to stand by the door, her arms folded. 'Have you told the police? Are you going to press charges?'

'No.'

Lucy was shocked. 'Why not?'

'Because I fucking consented, that's why.'

'You're trash,' said Lucy, while part of her marvelled at how you could go from being best friends with someone to blowing it to smithereens in the space of ten minutes.

'And you're slut-shaming. What would your new little feminist mates say about that?' said Charlotte.

Lucy looked away and shrugged, trying to cool down.

'Come with me to the rally,' she said, trying for a more conciliatory tone. 'Come and talk. We want you there. You can shine a light – we both can.'

Charlotte said nothing.

'We can't keep going like this,' said Lucy.

'It won't keep going like this,' said Charlotte, in the haughty tone she had always used with others, never Lucy.

'What do you mean?'

'Things will change course. They always do. This is just for now. A few months ago everyone was worried about Alfred, now they've forgotten. And this will be forgotten too. Things roll on. It's not worth getting so worked up.'

Charlotte turned the computer back on and resumed watching *Game of Thrones*.

Visiting hours to see Alfred were almost over when one of the rehab nurses handed Gary a card.

'The police were in here the other day. They were asking about Alfred and his injuries.'

'Did they say anything about what might have caused them?'

'No, but they asked if any cricketers from that college had been to visit Alfred.'

'Cricketers?' asked Gary, his heart beating faster.

'Yes, I know, it's strange, isn't it … cricketers …'

When Severin and Roman were asked to meet with the police to discuss the photos and the footage they brought their lawyers with them.

The lawyers told Tarrant and her colleagues the same thing: 'My client has not been charged with anything and is therefore not obliged even to be here. My client is attending this meeting as a courtesy, but at this point has nothing to say to you about any material found on any SIM card or memory stick, and is not prepared to answer any questions about the woman found on St Anton's oval, or respond to any baseless rumours about sexual assaults. I will be acting on his behalf, and I am the one you should contact if you need any further information – but at this point in time, my client has nothing to say.'

Tarrant had been expecting it – after all, Hadrien had brought along a Senior Counsel when the police quizzed him about the party in the tower. But still, bringing lawyers made these kids look shifty, like they had something to hide.

Grace told the police that Alfred had said nothing to her about going to the mountains, nor did he slip a note under her door or send her a text message or email.

'Is that unusual?' asked Lowell.

'I guess. Although we hadn't known each other for that long – a month maybe – we were friends. We saw each other every day.'

'What did you do together each day?'

'In the morning I'd wake up at eight to the sound of Alfred knocking on my door. I called him my little alarm clock. We'd go to the dining hall together for breakfast. Then, depending on when our classes were, we'd sit in the quadrangle for a bit, chatting or playing with the animals, or we'd go back to our rooms to study. If we had morning classes we'd walk to the university together and then back to college for lunch. Maybe in the afternoon he would text me and tell me he was in the library and I'd find him and we'd have a break. Then we'd walk back to college for dinner. In the evenings we'd play internet games in the Computer Room or play ping-pong, or watch television or study in our rooms. I was in the choir. Sometimes he came with me to rehearsals. He said he couldn't sing but he had a lovely voice. He was just shy and quite modest.'

'The Master tells us you're a practising Catholic, Grace. Is Alfred?'

"No – he is religious, though: he's Muslim.'

'Was he involved in any religious groups that you know of on campus? Or political groups?'

'Not that I know of.'

'Did he ever talk about going to meetings or meeting people in the Bio-med cafe?'

'No. He wasn't involved in politics or campus groups. He was studying Engineering. It's a hard course, even harder if English isn't your first language. He spent a lot of time studying. He also played ping-pong. He was quite good at it – quick reflexes.'

'Did he play cricket?'

'No – well, he may have back in Malaysia, but he never mentioned it.'

'Did he play cricket for St Anton's?'

'No.'

'Did he know the players? Socialise with the players at all?'

'No – of course not. None of us do.'

'Why not?'

'We may as well be at a different college to them. They treat us like we are invisible – literally invisible; I really don't think they see us at all. We are not from here but we have to live somewhere – so we come to colleges like St Anton's because they're close to the university and meals are provided. The brochures and the websites always look nice. They stress the convenience of it all but don't really mention the tradition. Then they put us in a building far away from everyone else and pretend we are not here.'

'What about bullying? Was Alfred ever mistreated by the students here? Was he ever mistreated by the cricket team?'

'He complained a couple of times about students – they would make a lot of noise late at night. Sometimes they would be sick outside the door of his room or run around with no clothes on. I think that upset him a lot. He felt he wasn't respected. He felt it wasn't a serious place, even though it looks very serious and grand. But I don't think anyone actually hurt him. Why are you asking me this? What does the cricket team have to do with anything? Did they do something to Alfred?'

They didn't answer her, instead asking more gently, 'What is Alfred like?'

Grace took her time answering, speaking carefully, wanting to get it right. 'He is … really quite incredible.'

CHAPTER 26

Ben knocked on Toby's door but there was no answer. How long had it been since he was last in Toby's room? A term at least – since that night he'd smoked on the balcony and talked about going to see the Master. When they were still wavering about what to do. When it could have gone either way. In other words, a lifetime ago.

Ben tried the handle. The door was locked.

A strange student they called the Lab Rat walked past. 'Toby's gone for a swim – he'll be at the uni pool.'

Ah, his amphibious friend, willing to brave the chemical-green, reputedly infected waters of the university pool when the beaches were too cold.

On campus he passed a large, noisy rally outside the Student Union building – a women's group by the looks of it, but with a few loud-mouthed, bearded men along for support. They were protesting against violence towards women. They were dressed in overcoats and scarves, gloves, hats and glasses, carrying satchels and backpacks. Some people with lightweight camera gear were recording the shifting crowd. They wore bright-yellow plastic vests like workmen with the words INDEPENDENT MEDIA on their backs, and moved about seriously among the protesters.

'Take back the night!' the protesters were crying as one of them thrust a leaflet into Ben's hand. 'End violence against women!'

Ben recognised a few students from his lectures, and a couple of those winsome Amnesty women who had so captivated him when he was a freshman, their pretty faces turned turbulent, their arms aloft, holding placards.

THEY PLAYED AND PREYED. The placard featured a large picture of college students Ben didn't recognise. They were in topcoats, arms thrown around each other's shoulders in drunken affection, smiles plastered across their soft cheeks, eyes blazing and alive. Alongside this image was what looked like a police or medical photo of a battered woman.

A small angry-looking woman (not one of the Amnesty beauties) didn't so much pass Ben a leaflet as punch him in the stomach with it. To his shock he saw it was a picture he'd seen on Facebook of the St Anton's ball: a group of boys, young toffs – was that Severin and Leeson? – with ice cream covering their chins, and girls leering at the camera, their creamy bosoms spilling out of their ridiculous dresses. He had seen photos like that a thousand times on the walls of his friends' rooms but in this context, on this leaflet, the scene it depicted embarrassed him.

He turned the leaflet over. The crowded type on the back was urgent:

He sighed and thought of the Jerusalems and how close their ideals were to this: common property, open doors, open hearts. It was all connected. Secrets – the secret societies, the secret initiations, the secret language of the colleges – were things to fight against. Let the sun shine in, Sylvan had said.

As more people joined the protest – streaming across the Science block into the forecourt of the Student Union building – he was jostled, pressed and pushed until he found himself jammed in the centre of the crowd without means of escape. 'They've kettled us in. Big crowd. Awesome. Here ...' said some excited boy from his Torts class, passing him a placard of a fist with a red line through it to hold aloft.

Ben received a further shock to see Lucy a few metres in towards the foamy head of the crowd, emerging from a knot of supporters. What was she doing here? And what had she done to her hair? In almost three years here her aim had been to visit the university as little as possible. Instead she had spent a lot of time in her room straightening her hair. But now some other woman, not from St Anton's, was helping her onto a raised platform. A microphone was thrust into her hand and – a little shakily at first – she began to speak.

It was a story he had never heard from her perspective before.

There were all the banalities, all the rites of passage for a young middle-class woman, the First World problems, the dance between self-control and the loss of it – the eating disorders, the binge-drinking, the self-loathing, the exam panics, the sleep deprivation, the laxatives, the sudden plunges in confidence, the hangovers and the classes missed because of them, and – most of all – the boys.

The boys ... The way validation was achieved through them, the way the girls would watch themselves being watched, the way the girls would come alive with a few grains of attention. The way, once you had their attention, the boys would want to photograph or film everything, and didn't respect a locked door, or a reticence to do *that*.

'It's taken a lot of courage for me to be able to speak out,' Lucy said into the microphone. 'It's like I've been asleep – really asleep – for almost three years. But I am awake now. And I can tell my story because of these women – my sisters.' She pointed to a group of women close to the stage. 'They have given me the strength to take on the patriarchy of St Anton's.'

Ben tried to reconcile this new assertive Lucy with the one who loved having her picture taken, the one who filled albums and albums and albums with photos of herself and Charlotte and the others on her Facebook page, the girl who had followed Toby around like a devoted puppy for the last couple of years despite his discouragement.

'On my first day at college, I hadn't even unpacked my bag when a couple of boys in masks and gowns broke into my room. They drove me and the other freshers out onto the quadrangle. They screamed at us and sprayed us with something, then made us drink alcoholic cocktails from a funnel. All around me frightened freshmen were being ill. The next morning they woke us at 5 am and we had to run around the oval and were not allowed to stop until we had collapsed with exhaustion. A lot of us were vomiting. People were force-fed stuff that made them sick – shampoo, dirt, dog food …

'After O-Week it was clear that it was important to be hot. It was important to be thin and popular. It was important to sleep with the footy guys, the cricketers and the rowers. That's how success is measured in college. It's not about your mind. How could I be so stupid as to think that university is about your mind? It's about your body!'

Ben thought about Lucy's body – always agreeable, although he had never seen it at close range in a bedroom at sunrise, never touched it. But now it was swaddled in bulky army-surplus clothes.

'At college women are called "furs" and "footy molls". They're plied with alcohol and sexually assaulted on a regular basis. At one party I had to lie under the open legs of a footballer as he used a bladder of wine to pretend he was pissing into my mouth.'

Ben looked around at the crowd. It had gone very quiet. People looked disgusted by what Lucy was saying.

'I have recently realised that women's place in university colleges is reflective of the sexist power struggles throughout society as a whole.'

There were a few hollers from the crowd. This they understood: the struggle, the long game, the virus of the patriarchy and how it infected everything. Then finally, this moment of consciousness, the bright light coming on.

'The heroes are the men,' said Lucy, sounding more confident, angrier. 'The cricketers, the rowers, the fucking chess players. And we women are expected to worship at their feet – actually, more like at their phallus. It's time to say it: these colleges nurture a rape culture by protecting the perpetrators. The Masters of these colleges cover up and protect these men from the law, from accountability, from consequences. WELL, NOT ANYMORE!'

Finally Ben felt something in him stirring. He felt his resistance to her words soften. Hadn't he had a similar moment of consciousness? Hadn't he been shaken awake – and now that he was awake nothing was the same and nothing would ever be the same?

He felt a brotherly pride as he saw Lucy shaking her fist into the rain. There was no way he would ever have the courage to do what Lucy had done in front of this crowd. His own transformation was still so new, fragile and special – too tender to expose – that he felt shy talking about it. He didn't know the words yet but he was intimate with the content.

'It's not only a few bad seeds; it's the way of the whole world. And I'm scared, really scared,' said Lucy. 'I will leave university and go into some firm or other, and these boys from private schools, who became the boys of the college – these boys will become the men who run the firms, the parliament and the media. And nothing ever changes, and nothing will change. The sexual assaults, the casual degradation of women in the language they use, the way they speak, how they act, it all continues unchallenged. Well, I want to challenge it now!'

There was a tremendous cheer from the crowd, and Lucy was carried aloft, like a crowd-surfer, from the stage.

The speeches finished (the last speaker was a girl who had been date-raped at the Chocolate Appreciation Society Ball in a disabled toilet cubicle) and the crowd started marching, accompanied by bongos and a weird lute and some fire dancers, heading in the direction of St Anton's. The mood was one of rage. Someone behind Ben set off a flare that died quickly in the rain.

Gibbs is going to have a heart attack when this crowd appears at the gates, thought Ben. He also thought, things will happen quickly now, and that excited him. Things will happen quickly and nothing will stay the same.

The voice of one of the date-rape girl's supporters rose above the crowd in a screech. 'Let's burn 'em down! Burn the lot of those places down!'

Ben was pushed along by the force of the chanting crowd for a while before he was able to weave his way out towards the university pool. He watched as the marchers turned towards the green fields at the back of the colleges.

As he entered the Aqua Centre, the first thing to hit his nostrils was the warm chlorine mist. The atmosphere was swampy, hot, chemical and grimy. Mid-afternoon and there was hardly anyone there; maybe all the swimmers were at the march.

Toby was the only one in his lane – his long, strong body lifting and surging through the water in a powerful butterfly stroke.

Ben felt both sad and proud watching his friend swim. Toby could do anything he put his mind to: the strongest swimming stroke, the most difficult exam, the most challenging women (Ben remembered the sharp stab of envy when he first met the formidable, complex, older Lisa). How had he allowed himself to drift so far from Toby?

Ben stood looming over the edge of the lane. Toby stopped and hoisted himself up in one smooth move onto the tiles, surprised to see him.

'What are you doing here?' he asked evenly.

'I need to talk to you,' said Ben. 'It's important.'

And where were you when *I* had important things to say? Toby wanted to ask, but didn't.

Instead they went to the change room, each footprint Toby made on the tiles light then fading like mist, contrasting with his own deep, heavy sense of dread. He felt strangely nervous around Ben.

The change rooms were worse than the pool itself: it was as if all the scraps of skin and blood and Band-Aids and hair had been brought in by a tide from the pool, and the waters had since receded, leaving the sad detritus plastered to the floor.

'Do they ever clean this place?' asked Ben.

Toby shrugged. 'I try not to think about it.'

They stood, almost facing each other off – Toby dripping, only one inch taller than Ben. Ben spoke quickly, as if sensing that he didn't have a lot of time.

He talked with an openness that Toby found distressing – about the things he had done in the bunkhouse to Alfred, and how he, Hadrien and Leeson had done these things to other boys at school, and how they had had their turn as well, with unpleasant things being done to them. He told Toby that the Alfred thing had gone a bit further, too far; he talked of his remorse, and the very strong feeling that came on him one night back at college that he could no longer live with himself.

He talked about his depression and how he had decided – for a day, possibly two – that he was going to kill himself. He was crying now, as if this admission had opened up a barely healed wound. He was wiping tears away roughly using the back of his hand, and talking very quickly, as if there weren't much time. It wasn't just the Alfred thing that had made him consider suicide, he told Toby, but its context. How nothing in his life seemed good, and things would just continue along this path – and he would end up like his father. He would become not a life enhancer but its opposite. There seemed to be no way out. Remember? Remember?

Toby nodded.

'All that rowing. All those boys. All that shit with the pact,' said Ben.

Toby nodded again, understanding.

'The only thing I could think of to stop feeling like that was to confess. I wanted to so badly. I needed to tell somebody – somebody not involved.'

Toby blanched.

'But I didn't confess, and I didn't kill myself either. I called this guy I met in O-Week – Sylvan. You don't know him, but he's nice, really nice.'

Toby nodded.

'He's religious, but not in a bad way. His group is called the Jerusalems, they're socialist Christians – and I joined. I was baptised last week. Everything I have I've given to them – all my money, all my shares, that ridiculous watch collection – but they have given me so much more.'

Toby felt embarrassed to see how his friend's face was shining.

'They've given me purpose. I don't feel so depressed anymore. I have a direction – you see, I'd lost myself.'

'That's great, that's so great you have this new thing,' said Toby. 'There's really no need to feel depressed. You know what? I've been reading a lot of Dostoyevsky lately – and you know what he says about a man who has committed a crime …' Toby recited the words he'd typed out a hundred times and deleted: 'He says, "If he has a conscience he will suffer for his mistake. That will be his punishment …" And that is you, that is so you. That's what I thought when I was reading—'

Ben interrupted. 'But I had to confess. I'm sorry, but I had to confess. I don't want to keep suffering. I have to try and live with myself.'

Toby was motionless. 'What do you mean confess? To a priest?'

'No, to Sylvan. He's not a priest. It made me feel better. I feel great. But it's not enough. Sylvan wants me to go to the police. Even if he hadn't asked me to I probably would have done it anyway. We should have done it at the start. I'll keep your name out of it. After all, you did nothing to Alfred. But anyway, I thought I would warn you. I've missed you and I'm worried about you—'

'You abandoned me!' Toby shouted, feeling a surge of emotion, as if Ben had taken an axe to the ice that sealed him off from the world. 'You went off with Sylvan and you just left me with all of them – all those creeps – and that secret. *You left me!*'

Ben went to touch him on the arm but Toby turned on his bare heels and stormed off to the shower, turning the taps on full, the steam making Ben and everything else in the room disappear.

CHAPTER 27

Ben's statement to the police

We got up to the mountains on Friday afternoon. It was a hot day. It had been a hot week. The trip had been planned for a week or so – we had won the cricket final and this was our end-of-season splash. Doesn't sound glamorous, I know, but we always made our own fun.

We didn't travel up there together. There were two cars, plus Dr Bath had my Jeep and Severin, Leeson and Hadrien were coming up later in a van they had hired. The whole team came up except the coach, Phil Matthews. I don't know if he was invited. He's an old boy but a bit of a dickhead, works in finance. Dr Bath doesn't have anything to do with the cricket team – he's a History tutor at our college, St Anton's. He was our chaperone on the weekend away, but it's more of a nominal role than anything else; it doesn't involve any actual supervising. I have to stress that Dr Bath had no knowledge of what we did up there – either at the time or after the fact.

Anyway, it was March, hot, and the drive was long, maybe three hours. Have you been to the western side of that particular mountain range? It's quite scrubby, harsh country.

The roads get worse the higher up you get. You have to be careful of road kill and hairpin bends.

I was in a car with Toby, Levi and Julian. It was Julian's car – an Audi. We were drinking on the way up and quite hypo – excited, you know … We got there before the others.

The key was where it usually is: in the fuse box above the woodpile. We settled into our rooms then went to the lounge to start drinking. The second car arrived: Sam, Niall, Ping and Roman. Some of the boys went outside and started playing cricket; the rest of us played a drinking game – it's American, I think – called Quarters. Severin, Leeson and Hadrien were coming separately because they were bringing something up to the house. We didn't know what. It happened every time we went away together: those boys would organise a surprise. Sometimes it was a girl, or several girls. This year it was a boy – Alfred.

Alfred Khoo was a first-year student at St Anton's but our circles didn't overlap so I didn't know him before that day. At first he seemed nervous but excited to be there. I think he was happy to be asked, really pleased to be included. But when he came out of the van with Hadrien there was a bit of confusion among the others as to what he was doing there, and what we were meant to do with him. They were expecting Hadrien to provide something quite different.

I knew what it was about, though – straight away I knew. A few of us in the cricket team had been to the same boarding school. There was this strange hazing ritual at our school; we called it terrorising. That's what we'd say: 'There's going to be a terrorising tonight.'

It was done to all of us by the older boys when we were very young, eleven or twelve – but it was the overseas students who used to cop it most frequently, and it would go on until they left school. They were weaker than us physically, and so quiet. They'd be upset, of course, but they never fought back. They tended to be loners. But while the Asian kids were probably terrorised more than the rest of us, we all had a turn.

The point of it was to see how much you could terrorise someone before you couldn't go on and they couldn't stand it anymore. Like a game. It was like: how much terror can this person take? How much terror can I dish out? Some of the older boys would joke about how this was where the real education happened – and you know what? They were right. We were studying Conrad when I was first terrorised. Some mad old prof in a chalky room talking about *The Heart of Darkness*. *'The horror! The horror!'* And there it was that very night. Afterwards I didn't just understand that book intellectually, I *felt* it. But it was never about hurting anyone, it was totally about fear. That's what terrorising was: making someone so afraid, taking someone so far into a black place, that when you took someone into that place, you would feel afraid as well. Because it's fucking dark in there and you don't know if you're going to come out.

That was the worst thing. You could find your way into the dark place with very little trouble, but finding your way back – well that's another matter altogether. As those of us who were involved in this Alfred thing know only too well ...

Can I smoke? Thanks.

You probably think we were little sadists. I guess you wouldn't be wrong.

So there would usually be a couple of ringleaders; by the time we were fifteen or sixteen it was Hadrien, with Severin and Leeson – always, *always* those three. They would decide when the terrorising would happen and who it would happen to. It was organised quickly – surprise was an integral part of it – and it would always start when we were slightly out of it – like if we'd been drinking or doing drugs (there were quite a lot of drugs in the boarding house), or at 4 am when we had been fast asleep. So when the terrorising started up it would always feel like a dream – as if it was not quite real. Actually, sometimes I felt like I was in a movie or a music video clip, it was so stylised. I guess that's what happens when something becomes a ritual: you're acting a part and then the director comes on and says, 'Cut!' And that's it – it's back to bed and the next day it's back to school and it really is like nothing happened, like it was just a bad dream.

It usually took place at the far end of the boarding house, the part furthest away from the Boarding Master's rooms. We'd be woken by someone shaking us in our beds – no locks on the doors, you see – and one of the other boys would say, 'There's a terrorising.' We'd get there and the boy would already be tied up with school ties – sort of like a starfish – to the ladder of the bunk. His back would usually be facing us and he'd still be in pyjamas. Masks were essential. Sometimes all the terrorisers would be in masks or hoods and the boy, the victim, would be unmasked; other times it would be the other way round – his head would be covered with a pillow slip or something so he couldn't see.

None of the main lights would be turned on and instead we'd have torches or those funny lanterns that some schools have – gas lights. It was eerie with all the shadows and the masks, but that's what it was all about: creating an atmosphere where fear would flourish. Sometimes there would be chanting – 'Get him! Get him!' – or it might be silent, which would actually be worse. The boy tied up would sometimes be so scared he'd shit himself, or piss himself, even before we'd laid a finger on him. And he might he saying, 'Oh no – please don't!', or praying, or crying out for his mother. [pause] That's what I did, whenever it happened to me when I was young: I'd cry out for my mother. They'd laugh at that and I soon realised crying out for my mother only made it worse, so I'd stay silent and just get through it. That's the key to surviving a terrorising: just get through it. Later – well, I never enjoyed it, but I relaxed into it, rose to the challenge of it almost: not to show fear, not to get scared.

So there we'd all be – either tied up ourselves or in a circle around someone tied up. And we'd do stuff to scare him, really dark stuff – but we'd never physically hurt anybody … well, maybe a little bit, but nothing too bad, nothing that lasted.

God – listen to me – you still don't know what we actually did, do you? To describe it sounds so disgusting, it even makes me feel ashamed to say the words. Out of context it sounds perverted. Anyway, somebody might pull the victim's pyjamas off and throw stuff at him – stuff that didn't hurt too much, like textbooks or trainers. We had a switch, like a light whip, and sometimes Hadrien or someone would pull down the kid's pants and would stroke the boy's body with the soft bit of the switch, like a caress, and the kid would be frightened, really frightened, whimpering and stuff, but also often [pause] turned on, and Hadrien would know it and would whisper in the kid's ear, 'You faggot,' and then bring the switch down hard across their thighs. God – it was pretty dark stuff when you were twelve years old. Then the other kids would be circling, poking you with sports equipment, jeering at your prick, mocking its shape, its size, commenting on whether it was circumcised or uncircumcised. Whatever. Probably a lot of boys from the school now have sexual problems.

But it wasn't always like that. Other times the terrorising happened in bathrooms – they would lead you in there and make you undress and get in a freezing cold bath and then they'd tell you that you were going to die as they lowered a plugged-in razor or alarm clock into the bath. Who'd flinch first? No one died but the aim of terrorising was to make you think that you might.

I remember when they did it to Leeson. They did all sorts of things to Leeson – and then he did all sorts of things to me, and to others. Not the stuff you reminisce about at the school reunion, not something you'd tell your wife. Um … what else? Things with electrodes, bags over your head and just when the oxygen is about to run out and you are thinking of struggling they untie you. But never a scratch or a bruise on you the next day. [laughter] I'd be too scared to see a shrink now – I'm sure I'd be far too much work for them. But strangely that sort of bad education does make you fearless. I don't scare easily, nor do any of the boys I went to school with. Prime ministers and captains of industry went there, people you read about in the papers who, well, don't flinch.

But in the mountains with Alfred it was different. For a start we were older. It wasn't just kid stuff anymore. And we were with other people who mightn't understand where it came from – people like Levi and Toby really don't understand. People like Sam or Ping, who weren't at school with us, well, they were there, they went along with it – but there was a point where they got freaked out; they didn't realise it was something that'd been fine-tuned over the years. It wasn't a St Anton's thing – it was a school thing. If it's happened to you, you know how far to push it with others. You don't burn someone, for example; you don't light a cigarette and push it into someone's skin. What you might do is light a cigarette and then hold it over someone's skin until they can feel the heat, until you aren't drawing pain out of them, but the anticipation of pain – there's a difference. It's a crucial difference.

But back to Alfred … There was a show-trial first – a literal kangaroo court. [laughs] Most of us are studying law, you see, and one of the classes is Trial Practice and Advocacy – we do a lot of mock trials. Hadrien thought it would be fun to put on a trial. Alfred was charged with a variety of terrorism offences, including planning jihad in the Bio-med cafe. It was just a sham charge, an excuse to give the terrorising a context. I don't even know if Alfred's a Muslim. Actually I think he's probably Christian – not that it matters.

I suppose you're wondering why I feel remorse now, with Alfred, when obviously I didn't feel the same way at school. But it was different with Alfred, way different. Sure, it was about fear, but it was also really violent; they were actually hurting him. I was standing next to him when Severin whacked him across the chest with a pole. I could hear his ribs cracking. Have you ever heard that sound? It's not very nice – and Alfred was tied up in such a way that his injuries could only get worse. I saw something blooming under his skin, like a rose. It was blood pooling; he was bleeding internally.

Severin gave the pole to Niall and Niall whacked him really, really hard in the knees. Kneecapped him. I couldn't believe it. This wasn't what was meant to happen. [cough] Niall's training to be a doctor – he's meant to heal, not hurt people. It was almost like they meant to kill him. I mean, how could you bring him back to college in that state, all banged up? What were they going to say? It was stupid and totally reckless.

I think I realised then this wasn't a normal terrorising. There was nothing cerebral about it. It wasn't Joseph Conrad or *King Lear*; it was just pure violence.

All this time while they were hitting him and beforehand, they kept asking him about some group called YIMA, some Islamic thing. They wanted to know about bombs and plots to blow up the university and Jemaah Islamiyah and al-Qaeda, and Alfred was crying and saying, 'I don't know what you're talking about. I'm not a terrorist. I'm not a terrorist.' I realised I was part of what appeared to be a lynching or a rendition ...

God, what else? Alfred was screaming in pain but he had a gag on so it came out a bit muffled, like a moan, and Hadrien was slapping him, telling him to shut up. [bitter laugh] Ah, Hadrien's way. He had a special way. First he'd stroke Alfred's hair and cheek, like you would with a girl, being so gentle – then he'd slap Alfred with such force! That one was an old school trick. And – this was the worst, I don't even like talking about it, but they, er, Hadrien and Severin, got the handle of a cricket bat, smeared it with Vas, and put it into Alfred. They asked Sam to take off his socks and then they shoved one in Alfred's mouth, and made Alfred bend over and then rogered him a few times with the handle of the bat, and there was lots of cheering and this feeling in the room of intense excitement and some of the guys were jerking off – and there was a lot of blood. Alfred's blood. I mean, it was everywhere, running all down his legs, all over the floor.

What was I doing? I guess you could call me a bystander. I didn't actually touch Alfred – no, that's a lie, I did touch him. Alfred's hands were tied to the bunk and behind the ladder. Towards the end, when it got really bad, I was holding his hand. Or was he holding mine? After they had raped him, then hit and cut him, they threw petrol on him. That's an old trick from boarding school days too. Petrol and a match. Your body's coated with petrol and some boy holding a match with trembling hands is almost close enough to your body for you to feel his breath. All you can do is grit your teeth through that one – try not to imagine what your own body would smell like on fire. Survive that and you're left with a curious mental toughness.

My mum once said I was a neutral boy, that I was opaque. She didn't mean it as a compliment. But after you've been terrorised a few times you do become neutral. It's like nothing can get at you anymore.

Of course, it went beyond all that with Alfred.

One of the guys, Roman, had been out in the bush with a hunting knife. He was outside yelling – he'd been trying to kill a kangaroo but he couldn't finish the job. God, he was so drunk, in his underpants, incoherent. Some of the boys went out there to have a look and came back inside with organs and blood and smeared it on themselves and on Alfred. It was chaotic already, but this made it worse, like bad physical theatre or something. The kangaroo blood was a funny colour – dark orange. A couple of the boys threw up at the smell, and also because they'd been drinking a lot. Julian saw them later washing the animal blood off in the showers, great clouds of pink steam billowing down the hall.

Alfred was hysterical by the time the boys came in with the bits of kangaroo. There was the blood and the pain and then being covered in petrol and now animal blood. And these stupid accusations of terrorism. They had some pamphlets with them that they kept reading bits out of, saying, 'You believe this, don't you – that there'll be virgins awaiting you in paradise after you blow up the Student Union building?'

And Leeson kept lighting matches. [weeping] Sorry. [weeping]

No, it's okay, I'll be okay. There's not much more to say, really.

Roman went back outside; like I said, he was having trouble killing the kangaroo. I'm not surprised, really. It was protecting the joey. Sam was shouting to come out quick: the kangaroo had kicked Roman in the head. Leeson dropped the matches and ran out with the pole – I guess to bludgeon the kangaroo to death. And suddenly they were all gone. It was just Alfred and me in the room.

The room was a mess and there was blood everywhere. It stunk. I untied Alfred and sort of lifted him down. That's when [weeping] … he – he looked at me and said, 'It's okay,' and sort of leant on me – a hug, I guess, or maybe he just couldn't bear his own weight after what they did to him. [weeping]

That was when I felt it – so hard to describe, and I know you'll think I'm weird, but something flowed from him to me. Some sort of energy that can only be described as good – it felt like forgiveness or, I don't know, absolution. It was the strangest thing, so powerful, so good, and then I realised what a very bad person I was. [pause] It was like I woke up – and I tried to hold him a bit longer and the blood and petrol on him was on me and I was crying and he was saying, 'It's okay, Ben, it's okay.' He knew my name. [weeping]

[break]

… Sorry, yes – I'll be fine.

He – Alfred, that is – said, 'I'm frightened here. I must leave.'

And he took his clothes and off he went. He just limped out into the night, out into the bush. I should have tried to stop him, I guess, cleaned him up, got him to a hospital. But I honestly thought he'd be safer out there.

The other boys came back. The kangaroo had got away. I told them I'd untied Alfred and he had run off into the bush. They called me a faggot terrorist collaborator, but suddenly everyone seemed quite tired, flat almost. That was when they went to the showers to wash off the animal's blood, and Alfred's blood too. No one said anything more about Alfred except Hadrien, who told me, 'You'd better hope that he's not found.' And I said why, and he said, 'Well, old chap, we went a bit too far this time. Not like school, where there were no marks on the body.'

Then suddenly I panicked – really panicked. We had to find Alfred. It was still night. I went to Toby's room – woke him up. He's my best friend, not morally fucked up like I am. Well, I thought he wasn't morally fucked up. I thought, Toby will do the right thing.

I thought we could make things right. We'd look for Alfred – he wouldn't have made it that far with his injuries. We'd find him and take a car and drive him to a hospital. It would be his decision whether or not to go to the police. But we'd go to the Master, tell the Master, and there'd be consequences and punishment and I'd be punished too. I needed that. I believed then that things could be undone, atoned through punishment. I thought we could turn it around and make it right with Alfred.

But of course, as you know, that wasn't how it worked out. That was overly optimistic of me. Even those less culpable … I don't know – they forgot about Alfred really quickly. They seemed more concerned about getting away with it than about what they had done, or how they had failed to protect him.

CHAPTER 28

Ben found Grace sitting on a blanket under the Faraway Tree, reading a book. He sat down next to her and told her what he had wanted to confess to her in the library on the night of the ball but hadn't been able to bring himself to say. He told her how he'd been alone with Alfred in the bunkroom just after the boys had run out into the bush, how he had removed the ropes from around Alfred's wrists and ankles. How in some places his skin had been raw and sanded down to the bone. He told her how Alfred hadn't been crying, which was surprising. How the two of them had sat together, not talking. How he had never felt as close to another person as he had for those few minutes. Their hearts were beating so fast together – synchronised – he could hear it (and oh, how he'd always thought he would experience that with a lover but instead it was there, then, with Alfred, after a night explicit with a kind of anti-love). Alfred didn't seem to be blaming him – instead he looked at Ben in a shining way, with perfect understanding in his eyes. He looked at Ben with forgiveness. God, it was incredible. The purest thing he had ever felt passed between them, between him and this boy he didn't even know. That feeling stayed close to him, expanded his heart and changed everything for him, but it also made him feel so, so ashamed.

Outside, as the creatures of the bush rioted, Hadrien, Leeson, Niall, Ping, Roman, Severin and Sam lit a fire, drank more, were sick, covered their faces with mud and covered the night with their screaming – their screaming for no good reason at all. They maimed a kangaroo and came back to the bunkroom, innards hanging off their hands ... And Grace touched Ben lightly on the shoulder and said, 'Enough, enough.'

Two weeks after the St Anton's Ball the Master, the man who held it all together, left abruptly for a conference in Montreal on David Foster Wallace – only days after his wife moved her things out of the college.

Around the cloisters and quadrangles Dr Bath heard the students speculate feverishly. Was there another man? How could she have just fallen out of love with him? When the police and Dr Bath went to their cottage, it seemed the Master had left in a hurry, barely pausing to pack. His wife's perfume still hung in the unaired bedroom and his ties lay coiled around the bedposts and on the desk next to where her earrings had been, just resting for a bit until he returned with all his vigour and energy, with all his assurances that everything would be okay. His wife would be on his arm, repentant, and everything would go back to the way it had been.

Left in charge was Dr Bath – who had begun to feel that the only thing he had a knack for was being on the scene at the worst possible time. He was uncertain how to handle the accounts or administration and so the college just spluttered to a halt. The garden grew wild and even the animals were neglected. They were fed at odd hours and roamed hungry and aggressive around the grounds during the day, and at night bleated and brayed in a way that suggested torment more than restlessness.

Then there were the police, still there, moving in on something, with their tedious questions and their endless patience. Would they ever go away and leave the college in peace? Dr Williams asked desperately one night after dinner. Without the Master's energy, the gatherings after dinner were morose and dispiriting. Most nights the tutors broke with tradition and didn't even meet in the Senior Common Room, instead each taking their own bottle and peeling off to drink alone in their quarters.

Bath felt too weak and depleted to resist all the new systems the police wanted to install in the college, until one day he realised it was now, after a court order, the police controlling St Anton's – like a coup at the palace, with the military materialising at the gates and bad new rules and curfews suddenly in place.

Students had to fill out yellow forms to tell police if they would be away for the night (*Attending: My aunt's for dinner. Return: In the morning before chapel*). The police slapped a ban on alcohol and suspended the college's liquor licence as they investigated the parties that had got out of hand and allegations that students had been raped. The Football Dinner still went ahead, along with the party afterwards in the Junior Common Room, but it was a joyless evening, with the police in civilian clothes (Lowell, Tarrant and Sanderson in neatly pressed jeans, tucked-in T-shirts) supervising the students, overseeing the service of lemon squash in plastic cups. Meanwhile, groups of freshers lurked in dark corners with hip flasks, a speakeasy was set up in Levi's old room, and Lab Rat danced by himself to Donna Summer in the middle of the JCR like he was taking part in a piece of bad performance art. Bath loitered miserably near the DJ's booth, craving a drink so badly he was sweating and his hands trembling, trying not to focus on the dreadful 1970s pop music being piped through the speakers. Could any of them listen to Abba now without it being a sickening reminder of that time?

Ben laughed to himself. He'd skipped the football turn, which was no alcohol anyway, and got drunk in his room instead. He'd missed it, this feeling of warmth that alcohol gave. He fell on his bed, smiling at the knots he had twisted himself in. What a strange business, life; he'd been taking it so seriously – always had.

This feeling was good. There had been a sudden shower and the quadrangle lawn had yielded up a soft, pleasant, grassy smell, the sheep baa-ing from their pens. Charlotte was asleep on the bed. They had got drunk together, talked about the most amazing things – the future, backpacking around France, their possible careers, all the bright things that awaited them. He had sung a stupid made-up song to her that had made her laugh: '*Got a missed call from you the other day/You rang my phone when I had gone away/But*

I texted you/Said I'm here to stay/I loved the trainers you bought for me on Christmas Day.'

It was so simple, being together again. They had got drunk, then fallen on the bed, laughing and stroking each other. They had made love. Ben said the words to himself in a sort of awe ('made love, made love') and for once they didn't feel stupid or sentimental or dangerous. God, it felt good – the heat of her – her skin. She was lying on top of him, voluptuous and soft. He felt enveloped and safe, like he was deep underground. He had sung his made-up song and she had laughed at all the wrong notes he hit, then she'd fallen asleep, an arm comradely over his shoulder. This was better than brotherly love, this was better than the cricket team or the rowing crew, this was better than the Jerusalems even. It was better than all the sport and all the religion. All the pain was gone – well, at least for tonight it was gone … or masked, maybe. It didn't matter: for the first time in a long while, he didn't feel like shit.

Yet he'd avoided passing by Toby's room and he fretted that by doing the right thing by Alfred he had done the wrong thing by his friends. All he had done was try to make his life into something he could live with.

He stood up after a while, naked, the smell of rain coming in through the open window, the moonlight like a torch. He poured himself the rest of the bottle of red wine. Music was playing softly, an old Pogues album, and he sang along to 'Rainy Night in Soho'– a song he and Toby sang once when they got drunk in the Irish bar of Toby's hometown, stumbling home fucked up through sheets of rain, fumbling with the keys, falling through the doorway laughing at nothing so hard it hurt. Only a year ago – before he'd found God and Toby had found drugs. This was a future of which they'd had no warning.

Charlotte slept on as he pirouetted a couple of times and pretended he was waltzing with her. God, it was nice, this feeling of pleasure – that was what it was. It didn't cost them much; it made them both happy.

Even when she was wrong for him she was right for him: damaged and brittle and afraid and bursting with mania at times when she should have been contained and silent. He remembered her slumped at his door – what an embarrassment, he had thought back then. Damaged, a disgrace. Now that he was a bit damaged and disgraced himself, he felt regret at the harsh judgment. Who wasn't a bit disgraced? Who wasn't a bit damaged?

He fell backwards laughing, lying down on the carpet, wine bottle in hand, and lit a cigarette. With his free hand he touched the part of Charlotte's back just before it curved upwards to her arse. He let it rest there, closed his eyes and hummed along to the Pogues.

He let his mind drift. Something in him was letting go. Something so deep within him that it had no name was uncoiling – he could sense it now, making him feel expansive, like the warmth of the wine and the heat of Charlotte's skin. This was it: he actually felt happy, so happy he could skip outside into the quadrangle and sing.

He didn't. He let the cigarette burn down to the tip and his hand rest on the small of Charlotte's back and tried to hold the feeling, cling on to it until there was just the memory of a feeling left, and tomorrow there would just be the memory of this memory, but that would be okay as long as there was a bit of light left in it.

He got up and lay beside Charlotte, and was about to fall asleep when his phone beeped with a message from Toby, and his heart hit his throat that this perfect night might include a detente with his best friend.

You around? Come to my room, we need to talk about Alfred.

When Ben got there the door was open and Toby was looking intently at his phone.

'I'm so glad you texted – I felt terrible about how we left things at the pool,' said Ben.

From outside there was the sound of chanting – another women's group protest, their troops replenished with activists from other campuses.

'God, I can't believe they're still out there – and in the rain, too,' said Ben. 'Did you see Lucy? I can't believe it, she's, I don't know, different … She gave this hard-core speech about female oppression at college.'

'Did you go to the police?' asked Toby tersely.

They looked at each other – stared, really – for what felt like the first time in months. Toby looked terrible, like he hadn't been sleeping. There was a sadness in his face that Ben had never seen there before.

'Yes,' he replied. 'You know I had to. I couldn't live with myself anymore.'

Toby nodded but didn't seem to take it in; instead he looked down at his phone and started texting. 'That's just fucking stupid. We were going to get away with it.'

'What do you mean *we*? You weren't even involved,' said Ben, confused.

There was a sound at the door, and Ben turned.

It was Hadrien, with Severin, Niall, Leeson, Roman and Ping behind him in a sort of phalanx. They stepped into the room and filled it up.

Hadrien was looking even more dandified than ever – wearing a white suit with a fine yellow pinstripe. In his pale clothing he was luminous, an angular quarter-moon. He took off his jacket and laid it carefully over the back of Toby's chair.

'Ben,' said Hadrien, leaning in to give Ben a brisk, dry kiss on the lips. 'Shalom, brother. It's been so long and we've missed you.'

Hadrien's mouth was hard and his skin smelt clean, like it had been freshly soaped.

Toby's jaw was twitching and he looked pale, almost as pale as Hadrien. He didn't meet Ben's eye as he closed and locked the door, as Leeson wedged a towel in the space between the door and the floor.

Ben flicked a quick look of concern towards Toby.

'Toby? What the …?'

Severin was flexing some revolting muscle in his forearm, a forearm that had been freshly, grotesquely tattooed with two 'S's intertwined, and the room was suddenly very hot and very still and quiet – quiet for one long second – then Ben, before anyone had laid a finger on him, curled up on the ground, arms protecting his head, knowing what would come next and accepting it.

CHAPTER 29

Julian turned and said coldly, 'You absolute cunt.' He and Sam had stumbled into Toby's room during the beating and dragged Ben out into the cloister.

Toby turned to Hadrien to see his reaction to such an unprecedented show of disrespect, but found instead that everyone was looking at him.

'Who *are* you?' continued Julian, flushed and angry, kicking the door shut, while dragging Ben out from beneath his armpits.

'He's right, Toby – you really have become a total cunt,' said Hadrien, laughing, as he and the others were leaving. 'I could almost like you.'

'Fuck off,' said Toby, before turning to Niall and asking if perhaps there was any of his pill stash left.

After taking some more Oxycontin (crushing and snorting was more effective than swallowing, he'd found), Toby lay on his bed, not even bothering to sponge the blood off the carpet, just chasing the steadfast old urge for oblivion.

He fell quickly into another one of those dreams – subterranean, disjointed, yet somehow more real than his waking life. A cricket match, players in white, looking like pale flames against the deep green pitch: a tableau as deliberate and composed as an art work.

A helicopter crashing on the pitch, an explosion, smoke, flames and blue gas in the air, and Toby still on the cricket pitch – about to bowl, his arm forever overhead, wrist dropped, the ball suspended in the sky.

Here is the helicopter, here is the fire, here are the screams as bodies fall out onto the turf and roll on the green to extinguish the flames. But the cricket match – both suspended and continuous – is doomed to always be happening, just like in a painting. *More happy love! more happy, happy love! For ever warm and still to be enjoy'd, For ever panting, and for ever young.*

Then he and Ben are in Sri Lanka, except it's Berlin and everywhere there are wild dogs, graffiti, abandoned buildings … They walk along Torstrasse and the sky is low and grey, puffy with the rain that's yet to fall, and Toby wants to ask (but doesn't): 'Where is the beach?'

The cricket pitch again and the flames, and no one is moving and he wants to scream 'Run!' but no sound is coming out. Then he is in a room – a room he has never been in – and Charlotte is in her yellow dress from the ball and standing very close to him, loosening his belt buckle, and he doesn't move. Behind her on a chair is Ben wearing a suit, and Toby is aware of Charlotte touching him inside, then outside, his underpants and back again, and this makes him embarrassed because Ben is there, but instead he asks Ben (heavy lids over green eyes, tired and pale) why he is wearing a suit and Ben says, 'Didn't you hear? I have to go to court.'

Toby opened the door, looking like he'd just woken up.

Dr Bath – feeling awful, stricken – pitched himself towards Toby, almost falling on him.

'Are you okay, Dr Bath?' Toby asked, still mostly asleep.

'I'm so sorry, Toby,' he said in a sort of anguish. 'I had to talk to the police. I tried to avoid it – I went to a conference, and then stayed away from the college as long as I could, but I got back and they were still there, they still wanted to talk to me. They knew I was at Evelyn that weekend and that I knew what went on, but oh my dear, I didn't expect you would get into trouble. You and I were in the lounge talking. I told the police that. I can't understand why your name kept coming up.'

Toby sighed. 'I don't care anymore. Anyway, it was Ben, not you, who was the rat.'

Dr Bath smiled. 'Do you remember that night?'

'Bits of it,' said Toby.

'That was one of the best nights ever,' said Dr Bath. 'Talking to you. Do you remember?'

Toby nodded dumbly. 'World War II or something?'

Dr Bath's smile broadened. 'That's right. Sitting on the couch with you, having a cup of tea and talking about military history. It really was lovely. It was the best night. I wish we could have talked all night.'

Toby seemed to look at him with surprise. 'Really? There was nothing lovely about that night.'

'I'm so sorry, Toby, I didn't mean to get you in trouble. You mean more to me ...'

And with that, his face blazing with affection and humiliation, he stumbled back out to the cloisters. It was the closest he had ever come in his life to a declaration of love.

One of Ben's eyes had pretty much closed over and a cheekbone was smashed. Below the neck he didn't even have the energy to inspect the damage done. Julian drove him to casualty; an easy feeling between them, even after all that had happened.

From the radio Bob Marley, softly singing 'Exodus', filled the car and the gaps in conversation. Ben lay exhausted across the back seat on bloody beach towels, and looked in wonder at the city buildings as they passed. They crossed a bridge lit up so beautifully it rivalled the Milky Way. The water under it lapped at the shore. Beneath them a ship moved upriver, its horn blowing in long bursts like a regretful goodbye.

'I love a river that's working, not just for show,' said Julian, and Ben agreed, nodding as much as his head would allow but not saying anything.

They left the bridge and drove onto the tighter roads around the business district. With his head back, the whole scene – the lights of the buildings, the streetlamps, the traffic lights and the skyscrapers towering over their grey, elegant Victorian neighbours – struck him as a work of moving art constructed just for him, seen only by him. It was a blur of colour, with small explosions of light. The dry air coming through the open window cooled his face and chest and ruffled his hair. The city at night: it was so beautiful he got a lump in his throat just looking at it.

'You comfortable back there, Benj?' asked Julian. 'You got enough air? You're not bleeding on my seats, I hope.'

'Where's Levi?' asked Ben.

Julian sighed. 'No one knows. He just left one morning – after the ball – and no one's seen him since. Left me some stupid note, Toby too. He unfriended me on Facie.' Julian's voice cracked. 'I think he's got a new number, because he's not answering his old one. I broke into his room – it looks trashed. Shit everywhere, clothes in the bin, all his posters ripped down. Leeson's turned it into a bar. Sam's going as well; he's leaving tonight. Don't say anything to him. I don't think he feels safe at college anymore.'

Julian sounded genuinely hurt and bewildered. 'I mean, Levi was my best friend. You don't just leave without telling your best friend, do you?'

'Did you think he might take you with him?'

'Yeah – of course that's what I thought. That we'd make a break for it, but we'd do it together. Kind of like how Toby thought he and you would stick together.'

'Ouch,' said Ben. Julian shrugged.

He left Ben at the doors of the casualty department with genuine regret. 'I'd love to go in with you and wait four hours before you get seen and hold your hand when you get stitched up, but I'd better get back to college. I'm thinking of going back to my parents' tomorrow. I'll need to pack. Sorry, mate.'

He shrugged again and ambled away, but not before turning around suddenly and saying: 'I missed you while you were off with that freaky cult. So was this interest in the Jerusalems just a fraud, then, or were you really into it?'

'It's not a cult.'

'But that guy you were hanging with was really weird … Tambourine Boy.'

'Sylvan.'

'So what's he like, then?'

Ben didn't have the words. 'Sylvan? Well he's – he's special, and I cannot do him justice.'

Julian grinned at him with his loose smile and said, 'Well I can't pretend to understand the whole religion thing, but I guess there's a lot I don't really understand.'

Ben nodded and hobbled inside. The bright lights hit him as hard as another blow. He took a number, aware that his appearance was causing other patients to recoil from him, and waited. It gave him time to ponder why, when he should be feeling so bad, he was feeling better than he had all year.

A man who'd sliced his finger off while making sashimi at a Japanese restaurant was called into a cubicle.

An ashen-faced child who'd choked on a chicken bone was seen by a nurse.

A teenage girl, so drunk she was almost paralytic, was collected by her worn-looking parents.

Why was he feeling so good? Could it be because finally he had spoken out about what had happened to Alfred?

CHAPTER 30

The hallway was unlit and gloomy. No one was home except the dog, who padded up to Ben, his wet eyes and tongue shining in the dark. Ben wished his mum were home. He wanted her to clean his cuts like she used to when he was a child and had tumbled from play equipment or fallen from his bike. That feeling ... being clean again, her touch on his face, his face on her chest ... After he had that elemental comfort he could tell her all that had happened to him: his long, strange journey from the bunkroom; Sylvan, his baptism; the police interview; being bashed in Toby's room; Toby sitting at his desk staring at the wall.

But she wasn't there.

He filled the bath tub and a large wine glass. It hurt to lower himself into the tub. He felt like an elderly person might and wished for the assistance of a hand rail. 'Arhhhh!' the water on his wounds made him cry out, and suddenly the water in the tub turned red.

'A blood bath,' said Ben, wishing someone were around to appreciate the joke, but then he stopped giggling when he remembered that the last time there had been that much blood in the water was that night with Alfred, and he had scrubbed it from his hands, trying to remove particles of skin and blood from under his nails like Lady Macbeth.

He got out of the tub and drained the bath, a red watermark clinging to the enamel. In his old room he stood naked, surrounded by childhood things.

There was a hush in the empty house and Ben responded with an equally quiet reverence when moving about his room, touching his things, all these old pieces of him, as lightly as if they might turn to ash in his hands. Holiday snaps, Ben with skis and a toboggan, then photos from London when his family had lived there when he was a child, the wintry expanse of Hyde Park behind him and his mother, ghostly trees and white skies.

Then summer holidays at the beach that turned his hair white-blond and his skin brown. A party at a cousin's house in the country. They had horses and ate only organic food – no sweets. Then that summer ended and it was off to boarding school.

He was ten when he first went, staring uncertainly up at his mother, the camera between them as she took the first photo of him leaving home. 'I'm too young!' he told no one in particular. He touched the face in the photo – his scared younger self – wanting to be back there and do things differently.

Then he came to a wall of what his father called 'the Glory Years': sporting trophies, academic prizes, certificates, rugby jumpers, team photos. There they were at ten, twelve, fourteen, fifteen and seventeen: he, Hadrien, Severin and Leeson in a crowd of boys in rows. After the first year the small, uncertain look on his face had gone, replaced by a blank expression. What sort of boy had he been? It was impossible to tell by looking at the photos.

More photos from boarding school: Ben in the debating finals, Ben in front of the boarding house, Ben holding a football, Ben in front of cricket stumps holding a bat, Ben at outdoor education classes, where in one week he hunted, killed and skinned his own dinner and was taught about Homer and *The Odyssey*.

He lay back on the bed, almost worn out now. The photo of him hunting rested on his chest. An unexpected erection had occurred during his trip down memory lane. He came with a choked cry into an old T-shirt just as the front door opened and a light was turned on. Mum! Ben dressed quickly, opened his door and went out into the hallway, standing in the shadows, not wanting her to see his damaged face just yet.

She was laughing. She sounded a bit tipsy, like she'd been out for dinner and had an extra drink. So he would have to talk to his father, then. He cursed softly in the dark. Gerald was away so often now Ben had assumed he wouldn't be home. His mother laughed again and said, in a voice that he'd never heard her use (lighter, girlish), 'I haven't had that much fun in years. Really, I haven't. I really needed tonight – thank you.'

There was a male laugh, not his father's. Ben suddenly felt sick again, all the welts and bruises on his skin suddenly coming alive in a pulsating dance. The dog came to Ben's leg and started whining for some affection.

His mother stopped laughing and said sharply, 'Who's there?'

'It's me, Mum,' said Ben heavily from the door, not wanting to come out yet, not wanting her to see his face, not wanting to see who she was with.

'Oh, hi, Ben,' said his mother, trying to sound natural as they talked to each other from their respective hiding places. 'You should have told me you were coming home, darling. I've just been catching up with a friend: Ray, from the Serenity Health Spa – you know, the one in Indonesia.'

Ben said nothing.

'Ray, thank you for seeing me home,' she said formally. 'You should probably go now.'

Ben peered out from his hiding spot and saw a tight grimace on his mother's face and a milder one of confusion on Ray's.

Ray looked to be around his own age, maybe a year or two older. Ben felt he had seen someone he wasn't meant to see. He felt he had interrupted something that was moving somewhere. He didn't want to think about it. He withdrew back into his room and left his mother standing by the door in the hall. Ray crunched back up the drive with a muted goodbye.

Ben and his mother. They were like actors who had forgotten their lines. No, worse than that: they were like actors who'd forgotten what parts they were meant to be playing.

Ben got back into bed, lay as still as a corpse. He lit a cigarette. His mother stayed rooted to her spot in the hall. A long time passed before she knocked on his bedroom door.

'Benj, don't be bothered about Ray. He's just a friend from the spa. He was dropping me home.'

'Why don't you hang out with people your own age?' Ben asked through the door.

Because I miss being with you, he wanted her to say, but she didn't. Instead she said, 'Can I come in?'

'Okay, but don't turn the light on,' said Ben.

She did as he asked and stood there in the dark.

'Oh, Ben, for heaven's sake – what are you doing smoking?'

'Shut up, Mum.'

'Don't tell me to shut up, Ben. Put that cigarette out. At least, when you're in my house you'll stop smoking.'

'I'll do what I like. Who was that guy?'

His mother was near tears. 'Where did you pick up such an awful habit? We didn't bring you up to smoke. And Ray is my friend – I do need them, you know.'

He said nothing.

A panel of light from the hall hit her face. She looked anguished; she had aged, his mother, who had fought so fiercely against it. Ben could barely have described what her naked skin felt like; when he kissed her cheek it left a greasy mark on his lips from all those creams she bought! Yet here she was, suddenly an old woman.

'Talk to me, Ben,' she sighed. 'I have no energy for this anymore. Just talk to me and tell me what's been going on.'

A new day, and through the curtains the sky was a deep winter blue. Ben came out of the bedroom, still groggy and half asleep. The enormous television was on and Ben's mother sat perched on the edge of her chair.

'Oh my God, your face!' she exclaimed, but uncharacteristically turned quickly back to the TV. 'St Anton's again.' Her voice was anxious. 'Isn't that your school friend, John Leeson?'

Yes, it was. Ben could hardly take it in, even though he'd been expecting it. There on the early morning news he saw Leeson, Hadrien, Severin, Roman, Julian, Ping, Niall and, most horrifically, Dr Bath cuffed and being led out of the college by police. 'Sorry,' he murmured to no one in particular.

There was a still photo of Alfred Khoo, a close shot that they'd probably got from his student ID. Then the vision changed to a dawn shot outside what looked like a terrace house and Levi emerged, glasses askew, handcuffed and head hanging, two grey-haired people in dressing gowns trying to get into the police car with him.

'Isn't that—'

'Quiet, Mum.'

The blood was pounding so hard in his head he could barely hear the reporter: something about charges of grievous bodily harm, and intention to cause serious injury, the words 'custody' and 'rendition'. Detective Tarrant was giving a press conference: assault of a fellow student, police investigation, many witnesses, acted in concert, cover-up, further investigation, serious assault, racial hate laws, animal cruelty. The protest outside the gate had swollen so much they had needed to block off the streets.

No Toby, though. Where was Toby?

He prayed Toby had been spared even though his former best friend had sat detached at his desk, out of it and glassy-eyed, as Hadrien, Leeson, Severin, Roman, Niall and Ping had beaten him savagely the previous night. His impassive, corrupted best friend, who'd summoned him to his room via text message – who'd set him up in the coolest manner. Toby hadn't even blinked at the blood, hadn't even flinched when Ben was screaming.

He turned and his mother was staring at him, scared.

'Oh, my God. Will they come for you?'

He nodded. Yes, they'll come for me. He tried to imagine how the handcuffs would feel. How everything now would feel, the trade-off he had made: that to feel free on the inside, to feel free in spirit, he would no longer be free in body. He could live with that.

His mother was standing in the kitchen, arms folded, tears dripping down her face. She still didn't understand.

'I'll be okay,' he wanted to say. But the words caught in his throat as he heard a rapping on the door.

The next winter there was a trial. The judge called it a crime of 'grave moral turpitude'.

One newspaper wrote:

> *The police told the court there was a culture of bullying and rumbling that had escalated into torture and sexual assaults. The college, and boarding school that many members of the cricket team had attended, were breeding grounds for violence.*

The Crown-appointed psychiatrist took the stand and said, 'The cricket team peer group was regulated and maintained through collective oppressive practices characterised by the boys' attempts to acquire power, mark prestige and validate or prove their own ways of being male.'

The newspapers followed the story closely and there was even political fallout when the sentences were handed down. They were a bit on the light side. Media identity Derryn Hinch organised a 'Rally for Victims' at Parliament House, protesting against soft sentencing. But it was too late. The deals had already been done. The Crown had dropped twelve charges against the accused boys – Roman, Hadrien, Severin, Niall, Ping, Leeson, Sam, Ben, Levi and Julian – in exchange for guilty pleas to the lesser charges of aggravated indecent assault. They were all given community corrections orders, which specified counselling and psychiatric treatment. The boys' lawyers tendered psych reports on plea, confirming private counselling had been taking place since their arrests. All the boys were required to complete one hundred and fifty hours of community work over twelve months – hours of chopping vegetables in a community kitchen, planting trees in a national park, sorting out recycling at a depot. Some of them complained about this bitterly, but their lawyers advised them to accept it with good grace. Hadrien, despite the skill and expense of his barrister, was given the heaviest penalty for his role as the 'ringleader', but even then his fourteen-month sentence was wholly suspended due to his lack of prior convictions and excellent references from a number of youth charities he supported.

Toby was charged as an accessory (found guilty, given a community corrections order), while Dr Bath and the Master avoided any accessory charges due to their co-operation with police.

There were civil suits against the college, and later against Ben's old school. They dragged on for years. A number of boys had had psychological problems after being terrorised in the boarding house ('some up to sixty times', journalists reported, a bit lasciviously, Ben thought). They sued the school and the college that should have been protecting them.

After the criminal trial, Alfred sued St Anton's in a personal capacity for lack of supervision, breach of duty of care and compensation for his physical and psychological injuries.

He had been repatriated to Malaysia in October when he was well enough to fly. Two years later he was due to return to present evidence when the case opened in the Supreme Court. On the eve of his arrival the college asked for mediation and settled for an undisclosed sum. Newspapers put the figure at $750,000. Alfred's father – through a translator – said Alfred had made a full physical recovery and had finished his studies back in Malaysia but required weekly therapy. He'd been diagnosed with post-traumatic stress disorder, and was still living at home, 'a fragment of the boy he once was'.

The year after the arrests the College Council appointed a new Master: a middle-aged, dour-faced Scot who was more administrator than academic. He moved his wife and teenage children into the cottage. The wife, with her sensible slacks and her slightly sad smile, saved her attention for the rosebushes. The children were sent to a nearby minor private school and were forbidden from frequenting the Senior or

Junior Common Rooms and the banks of the river. The new Master's friends were the clergy or Scottish academics he had known from St Andrew's. He relied heavily on the Old Boys' Association for advice on running the college – suffice it to say that no Hollywood movie was ever made at St Anton's. At the High Table the new Master rationed the wine to one lone bottle a night, with port taken once a week on a Wednesday. The decadence and blazing life force that had powered college life were finally extinguished. All that was left were rumours and legend.

It only took another two years – another two cricket seasons, two Easter breaks, the onset of two winters, two more college balls, two women's hockey finals, two debating championships, two losses in the rowing, two springs of newborn lambs in the stables, two final swot vacs, two blistering summers – for the students who had been there at that terrible, notorious time to leave.

Two years and they were all in share houses, or inner-city flats, or back with their parents, or travelling overseas. Another two years after that and they were in law firms or working as judges' associates or articled clerks – or were famous for working as a muse (Octavia), or as a celebrity vet (Giles), or for dying in Afghanistan after joining the army then promptly getting blown up by a roadside bomb (Sam).

Everyone from that terrible year who had talked about Hadrien, who had worried about Ben, who had longed to be taken into Toby's confidence, who had gossiped about Charlotte, who had speculated about Levi, who had been frightened of Leeson, who had been disgusted by Ping, who had been enchanted by the Master and his wife; everyone who had loved Alfred briefly and from afar, who had prayed for him; everyone who had sat in the sun in the quadrangle and felt the sweet soft summer air skate lightly across their skin, who had sighed and shut their eyes and let a snatch of song distract them from their study; everyone who had fallen in love under the Faraway Tree, who had wandered drunk from Elysian Fields to Isolodes Towers, who had been summoned to the oval by Grace's screams, who had seen – as if in a dream – a woman collapsed and trapped by croquet hoops on the cricket oval; everyone who had been there then was now gone.

A few new batches of freshers acted to rinse the place clean. Initiations were over. The Savage Society fell back into mystique and urban myth. Hadrien and the cricket team joined them in this exalted space.

The college stopped recruiting jocks, and instead recruited students strong in the arts and sciences. They integrated the overseas students, moving them out of the Fraser Wing and into the main buildings. They gave women more leadership roles in the Students' Club. Gatherings of more than three students in any student's room were banned. Parties on campus were promoted as drug- and alcohol-free events, with money raised from entry fees used to sponsor some of the students on a walk of the Kokoda Track. Alcohol was banned in the quadrangle. Balls finished early and there was a strict new curfew of 1 am.

Following the police investigation, some of the more vulnerable animals were removed to a farm and the stables were converted into a gym, but the choir continued to enchant. Dr Bath moved to New Zealand where he took a job at a small, private university; Williams finally retired; Dr Childs returned to Cambridge alone.

The college promptly sold Evelyn. It had become as notorious in the local media as Australia's Abu Ghraib – where it was forever night-time, where unseen renditions and revisions would take place after cakes and scones at the tea break.

After the trial and their eventual graduation, the members of the now notorious cricket team embarked on permanent global roaming, living restless lives – business school in France, secondments in Singapore, on-site projects in Dubai, transfers to New York, London, Beijing, Moscow, Hong Kong, the hubs of finance, where they joined the throngs of young city meritocrats, moving from one old financial power to the emerging markets and back again, getting out and moving on, as superpowers fell and new ones rose.

Toby tried to separate himself from them. He travelled a lot and didn't check his email or Facebook. Once he ran into Hadrien in a bar in Jakarta – Ramadan, martinis, smoking with an impassive group of generals, a deep scar on his lip, hair gone all white, everything in his eyes communicating complete corruption, like a character in a Graham Greene novel who had stayed East for too long.

'Do you see Ben anymore?' Hadrien asked.

'I don't see anyone,' said Toby.

After several years working overseas, Toby returned home when he heard his father was dying, but never went back to

St Anton's – except most nights in his dreams. Sometimes he felt like he'd never left.

None of them had. It was unbelievable – how could they make sense of it? Had they really swayed under the giant gum trees, so drunk they could hardly think, but so strong they could mutilate a kangaroo with their bare hands? Had they really all howled at the moon? Had they really been so dumb as to film every single thing they did? Had a boy really almost been killed in a stupid prank? Had he really? No – it couldn't have happened – it seemed so unlikely … But then, later, as the years sped up and got harder and there were things waiting for them like the payment of school fees and divorce settlements, cancer and loneliness, and the knowledge of the treachery that surviving in this world entails, well, that was when they retreated – back, back to their consolation, the past. And they were really back there – in the Elysian Fields of their youth, the prison of nothingness, trapped in a quadrangle with music and animals and books and each other.

ACKNOWLEDGEMENTS

As well as the love and support of my friends and family, I would like to acknowledge the following people who read the manuscript at various stages and gave me advice on how to proceed: Robert Wainwright, Bonnie Malkin, Lee Glendinning, Tom Dobson, Andrew Charlton, Hannah Westland, Pippa Masson, Stephanie Peatling, Michelle Jana Chan, Victoria Gosling, Hal Crawford, Erik Jensen, Peter Bishop, Sarah Klenbort, Penny Bradfield and David Wroe.

At HarperCollins: Jessica Dettman, Jo Butler, Catherine Milne, Amanda O'Connell, Dione Fiford and Ali Lavau.

For a place to write: Varuna, the Writers' House.

For legal advice: Matthew Goldberg.

And to my parents – Jim and Mary Delaney – for everything else.

www.ingramcontent.com/pod-product-compliance
Lightning Source LLC
Chambersburg PA
CBHW030514120726
47904CB00005B/1451